Quantum Marlowe

By Glenn Lazar Roberts

2019, TWB Press
www.twbpress.com

Quantum Marlowe
Copyright © 2019 by Glenn Lazar Roberts

This is a work of fiction. Names, characters, places, and incidences are either a product of the author's imagination or are used fictitiously. Any resemblance to any actual person, living or dead, events, or locales is entirely coincidental.

Edited by Terry Wright

© Cover art designed by Terry Wright
Images from shutterstock.com

Published by TWB Press, Centennial, CO
www.twbpress.com

ISBN: 978-1-944045-51-7

CHAPTER 1

inero or die. The words splashed in my brain like drops of tequila on the floor of a Tijuana bar. The smirk on the face of the jailhouse guard as he imagined fifty grand wired from my Ex in Idaho as ransom might still be glued in place. I didn't know. And didn't give a damn. I stepped through the wall and the molecules that formed the gypsum and paint on the building that was the pride of Ciudad Juarez again became impenetrable. Outside, I re-attached my finger and turned and snorted. Pinky—I smiled at the nickname. *'Pinky' this, moronista.* I told you last night no jail could hold me.

How many times would I have to play this game? I could have cut another notch in my belt, if I bothered to keep count, and if that jailhouse jerk had not taken my new Italian belt along with my new Italian tie. Squinting in the blazing sun of late afternoon, I clutched my pants and strode casually up the deserted alley behind the jailhouse, past soiled clothing and discarded plastic bags. I looked up at the mayor's office where a light shined bright in a lone window from the third floor as darkness slowly crept. Yeah, keep it up, José. You'll learn soon enough. Once your pals find out, they'll be jerking your chain, and a lot more besides. Welcome to the Club of Sudden Bad News.

At the only exit not blocked by barbed wire, the alley gave onto a parking lot cratered with potholes. The moronista's twin had propped his taco-eating bulk in a sagging chair that wondered what it had ever done to deserve a daily crushing by Godzilla. One eye peered. Seeing no car lurching from pothole to pothole to make a break for the street without *El Generalissimo de Tacos'* permission, the eye settled on me. Hand over face to block the sun, I stared back with one of my own. I upended an imaginary bottle, stumbled to a halt for his reply. The gate-guard frowned and jerked a silent thumb. *Salir de aqui, borracho.* As his baggy eye shut, I dragged my feet to the street as if to beg for booze elsewhere. Silently smirked. Civil servant exams are the same everywhere.

Across the four-lane road and around the corner I glimpsed a pair of young boys offering younger girls to Escalades and BMWs as the vehicles paused at a streetlight. Another time I might have donated some pesos. Today was different. Alert for a pair of black Land Rovers, I halted in front of the nearest taquería and snapped my fingers. The pair turned their dirt-smudged faces to the short earnest stranger even more unwashed than they. They hesitated at first. But with no more suits in cars filled with mountain-cold air rushing for the International Bridge to get the hell out of Juarez before dark, *los jovenes* took a gamble with their precious time and sauntered near.

They stared. I stared back, one hand holding up my chalk-dusted ivory Canalis. I fixed my gaze halfway down the nearest boy. If this were Bangkok, a fat over-aged Madame would have leapt from the shadows to close the deal with a grin. But this was Shitty Juarez and the punk handed me his belt, his hand upturned for dollars in exchange. Snatching his belt, I strung my pants, hooked the buckle, and reached for my wallet. Being Napoleonic in size sometimes has its advantages. As I made the usual moves to fling out a bill, the boys' eyes lit up—then froze as I crossed my arms.

Frowning, I raked a finger across my throat.

The punks bolted. Tie or no tie, I knew they would not harass a gringo in a suit. My ears alert for signs of angry pursuit by City Hall and Company, I turned and slouched through Jerusalem—or what was as close to the Heavenly City as Shitty Juarez could become.

Blocks from the bridge, I turned down a familiar street, hugging the deepening shadows. Way familiar. The same green Oldsmobile was still double-parked in front of the same grey-steel-plated shop, the ramshackle building cased in metal and plastered with full-color photos of girls engaged in acts that could have taught that Bangkok Madame a thing or two.

As I stared, the last cars faded into night along with the posters. The street did have streetlights. And during the day they were impressive. But this was night and the City was descending into darkness more complete than London during the Blitz, not a single streetlight working. Night in the City of Juarez, named after a Mexican who hated gringos so much that he shot every Frenchie he captured during some War against the Frogs, which made his pals so happy they married his name to Shit.

I was here and I was stuck and it wasn't my goddamn fault.

But I knew whose fault it was.

I laid my glance up and down *la calle*. Night in Juarez was not a place anyone wanted to be, and the street was already clear of the usual parade of two-legged fleshpots. A pop reverberated in the distance as if celebrating the death of the sun—another source of ecstasy to members of the Bad News Club. I knew better than to remain for long. Just as I knew better than to do the tango where laymen could see, or make a strange appearance that might trigger lots of gab.

A glance inside the Oldsmobile showed nothing had been touched—which was all the proof of guilt I needed, since otherwise not even the car doors would remain intact. Reaching under the back fender I felt for a strip of thick tape. Ripped it off. My palm closed on a cylinder of steel. I tossed the tape in the gutter and perched the barrel in the small of my back behind my new kid-sized belt.

Shuffling drunkenly next door like I had sighted a half-empty bottle—to ward off any curious eyes—I leaned against the only door on the block that lacked a Chinese Wall of steel reinforcement. Not that the type of molecule mattered. I pretended to inspect the ground, my eyes again scanning the horizon for eyes and ears, especially those peering *jovenes*, sharp beyond their years. Barely taller than them, I could generally count on being mistaken for a *joven* myself, and the growing dirt on my Italian custom suit and the scuff marks on my Italian shoes were beginning to make me one of the crowd, only the absence of a Pancho Villa broom on my upper lip to match my gringo Elvis hair giving me away.

Without a sound, I slid off the tip of my jack-leg finger. My hitch digit punched the red button implanted in the stump and a change in the color of the rusty wood of the door told me the tango was working. One last look at the deepening shadows of *la calle* and I faced the wall. My ears rang with the high-pitched whine I had learned to expect each time I fucked with nature's giblets, and again I wondered why the hell *they* had done this to me. Who the hell fucks over his worst enemy, gives him the keys to the universe, then fucks him over again? Well, who gives a fuck. That's their hard luck. I stroked the barrel behind my back—it was just about to get harder.

Istanbul was Constantinople
Now it's Istanbul, not Constantinople
Been a long time gone, Constantinople
Now it's Turkish delight on a moonlit night.

With that, I stepped forward and the tango was done, and round lights stabbing the darkness morphed into a single night-lamp. Behind me was the nether edge of the joint's double-jointed triple-locked door, the molecules back in place, not necessarily where they should be, but back where they had been.

The room turned out to be barely larger than a Greyhound restroom stall and I gave one quick rubber-necked turn to make sure no stray Garcia or Gonzalez was camped inside—or, worse, Montez & Muck. An absence of chainsaw snoring signaled clear. I slid the fingertip back on. Gave it the usual twist. Felt it contact the tiny O-ring that ensured silence in use. My smirk turned into a smile. When Pinky gives them the finger, they stay fingered.

I paused to catch my breath.

Crossing to the stall's side wall that stretched ocher under the night-lamp, I again plucked it off. My pinky was getting a lot of action—more than usual. My thumb squeezed the red button. Bubbling spumed on the wall, the ocher transforming into a miniature version of that volcanic pit on Mount Kea that never fucking heals. The tango had different moves on different dance floors.

Istanbul was Constantinople
Now it's Istanbul, not Constantinople...

I stepped through and emerged on the far side, the high whine of pained giblets again receding in my ears. In front, videocams and backlight frames and sound booms littered the place. I smiled again at the irony. The most secretive operation on the planet brought in spare cash by making video shoots for *los pescas grandes*, 'the Big Fishes', the operation sucking up *el dinero* from the very same *los Jefes* who 'offered' it protection—and not only of the shiny steel type that covered the joint's windows after dark.

A glance at my pants reminded me of the jailhouse dust and dirt and I brushed off what I could until my new Canali suit regained a semblance of its former glory. Ain't no point in shuffling onstage looking like a bum. After all, when you're four-foot-eleven, you gotta do something to get noticed. Shining each shoe on the back of a pant leg and rubbing my nails on the inner side of each underarm till they gleamed, I walked. Halfway across the room I climbed the step that divided the room in two, steps always more of an effort for me than most, but hell if I would ever tell. I had just learned what it meant to give a clue to M&M. And they were about to learn that not everything melts in one's mouth.

A soft glow betrayed itself from a back area.

Inching closer, I fancied I was back in the Vatican, my new shoes stroking luxury carpet beneath the silent gaze of ancient statues of long-dead big-shots. As distant as those frozen gazes were, mine was up-front, in the here and now.

This was personal.

My eyes focused on two figures whose backs were turned. In a mostly darkened warehouse, they sat on four-legged stools before a dully lit wooden bar strewn with scribbled papers while they stared into wide computer screens. On the left, a full head of white hair ended in a long white ponytail. On the right, a bald head reflected colored lights from the rows of monitors as if in a discotheque.

My smile broadened to a grin. This was better than I expected. Withdrawing the pistol from the small of my back, I leveled the business end at the pair.

"*Plomo? O plata?*" My voice echoed through the otherwise quiet warehouse.

The two heads stiffened. Slowly the bar stools swiveled till both faced me. My innards melted with joy at the panic that crossed their faces as recognition dawned.

"That's the preferred language, *mis amigos*. Not 'dinero or die'." I sniffed scornfully. "I mean, who talks like that this side of the Big Ditch? Next time you stab a friend in the back, you should learn the lingo, then you could coach your *compadres* better before sending them to do your dirty work. If you have any questions about how things work hereabouts, ask *me* first. After all, I've had lots of spare time to learn since you dumped me here."

Baldy and Ponytail exchanged nervous glances, but said nothing. Only their eyes moved.

I turned to Ponytail. "What's the matter, *Bob?* When the hell has the great Bob Montez ever been short on words? *Gato* got your tongue?" My eyebrows rose in mock seriousness. Baldy, also silent, shot a panicked glance at his white-haired comrade. My heart swelled with satisfaction to see his eyes round with terror.

"And what about you, *Jack.* Nothing left for you to *muck* around with?" I turned the pistol horizontal gangsta-style, unable to resist a little intimidation in his direction too. A nervous tic took hold of Baldy's chin. Slaver drooled as he struggled to speak, too terrified to utter a word. I watched his eyes flick imploringly at Ponytail, then back to the gun that I weaved evilly in his smooth hairless face. I continued to stare into Jack's eyes, upward despite the fact that he sat while I stood. Sometimes being Napoleonic in size is merely napoleonic.

"That's right, Muck. It's *Pinky*—Pinky as ever was. Say Hi to my newest finger, Jack. Only this one is blue-steel Colt." I laughed, unable to contain my joy. "How do you like that? Jack Muck as speechless as Bob Montez. *Gato* got your tongue, too? Or should I say *perro?*" I threw my face to the shadowed ceiling and howled like a dog. Danced a jig on my hind legs. "Awooo! The great Jack Muck, Founder of Sirius Enterprises, helpless as one of his prize poodles." I stepped closer, thrust the barrel of the Colt in Jack's flabby face. "What do you think of this, Jack? How does this fit into your little scheme? Why, I oughta..."

But I calmed. Breathing deeper to regain control—another little thing I learned in the Vatican—I stepped back. Double-checked the cylinder of the old-fashioned piece I had picked up for a few pesos when M&M first dropped me in Shitty Juarez with hardly a doubloon.

"After all I've done for you. And after what you've done to me. With that kind of history, you throw me away like a piece of meat, give me up like day-old coffee, and let that Nazi José..." An angry look emanated from Jack's hairless face. "Oh, *scuza mía*—that *Peronista* Mayor José." The look relaxed a trifle. I thrust the barrel in Jack's face till he relaxed no more. "That *jerk* mayor who is still a fucking Nazi to me, so don't cry to me Argentina."

I stepped back again. I love gloating. Always have. Almost as much as complaining. This was my chance to do both, topped off by a sweet cherry of revenge. I pressed the barrel against Jack's bald temple.

"Why'd ya do it, Jack?" I hissed. "It wasn't enough to drop me in this hellhole? Couldn't you just be happy raising your poodles? Did you have to go back to the Man in the Moon? You said you were over that phase of your life."

Still no response from the blubbering bald poodle-lover squatting on the swivel chair before me, the range of busy monitors behind him showing windows on unnameable places, including some that looked like craters. It was starting to get weird.

"And you, *Bob*..." I stretched out his foul name like its letters hid an infinitude of secret meanings. "How could you let Jack do it? You've always been Jack's gabby sidekick. Why did you let him turn me over to El Chapo? You know what Chapo does to snitches, *Bob*? It has a lot to do with chop-suey, but not so pleasant. Chapo was already on his way to Mayor José to take me for a 'ride' when I managed to do the tango and *vamoos* the hell out of there. But our appointment was way too close to keep me cool and dry."

Bob flicked his eyes back to Jack. Still neither spoke. Or moved.

"Okay, so you wanted me to put the finger on Nazi José and El Chapo. I got it. So you said 'Find them' and sent me to Juarez. Well, I found them. But I never gave permission for you to do what you did to me, and I never wanted any part of this little enterprise of yours. Still, I did the tango on your promise not to touch my Ex—not that I give a fuck about that bitch anymore. But old times is old times. I thought you understood that. And what did you do to repay me?"

Lurching forward, I thrust the short-barreled Colt against the side of Bob's head, almost entangling the rod in his thick white ponytail.

"You squealed. You sang like a capo in spring, like a canary in Hackensack, like a Bonanno wearin' a wire *at his daughter's weddin'.*" I spat a big one on the floor. "Turned me over to the Bad News Club with nary a thought, left me to be sacrificed to their Sun God of Death. You know what that does to one's yoga high?" I pressed the barrel harder. "Huh? One's meditation kinda takes a nosedive after that. You think it's easy escaping from that kind of bear trap? Red button or no red button, you can't just walk away after the Club has your number. They'll be hot on my trail soon, if they're not outside already. They may be stupid, but they ain't dumb. They know where you are. And they know I'll be coming after *you* to get even."

Bob and Jack exchanged those silent glares again, this time their brows showed signs of movement. Unpleasant signs. For some reason they didn't seem happy.

"But you know what, *muchachos*? It's time for lights out. Yeah, buddies, since it always has to be *all about you*, I see no reason why this shouldn't be about you as well. You gotta pay, my friends. You can't do what you did to me and *not* pay. This lap dance is over. It's time to pay the cat-house Madame."

I took a deep breath, let my lungs take a walk. Opening the cylinder of the Colt, I inspected the chambers to make sure it still contained *plomos*, and snapped it shut. With the deliberateness of an undertaker, I raised the barrel and aimed...

CHAPTER 2

Three months earlier, a newly divorced man happily soft-shoed to the front door of a small but adequate office on the fourth floor of the latest foreclosed building in Albuquerque, New Mexico, pausing to admire the small but adequate sign: 'Pete Marlowe – Private Investigator'. He inserted the key in the lock and entered big as Gulliver, for once unconcerned at being sighted by the first floor's spray-bouffant manager. She had ignored him. Deprived of half her salary by her boss's bankruptcy, Big-Hair no longer bothered to collect the rent.

That man was *mío*: Pietro Quinn Tiberias Marlowe. 'Pete' for short. In those antediluvian times, the birds sang sweeter, the rain fell wetter, and the fairer sex had no muscles stronger than needed to climb a steel pole to the sound of pixie trumpets and two-fingered whistles. Originally just 'Peter'. But as I grew older without growing taller, my *loco* parents added names as if to inspire a shy hormone, then, as biology stayed AWOL, in futile attempts to compensate.

Yeah, I got the Freudian angle. Quinn as in Mighty. Tiberias as in a king commanding armies. And if two fancy names were enough for some, I had to have three. Then four. More incentive came with each passing year. 'Peter' soon wasn't good enough. It had to be *Pietro,* even though my dame-and-dunce *au pair genitori* were only Italian through a con pulled off by my father's '*duncer'* brother—a sham Irish priest named Flynn who convinced a senile pope that the Blarney Stone was the real Rock of Saint Peter stolen from the Vatican in caveman days by King Henry the Seventeenth, or some multiple thereof.

Fast-talking Flynn claimed he had smuggled it back into the Vatican and substituted a fake in Ireland for the rubes, the grateful and half-blind Pope kissing the Blarney Stone under his lumpy bed each night when no one else could see. As a punk kid, I saw the knowing wink the myopic Pope laid on me, mistaking me for Uncle Flynn, sharing their secret. Memories last long in those carpeted and marbled halls. If you don't bring them with you, you carry them out like fast food when you leave.

Which explained the other secret that lurked in my name. The family secret of the true location and purpose of the Blarney Stone seemed to lurk in the initials Q and T. Everything with my parents was 'on the QT'. Quiet about this. Don't say a word about that. Or the Pope will be forced to reveal the Truth and go to war with Ireland and the whole fucking world would have to invest in fleets of paddy wagons for angry drunken redheads demanding the return of their precious Stone.

I didn't see the problem. Who in hell can handle the truth, anyway? Not many this side of Limbo. True believers least of all. Fast as the world finds them, the world reburies its truths like yesterday's garbage, breaking every streetcar mirror on its race to Knob Hill cemetery so even the memory will die.

The private investigation racket slams this home every time I pop the lock on the glass and wood door to my little behind-the-rent office, the click coming to sound over the years more like the electric gate of the Big House than a quick way to pay for lap dances and pole calisthenics. Only my clients enjoy the sound. Without exception, they bring their Big House with them—and just as often an invisible sack of trash, wanting me to bury it with their carefully hidden truth-of-the-day.

That was when *She* appeared. From behind my desk I had a better view than front row at a Yankees game, her moves more obvious than a clumsy umpire's bad calls. And just as below the belt. She sauntered through the door with her hips leading the charge, a short lime-green skirt leaving little to the imagination—and launching mine into the stratosphere. Like a predator, I sensed immediately she was on the prowl. The overly demure smile that read my thoughts as if telegraphed, the orange-swirl, see-through chiffon blouse showing more cleavage than Lincoln's forehead, framed by green-fringed black hair that circled her smooth neck like a Navajo snake charm. Her black leather jacket came with red-spotted black feather epaulettes that stretched down her arms to her elbows, the fringes also green. Black boots laced behind and above the knees completed the ensemble. Had fate turned to destiny? Hard luck to winning Harlem's policy lotto? Or had my stars crossed into Indian country, ensuring that after meeting her, if not for real bad luck, I would have no luck at all.

"Velvet becomes you."

For a moment I thought my voice had skipped an octave and switched sexes. I did a double-take and realized that Leopard Woman had spoken and was looking beyond me at the Velvet Elvis painting that graced my office's back wall like that picture of Moaning Lisa in Paris so admired by those eaters of snails and fungus. I was surprised that such a smooth sound could exit such a cat-like neck.

"Velvet becomes *Elvis*," I corrected. I stretched out my arms clad in a new Canali jacket fresh from my Italian tailor, an ivory-colored suit accented by glittering Elvis cuff-links. The Ex had hated Elvis.

I blinked.

A smile crept over her lips. She purred and leaned over my desk, displaying more flesh than a kosher grocer turned meatatarian.

My eyes struggled to defy gravity and avoid vanishing in those cliff-like chiffon depths.

"Either way, it agrees with you." She smiled, her eyes running over my body like gasoline seeking a fire. Her gaze settled on the maroon wave on my cranium. I sat taller, conscious that the wave in my Elvis hair imitated the bend in Elvis's coiffure in the velvet painting. She crooned, "So soft. But so masculine." One delicate leopard paw hovered as if deciding whether to caress or carve.

I broke the connection. Leaned back in my un-oiled squeaky chair. A man with a smile means one bag of garbage and a short stretch in the Slammer. A woman in spots means a truckload of garbage and a lifetime on ice. Whatever her problem, it was hotter than a godfather's offer and more explosive than a grenade on a gun range.

But a memory flashed—baby needs a new pair of shoes, the one part of my Canali suit that I didn't have enough dough to buy. In this business, grenades mean money. And more besides.

Nodding to a guest chair, I let loose a half-smile. My elbows propped on the desktop, my eyes flicking back to the Imperial Valley fruit just waiting to be picked by the right guest worker.

She took the offered chair. One hand cracked an alligator purse and extracted a handkerchief. I focused on the kerchief's gold embroidery and made out the words 'Bourbon Street Tailor'. High-priced as they come. Leopard Lady could not only change her spots, but bring home the gator. The gator she could keep; but I could hardly keep my mind off the famous bourbon any more than the White Cliffs.

She averted her gaze and gushed into the handkerchief. Tears came from somewhere—maybe from her eyes. I'd seen better acting at weekly probation check-ins.

"I'm sorry," she muttered. "I didn't mean to come on strong. It's my sister." Another blubber.

"Your sister?"

"My brother."

"Your brother?"

"My mother."

"Your mother?"

"My sick father-in-law."

She paused so she could get her story straight. They all do.

"Married, then?"

"No. Rather, that's all in the past..." She lowered the kerchief and sniffed. "Perhaps I should start over."

"Perhaps you should." There may have been a red rim around one of those pretty eyes. Yes or no, from somewhere a feeling of joy spread over me at the news that her spouse was as Ex as mine. I pursed my lips. Sat tall as I could in my special seat with the extra padding so my elbows could reach the desktop.

She sniffed. "It's like this, Mr. Marlowe..."

I waited for the bag of trash to appear. Hoped there was enough room for it in my little office.

"I need a...bodyguard."

"Bodyguard?"

"I have what you might call an appointment. Across town. And it would be best if I didn't go alone. It's not in the best part of

Albuquerque."

"There's class—and there's class," I cagily observed. "Unless you have something else in mind." Climbing out of his cellar to perch on my right shoulder, my alter ego Pietro wondered if this leopard could be caged. I warned him to keep his pants zipped.

The sniffs disappeared. "I need to make a delivery. For my sick father-in-law."

I folded my arms. "Wanna try again?"

Her green eyes stared back. "To my sister and my brother and my mother. *For* my sick father-in-law."

Leaning back, I half-smiled.

"Really. I know it sounds strange, Mr. Marlowe, but...well, this is a family affair. You see," she glanced down again, "I'm being blackmailed. By my own relatives." She looked up, eyes round.

I stopped smiling. Family trouble I understood. That's always a prime ingredient of any bag of trash. "What's wrong with the Albuquerque P.D.? Their Criminal Investigations Unit can be found with a two-second online search."

Her eyes widened. "No. I can't have the police involved. At least...not yet."

So there was more in the bag of trash than rotten relatives. I sensed the Big House lurking in there.

"They're demanding I give them money. They say they'll hurt my father-in-law if I don't...my *former* father-in-law. He's so ill that I feel I can't say no. And," her green gaze dropped to the floor, "if I don't pay, they say they'll go to the police about...my past."

"What have you done wrong?"

"Nothing."

"Then that's not blackmail. It's extortion."

"Oh. Extortion, then. If I said it right."

She said it right, all right. Whatever she was, she hadn't just fallen off the turnip truck.

"Maybe I should introduce myself."

"Maybe."

The enigmatic smile returned, just like Moaning Lisa. "Antonia Massolini." She offered her hand like royalty.

I didn't feel like sucking up, but as she leaned forward I

thought I caught a glimpse of zeros on slips of chlorophyll lurking in her gator-hide purse. My other alter ego, Quinn, climbed up from his cellar to my left shoulder. A quick preemptive smack in Quinn's face and I sat up again. No harm done.

"Sounds familiar. Any relation?"

"To who?" she asked.

"Forget it. Just thinking aloud."

"I'm sorry, Mr. Marlowe. We're a big family but close-knit. We don't mix a lot with outsiders."

"Sounds like you against the world."

The sniffs returned and the kerchief came back out. "That's exactly how it is, Mr. Marlowe. You understand so much." The pretty eyes glanced up again. "So much about...*women*."

Oh, those lying eyes.

"I need your services tonight. You came recommended. I need a strong wise man to help me make the delivery, someone who can handle his own in case things get rough."

"You sure you don't mean a 'wise guy'? Cause I try to avoid that kind of wise."

"Close enough for what I need." Another tear appeared.

Quinn was smacked down from my left shoulder, but on my right Pietro was back to grinning. He followed the tear's trace down her sweet neck toward the magic cliffs. I tried to switch off both alter egos, but Quinn waved a fistful of green at me, his favorite topic, as flirting with the opposite sex was Pietro's.

"I don't come cheap, Miss? Mrs? Miz?"

"Miss. I hope you don't mind. I'm old-fashioned, Mr. Marlowe."

Still grinning, Pietro shoved Quinn to one side. "You're looking at Mr. Old-Fashioned himself, Miss Massolini."

"Antonia, please. Tonya for short."

"Tonya it is." I held out my hand and we shook, breaking a bit more ice for our verbal liqueur.

She dipped into the gator pool and extracted the wad of bills I had glimpsed. "Will a thousand dollars be enough?"

Now Leopard Gal was talkin'. "Just covers it. As a retainer, that is." I learned long ago never to make an open-ended commitment without open-ended payment. And I knew now that she hadn't just stepped out of a soup line. She stripped off ten hundred dollar bills into my hand and a quick inspection of the notes sufficed to prove she was the real McCoy, with the real gin—not bathtub. I stuffed the bills into a special pocket velcroed shut. No telling what other talents she may have, perhaps some regarding picking pockets. Quinn signaled caution. But at the mention of pockets, a horny Pietro reappeared and flashed 'Go' as big as green Nascar flags.

She smiled again, this time a shy girlish smile without the carnivore eyeteeth she had displayed when she first entered. "But I need you tonight...midnight. I'm supposed to deliver the money off University Park at a small restaurant near the airport, up a back-road called Cartagena. I don't know why they're insisting on that place, and at such a late hour...unless they're not telling me everything."

Fancy that. Partners with something to hide.

"So I need an escort to meet me and help me hand over the money, and to make sure we both come back. Is another thousand enough to rent you...*after hours?*"

Pietro did a back flip. I stuffed his grin into my own bag of trash—but not so far that it couldn't be summoned by the clink of happy hour shot glasses. I nodded. "To rent me. Or buy me out." I allowed the grin to half-surface. I pulled out my one-size-fits-all electronic cigarette and jammed the ON button till Strawberry flavored white smoke enveloped me.

"But one night only. Tomorrow's birds always sing another song."

She tabbed off another ten hundreds into my callused palm, which promptly joined their cousins under Velcro.

We both stood, my eyes coming face-to-face with a pair of darker curves smoldering beneath the sheer chiffon. Green Eyes had a good three inches on me. At times I have to admit Napoleon never had it so good. Suppressing a gulp, I reached for my pencil-pad to hand her what the IRS boys call evidence.

"Receipt?"

"No, Mr. Marlowe. I trust you."

My eyes half closed. Now I was truly nervous. The only thing one should trust in this crazy world is that last lonesome stroll down

Deadman's Walk to the Hot Seat—but the hole in the bottom of my left sole stiffened my spine like a dose of Dr. Feelgood's mail-order tonic.

Green Eyes turned and left.

After she clicked the door behind her, I stared down from my fourth-floor window to where a few moments later the setting sun threw its red-devil cloak over a green-tinged figure emerging from the building's entrance onto the hot New Mexico sidewalk. A limo pulled alongside, every seat behind the car's tinted glass doors darkened with shifting shadows, hinting 'occupied'. Even from this height I could see Green Eyes' face light up as if delivering good news to close kin.

I heard a muffled clump. The limo wheeled away.

Compulsively, I fingered the six-chambered Colt that I keep holstered under my left underarm and glanced up at Elvis. I rubbed the back of my neck. Had I just bought the farm? Or rented an overnight room in Heartbreak Hotel? Either way, I knew I needed to find the biggest empty trash bag ever made.

CHAPTER 3

Red spots. Red volcanoes. Red hair. I don't know why these images merged in my mind. When I stepped out of my taxi ride with just minutes to spare before an invisible local church rang twelve, the red dust of a New Mexico sunset had long faded into night. Only the ashen glow of my dark-red black-Irish hair remained to match the ivory of my new Canalis.

"Keep the motor running, Joe." I tossed an extra peso to the cabbie. My usual driver. Not because he drove well or smelled good, but because old times is old times. I'm just that kinda guy.

I had barely donned my gray-banded ivory fedora—like the rest of my suit, part of my divorce celebration after signing the papers—when she slid out of the shadows behind a warehouse streetlight like a snake in heat. Her eyes were wide and her lips trembling. I could not account for it. Puppy love I understood. First dates and prom dances I got. But why the eagerness of a kitten that has just sighted mommy's teat? I struggled to keep Pietro under control. After all, I was just as vulnerable to the underside of life as any other man this side of senility—but this was business. So I slapped Pietro back down to the catacombs.

Green fringes. Green eyes. Emerald Isle. I don't know why these merged as well. But at least two in the list were visible, despite the hour. Still fringed with verdant fronds, Tonya blinked her florescent eyes like an Irish lighthouse summoning ships to dock at a Gaelic Jamaica Inn. Except this lighthouse shed tears.

"Mr. Marlowe."

"Pete."

A quick nod. "Yes...*Pete*." She swallowed.

Wondering where her limo had gone, I glanced furtively about, searching for deeper shadows in the shadows cast by the lone streetlight, the dull pockmarked adobe warehouse stretching down University Park into blackness, its obscured far end anchored by the North Star. My eye settled on a chartreuse valise beneath her arm that had replaced the maroon gator purse. The folder seemed far too small to carry the amount of cash that all her drama suggested. Money orders and bank checks aren't in this line of work. But my digits fingered several bills stuffed in my left pocket—those hundred dollar bills, that is, which I had not entrusted to my friendly neighborhood Savings & Theft.

I reached for my 'brain', punched the code in the cell phone, making ready to GPS the target address. Looked at her and paused.

"That won't work," she said. "You won't find this place on any map." She turned and stared up into the pitch-black hills blotting out the sky behind Albuquerque's airport. "It's too recent. My father-in-law opened it just last week."

I shrugged. There was always some reason why a simple 9-1-1 wasn't good enough, or why the Operator won't answer, or why the Postman no longer rings twice.

Green Eyes pointed to a poorly paved road that wound behind the shambling one-story warehouse and curled up into foothills. I followed her gaze to a faded street sign bathed in shadow that might have read: 'Cartagena'. The back of my neck itched again and I pulled out my e-cig. A squeeze by my thumb sent its aromatic fumes curling about my fedora like my own version of Green Eyes' snake charm. Better than Xanax.

"The restaurant is up there. It's not far. Your driver can drive us." For a moment she stared at me with a quizzical, almost sympathetic look. She extended a palm crossed with paper that bore a picture in badly scribbled crayon. "Look for this sign."

I stared. After a moment, my neurons aligned and I saw the outline of a bell.

A quick glance and a nod, and Joe pulled his taxi alongside. With a squeak, I opened the back door and slid in beside her. I don't know why, since it was no protection from Leopard Gal, but I was instantly comforted by the two tons of glass and metal. With the distant ridges blotting half the stars, and the road spiraling into emptiness, the night was dark. Too dark. Despite the cool night air, my Colt sweated bullets.

We rolled onto the cheaply laid asphalt. After a minute on the road, Joe glanced at me, questioning. I questioned back. I could not help wondering at the marketing genius of a restaurant owner who opened his shindig on a lonely country road without neon. He couldn't be more hidden than if he was selling contraceptives in Saint Peter's. Not my problem, I shrugged. A fool chef and his lettuce are soon parted. That's his lookout. Except in this case, the chef-in-law had fallen ill just as the lettuce was chopped, and like famished goats, the rotten relatives had rushed to consume the Waldorf salad. He was shit out of luck. It happens.

The road wound left and right but always up. Desert shrubs and cacti loomed in the taxi's headlights with glimpses of misplaced petrified wood, throwing their ghostly swirls past the corners of our eyes to disappear with each bump in a pothole. Still searching for neon, I risked a sidelong glance at my employer-of-the-day, not wanting to risk future paychecks or a fine for breaking her speed limit. Her strong come-on had had its effect, whether I wanted to admit it or not. I didn't get it—her tear was still there. Kittens don't cry once they find their teat.

One more speed bump and an edifice popped into view from behind a hill. How do you like that? Neon after all. In the middle of the desert, bozo-in-law had thrown up a small but bright sign that broadcast 'Rick's Americana' to the coyotes and gila monsters. Well, who could blame him? After springing for my new suit, even Mother Nature's vagrants had more pesos than I—that is, until Green Eyes had paid her bill.

Beneath the sign was a glass door lacking the usual pin-pricks by air-gun pellets, another sure sign that the place was baby-spanking new. Otherwise the glass would have enough pockmarks to make smallpox envious. On either side was more glass and pristine elaborate menus were pasted from the inside, boasting unlikely combinations of Tex-Mex and Coney Island fare. Americana comes in all flavors, I guess.

No red carpet, but freshly laid asphalt with just-painted yellow diagonal stripes invited Joe to park his jalopy. He could take his pick—only two other cars were present in the wide lot, both of them plain-Jane and unfamiliar, though an oil stain or two indicated others had already experienced Rick's brief hospitality.

Through the wide display of glass I could see Rick's interior: soft chairs, hard tables, off-white lights, white smoke drifting from swinging doors behind a cherry-red counter that traveled the length of the place except for a bend that created a flat L ending in a blank wall on the left. Rows of bottles graced a backsplash mirror. Now they're talkin'. Why In-law-Rick didn't put 'Bar & Grill' beneath 'Rick's Americana' and lasso in the scarce thirsty traffic, I couldn't say.

Joe lurched to a stop and jostled his taxi between exactly parallel bright yellow stripes. Like me, Joe was a creature of habit. I glanced sideways. Joe's bumpy nose was always alert for trouble, even when Quinn's bloodhound schnoz was distracted sniffing carpet. Joe raised his eyebrows, shifted his checkered blue taxicab cap down over his forehead and leaned back to rest. I breathed more easily. No sirens from that angle.

I stepped out. I held the back door open for Green Eyes, and she followed me and stood staring at the unlikely neon apparition, one jacketed hand holding down the green-tinged feathers that adorned her jacket's other arm as if it might take flight and magic-carpet her away. Another sideways glance from her still-tied felt boots to her swirling green-tinged hair revealed nothing screwy about her reaction either. Even Pietro paused in his eyeing of those jungle-fringed feathers and verdant skirt to give me the thumbs up. We were *A-OK*.

When I swung open the door to the eatery, a tiny bell dinged. For some reason it reminded me of the invisible church's bell that had announced midnight at the foot of the road, sending its timeless message into the wilderness, and leaving me half-expecting eleven more door-dings to keep things even. But the day had ended and we had begun again—one ding for one o'clock, though it didn't seem to me that a full hour could have passed since we hit Cartagena Road.

At one end of the walnut bar curled a wide horseshoe booth. Three seated faces stared us up and down as the mist from the swinging doors dissipated in the blast of dry New Mexico air. Behind the bar appeared a short man who trotted about making drinks and washing pots as if the place were full. His dark face and squat size broadcasted El Salvador, maybe San Miguel. A quick glance revealed only two others, at the opposite end, a pair of gringos whose well-tailored elbows kept another table anchored while they sampled Americana concoctions. Three plus one plus two. I count. All PIs do. Part of living in a habit-hole.

I tried to nail down the trio of faces as Tonya and I approached. They had seen Joe and me park but had remained seated, watching. Though the mist was dissipating, a new cloud hovered about their table. Tonya slid comfortably into the booth and slapped her folder down in a tiny puddle of water that had condensed on the sides of two lime tequilas and a red vino, vintage three o'clock, I noticed wryly. So much for her *delivery*. Still, something about the way Tonya sat and the way her muscles tightened on the flanks of her gorgeous chin suggested maybe there was some truth in her tale after all. Maybe she was just too innocent to know how to cover her backside. I had no such monkey on my back. Reversing a chair, I sat with its back turned toward our hosts. Every layer I can put between me and a bullet is welcome.

The mist slowly vanished, leaving an acrid fruity scent in the air. An older matronly woman—older than Green Eyes by at least three decades—flicked a live flame and relit her cigarette pipette. Cherry flavor. A new cloud emerged. Beside the older woman sat a younger woman and a still-younger, dark-haired man. The tricky trio I presumed. Draped in a purple evening dress with a collector's repertoire of red rubies and white pearls about her neck, the matron's pert mouth still managed to give a schoolmarmish air to match the cherry smoke that constantly enveloped her. The more Schoolmarm puffed, the more the younger woman beside her coughed into a curled up fist. Finally the younger woman—older than Tonya by a few years at least—settled into a stoic frozen-faced glare, resigned, or condemned, to share Marm's lung-destroying pollution.

Habits. There's all sorts of furniture in people's habit-holes. It comes delivered free of charge if one doesn't keep the door locked.

A wide grin was plastered on the young man's face. Before I could kick the can of conversation into gear, the grin erupted in laughter.

"Hand it over." Like a dog he panted, his pink tongue thrusting out of his mouth every few seconds as if the roving target in a game of Whack-a-Mole.

Marm flicked ashes onto the table, depositing some on Tonya's dampened chartreuse folder. Purple Dress inhaled another long stream and blasted the exhalation into the grimacing face of the young woman whose misfortune it was to sit next to her. "Credit where it's due, I always say." Marm's eyes glittered behind the white cloud like twinkling stars. "Credit where it's due." A faint New England accent? She turned to the frowning totem. "Licia, dispense a wafer." Marm's mouth was still pert, determined to remain flatly horizontal.

Frowning deeper—if that were possible—Licia popped open a handbag in her lap. Sweeping aside the wet puddle of water on the table with the handbag, Licia oddly touched the same fingers to her tongue to moisten them, then carefully extracted a small round flat pastry. With exaggerated poise she handed the pastry to the young man seated next to her.

"That's the crank," he blurted. Without eyeing the wafer, he swallowed it. The grin faded, then just as suddenly returned wider than ever, and out came his pink tongue. I could not shake the image of a desert reptile tasting the air for prey. Not much unnerves me. I've had theater tickets to everything from knife fights to barroom chokings and confessions beaten out of border-jumpers with vacuum tube TVs. But the staccato punctuation by tongue of every change in mood by this otherwise well-dressed man of twenty-three-ish did the job.

"What do we do when we receive a wafer, Andrew?" asked Marm.

His frown returned. A quick glimpse at Marm to ensure he was still in Marm's good graces, and he flashed his grin at me in triumph. Crossed himself left to right while Marm watched.

"Thank you, Andrew." Marm breathed contentedly.

"She's got my jacket." Licia pointed a finger at Tonya. "I told you, Mother, I told you she stole it." Another blast of smoke triggered a brief fit of coughing as Licia tried to breathe.

"Hush, child. Do a deed, get a deed. That's what I always say.

Charity is the soul of godliness. You must not forget that, dear."

"Give it back." Pushing the chartreuse valise to one side, Licia snatched at Tonya's sleeve and ripped off a feather. Tonya yanked back her arm, sending the valise sliding to the floor, hydroplaning on the drops of water. On impact, it burst open.

I focused. Squinted. A small avalanche of currency spilled free across my shined shoes and, before I could anticipate, Mother slid off her vinyl booth cushion and, ignoring the dirt that must have been accumulating on her purple dress, snatched them up while on her knees, displaying no trace of embarrassment as she scrambled below me on the floor, grabbing the notes and plopping them onto the table with her one free hand.

Andrew and Licia watched unconcerned. Licia breathed more easily; Andrew paused to play tiddlywinks with his fingers in the little pool that remained on the Formica surface, then paused to place the money in little stacks, till Licia slapped his hand and commandeered making the little piles. Still seated opposite, a look of accomplishment settled on Tonya's face, her jaws relaxing a trifle.

I kept squinting, not because of the unlikely behavior of Mother, but because of the value of the notes. I had supposed Green Eyes was in hock up to her pretty neck, whether or not she was as rich as Rockefeller, being forced to hand over enough cash to buy Monte Carlo. She had thrown me a thousand like it was nuts at a zoo, and a thousand more besides. The cash that Marm and Licia IDed in that back-road joint was only seventy-five dollars: fifty ones plus two tens and a five. I counted.

I'd seen men killed over quarters. But only when Skid Row had missed its nightly booze and pill run by part-time entrepreneurs trying to squeeze a quick buck from the hopelessly hooked, naive college kids doing an Uber version of gangsterdom. And not when the bully was dressed as highfalutin as the victim. In this case, Green Eyes not only wore the finest from Rodeo Drive, but there seemed nothing part-time or entrepreneurial about jewel-laden Marm.

Eyes glittering, Marm recounted the cash, mouth mumbling. Maybe I didn't get the full picture. Wouldn't be the first time—I had barely begun sorting this family's trash.

El Salvador stepped lightly to the table. Before Marm finished recounting, she took Licia's purse and unceremoniously swept the money into it, which dove back to its hiding place in Licia's lap beneath the table, on call at Mother's whim. Her matronly smile wanly greeted the waiter.

"Diego, I'd like the best for our guest." For the first time, everyone acknowledged me—by look, though still not by name—not that it mattered. With a hint of resentment, I realized that even Diego was a trifle taller than me, the rest of the Massolini clan taller than both of us by four inches and up. Marm smiled in my direction. "Our guest will have the..." She inspected the menu. "Chicken-fried taco." Mother turned. Bestowed a beatific glow, all white paint and red lipstick beneath crusty-sprayed hair, reminding me of nothing so much as those white statues of the Great Mother Mary that suddenly bleed red. "And...some of your wonderful Zen green tea." Her smile broadened.

What could I say? There was only so much overlap possible between Americana and New-Mex-Tex. Story of my life, I reflected. "That'll do."

The trio stared at me. As the stares morphed into glares, I ventured, "...gratzi."

Smiles burst. Andrew finalized the result by winging the plastic single-page menu at Diego, who dodged it, apparently used to fielding orders this way. Diego did not react to the pink tongue that darted out in emphasis, but I felt the back of my neck creep. I had an indescribable urge to grab a shovel and chop off Andrew's head. Would I truly have to endure this reptile for...well, however much longer it took to ensure my client's safety, all the way to Pietro's fevered *afterhours* funland? Though it seemed less and less likely that Tonya had anything to fear from these her family members, and certainly not after having completed delivery of what they wanted.

In an improbably short time, Diego slapped down the house specialty and the tea. I blew on the brew, then sipped. Out came Andrew's tongue—Licia paused in her coughing to smile and adjust her Etrusco-black hair. Marm stared at the ceiling where the headlights of a lone vehicle drifted onto the parking lot from the darkness. As a trucker's joint, maybe we weren't so far off the trade routes after all.

Tonya swiveled and turned strangely sad eyes on me. She looked back at Mother. "Rick," she uttered. I caught the unsureness in Tonya's voice. So the deed wasn't quite done yet. "You have what you wanted. I did what you said. Will you let Rick out now?"

Mother's eyes narrowed. A quick glance at me and I instantly realized that Tonya had spoken an indiscretion—some family trash had dropped on the floor. "Do a deed, get a deed." The pert expression returned, emerging through another hastily puffed cloud of cherry. "We all get what we deserve. That's Mary, Mother of God's plan, you know."

Tonya pouted. "But the Bell. You said that once I do as you say, you'll let him go. You don't need him anymore for the Bell."

"Hush, child." Marm's eyes resumed narrowing. Her fingers tapped a forearm in irritation and her eyes flicked back to the ceiling. "Can't you do *anything* right?" Andrew and Licia snapped their gaze on their errant sister, grinning with *schadenfreude*. "You'll get no wafers misbehaving like this," Marm added. Mother resumed smiling. "Credit where it's due, my child. Credit where it's due."

Green Eyes pouted. Her gaze dropped. "So you're going through with it?"

In reply, another puff of cherry smoke cast its pall over the table, and Licia resumed hacking her lungs. I could no longer resist and reached for my e-cig. For some reason my arm responded dully, as in slowed motion. Managing to extract the device from the inner pocket of my Canali jacket, I stared double, the e-cig splitting before me, duplicating. With a supreme effort I punched the button, sending my own cloud of fruity flavor erupting as if to do combat with Marm's. What was Mother's name again? No one had said—just as no one had formally introduced themselves to me. It seemed almost as if no one expected our little meeting to be repeated, so introductions were pointless—yet, all clearly *knew* me—or at least *about* me...

My doppelgangered eyes strove to focus on the blank wall of the tail end of the flattened L, where the undecorated canvas beside the bar's hook-end reacted strangely to the twin waves of smoke. The white waves mixed with another blast of mist that emanated from the kitchen's swinging doors as Diego stepped out—funny how he suddenly took on the high-cheekbones and long hair of those cast-iron statues that grace the front of even the smallest churches in god-forsaken El Salvador. The statue vanished in the waves of mist. The waves stuck to the blank wall, accumulating until gravity sucked them into its depths, the surface reacting bizarrely by erupting into a pizza-scape of bubbles and spume.

A smudge emerged. It became a man's back, enlarging until the whole man appeared, walking backwards like a film in reverse, gliding blindly but confidently toward our table, his face obscured, only a long white ponytail visible between his shoulder blades. Before he cleared the volcano, a second figure appeared, also walking backward, face invisible, just a bald head. Ocher and off-white jackets reminded me of mariachi players in Acapulco.

My hand drooped. The e-cig cracked on the tabletop. For a moment I counted the cost of replacing it, which made little sense given that the interior of Rick's Americana had begun to warp and swim as if viewed from the bottom of an Olympic-sized pool, making me wonder if I had just been selected to pay everyone else's check. From somewhere a postman delivered the bill. It read: 'Mickey Finn' in letters that Quinn insisted on spelling 'Rohypnol'. In even slower motion, I turned my gaze on the Zen green tea and wondered just how much Zen Marm had put in the recipe.

From somewhere, and nowhere, the blank face of a Ming Dynasty bald Buddha appeared alongside me. A set of arms on either side lifted me from the booth and transported me out of the neon light into the darkness of the night where the North Star sent its emissaries swirling in rings to rest over a dark blue taxi. Out of the depths—a sleepy "That you, Pete?" From under my armpit, blue steel came to life and I wondered how my rod could penetrate Green Eyes' female jungle since my legs had turned to rubber.

Sleepy eyes stared in surprise at me through an open car window.

A pop rang again. And again. "That's the crank," squealed a voice. Something forced a smoky hot blue-steel Colt—or was it my e-cig spilling more white smoke?—into my numb hand. As the walls closed in, I glimpsed a limo parked absurdly in trapezoid yellow lines behind the taxi, and a snake flicked its pink tongue in my face, the appendage evading grinning ivory teeth to the upbeat sounds of a woman's coughs. From somewhere echoed two rings of a church bell, ear-splitting loud, followed by a bright voice in thick European accent—Czecho? or just plain Slovakian?—utter, "What a *little* man he is..."

CHAPTER 4

I awoke to the chirping of nightingales. Hardly the state bird of my adopted home New Mexico, but more to my liking than bats, the *unofficial* official state bird. Bats do chirp. But with the crack of dawn, which sent its shivers of light into my crusted eyelids, and was hardly more welcome to my aching head than the butt-crack of Don, the building's plumber, the bats had flown to greener caves. Like the coyotes and gilas, they were apparently smarter than me.

The scenery seemed strangely urban. The phantoms which a moment earlier had been infecting my dreams, making me sweat cold sweat, returned to their dark refuges to be replaced by the back-ends of a pair of downtown buildings. I blinked. My vision remained obscured. Deciphering that I was peering through a car window, I reached out and with some effort managed to curl down the glass with the old-fashioned window crank.

I gazed at the rear door of my office's edifice. Glancing up, I could just see the fourth floor, though I knew my rented digs looked out on the main avenue, not the building's back alley. That's where I was. Or rather, that's where the car that I sat in was stopped.

I turned to see who drove—a silent presence already alerted me that I was riding shotgun. With relief, I recognized Joe. I smiled. Face of Joe was no more photogenic than crack of Don, but that never bothered me. I'm just that kinda guy.

Surrounded by dark blue taxi, I was finally awake. "Helluva ride, huh, Joe?" I mumbled, running my fingers through my jacket and pants pockets, searching my habit-holes. "But I can't seem to squeeze any juice outta my brain cells. Are we coming or going?" Unconsciously I counted the boxes and dumpsters that littered the alley behind him. Lost count at three.

Joe's window was rolled up. And his head rolled down. It

didn't seem comfortable, his head at that angle. Must be napping, I supposed, like me. I reached for his shoulder and tapped.

He slumped over.

I jerked. Not because Joe is that ugly—which he is—but because the driver side of his head was gone. Half his ugly mug. Blood drenched his left side like a herd of nuns had foot-stomped roses into wine.

Snapping open my side door, I struggled to stand. Slower than I should have. Then it all came back. The Mickey Finn, the snake-like tongue, the Schoolmarm dispensing 'wafers' like a female cardinal but without the red hat. And the Czech Buddha, with his ponytail pal. And Green Eyes herself, obsessed with invisible chefs named Rick. And...church bells. Very loud church bells.

Damn if it didn't add up to one helluva mystery.

I sighed. A last look at what was left of my friend and a tear tried to jump from my eye. And would have, had any of those salty symptoms of debt remained in my memory bank after so many years eye-to-eye with nature films of back alley melodramas.

My first impulse was to whip out my cell phone and put in a report to the local gumshoes. So of course that was the last thing I would do. First impulses are like Jehovah's Witnesses at the door—something to be resisted at all costs. But that option was missing anyway as I realized my pocket search had failed to find the thing. Phone gone. *And* gun. But wallet where it should be, and my cash still there. Now thoroughly puzzled, I felt the rest of my pockets, and, just to be sure, every hidden fold between my pockets, finding nothing but my ivory fedora that someone had carefully placed in the taxi's back seat.

I tried to think. Not only my legs felt like rubber...my brainiac cells had also still not kicked into gear. And wouldn't till I drenched them with Ecuador's finest dark brew. Hands in pockets, I stood dumbly staring. At the taxi. At Joe. At the backs of buildings. Up and down the alley. Thank Providence and JesÚ that no one loitered to see what the hell had happened. All I knew was someone had to report this—and that someone couldn't be me. That someone, in fact, had to be *no one* till I managed to find the rest of my shit. My own bag of trash waited for the next deposit.

A ring sounded.

Mechanically I reached inside my jacket to answer the phone. Pavlov's dog couldn't have responded more predictably. I had once felt sorry for the mutt, but Pavlov's bitch never had to deal with date rape drugs and cell phone thefts and gangster executions using someone else's gun in the middle of someone else's night. Yeah, I may be stupid, but I ain't dumb. Even that blind umpire at the Yankees game could see what was about to happen.

I swallowed. Knew in my bones better than a three-eyed fortune-teller what was coming...

Reaching into the taxi, I lifted Joe's lapel and pulled my phone out of his breast pocket as it rang. For a moment it reminded me of those timbrels crashing from that invisible bell tower, and my head again ached. The phone went silent. I stroked my magic code and a text popped into view. A picture—just a picture: a blue-steel Colt with a Canali-clad paw on the handle, the barrel pointed at an exposed head at the moment of impact.

Nicely done, I thought. Must have a lot of practice with split-second photography to have gotten that just right. And split-second gunnery. There was no point in spending calories wondering whose hand and whose gun it was—the gun was my government-registered blue-steel Colt. *Or* whose head. He slouched beside me now, un-gently sleeping. As pretty a setup as I'd ever seen, with my fingerprints and all.

Only the fine print was left to be read. They had me and they knew it. But why wasn't I as dead as Joe? And why didn't they take my money? And who the hell were 'they' anyway? Despite my years of taking slugs in this thuggish business of sorting through people's trash, my intuition had failed me, had left me with little notion of who 'they' were. Oh, 'Andrew' of course. And 'Mother'. And probably 'Licia'... But who exactly *were* these goofballs? Somehow I felt sure there would be no Massolini clan in the phone book, or online. And Green Eyes? My memory banks clearer, I ransacked her comments from the night before and detected more than *innocent victim*. A client not telling the truth—fancy that. I kicked Quinn for having opted for the quick buck. While at it, I kicked Pietro too because his obsession with penetrating Tonya's green jungle had helped sink us all.

The phone beeped and I glanced down.

A smiley face.

I was not amused.

But I began to breathe again. That smiley face meant a lot. It meant I wasn't dealing with desperadoes intent on deep-sixing me in the Big Ditch, or with the non-politics of dirt-dwelling insects, but with living, eating, crapping, two-legged humans. That was good news because humans can talk. And that face was talk. It was more than that—it was negotiation. Whoever it was, they wanted something, or I would already be in cuffs and blinking in the glare of red and blue cruiser lights, headed for the Slammer. And, seeing that my gun was someplace besides the inside of Joe's taxi or the inside of Joe's jacket, meant I could walk away from what was left of him without calling the cops. Since pictures can be faked, that photo would be useless to them without my gun. My gun with my fingerprints was their insurance...

But for what?

How was just barely conceivable—a before-dawn ride behind a tow truck to bring the taxi to this alley, though I saw no sign of the truck or recalled any sensation of the taxi being lifted. But what the hell for?

I intended to find out. *Had to*—unless I wanted to spend the rest of my meager life living in cardboard boxes in Borneo as Señor Pavlov. And *had to* before their plan kicked into gear, whatever that plan might be.

First things first. I needed a new gun. Luckily I still had my underarm holster, so, after paper-napkining my fingerprints from the car handle, and a last swiveling-sniveling glance to ensure that I was still incognito in Las Crueles, I bid *adidas* to soon-to-be-gone Joe DiMaggio and strolled in the back door of my low-to-no-rent office building.

It had no videocams. Or rather, Big-Hair's Landlord's bankruptcy had terminated her contract and she no longer plugged in her boss's video server as a match to no longer collecting the rent. Still, I was glad to see she had not yet come to 'work' and no one remained to see me hoofing it from the scene of the crime.

Taking the stairs, I keyed myself into my little glass and wood door. Paused before the 'Pete Marlowe – Private Investigator' stencils. Someone had sure done some investigating, all right. But into me. There wasn't much *private* left.

I used the desk phone. Not because I'm old-fashioned—which I am even more than Green Eyes—but to avoid being spied on using my cell, which might have been the little ear that had copied my privates onto somebody's front page. With my cell phone dismantled on the desk before me, and battery temporarily removed, I used old-fashioned Ma Bell to touch a local fence. Yep, he still had my other blue-steel Colt in pawn. Twin of the first. But this one unregistered, the numbers altered by one of his minimum wage Rembrandts. I ordered extra bullets.

Stuffing a stack of Uncle Sam's own declarations of bankruptcy into hidden velcroed pockets, I grabbed my genuine Movado watch and Loreto rose gold sunglasses, both bought a year earlier in a Bangkok stall, and snuck down the stairs. I glanced around the corner into the manager's marbled office. Big-Hair was still AWOL. I slipped a plastisteel lozenge the size and shape of a credit card—complete with fake numbers raised on its face, another trick of the PI trade—into Big-Hair's door lock, and the door opened.

I slid inside and plugged the server back in. Within moments it was recording again, and I made sure it got me as I exited the building via the front door, though with my fedora pulled low over my face. That way I could claim I had been where I was supposed to be when Joe's body was discovered. Or the opposite—that someone had only pretended to be me. Nothing in life like choices. A siren growing louder by the second indicated a local had called. I sniffed. Bumpy Joe was already a statistic in the City of 'Querque's Doomsday Book.

Down the street and around the corner, at the bus stop I paused. Right on time, the eight-thirty a.m. special to Town Center appeared and I swung aboard. Tinkling change into the collection box, I sat, and in minutes arrived at Pawn & Loan where I surprised the proprietor by at last settling my debt. I exited with my holster again filled and shells in my pocket. Only a close inspection would spring that I had switched rods and no longer had a registration for this.

Next stop was wheels.

I decided to upgrade from taxis. Checking the cash balance in my memory bank, I recalled that not much had been there before Green Eyes' deposit, having dropped my last dime on my suit, which meant that not much remained to throw at Taxicab Joe's chop-shop cousin who posed as a used car pusher during the day—Honest Juan. But there was enough. So I flatfooted through the sterile dry air of the New Mexico plateau, keeping my fedora close. Who knew how many eyes may have glimpsed my exit from Joe's taxi, or how many ears may have heard my grunts while I reenergized brain cells and squeegeed the taxi's door handles. A video of me on a server was proof of nothing—just one brand of insurance. Another trick of the PI trade: there are no sure things, just layers of protection. Like guns in reserve, buried 'lotto' winnings, and the backs of stairs and chairs; every good suit of armor has more than one layer, and more than one blacksmith.

Not a consignment guy, Honest Big-Money Juan held the Guinness World Record for repossessing the same car from the same guy—*mío*. Sauntering up the back way, I verified that my antique green Oldsmobile rested in the same spot as usual, and I slipped in the back door. Though the Olds was technically for sale, it was too darn ugly for anyone to actually buy, except the car's serial owner. Every four months I bought it. Every four months he repossessed it—after the usual nonpayment of a single dime and after figuring out what part of Albuquerque I had stashed it in this time.

I'm just that kinda guy.

Our little dance was never voiced, but after a decade we both knew that the combination of my lousy credit and his lousy car was making it the most expensive rental in history. So as soon as his eyes landed on me, he smiled big-time, and as I laid my cash on his table, he eagerly handed me the keys.

He's just that kinda guy. Old times is old times.

Wondering if behind a warehouse on University Park would make a good hidey-hole for the Olds for the next four months, I exited Juan's makeshift office, rounded the corner of his repair shop, and strode into his vast barbwire parking lot of fifty feet with its vast repertoire of eighteen hulks to where the Olds was contentedly rusting. I slid into the front seat and turned on the '85 engine. *Smoooth.* One last check on wallet, fedora hat, seat-belt, shades, and wristwatch and I reached for my Colt to verify to doubting Quinn that I was indeed ready, that the Enterprise was juiced and the photon torpedoes loaded for my emergency road trek back to Rick's.

My left arm refused to budge.

I had left the windows down, and someone had laid a ham hock on my shoulder.

"Where do I send the china?" graveled a voice in my ear.

In the opposite door's lowered window, another elbow leaned in. "Maybe ya should postmark it: 'To the happy bride'."

Full-size human number one released my shoulder. He reached over my seat-belted body and turned off the motor, extracting the keys and dangling them noisily.

"Does he look happy to you? He don't look happy to me, Krupke, like he just missed his bridal shower." In the left window, number one pushed his mug closer to mine. "You in a hurry, Marlowe? 'Cause it looks to me like you're in a hurry. A *big* hurry."

"Where's the lingerie sale, Marlowe?" added the other, leaning in the right window, his fat round face pasted with a half-smirk. "Ya gettin' short on pink undies and need a new pair by noon? Or did Victoria's Secret finally put your bra size on sale?"

Both gave a bare hint of a smile, their formal dull black polyester government-issue suits showing specks of dust.

Their clean-shaven faces were familiar. "Detective Dorkman," I exhaled. "How do you—"

"How do I *what*, Pete?" he interrupted. "Now do I have to shove my badge in your face again? Or run off to the judge for another piss-ant warrant? What kind of monkey gym are you gonna make us climb through *this* time to get an honest answer outta ya?" Dorkman glanced at his partner. "What do *you* think, Detective Krupke?"

"Oh, I think our little lady here is gonna cooperate." Krupke squinted in the sun and pursed an exaggerated kiss in my direction.

Dorkman pulled open the driver's side door. "How 'bout at least gettin' outta the damned car while we interrogate ya?"

Honest Juan's face appeared briefly in the back door of his Taj

Mahal. I couldn't tell whether he was upset over having to repossess his dead cousin Joe's taxi, or worried that Albuquerque's true-blues might add my blood to the oil stains on his concrete. Either was possible. Or both.

Unclicking my seat belt, I stepped out. "Always happy to oblige, Dork."

Dorkman frowned. "Watch your language, Pete."

"I always do, Detective Dorkman. Just like the porn channel at midnight. Never miss a second."

Krupke rounded the Olds and stood behind me, his fat frame sweating from that little effort. "We don't need no stinkin' badges for this dipshit—or warrants."

"Season's greetings to you too, *Krapke*." I glanced at a plastic fork peeking from his suit's shirt pocket. "Still goin' back for fourths at your favorite buffet? Well, *laissez les bon temps roulez*." I smiled at him. "But if *you* eat any more *bon temps*, they'll have to *roulez* your fat ass to the cemetery."

Krupke did a fast burn. He lunged. Dorkman managed to stiff-arm him to a stop before I had a chance to judo-chop his Adam's Apple, which had fattened so far beyond Adam that it looked more like Zeke's Zuchini.

Krupke regained control. "I told you last time, Dorkman, if this little shit starts in on me again, I'll fuckin' kill him." Krupke's face turned into a dirty strawberry. Not that there was much difference.

"Take it easy, Krup." Dorkman pushed his partner a few paces back. "You know the rules. Maybe little shits like Marlowe don't know and don't care, but we're better than that. We got rules."

Krupke calmed. From behind Dorkman's back, I removed my Loreto sunglasses, the better to grin at the fat man as I fed invisible boudin into my mouth with an imaginary fork.

I'm just that kinda guy.

Krupke's eyes drilled hate but he didn't lunge.

Dorkman turned to face me and I dropped the pretend fork. "We ain't here for our health, Marlowe. Or 'cause we think you're more fun than monkey gyms. We're here 'cause a body turned up in the back alley behind your office, and we got word that you came into some money and you're suddenly payin' off debts." Dorkman and Krupke exchanged glances like they knew more than they let on, though in my experience the reverse was usually truer.

I shrugged. "Don't know nothin' 'bout nothin', gentlemen. All I know is a client paid what he owed me so I came here to buy a new car."

"Honest Juan don't sell new cars. Just old ones."

"An old-new car. You know what I mean."

"'Fraid we do, Marlowe. Too bad the PI business ain't more lucrative. You're lucky to be back in that ancient heap of yours."

Krupke smirked again and kicked the Olds. "He likes ta ride *in style*, don't he?"

"Old times is old times, Krapke. I'm just that kinda guy."

Krupke narrowed his eyes. "Make him shut up, Dorkman, or I swear ta God..."

I raised my chin. "Breathe slow, Have-Fork-Will-Travel. It sometimes helps."

"Watch your mouth, Marlowe," said Dorkman. "You may not know it, but you're in deep. Maybe deeper than you know."

I omitted the memoir and footnotes of the past twenty-four hours. Deep was hardly the word.

Dorkman continued. "You sure you didn't take a contract on a taxi driver?"

"Now why the hell would I do that, Dorkman? Is there a hot market for ugly cabbies and their junk heaps?"

He stared. "Maybe you didn't like him takin' the long way to Vegas."

"Or to Victoria's Secret," said Krupke.

"County Line Thoroughbreds is only a skip and hop away," Dorkman added.

"He don't look like no thoroughbred to me, Dorkman. Not even an also-ran. I mean, if I was like real desperate and had a choice between him and Gilligan..."

"Hate to break it to ya, Marlowe, but I'm with Krupke." Dorkman dead-panned. "Ain't no time long enough."

"Or island small enough," added Krupke.

"Though small in your case means somethin' *completely* different."

"Completely."

"A single tree, a mighty jungle."

"Few grains of sand, the Sahara."

"A twig, an elephant's happy stick."

"None happier than a tiny guy like you."

Dorkman and Krupke traded their quiet smiles for quiet looks.

"Which brings us back to what we said, Marlowe. Where'd ya get the dough?" Dorkman squinted again. "And what were you doin' around midnight when your buddy Joe got his? Did he win the lottery and you couldn't stand not bein' invited?"

"Did he win a card game and the loser boo-hoo on your shoulder?"

I stared straight. "I suppose it's beyond you two dicks that a satisfied client might have paid me for my services."

"Way beyond."

"Completely and past."

"Beyond and beyond."

I narrowed my eyes, focused on a billboard behind Honest Juan's Taj Mahal that touted bus trips to Vegas at discounted rates, a pair of D-cup silver headlights thrown in as incentive. "You guys should know by now that I only play stud to hi-class fillies. And I don't mean cards. I go only by the book. Legal all the way..." I reached under my arm.

Dork and Krupke's hands moved to their own underarms.

"Whoa there, Pete," said Dorkman. "Don't get burs under your saddle. Just tell us where the hell you were last night around midnight."

I paused. "I was only going to show you my permits, gentlemen. All up-to-date, as I'm sure you reviewed before you followed me."

They didn't deny it.

"We're waitin', Marlowe. It's awful quiet out here. And hot. I'm gettin' darn tired of standin' in the sun, feedin' you your bottle."

Pulling a laminated PI license, and the gun registration the license required, out of the inner pocket of my Canali jacket, I handed them over. "I was on a job in the Petrified Forest, Dorkman. All evening. My client can verify that." I hoped they wouldn't call that bluff, though there had been some fossilized wood on Cartagena Road. After all, a few stumps, a forest.

One quick glance too brief to read a word, and they handed my documents back. "Better be sure, Marlowe. 'Cause we might just ask." Dorkman paused, then looked back at me.

"Now your piece," he said.

With a hint of a pause, I slowly pulled it out of its holster and held it out ass-end under Dorkman's nose. He sniffed the barrel, not taking his eyes off me. A glance at his partner and he nodded. I slid the blue-steel back in its place.

"Does he live in Albuquerque?"

"Who?"

"Don't get stupid on me, Marlowe. Your Rockefeller client."

"He's in the phonebook."

"And?"

"And what?" I asked.

"What's his number?" Dorkman glared.

"That's in the phonebook, too."

"Name?"

At the same time we both said "Phonebook." I crooked my mouth. "That's all I can tell you, guys. Confidentiality, etcetera, etcetera."

Dorkman spat on the concrete, wrinkled half a lip. "Get a warrant?"

I smiled a broad one. "The piss-ant kind."

Their dead-pans turned into bed-pans, flat and raunchy. But hell if I would ever let this dead-namic duo hold me back. I had an errand to run. My gun, paper, and laminated plastic back in my jacket, I tipped my fedora and held out my palm. Dorkman pointedly dropped the keys on the concrete. I picked them up—easier for the napoleonic than for most.

"By the way, nice suit."

Back in the front seat, I fired the engine and jerked the shift into gear. Slowly I cruised out the back gate, watching through my rearview mirror the two gumshoes in Honest Juan's car lot silently glare. Krupke kicked the back of my Olds as I rolled away.

He's just that kinda guy.

CHAPTER 5

I was more tired than a Canadian duck in Yucatan, but hell hath no fury like a private dick scorned. Not only was Pietro pissed at having missed the trolley bell for Green Eyes' Emerald Isle, but Quinn wanted tit-for-tat for what the Massolinis had done to ugly Joe. Knowing that Pietro would accept teat-for-tat hardly helped. Green Eyes was as AWOL as Marm & Co.

Besides, I had to figure out what the hell had been worked on me. And something had sure been worked. The second shoe had yet to be dropped and I didn't want to be caught in the open when the footwear fell. Albuquerque's twin dicks already carried sand in their pockets to sprinkle on my gravestone—all Dork and Krapke needed to make their day was a tap-dance menu.

I had muted my phone, charged its prostate, and finally—out of sight and hearing of the dancing duo—puttered west, then north, then finally southeast. Whatever it took to ensure privacy in my route back to the scene of the crime. Was it smart? All I knew is that it was dumb to sit and wait for the weather to change without an umbrella. Given the nonexistence of the Massolini clan, one and all, even Green Eyes, there was no other way to get to the source. Sure, a lot could happen. But I made bet on one thing: they wanted me above ground—not under it. I had not forgotten the smiley face.

So I drove.

The sun had crossed midpoint and hovered in the shimmering heat thrown off concrete and asphalt. Again I viewed the pockmarked warehouse that seemed to stretch to infinity, the heat waves wrinkling its far end into invisibility as had the previous night's darkness. Squinting barely helped.

I slid on my Loreto sunshades. Not that it accomplished miracles. Nothing could do that in this corner of the universe.

Godforsaken, the Indians had called it, ignoring the earnest counsels of the Spanish missionaries who had attempted to drag their resisting souls into the modern world. Heat and God don't go well together. The Indians knew that. And after three centuries of failed conversions, the Spanish learned it too and gave up trying to colonize this hellhole, leaving it to brash immigrants from the east to smash and grab, and cover up the superstitions of the pueblo dwellers by calling it New Mexico, though it was not new and barely Mexican. The Indians knew that souls don't meet their Maker in the desert without a fight. The desert is like a pizza oven—it delivers. And the snakes, gilas, hawks, and of course *los coyotes* do the same, delivering souls of the damned to their Sun God with or without fast-food orders.

Creeping the Olds up the boulevard, then back down, I turned suddenly east at the same cutoff as the previous night, watching the sparse traffic to make sure I wasn't followed, or my escape blocked.

No car appeared.

I let the throttle run.

Bouncing potholes like on a trampoline, the Olds wound through the heat. I scraped the shoulder here, then there. The view was better this time. The road was flat underfoot, but slowly climbed into gray foothills that streaked skyward up ahead where other roads led to other districts, other worlds where real Rockefellers cavorted and splashed in private gardens, hidden in their Shangri-Las by vertical cliffs and frowning gate-guards from the staring eyes of white-pocket gumshoes like me.

Petrified shards of prehistoric wood threw occasional flashes like ancient sacrifices. Furtive movements behind burning rocks and bloated cacti reminded me that only mad dogs and Irishmen venture out in the noon-day sun. Much more of this and I might wonder which one was I.

For minutes I drove without seeing another car. The trucks I fancied I had seen last night were gone, leaving no trace, not even a tire track. At the top of a slope a craggy hill appeared. The road circled round and I inched forward, avoiding a new set of potholes, bone-dry, as if this portion of the sky had never known rain. Pulling into a wide rectangular patch of sea-shell strewn awkwardly in the desert, I came to a dead stop.

I stepped out of the Olds. Scratched the back of my neck.

A church?

No neon.

No glass front, no 'Rick's Americana' sign, no cherry-red bar, no phalanx of Kentucky's finest. My foot crunched scrabble and I glanced down. No paved parking lot either, no yellow stripes or ugly Joe's blood. Just raw primitive shell that drifted up to a blank pale wall punched by a simple wooden door.

A bell rang, louder than it had any right to ring. I brought my hands over my ears to block the clamor. Above the door rose a modest bell tower, its old-timey metal clanger sending its call into the baked desert as if summoning a reluctant ghost-congregation to Church Mass.

Saint Peter's of the desert—a simple adobe church.

Now I understood the bells I had heard from University Park. This damned bell was loud enough. I could see its enormous girth through an open window in the tower. As if in response, the bell rang again and proceeded through the litany of a full twelve clangs announcing the advent of noon while I stood there, hands over ears. And still the door remained shut, no one scurrying from the countryside to attend services. Four centuries and the local padres were still shit outta luck.

That's what I call slow to learn.

The ringing stopped—but didn't stop. Instead, static infused with melodious sounds lingered, unplaceable, incomprehensible, like a backdrop buzzing of insects.

Finally silence returned.

Stepping forward, I tried the door. Locked. From the other side I thought I heard a light padding of quadruple feet, together with short energetic breaths as if dogs patrolled the joint. No one answered and I wandered back to my Olds to get the big picture.

Maybe the church had a back entrance.

I stumbled around the corner, across cacti and stray weeds, taking care to avoid getting any more dust on my pants legs than necessary, silently thanking the Hollywood gods that no one had written quicksand into this real-life script. A hundred feet and I found the ass-end and ascended some old wooden stairs to a second door. It stood ajar. No need for Katy to bar the door against intruders in this neck of the weeds, though. Gila monsters never yet stole church silver.

Inside was empty. No furniture. The adobe walls devoid of pictures. Not even an 'our first peso' framed on the wall, or 'Our Founder' posing in old-timey ermine and neck ruffs like a big-shot conquistador of untamed Indian souls. In the center of the church, I gazed about, puzzled. There must be someone—or something—to give me a clue as to what the heck had been done and what the hell was up. Even a private dick needs a clue, but they'd been sucked up by an invisible vacuum cleaner.

I blinked. Someone must have yanked that bell rope a minute ago. Switching a modern bar and grill with a decrepit has-been museum was more than a trick. It was mind-blowing.

I sighted a stairwell. A metal one that wound upward directly into the bell tower.

Then I remembered. Putting my hand in my pocket—the tiny velcroed pocket inside the larger one, where I kept my cash—I withdrew a slight paper scribbled in crayon with a picture of a bell. My brows arched. Only one way to find out.

Approaching the stairwell, my hand crinkled old paint and rust off the railing—it had clearly been there for decades, if not centuries. I climbed. The top gave onto a small platform of wooden planks. Above me, circling the upper portion of my body was the church's antique bell, even larger than it had appeared from below now that I stood within its circumference, its noon-tide ringing only recently stopped. Standing there, my gaze penetrating the simple un-shuttered window that let onto the shell lot below, I fancied I could hear the bell's reverberations still echoing.

The echoes took form.

"Mios Italianos... Mios Italianos... Let me back into your hearts. Do not forget me."

I froze. I've heard damned funny things in my short mortal life, and things that were damned hard to understand, and things that I'd damned sure like to forget, but I had never yet heard a radio broadcast from Heaven, in church or out, and sure the hell not by a man's voice in Italian. Swinging down the staircase like a Versace Tarzan, I popped the deadbolt on the front door and ran into the parking area till I had returned to my car, only then pausing to catch my breath. Calming, I stared up at the tower, the voice still echoing in my ears, like an Easter Annunciamento by the Pope from his favorite Roma balcony. Mary, Mother of God it wasn't. God, son of Mary...well, who the hell knew? But last I heard, Jesus didn't speak Italian.

The echoes finally vanished.

Or had they?

The new sound was different. Tires crunched. From around the hill something was coming. I leapt into my car, kicked it to life, and sped past the adobe church to pause behind an outcropping of enormous cracked stones. Stepping out, I peeked over the crag to see who or what was interrupting my yoga high.

A white government-issue four-door crept into view and rolled forward until it occupied almost the space where my car had been. Out stepped a pair of dull black polyester suits.

"Dork and Krapke," I whispered, my palm shielding my sun-spectacled eyes. Maybe they knew more than they let on after all. Or maybe they were just too pissed to let things slide.

Either way, I had no time for their shenanigans. I reentered my Olds. Loosening the brake, I let gravity take my car away down the hill and out of sight. When the road flattened, I keyed the motor and floored the pedal just in case their hearing was as good as mine, and before long I was tracing cork-screws among the cliff-like ridges that border eastern Albuquerque until no chance remained of being tracked by those flatfoots.

My cell phone blipped.

Pulling to one side of the road beneath the shade of a giant limestone slope, I punched the code and viewed the latest message. Somehow I knew in advance that this would be no smiley face. I opened the attachment. A naked girl swung hips around a vertical pole. Her face wasn't visible. But there was no need. The message was as clear to me as midnight porn.

I had no appointment, but I knew when to arrive just as well as I knew the closing time of every Irish pub in Albuquerque—both of them. This could not be handled during daylight hours. Like white zombies and pink-tongued snakes, pole-dancing only comes out at night.

Meantime, my dogs and my brain were exchanging pathetic yelps. Each wanted a break. I had been up for most of a day on half-a-night's sleep and the Mickey Finn was still making both brain-work and brake-work difficult. There was no more to be done till the pole opened—9:00 p.m. So I surrendered to Pietro's and Quinn's demand that I recharge my batteries and headed home.

Giving the adobe church and its lonely road a wide berth, I carefully motored to a minor warehouse district southwest of town where I slid the Olds into my on-again-off-again spot with its eroded blue wheelchair logo. Hardly any of the logo remained after rolling my bald tires over it so often. Not that it inconvenienced the truly helpless. Parking spots lined the warehouse up and down, some taken, some not—all eroded, all unused. They were all the same to anyone who went about their business without a government-issue microscope in their pocket.

Home.

Since my Ex had put her X on the ownership line of the shotgun shack I had shared with her, by order of her ex-stripper friend who had finally made good as a gold-digging divorce judge, I had opted to spend my a.m. hours in a cot behind the warehouse's chief tenant—a wholesale laundry service. Secluded, just the way I like it.

After depositing my wallet in a wall locker sporting a hefty lock that only I knew the combination of, I collapsed on the cot hidden in a darkened corner. Lulled by a combination of Honduran gibberish and the spinning of eternal mixmasters, I drifted...

Not secluded enough.

A stern-faced Oriental who looked as if she were just off a slow Boeing from China jerked my arm. "You pay. You behind rent again. You pay."

It was too late. I could not combat the Rohypnol remnants reclaiming my brain and slipped back into la-la-land where I chased spherical laughing Honduran females trying to penetrate their jungles with Colts while a frowning Empress of China flew above us like the wicked witch of Oz. Cloud Nine—not to mention Clouds One through Eight—later, I finally returned whole to earth, fluttering like a kid who had lassoed a kite.

Rubbing my eyes, I rose on one elbow.

Stood.

The Empress was gone. Stumbling to my feet and throwing my numero uno suit into a machine cycler, I staggered to my locker where I kept my spare—it was still locked shut. Sometimes a man's gotta do what a man's gotta do, first of the month or not. That's pay the rent. Anyway, the Empress had already blocked the back door preventing a quick dodge. I smirked. I've seen dogs in her nightly stew that learn quicker than her. But this time she had me.

Dry-cleaning my Canalis, I snapped them free when they were done and draped them on my body, taking care to prep my white shirt with a pink tie. One eye remained open for the Manchurian Candidate as I resigned myself to finally handing over the filthy lucre—but hell if I would do so without a fight. Two Jacksons in hand, but concealed in my still-warm pants, I braced myself for another confrontation over the price of a soiled cot in the corner, a locker stuck to the wall, and a parking space with a worn-out blue logo.

Near the exit, I sighted Her Imperial Majesty. Behind her, a herd of way-down-south unsmiling maids circled like a collection of silent moons, making a timely exit impossible.

She turned. Saw me.

Was I still drifting in Honduran land? The Empress wide-smiled, and with a wave of her hand brushed the silent moons aside. Her own lacquered fingernailed digits opened the back door, without the assistance of even a single court eunuch.

"*Thank you*, Meester Marlowe," she grinned, nodding. "*Thank you*, Meester Marlowe."

I never understood why a broad from East-Alien-Land would speak the King's English with a Spanish accent, unless it was from her endless machine cycling in the presence of Centro-Americanos. Takes all types, I suppose. And I could not understand why Dragon Lady had melted into Snow-White when I hadn't paid a dime on my account in weeks.

But good times is good times.

I walked out.

Out of booze, coffee, time, and explanations, I parked my ass in my parked Oldsmobile, stirred the engine, and rolled about my business, as the sun—having risen that strange morning *like* a phoenix—vanished into night on its way *to* Phoenix.

Puttering back toward town center, I entered a forest of neon and finally wheeled into a back lot adjacent to one huge neon: 'Suite Chicas'. Yeah, I got the pun. It was my Ex's sweet cheeks that had sent me down tobacco road in the first place, every spare dime going to drape her in furs and German engineering while I hid my Olds from Honest Juan, and cleaned acorns and bat-poop from the roof of our shotgun shack. In the end, after a brief year of my being joined at the hip and drained at the wallet, she decided that size mattered after all and went back to climbing the same silver pole and flashing those same sweet cheeks that had snared me. She got the German car, the house, the bank account, the furs, and the jewels. I got the right to remain silent.

But old times is old times. As nine o'clock rolled around and the dead-heat of late spring seeping in from the Chihauhuan Desert turned ten degrees cooler, the world and its cares fell away. The Chicas sign flicked on, and blue and red outlines, female down to their neon hips, flashed one way, then the other...one way, then the other. Despite Quinn's veto glaring as red as a traffic controller's emergency blip, Pietro waved his tarmac-flares inviting Airforce Marlowe to land. Sweet sounds softly drifted as I approached the door.

A giant in an open-chest stretch-shirt with a gold medallion resting on a bed of hair stared down his nose. "How many?"

"You can't count to one?"

King Kong snorted. Opening the door wide, he sneered, "Entry for one-half." As I paid the full-price entry fee and walked through, he stopped me with one giant arm and stepped on my toe. He grinned until his ape-like mind finally got the info that I would never react to the pain, and, bored, he finally stepped off and lowered his arm.

I sauntered through. I had business that I didn't want side-tracked by a muscle-brain.

Inside was a different world. Through smoke and mirrors and florescent lights glimmering through the darkness like Venus and Mars through a dust storm, a wail of saxophones enveloped me. I melted. Under a canopy of Coltrane my mind folded into a Picasso clock. Walking to a bar that bordered two-thirds of the joint, I fumbled and slid a stack of bits onto its sticky surface.

A thin bird in glasses scraped it up. He arched his brow. "The usual?"

I nodded. "White Zombie."

He turned to assemble the components—*sans* green tea as I carefully observed. I may be slow, but I ain't sub-zero.

I let my eyes do the walkabout and, despite the gloom, saw a dozen other patrons. Some might have been Irish. The rest looked like they had just bounced in from Mexican cantinas after an evening of up-and-down polka, like mini-me versions of those Masai cowherders who can leap cars. I almost smiled at the prospect of blending in again with a Grand Armée of petit napoleons even if they did play trampoline bean.

I recognized no one. But the latest picture had clearly been a warning. Divorced and sent to the cleaners—literally, complete with cot and Mixmaster—still there were some things a man cannot do. Like fink on an Ex, no matter how many Exes he has, or allow someone else to poke his schnoz where it don't belong. Alien schnozes don't belong with Sweet Cheeks. Not even appendages signed Massolini.

I slid my e-cig out of its jacket pocket and pressed the button, sending a cloud of white mist into the night to mingle with the smoke and mirrors. The music switched to Charlie Parker and my soul relaxed more. Bogie never had it so good. And I even got to enjoy a leg up on the evil tobacco weed, imagining a future filled with job-destroying robots happily puffing tobacco-free e-cigs on their mid-morning break around an oil drum, like illegals from a planet of steel.

An explosion of light made me blink, then squint. When I opened my eyes again, an upraised stage at the back of the place shined in the harsh glare of a row of kliegs along the bottom edge outlining a single silver pole, a wide curtain of party-collage Mylar draped behind. It glittered like an aluminum waterfall. I wondered if the shiny drapes would block alien brain waves as effectively as tinfoil hats and which category of alien the Massolini clan fell into.

Like a Dallas Cowboy cheerleader on a New York sidewalk lift, she rose into view. All blonde hair and skin to match the blond Norwegian wood of the polished furniture, the Mylar glittering with her blinding beauty. Immediately, cigars appeared all round and, as if on command, goose-stepped erect, saluting her Nordic pulchritude like a Nazi allegiance from some weird crowd of Mexican skinheads. I fancied I saw Playboy and Penthouse reps duke it out under a table for the prize of her centerfold contract, and I thought briefly of joining in, but the shadows resolved into a pair of sodden rancheros searching for dropped coins. I already been there, done that.

My e-cig too was erect. Couldn't help it. I always had a thing for Ikea. Just like I always had a thing for Irish peaks. As long as the peaks were twin, I was always ready to mountain climb. And right now my attention was on the Swiss Alps and the rounded hinterland that backed them up, knowing every detail of the international tunnel that joined them. Her hinterland swayed and spun around the silver pole with all the fun of a kids' merry-go-round, while her Alps shook free of their nylon glacier and boldly swung, causing the phalanx of Rocky Patels to explode in smoke. My e-cig, no exception. All my boiling brain could think of was how to buy one more ticket so my train could release its load of freight in her tunnel—new times for old-times' sake.

Yes, Pietro dreamed, but I was no fool. That train had left months ago and, at length, he whimpered and re-holstered his gun. After the crowd of fans tossed bales of minimum-wage money on the stage to show their appreciation of 'modern art', the map of Switzerland went blank. The stage lift dropped, the lights lowered, and the blond décor went back to the kind of grubby furniture that usually infest cheesy strip joints.

Jack Ruby strode on stage to introduce the next Chicago act— no it wasn't Ruby, but he looked so similar that I checked myself to see if I had just killed a President and I almost yelled "I'm a patsy." to scare him off.

Ruby introduced the next nude act.

Pocketing Pietro, I got up. I left my bar seat to the tender mercies of an actual skinhead, and put distance between myself and Ruby, proceeding to Part Two of my plan—my stiffly erect e-cig still testifying to the success of Part One. Taking advantage of renewed bursts of smoke, I sidled past—or more precisely under—the radar of King Kong who was now serving as the girls' changing room hallway bouncer, and I gave a certain door a certain familiar scratch. Wasn't sure the code was still good. Hadn't been the last two times I tried it. But this time it needed to work; it wasn't just me in the proverbial pickle jar.

Several moments passed with no answer. I was about to raise the ante by banging loudly despite the certainty that bouncer Kong down the hall would be alerted and force me to karate chop him down to size. That would be his hard luck.

But the door cracked. Saving Kong from a drubbing, a slit opened from top to bottom revealing an interior that was better lit than the hallway.

No face? I blinked and pushed my mug forward. Somehow I didn't think the Ex's taste in art would change so fast that she would prefer me without a nose.

I was wrong.

An eye peered through the crack, then the door slammed shut, almost condemning my future carpet sniffing to crystal balls and Gypsy fortune-tellers.

"Wendy," I hissed. Glancing behind me through the hallway's smoke, which seemed in danger of dissipating, I blew another expansive cloud of mist to cover my tracks. Time was short. "It's *me*, Wendy."

More silence.

Suddenly she answered. "Go away, Pete."

"Baby doll, ya gotta listen. I've got somethin' to tell you, somethin' you gotta hear."

"You got nothing to say that I want to hear."

"Come on, baby, it's me. You know I still love you—"

"There's nothing you can say that you haven't already said, Pete. A thousand times."

"Wendy, open the door, *please.*" I glanced behind me again at

King Kong, my palms getting clammy. "I only have a few minutes. Then I'll leave, I promise. But, believe me, you really want to hear this."

The door cracked. The eye reappeared. Blue. My favorite when coming in pairs. "What do you want this time, Pete? I told you not to come around here again."

"Ya gotta listen, baby. No kiddin'. Something has happened. It's about you."

The second blue eye appeared.

"And money...lots of money..."

Both eyes blinked.

The door swung back. She continued hiding behind it, but I stepped inside, and she swung the door shut with a bang and locked it. Progress.

The Picasso clock melted across my head and shoulders as I realized that Wendy had not had time to dress after her last performance. Like old-times spouses in an old-times marriage, she stood raw and unassuming, entirely unconscious of her centerfold-class nudity. That's my Wendy—just like old times. I got busy strangling Pietro to keep him from jumping her bones. He never could get used to it.

"Well?" She folded her arms under her snowy peaks, framing their Matterhorns. Ignoring my hands about his throat, Pietro gave a fierce thumbs-up to spelunking. Like always, Wendy's prim face when annoyed looked cuter than kittens, and, sporting a good four inches over me, left me eye-to-eye with her mountain summits. Even when angry, she put the hi in hi-class filly.

"You're staring, Pete. Ain't nothin here you ain't seen a hundred times before. Which was a hundred and one times too many."

I blinked. "Don't say that, babe. I'm all yours. Always have been. You just don't know which side of the bread to butter anymore, that's all."

"The hell I don't. I've got news for you, Pete. Past-times is past-times. So don't come calling on me anymore." She paused, flattened her brows. "Now about that money..."

I noticed her eyeing my new suit. Quickly guided her back on track. "You got it all, baby. Every last cent. There ain't no more, no-way, no-how. That is, not after I bought my suit."

Her brows arched. "You bought a new suit? I *knew* it. There you go again with the lies." She dropped her arms. "That's why I left you in the first place. Lies, lies, lies! Can't you just for once tell the truth about anything?"

I wasn't listening. My eyes inches from the teats of my dreams, I almost dropped dead as my heart skipped a trio of beats. It was cruel and usual punishment. Of their own accord, my hands reached out.

"Mommy."

Wendy slapped Pietro down with a palm to the face. "Nothin' doin'. You had your chance, Pete, and ruined it. We're divorced now. You got everything you deserve. And after you spent every last dime that I earned from five years of hugging a pole, all I got was bills." She flung one precious shoulder, jiggling my brain along with her breasts. *"Now* look at me. I'm back in this place again, right where I started. And after you promised I'd never have to do this again." She refolded her arms. "So don't cry to *me* Argentina."

I calmed, rubbing the imprint of her palm on my chin. "Touché." The filly had a point, even if she was plagiarizing. "But, baby, I'm not here to ask you to come back. I know that's all old times now. I'm here to let you know there's a new problem—and it's a big one."

Wendy threw a shiny gown on, leaving Pietro whimpering. Her eyes narrowed. "What did you do?" Narrowed further. *"This* time."

I took a deep breath. The PI business is always hard to explain to lay-women. Especially ones named Wendy. That was another straw that broke the marriage.

"I can't go into details—there ain't no time, and it wouldn't help anyway. Just believe me when I tell you that you need to get the hell out of Dodge. Now. Tonight." For the first time I seemed to have her full attention. "There's a case, see? They're puttin' the squeeze on me. And they know all about *you*." I stared harder. "Do I really have to draw you a picture?"

Tying a belt around her waist, she tossed a nervous glance behind her as if black-shirted thugs with silver ties lurked in her closet. Sometimes Wendy got the drift. Especially when it involved money or safety. Strip joints will do that to a gal.

"That's just great." She dropped her eyes. "I swore I'd never let you screw me again...but you found a way." She shrugged. "Well, why the hell not? I was going to tell you soon, anyway. I'm going to Idaho, Pete. I've got just enough cash to start over. *If* you let me alone."

I dripped earnestness. "You bet, baby. Whatever you say." I too glanced at her closet. Who knew how long it might be before real thugs were lurking there. "Don't waste any time, baby." Taking a deep breath, I gritted my teeth and, reluctantly, cut the last apron strings—for her sake. "And don't tell me or anyone else exactly where you're goin'. For your own good, just go."

That was it. No point in this jockey giving the filly the whip as long as she was already running. As Wendy turned away, I backed out of her dressing room—Pietro refused to miss one last gander at her hinterlands. I had to give him that much, considering how he had just suffered. Few men can survive such punishment.

Luckily, King Kong was gone. Or, more accurately, had business back at the front door. Seems someone had tried to slip into the joint and he and a couple of bouncer pals were blocking them. Smoke and mist laid down such a blanket of fog that moving through the interior of the place, now that the dancing was done and the lights doused, felt like trying to maneuver a coal barge up the Thames.

By London Bridge I halted.

The infiltrators were the same familiar clowns: Dorkman and Krupke. Sliding my fedora over my brow, I returned to the fog bank of the hallway where I peered at the front entrance. How the hell did they find me? Well, who gives a damn. I guess it wasn't that hard to figure out my movements, though I was a bit surprised that a couple of dullards like them had the gray matter to get it. Too good, in fact. I wondered if they had planted a GPS on my car, but what difference did it really make? With all the nosey emails from Massolini and Co., it might just come in handy for Dork and Krapke to have my back. If only they could handle a gun as well as a fork. I knew better. Meanwhile, I still had business to tend to, which would be best done without Laurel and Hardy to gum things up.

I steered the tugboat to the strip joint's back door and made a quick exit into the darkened back lot of Suite Chicas, where once upon a time I had wooed Wendy in her off-hours with cold bracelets and hot burgers. I could almost see her now, her icy Nordic beauty freezing the blood in my throbbing veins, hormones thirsting to burst free, to mingle with their opposite.

Could it be? There she was, standing between the Suite Chicas' taco truck, one of the strip joint owner's side bets, and his latest toy, a maroon BMW. Her back was turned. For a moment, I breathed easier. Not because I was relieved to see Wendy dressed and heading for her Volkswagen faster than I thought possible, but because Pietro still thirsted for one last glimpse of her charms. I glanced at my right shoulder. Some people never change.

I stepped closer and paused. Something about her was different. Still gazing at her perfect backside, I noticed she seemed a trifle shorter than she should, a bit darker and a little less hard-edged, as if feathers smudged her outline.

She turned.

Green-fringes enveloped emerald eyes. Tonya! Yeah, she still wore the same outfit.

Before I could react to Tonya's unexpected presence, two pairs of hands grabbed me and shoved me against the taco truck. For a split second an image of a crunchy shell filled with spicy ground meat implanted itself in my brain to reside alongside a sultry green-eyed smile.

She'd done it again.

"Hold him, Frankie," said an upbeat voice. "This means wafers for both of us." It was Andrew's optimistic cackle and, as his friend's face brushed mine, I recognized the rat-face of one of the gringos in Rick's cafe who had seemed so disinterested the previous night. Andrew yanked the jacket off my back, thankfully not tearing the imported material, and pulled up my sleeve.

Before I could ID the device, a wasp stung my forearm, and Andrew stepped back with a satisfied smile on his mug. "Look at him, Frankie," he squealed. "He's sleepy already. It don't take much to put these little guys under." As the chatter died down, I wondered if I was about to have a need for yet another blue-steel Colt...and whose corpse I would wake up next to this time.

From a vast distance a last sound penetrated. "By the way, Pete. Nice suit."

CHAPTER 6

No corpse. But who would have believed it? For the second time in twenty-four hours I awoke inside a car. Except this was no taxi or broken-in Olds, but from the cream and black interior with wine bar and backseat tablet displaying overhead, I had more than a suspicion whose car I was in.

Green Eyes' limo.

From somewhere came snoring. Chainsaw loud. I wobbled my groggy head to the right and had the shock of glimpsing the out-thrust tongue of the desert reptile himself. Andrew grinned and flashed the pink monster at me. Where does he get off with that? Who the hell could endure this creature's company more than one moment without muzzling his ugly snout? Apparently several.

Andrew was seated to my right in the back row of the limo, which rocked gently as the car wound through the heavy traffic of noon-hour Albuquerque, not far from city center. Its famous convention hall loomed directly ahead. Two seats faced us, empty. In the forward seat, on the left with the wheel, was one of the gringos from the other table at Rick's, the one with the rat-face. The name Frankie dripped to mind. On the right—a white ponytail was draped over its owner's left shoulder as he slept reclined with his back to me. I wondered whether his hair color was perennial or due to age. He didn't seem that old. I didn't wonder who it belonged to, though—it was clearly the same ghost who had emerged backwards from the misty cloud that engulfed Rick's bar the previous night.

Did he have a face, or was he all hair?

Andrew nudged Ponytail's seat. "He's awake."

The snoring stopped like someone had tripped over the amplifier cord. Ponytail shook his head and yawned. Turning, he flashed a morning grin. Then winked. The left eye. Clean-shaven.

Brows as white as his pony, and teeth too. Not only did he have a face, but the complete package. Straightening his chair, he lurched his skinny body forward to compensate for lack of headroom for his very tall frame.

He twisted his neck to glance at Andrew. A high voice, but still lower than mine, squeaked. "Don't worry, Andy. Mr. Marlowe won't hurt us." He looked at me. "Will you, Mr. Marlowe?" Another grin.

I wasn't sure yet if he was idiot or savant.

I blinked, trying to reorganize my brain cells. Two doses of mind-ice in one day will do that to a guy. And the most recent was a direct line to the blood. I rubbed the spot on my right arm where Andrew had injected the drug.

"Ohhh."

Ponytail grinned at Andrew. "Heh. He's gettin it now." At me again. "Almost." Ponytail was back to full-tilt a darned sight faster than me.

Out came the tongue. "Is your *arm* a problem, little guy?" Andrew winked at Ponytail.

What arm? I clutched my left hand with my right, covering it as best I could. Something was wrong. More than wrong. Something *else* had been worked on me.

"He's gettin it, Bob." Andrew smiled down from his pompous height.

"I think you're right, Andy. I think you're right."

Frankie honked at another car. The limo jerked as he negotiated the busy street.

I knew these guys had no problem removing half a head, and no hesitation in putting a guy in the brig or making him dance to fancy tunes, but the realization that they would also break fingers somehow came as a surprise.

Now I was awake. "What's the deal, guys? You tryin' to cash in by mailing fingers now? Hate to tell ya this, but there ain't nobody nowhere gonna pay you a dime for a piece of me."

"He doesn't get it." Andrew smirked.

"Give him a minute. He will." Ponytail looked ahead as Frankie pulled off the main street and maneuvered the car into the Convention Hall's parking lot.

Cautiously I felt around my left hand. The bruising was not general but seemed confined to my little finger. The tip seemed hard and registered no feeling, but the rest of the digit was definitely wailing loudly about the punishment that had been inflicted.

Still cradling my finger, I stared at Ponytail. "All right. Just who are you? And what's your angle?"

Pony glanced back. "Bob Montez." He flashed ivories. "And we're there now."

So far I had not wasted energy viewing the backseat overhead display, where confused movement had crossed and re-crossed the screen as we drove, like much ado about zilch.

Bob pointed out what I was missing. "There it is, boys. We're rackin' up another one."

The tablet's display crawled with dogs. In Albuquerque's Convention Hall, the final judging in a dog show contest was in progress, my eye confirming this by sighting through the limo's front window a huge sign on the side of the Hall: "Dog-Gone Annual Show – Public Welcome." The tablet was streaming the events live into the limo.

"Chalk it up. Is that Jack's fifth?" asked Andrew.

"Sixth, Andy. Sixth." Bob Montez gleamed vicarious pride.

In the display, a stocky bald man trotted a brandy-colored poodle before an adoring crowd, the animal pausing, jumping, and trotting again on Jack's command. His shrunken head in the display looked as proud as Bob's.

Where had I seen that face? The pain in my finger was still clouding my brain, throwing everything off.

The car lurched to a stop. Frankie got out and opened my door. Easing out, I noticed Frankie had a lump under his left armpit. No mystery there—these guys may make conversation, but they were in charge and taking no chances. Andrew handed me my fedora; that didn't make me like him any better. He and Bob joined Frankie who beeped the limo locked behind us. No retreat there either.

At least I could still walk—though not yet run. I wondered just how far ahead these jokers had thought. And what the hell was the jackpot in their little game. There must be a jackpot; no one but no one plays games if there ain't no jackpot.

I felt something metal poke the small of my back. When I turned, Frankie met my eyes with his and nodded toward his hand stuffed in a jacket pocket. His pocket held more than handkerchiefs. I dropped all thoughts of tripping my hosts and making a run for it and instead joined them as they headed into the Hall, Bob grinning in front, Andrew by my side, Frankie frowning right behind.

At the edge of the Convention floor we paused. Jack was on stage with three decked-out poodles, beaming joy while a pair of judges pinned blue and pink ribbons to his frilly-sleeved eggshell-colored shirt. Even from this distance, I fancied I could see their faces in Jack's gleaming bald pate. A little too orange. And despite the frilly cuffs, the long-sleeved shirt was more than a little off-beat since most of the other dog owners wore suits, or at least near-formal clothes. Apparently used to Jack's attire, the crowd seemed not to care and clapped their enthusiasm for the winner of the top prize.

The microphone recited names and events. I couldn't make out details. The announcers were too loud to hear clearly, though the metal cylinder jammed in my back by Frankie may have blown my concentration. Maybe it's just me, but loaded guns tend to do that. Especially when their owner twitches his upper lip.

At last the mic went silent. Jack shook the judges' hands with enough energy to make them wince, his jaw slack with the emotion of his win. He gripped three reins and descended from the stage to the floor, his well-trained poodles taking the lead. A single glance from their owner and they pranced obediently in our direction.

Bob laid a warning eye on me. Andrew and Frankie stopped at the edge of the arena and hugged the wall with me caught between them, while the crowd squeezed past. Was the crowd my chance to slip between the Massolini thugs and vanish in a torrent of bodies? More harsh glares from my escorts made clear they knew what I was thinking. Not this time. I could not forget those emails anyway. There was a certain compromising picture and a certain compromised gun, not to mention a particular twin-peaked Ex who'd done nothing to deserve losing half her mug.

I had to get to the bottom of this cup of dregs. For now that meant being a good boy.

Despite the crowd, Jack wasted no time in joining us, his prize poodles nosing a path through the attendees as if cross-trained as bulldogs, the admiring crowd stepping aside to make way. The rich smell of a hundred canines drifted from the Hall's interior.

Frankie jabbed me again. We were backing out.

In the parking lot we joined Jack. The dry Albuquerque sun baked down on his hairless scalp, which I was now sure was slathered with spray-on artificial tan, and I thought I spotted a small swipe of the stuff staining one long off-white sleeve. Bob grabbed and kissed Jack on both cheeks, who kissed back. Nope, the orange didn't transfer. But I got the Mediterranean cheek-kissing thing. I'd seen that in the Vatican, too.

The vertical embroidered stripes on Jack's burgundy shorts suddenly alerted me to the possibility that what seemed casual, or even disorganized, with this guy may be more deliberate than I had supposed. Standing there in the bright New Mexico sun, Jack with his embroidered shorts showing short muscular legs and skinny Bob with his light lavender jacket bordered by wide white lapels, reminded me again of mariachi players. All they needed were a trumpet, a sombrero or two, and a fat *guitarra*.

A squeal of tires sounded behind and I realized Frankie had fetched the limo. He popped out and raced to open doors. Everyone piled in—yep, even the brandy hounds, who Jack directed into the back of the limo where they squeezed their delicately manicured puffy bodies among us, apparently taking no insult to their dog-territory by the trespassing of our legs.

Bob again took the right front seat. Jack sat back-to-back to Bob, and leveled a happy stare at me, managing to seem even more condescending than Andrew, who stubbornly shot out his snake-tongue every few seconds no matter who he stared at. Frankie took the wheel. One poodle took the seat opposite me, and I could swear stared at me out of a round fuzz-ball of gray-trimmed fur with the same condescension as his orange-sprayed master.

Now Andy had the gun. He held it in his right hand, which he kept aimed at me, like his eyes.

So why was I so popular? Bob was right, I just didn't get it. But my left finger sure had. My mind cleared further and it suddenly hit me. Last night's Ming Buddha was Mr. Poodle-King himself.

That injection had kept my brain skipping grooves. My gaze scanned his shirt for signs of Ugly Joe's blood on top of his orange spray but found none. Seeing the way the stupid thugs filling that limo listened when he spoke, there was no mistaking who was the Chief Honcho of this litter. My firecracker pop of recognition must have plastered itself on my face.

"Jack Muck." Poodle-King grinned.

I blinked. "Nice ta meet ya, Muck. I'm—"

"Pietro Qvinn Marlowe," Jack interrupted. Bob glanced once at Jack. Jack got the message and repeated himself, "Pietro Qvinn *Tiberias* Marlowe I should say. Pete for short."

No doubt remained. Poodle-King was definitely Czech, or at least from somewhere to the east of the Land of Snail-Eaters, which as far as I knew meant either Czechland or Germanistan. Either way, he was definitely the finger behind the trigger that killed Ugly Joe. Somehow he had to pay; but not yet. Patience is what this doctor ordered.

I frowned. "How—?"

"Oh, ve've known about you for some time, Mr. Marlowe," said Jack, his Czech accent coming through. "Indeed, you are famous in a vay..."

I knew that, of course. Wondered why it took the world so long to see. But why *this* guy? "So I'm the famous guy with four names. And you know them to a T. What's your angle, Muck?"

"To be exact, Mr. Marlowe, not an angle—but parallel lines."

"Huh?" Now I really didn't get it.

Jack sank further into his cushy leather seat, staring down at me from what seemed higher and higher altitudes.

Ponytail poked his face from the front seat. "Heh. He won't understand. Not *this* guy."

"Everyone understands pain," Andrew butted in.

I wondered how he managed to speak at all with his appendage playing hide-and-seek.

Jack continued. "Ve vill vork it out, Bob and I. There is no need for Mr. Marlowe to confuse his mind vith the details of our little enterprise. Or for you, my dear Andrew." Jack was still smiling, but Andrew went quiet at what was apparently a spanking from his boss. He kept the gun, though, which remained barely visible in his right hand.

Without speaking, Frankie at the wheel glanced once over his shoulder at Jack, then looked back to the road. The limo left downtown Albuquerque and headed east. I had more than a strong suspicion where we were going. I suspected I was about to learn more about gilas and alamos and maybe how deep one buries bodies in the desert to keep them safe from crows and serpents.

As University Park appeared, I tried to reposition my left hand and got another stab of pain. I winced. "Okay, jerks," I blurted. "I want to know right now what the hell you did to me. And I mean my hand, not my life, which you also seemed to have screwed up."

"Oy, oy! Such a little firebrand," Jack said. "A bantam-veight vith an elephant complex." He smiled broader and leaned closer to me, his poodles squeezing aside to give their master room. "Vhich is partly vhy ve vant you. There are other parts, too, my dear Mr. Marlowe."

"Tell him about his finger, Jack. Before he does something stupid."

"Yes, yes, dear Bob. Ve can't have Mr. Marlowe...how do you say in English...screwing up the vorks."

That was it. I lowered my eyes to my left finger and stared. Carefully I cradled my finger and raised it into the light streaming in from a sun in full bloom and saw a rainbow of colors reflecting from its skin. No, not skin. Plastic. Dull, unfeeling plastic.

"Not yet, Mr. Marlowe. Not yet. It must heal a little longer before you can use it. It vill be a vhile before you can take on the vorld. But soon, soon..."

Bob yawned.

"Tank you, dear Bob," Jack continued, "for stepping in last night. How do they say in English...all vork and no play makes Jack a dull boy?"

Bob's ivories flashed again. "Heh. You got it right, Jack. Right on the nose. As usual."

Jack looked back at me. "And Jack had to play vith his poodles." He vigorously rubbed the heads of his three dogs, who beamed happiness. "After all, ve must keep our priorities straight. I think the finer things in life are the least appreciated. Vouldn't you agree, Mr. Marlowe?"

I shrugged. "Hard to say, Muck."

"Oh, do call me Jack. Please."

Frowning, I winced again. Stared out the window where the foothills leading to the Rockefeller estates east of Albuquerque appeared. Where was the adobe church? This wasn't Cartagena Road. Frankie was headed elsewhere. "What the *hell*, Muck? You wanna finally spill the *hopalenos*?"

Jack swiveled to look at Bob, who twisted to return his quizzical look. "He means *jalapenos*, Jack. Beans."

"Oh." The Poodle-King looked back at me, brows up. "Another cute colloquial expression from a native. Soon. In due time, Mr. Marlowe. In due time."

The foothills rose to ridges, gray and dry like a beached caiman. The limo raced its box of iced air on the same road that had provided my silent escape the day before, giving me at least some idea of where we were in relation to the church. Was that another ringing of its bell I heard? I shook my head. No, impossible. Must be merely the aftereffects of the injection.

The road wound upward into the mountainous ridges, our limo shrinking to toy size as it entered boxed canyons. Hard-eyed gate-guards in street clothes came into view, staring from behind a carefully tended entry stand like extras from a Godfather movie. The limo came to a stop. Frankie rolled down his darkened window and with a brief nod the guard punched a hidden button. A metal grill grated to one side.

Frankie gunned us through.

The road wound about and steeply up, coming to an abrupt end in a mini-circle under a heavy overhanging ledge shouting Frank Lloyd Wright. A square pool with a perpetual shimmering waterfall matched the ledge, more square angles and rectangles defining the rest of the sprawling house. The view was better than your average twin peaks—but didn't make me want to suck nipples.

CHAPTER 7

W e stepped out of the limo and Frankie drove around a projecting corner where the engine grew silent as the car parked just out of sight.

The poodles led the way. Straining at Jack's leashes, they pulled him forward barely giving Andrew time to hurry to a pair of wide glass doors to open them for Jack. Before Andrew arrived, the twin doors angled inward and a woman dressed in purple and sporting Christmassy jewels materialized in the gap, her pasty face topped by a round halo of sprayed hair.

Andrew paused. As he locked eyes with Marm, frowns and tongues alternated like the heads and tails of a tossed coin. His peepshow continued while Jack and Bob and the poodles walked casually up the several hard-edged steps that led to the threshold, passing Marm and ignoring Andrew.

I stood at the bottom of the steps, my brain cells comparing the architectural monstrosity of the house with old-timey castles, noting that the pool was fed by a deep concreted stream of water. Alligators, or sharks? I peered into the deep. Everyone knows that every madman's lair has one or the other, not to mention movie-lot quicksand in the back.

Frankie reappeared and motioned me up the steps with his gun.

Inside was no more happy than the front, to my street-wise taste. Hard silvery surfaces and spare functional furniture of black and white yelled Art Deco gone wild. I gave a disappointed stare in Jack's direction. Busy kissing his sloppy-tongued dogs under Bob's attentive gaze, Jack didn't notice. It seemed Muck and Montez had forgotten me.

Marm and Andrew remained on the threshold in their mini-Mexican standoff. I'd seen this before, knew how this drama played out.

A slight tap drew my eye. Turning, I gazed upon She Who Must Not Be Trusted. In strode Green Eyes herself and my face conscrewed into a tangle of scorn. After two betrayals, Tonya had more nerve than a Cirque de Soleil acrobat by showing herself to me again. I planned a very public and humiliating revenge while Tonya swept brazenly forward till she stood next to Marm.

Marm raised one hand and the fingers delicately pinched air. "Licia, dispense a wafer. Andrew has been a very good boy."

The tongue stopped its steam-hammering and for once actually stayed where nature intended it to be.

Licia? In a flash, I realized my mistake. Marm's good-witch daughter, Licia, had got her way and been granted Teacher's permission to retrieve her green and black feathered jacket from bad-witch daughter, Tonya. And mistake number two: the delicate waist I had glimpsed from behind in Suite Chicas' back parking lot, which had drawn me recklessly into the Massolinis' trap, had also been Licia. My barely conceived plans for revenge evaporated. Green Eyes had still only one strike against her, while the rest of the Massolinis were fast racking up enough strikes to harm even the Mets' reputation.

"He doesn't deserve it," burst out Licia. Getting to be a habit with her.

The cold stare that came suddenly from Marm made Andrew's frown look meek. Licia fell silent and seemed to shrink. "Do not tell me my business, daughter," Marm said. "I'm responsible for this family. It's my love and my sacrifices that keep us all going, especially since I no longer have a husband to help me in my time of trouble." Marm's mackerel stare melted not a bit, despite her words.

"But Rick—"

Marm raised one hand, palm flat, ready to slap. Her eyes grew big, daggered once at me, then back to Licia. "Must I discipline you *again*, young lady? Should I take away all the wafers and give them to Antonia? Or to your brother Andrew?"

Andy grinned at Marm, anticipating a promotion.

Licia dropped her gaze to the floor. "No, Mother. But what about *father*?"

"I'm in charge here. Not Rick. You know I give no wafers for misbehavior. So be a good girl and obey your Mother, Licia. And that's that!"

Marm's good daughter—her favorite of the hour—withdrew a tiny white cracker from her purse and handed it to Andrew, who greedily consumed it. The way he relished the cracker gave me even more doubt about what seemed real around here. Munching his reward, his eyes briefly rolled up like the eyes of addicts I had seen in those weekend Uber runs, fed by part-time pushers of ice and heroin. Licia quietly snitched one.

So this was how Marm, the head of the Massolini clan, kept order in her ranks. Marm, the pusher. It didn't surprise me. Neither did the realization that Missing Rick was Marm's husband, and Andrew's and Tonya's father, *not* Tonya's father-in-law, and my gray-matter forced me to the conclusion that Rick's 'loving' family had done something to him. Nothing in this family could any longer surprise me.

Or so I thought.

That was mistake number three.

Jack dropped his dog leashes and clapped his hands. Wildly, his three poodles leapt free and ran about the interior of the Art Deco-strewn castle, tramping thick adobe and Aztec carpet. One paused to glare at me with ears forward and teeth bared until I put my hands in my pockets. Then the animal joined the others in scraping at the twin doors. Bob let them out. I had the definite feeling they would patrol the surrounding desert gardens as fiercely as any Dobermans, had I a notion of breaking for freedom. Gazing through the several panoramic glass windows that graced two walls, however, it was clear that only a veteran of Ironman competitions could avoid the cacti and gators and survive the long trek to civilization. I had heard much about the Big House. But I never knew that it was decorated in Art Deco and patrolled by poodles.

The Czech Buddha stepped near, his hands propped on his hips, pointing casually backward—affectedly casual, I decided. "Mr. Marlowe," he said, his endearing smile reappearing. "Please to...how to say...grab a seat." He pointed to quadruple white divans squaring off a transparent glass table on four steel legs.

"*Take* a seat," corrected Bob.

"Tank you." Jack nodded, then corrected himself. "Th-thank you." He struggled with the 'th'.

As I sat, Bob Montez walked up and perched his skinny self on one side, while Jack Muck took the other. Frankie planted himself by the front doors, hand in pocket and eyes on me. Andrew stuck close to Marm, and he and Licia trotted after her to the back of the broad room where the Elder Stateswoman addressed her brood in quiet tones. Her stoned brood listened while staring submissively at the floor. Marm's expression had all the marks of a spanking. Situation normal, I thought.

Bob Montez pointed to my pocket. For a moment I was puzzled, then I understood and handed over my cell phone. Bob snapped it open and removed the battery, before handing both items back to me.

"Mr. Marlowe." Jack smiled. "I vant to congratulate you."

Bob joined in. "Take it or leave it."

"No, my dear Bob." Jack glanced at his friend. "Ve must be nice to our guest. After all, he is going to *help* us." Jack looked back at me. "Aren't you, Mr. Marlowe?" His brows rose expectantly across his orange-sprayed forehead.

I didn't know what to say.

Bob said it for me. "He sure the hell is. Like it or not."

Jack displayed a grimace, flat as a carpenter's level. "My dear Mr. Marlowe..."

Having called me 'dear' for the first time, Muck had my full attention.

"...ve have vhat I call a...little enterprise."

"Little." Bob snorted. "Way to put it, Jack."

"Ve provide vhat you might call *public relations*. Have you ever heard of...how do you say?" Jack glanced back at Bob.

Bob looked at the ceiling, thinking. Back down. "Bloopers."

Jack laughed. "Yes, that is the vord. That is indeed the vord—bloopers."

His eyes returned to me. "Everyvon, you see, my dear Mr. Marlowe, has at von time or another had the experience of making a big mistake, committing an error, damaging their public image through vhat the French call a *faux pas*. Once the mistake has been made, they realize that they have goofed. But vhat can they do? The vay communications are today, the vorld already knows vhat has happened and their blooper is already sent out to the ether for the whole vorld to see. It gets repeated and repeated, often vith, uh... magnification... exaggeration." Jack waved one hand in the air for effect. He shook his head. "Veery unfortunate for the poor person who has made the error."

I ventured in. "That's pissing on a guy when he's down, Mac. But he can fight it. He can sue, protest, slap around the bad guy's wife."

"Yes," said Jack, one finger pointing up. "All these are the possibilities. As is hiring somevon to run around the Internet deleting photos, correcting blogs, posting favorable comments about the poor pissed-on person."

"You got it, Muck. Seems you have it down pat." My eyes wandered, scanning the joint for anything that might reveal a hidden exit and avoid Frankie at the door.

"But, Mr. Marlowe, there is another vay." Jack glanced up at smiling Bob, then back to me. "My dear-dear Mr. Marlowe, have you ever heard of gene therapy?"

Now they got me. Despite my promotion to double-dear, I still did not understand. I barely shook my head.

"I told you he wouldn't get it." Bob sneered, his white ponytail swaying behind him.

"Maybe, ve vill see." Jack leaned forward, more earnest. "Let us say, Mr. Marlowe, that a person is ill, is dying of...cancer, for example. How do you cure this poor person once the cancer has spread... how to say..." He looked back to Bob who mouthed a silent word. "...yes, *metastasized* is the vord."

I knew the answer. "Ain't no cure for cancer, Bud. You know that. Not after you've rounded the bend and your dog is in the last lap of the track."

Muck wasn't fazed. "Ah. But vhat if you could reprogram the poor person's DNA, reboot that person's operating system, so to speak? The boot code vhich vas corrupted and vhich resulted in the appearance of the cancer?"

I shrugged. "That sounds jake to me, Jack. But what's that got to do with neon blimps and getting your sister-in-law to go online and tell everyone what a great joe you are?"

"My dear Mr. Marlowe, information is information. It does not matter vhere it comes from or vhat form it takes. Vonce it is written in the book of life, so to speak, it is written in the stars."

"Forever," added Bob, more to himself than to me. "In the universe's hologram...*permanent-wise*."

Jack continued. "Our unfortunate person whose reputation has just been ruined can no more change vhat has happened, and no more avoid getting *pissed on*, perhaps for the rest of his miserable life, than can a cancer patient cure his cancer by trying to transplant every organ in his body. The cancer vill spread faster than the transplants could possibly be performed, as the incorrect information gets replicated throughout his chemical universe."

"Tough break for both. But that's life, buddy. What can anyone do?"

Jack grinned—a real grin—without the level. "I propose," he leaned closer, "a *do-over*."

My brows lowered the boom. "A what?"

"A *do-over*, Mr. Marlowe. Gene therapy for *bloopers*."

I shook my head again. "I don't get it."

Bob crowed, "Heh. I told ya, Jack. He ain't never gonna get it. Principle of Computational Equivalence."

"Perhaps you are right, Bob. Ve should perhaps consider Rule 30 instead of 110."

"For this guy...Rule Minus-One." Bob cleaned his nails.

I got the feeling I was the dirt.

"Ve shall see." Jack turned back to me. "Mr. Marlowe, ve have a vay, a special vay, so to speak, to reboot his personal universe. The pissed-on person's universe, so he can eliminate his blooper."

My brows lowered further. I think beetled is the vord. I shook my head and silently corrected myself, without Bob's help—'word'.

"It all starts vith parallel lines," Jack continued.

I matched my beetled brows with pursed lips.

"Or more precisely, slits. You see, Mr. Marlowe, vhen electrons are emitted through parallel slits onto a screen, they emerge as *vay—*

" Jack struggled to pronounce a W, "*vaves*. You know, like vaves in the sea. These form an interference pattern on the screen, exactly the kind of patterns that ve see in a quiet pond vhen ve drop a pebble on its surface. Or more precisely, two pebbles next to each other."

I nodded, not sure where he left his straitjacket.

"But if ve emit electrons through parallel slits onto a screen and then measure the vaves, they turn into particles. Instead of an interference pattern, the impacts clump together like vertical strings of bullets on two targets, just as if the electrons had been particles all along. In fact, if ve measure the electrons *before* they pass through the parallel slits, they still emerge as vaves on the screen, but vhen ve *observe* the previous measurement, once again they are particles. This means they somehow reached *back in time* to change their nature to vhen ve measured them, merely because ve took the time to observe them."

"Took the time." Bob grinned. "That's good, Jack."

Jack returned his grin.

Ponytail Bob looked back at me. His lips curled up, but I didn't mistake it for a smile. "Can you spell entanglement, Pete? Cause that's what observation is."

"Yes, my dear Bob." Jack smiled. "Entirely correct. And entanglement is vhat our little enterprise is all about. Measurement and observation *is* entanglement. But vaves are only probability, Mr. Marlowe! There is no reason vhy an entire baseball cannot pass through that vall over there vith no problem at all if ve have enough time and energy to make it happen, and if ve can entangle our consciousness through observation of the baseball." Jack grinned like a kid with a new toy. "This can in fact be done using vhat ve call a Universal Indexer to index each universe in the Multiverse until ve find the von universe that has the probable outcome that ve vant. Then ve merely transfer the entangled consciousness so that everything remains...uh, vhat is the vord?" Jack looked to Bob.

Bob screwed up his face again. "Hunky dory."

"Yes." Jack laughed. "Tank you again, Bob. Hunky dory! That is our *reboot*, vhich can be either a big reboot, or a little reboot."

I stared straight ahead. Wondered how many hits the Mets would have to miss before this probability stuff finally let them win the pennant and avoid getting the boot.

Bob flipped his ponytail. "Might as well be a Gordian Knot to this guy. He'll never be on board."

Jack sighed. "Perhaps you are right, my dear Bob. There really is no need to explain our Sirius Enterprises to our famous guest. I can see from his face that it may require more time than ve have available to...how do you say...bring him up to speed."

"Told ya, Jack." Montez laughed.

I folded my arms. I kinda like to think of myself as a cut above dirt.

Jack's brows drifted down. He leaned back into the divan. "But understanding is not necessary. All you need to know is that ve have a purpose for you, Mr. Marlowe, vhich takes advantage of our little reboot, our little technique vhich *takes the time*."

I had my corporal's stripes back with 'dear', but I wasn't out of the bag yet. "So how does Yours Truly fit in with this little Sirius Whatchamacallit?"

"Enterprises," said Jack, back to grinning. "Like a peach. You see, dear Mr. Marlowe, there is a certain object in a certain place, vhich vas placed there by a certain person. And *you* know vhere it is."

"You're not helping, Muck. How about coming to your point so I can be on my way out of this circus." I jammed my crossed arms crosser.

"Starts with an F," said smiling Bob. "Getting it, little guy?"

From across the room, Andrew stepped closer and managed to find time between pink tongue-thrusts to utter, "Sounds like..." He shoved his arms one up and one horizontal in the shape of an L, like a high-school cheerleader ready for charades.

I still didn't get it.

"Y not?" Andrew joined in, between tongue thrusts. "N...then N."

"Even Pistol Pete must be on board by now," smiled Bob. "Got the hint? What's that spell, player?"

My brain clicked. Slowly I spelled out "F-L-Y-N-N."

CHAPTER 8

"**Y**es, my dear Mr. Marlowe," said Jack. "Your *Uncle Flynn.*"

Lightning stabbed my brain. "My crackpot uncle? Is this for real?"

"Keys to the universe real." Bob snorted.

"You see, Mr. Marlowe," continued Jack, "your Uncle Flynn vonce secretly took an object from its place in Ireland and delivered it to the Pope in the Vatican. Ve vould like to retrieve this object."

My jaw dropped like a cheap Cessna. "The Blarney Stone? *That's* what this is all about? That flaky piece of junk?"

Bob and Jack exchanged silent stares. Back to me: "Yes," said Jack, "that flaky piece of junk, vhich you so endearingly call the Blarney Stone."

Smiling Bob no longer smiled.

"Yes, this is the object vhat ve vant and ve are asking of you to get it for us."

I could stands no more. "Ho-ho!" I let out all my air. "I don't think so, gentlemen. Boy are you guys poodling up the wrong tree. First, it was not me but my Uncle Flynn who gave the Stone to the Pope. Second, Flynn disappeared ten years ago without even a Fuck-You-Have-a-Good-Life postcard to anybody. And third, it's just a hunk of rock anyway, so who gives a damn?" I snorted. "Besides, how the hell would I know where it is now? I was barely out of diapers back then. The Pope put it somewhere that I don't know, and how the hell could I even find out?"

I paused to catch a breath. Refolded my arms. "You wouldn't be some kind of Opus Dopus hit squad, would you? Cause the Blarney Stone ain't no Rock of Saint Peter. That was just Flynn's line of trout that he fed pigeons until he found some joker who finally took the bait. The joker just happened to wear a split pointy hat and cross himself on Sundays."

Smiling Bob was smiling again. "It ain't the rock that interests us, Marlowe. It's what's *inside* the rock. We could explain it, but you still wouldn't understand."

I shrugged. "Don't make a Dutchman's Difference. The Pope don't know me from Adam."

"Precisely." Jack reached into his pocket and extracted a small stiff paper. He held it up. It was an old black and white photo. "Look closely, Mr. Marlowe. Vhat do you see?"

With Frankie at the door and Andrew crowding closer and Jack and Bob already too close for comfort, and Marm and Licia—not to mention a trio of dogs—staring at me from across the room, I postponed my plans to judo-throw them all in a giant pile and instead stared at the photo. The guy looked familiar. Real familiar.

"Yes, my dear Mr. Marlowe. It *is* your Uncle Flynn. But who does he look like?"

Yours Truly, I thought. "Yours Truly," I said.

"Doppelgangers," said Jack. "How do you say? *Doubles.*"

"Or as we say in Des Moines..." Bob cracked his knuckles, "...his spittin' image."

"You knew your uncle vell," continued Jack. "Vell enough that you could be successful in pretending to be him in a visit to the Pope—who, as the whole vorld knows, is old and almost blind and used to mistake you for your uncle each time you visited vhen you vere young. Flynn vas a velcome guest in the Vatican before he vanished." Jack's smile lit up again as he stared at me. "Vith your cooperation, he vill be a guest again."

I shut my mouth. It was more fantastic than ice-wagons in the Chihuahuan Desert.

"So vhat ve propose to you, my dear Mr. Marlowe," again Jack dropped his grin, more serious, "is that you, as your Uncle Flynn, make an appointment vith the Pope in the Vatican, catch up on old times over a cup of coffee, find out vhat the Pope did vith the Blarney Stone, and then...*steal it.*"

My jaw dropped again. "Oh, is that all? Just steal it." I sniffed. "Just that little thing... Well, you know what? Even if it were possible for me to be my own uncle, which I doubt, and if I can even find out where the hell the lippy rock is, I guess I should just walk right out of the Vatican with the damn thing tucked under my arm."

Bob and Jack exchanged silent stares again. "That's exactly right, Mr. Marlowe. You vill just valk right out."

"Ha-ha!" I guffawed, holding my stomach. "And just how the hell am I supposed to do that?" I paused to cradle my left hand again, the pain returning.

Jack and Bob looked at my hand.

I finally got it. "No... Oh no..."

Grins all around. "Now for me to tell you, Mr. Marlowe, in answer to your... insistent earlier qvestion: *Vhat the hell did ve do to you?* Oh, before I forget..." Jack glanced back at Bob, "...tank you, my dear Bob, for stepping in and performing Mr. Marlowe's little operation last night vhile I vas busy playing."

My stomach turned.

Bob nodded. "Gotta keep our priorities straight, Jack. As you said, all work and no play. Da-ba-da-ba-doo."

"Tank you, dear Bob, and I am sorry that you had to stay up vith our little friend vithout my help." Jack turned back to me. "Anyvay, vhat the hell did ve do? Ve simply installed a Universal Indexer in your little finger." Jack shrugged like he had just described the weather. "Now, for our purpose the healing is almost complete. A little steroid goes a long vay, though, unfortunately, it vill still be a vhile before the pain is gone." Jack scooted forward on his seat. "But now at least ve can check things out."

Operation? I was sitting in the middle of this drum circle of mad scientists and insane Italians like the Madwoman of Chamois, listening to their crazy talk. My eyes searched for moons and stars through the wide glass ceiling-to-floor outer windows, trying desperately to restore sanity. It had to be the drug, my brain insisted, the aftereffects still screwing with my gray matter. To my screwed-over brain, even Dorkman and Krapke sounded welcome at this point. They didn't appear.

Marm cleared her throat. She had stepped quietly closer like a cat stalking a bird that might flap suddenly away.

Without turning to face her, Jack announced, as if responding to radar, "Ve have not forgotten you, my dear Mrs. Massolini. Not to vorry, vithout a doubt there is more money to come. More money than even *you* can imagine, dear lady."

Her face lit up at the mention of golden loot. She replied, "That's the soul of the business, Mr. Muck, after all. It may be *your* enterprise—but it's *my* money."

"Do not vorry about little things like money, Mrs. Massolini."

Did I hear a trace of contempt in his thickly accented voice, perhaps for someone of such limited ambition as to be obsessed with mere money?

She smiled broader with the mention of her favorite subject.

"Dear lady, you know it makes my heart happy to get you everything you desire, including money. Lots and lots of money."

She beamed, hands ecstatically gripped together as in prayer. And was this the stirrings of a sexual thrill now passing through Marm's stolid body? I could almost swear—

Licia and Andrew trotted up behind her, extending hands for their share and eyeing each other in their sibling rivalry.

"But are you certain, Mr. Muck?" A trace of doubt remained on her face, despite Jack's Czech-accented assurances. "Rick, after all, was my husband. And there are laws..."

Jack stood and turned, the carpenter's level smile pasted back on. "Have you forgotten vhat Bob and I have done for you, my dear Mrs. Massolini? Have you already forgotten vhat you happily call 'the Miracle of the Desert'? Do Bob and I really have to prove our abilities again so soon?"

I wasn't listening. My mind had focused on the 'was' in *'was* my husband.' Bad news for Rick. The size of the Massolini's trash bag was growing by the minute. Still smarting from my goof regarding Green Eyes added to the pain in my finger, I wondered how much she had contributed to the bag.

Marm exhaled. Licia and Andrew did likewise, equally oblivious to Marm's use of the past tense in regard to their father. "No, Mr. Muck..." Marm glanced at Bob, "...and Mr. Montez." Her head nodded in satisfaction, though it still seemed to Yours Truly that Marm's trust was AWOL—if it ever existed in that pasty jewel-crusted head. "I don't know how you did it, but I'm glad it's done.

Damn that Rick. What a stupid idea to build a bar in the desert. Well, he has paid."

"We ain't passing judgment, Mrs. Massolini," interjected Bob. "Just doing our part. You get the money, we keep the rest."

Again she beamed happiness.

"Now, as for Mr. Marlowe." Jack turned back to me. "I apologize, dear sir, for the interruptions."

I stood. My peepers may have been on Muck's shiny skull, but my brain cells were in orbit around my little finger. "Not to vorry, Muck. Uh, I mean *worry*. No offense, Jack. This is personal...but it ain't personal."

"I get you completely, Mr. Marlowe. No vorry taken."

"No *offense* taken, Jack," Bob said.

"No offense taken, I mean, Mr. Marlowe." Jack nodded.

I raised my left hand, the tip of my little finger standing out like a plastic weather-vane, to me, at least. "What operation?"

Bob pointed. No missing fingers on him, I noticed. "Pete, pull off the tip of your pinky."

Staring at my digit, I slowly raised my left hand. With my right I gripped the end-bone of my left little finger and pulled. Without a sound, it slid off. I let my eyes peek under its skirt. Plastic. Pink on the outside, pinker on the inside, with a black plastic O-ring for a firm connection. I spent little time examining the chunk of plastic, however, as my eyes were drawn immediately to a small red button implanted in the stump of my next-down knuckle, the middle one.

Jack stepped closer. He grabbed my attention with a glare into my eyes. "Do not touch the button, Mr. Marlowe. Not yet." He glanced at Bob. "Ve vould not vant our dear Mr. Marlowe to disappear into the earth now, vould ve? A Universal Indexer has infinite power, dear sir. Its micro-vaved crystal draws its power from the MultiVerse." He laughed.

I looked back at Jack. So there was quicksand in this Big House after all. But I didn't get the humor.

Jack lurched to his feet. "Please to valk this vay, Mr. Marlowe." Jack walked across the room, one arm motioning me to follow. He halted by the room's back in a corner where two walls met at right angles, a lacquered grandfather clock on one wall and what looked like a giant copper pin cushion on the other. More modern art. I couldn't help but notice that the Massolini clan stepped carefully away as if I was waving a loaded gun. Frankie remained by the doors, but Bob followed Jack and me, halting a few feet behind Jack.

Jack continued to grin, apparently happiest when lecturing. "Mr. Marlowe, you are something of a... how to say... *pioneer*. Like Columbus. Vhat you have the privilege of experiencing is something that everyvon of education and breeding vould give his right arm to experience. And all you had to give vas your...how to say—*pinky*."

"Heh. That's putting it well, Jack. His *pinky*." Bob put his hands on his hips and laughed. "You're a lucky man, Pinky. Damned lucky."

"That's a good vay to put it, dear Bob. Pinky. Columbus is such a *big* name—vay too big for a little man like Mr. Marlowe."

Pinky. I guessed that beat the heck out of Mr. Missing Right Arm or Mr. Knee-capped Left Leg. But down below I began to do a slow boil. Montez & Muck. Taking me for a ride was one thing, doing a Yakuza on me was another, but hanging me with this *Pinky* sign was crossing the damned line. My plans for the revenge business were piling up.

"This, Pinky, is how you are going to steal the Blarney Stone." Jack stood in front of the wall. "You vill stand like this. Remove the tip of your finger. Then activate the Universal Indexer...that is, press the red button. Vait five seconds...then-and listen to me carefully now, Pinky—*you vill valk straight through the vall* vithout stopping until you are standing on the other side. Do you understand me, Pinky?"

My eyes saucered. "What?" I'd heard cockamamey nonsense before, but this was the cockiest mamey I'd ever heard. Was I surrounded by morons and lunatics? I burst out laughing. "Ah-ha-ha-ha!" Doubled over. Tears poured from my eyes till finally I stood straight. "I gotta admit, guys, you almost had me there. It was a good one. A real good one. But I'm tired of screwing around waiting for you to come clean with this hocus-pocus and get to the real point of how the hell you expect me to get your god damn rock. I ain't no mule. Not for drugs, and sure the hell not for flinty pieces of stone from some filthy corner of Ireland."

Montez looked back to Muck.

"Told ya so," muttered Bob.

"Plan Two," replied Jack. Jack looked at Marm.

The Godmother of the Massolini family walked to my side and reached into her purse. She pulled out a slip of green. Reluctantly she offered the money to me. Reluctantly I say because her arm kept sliding forward then back as if refusing to obey her brain. Now I knew they were serious. For Marm to offer money to anyone, after having seen how far she would go just to grab seventy-five dollars from her own daughter, suggested she was all-in for what Montez & Muck had planned.

I put my hands behind me.

Jack frowned. "Pinky, please to cooperate. Ve know how much you have in your bank account. Ve are prepared to pay you a *whole twenty dollars* if you vill just press the button and step through the vall."

Marm backed away. "Ten," she exclaimed, directing a look of outrage at M&M. The money disappeared back into her purse.

"My dear dear Mrs. Massolini," Jack said, exasperation in his voice. "This is no time to...how do you say—*go cheap on us.* Pinky must learn how to use the Indexer. And ve already negotiated vith you from von thousand dollars down to tventy. Now you object to a mere *tventy?*"

A shaking seized Marm's body. Her eyes rolled up like Andrew's, her hands clutching her closed purse as to an anchor in a storm. The violence of Marm's seizure grew and Andrew and Licia hurried to her side and propped her up by her arms before she could collapse onto the Aztec carpet.

"Oh vell," said Jack. "Back to Plan Von."

Frankie stepped forward, hand thrust in his pocket.

"Guns won't work either, Muck." I folded my arms. "I've seen your worst, and my life insurance is paid up."

Oops.

"Yep, Pinky," said Smiling Bob. "Plan One was *not* your taxicab buddy. That was just to get your attention. But your pole-climbing Ex, Wendy. *She* is Plan One." A look of triumph came over Bob. "You would not still be paying your life insurance if you no longer cared about her. We know she's still your beneficiary."

I sighed. There weren't no arguin' with that. "Okay, M&M. You got me. When, where, and how?"

"Ve thought you vould see things our vay, Pinky." Jack grinned.

Bob pointed. "Stand there, beside the grandfather clock."

I stood by the back wall, close in the corner, taking care not to entangle my Canali jacket and fedora in whatever the hell was about to happen. With my right forefinger and thumb, I slipped the plastic digit into my right pants pocket.

"Aim the red button at the center of the wall," Bob said.

"And vith your left thumb, press it," added Jack.

I aimed the button.

I pressed it.

A stab of pain from the operation raced up my arm but I soon forgot it, as, from somewhere, a high whine sounded. It gathered strength. I wondered if this was how dogs heard whistles above the hearing of humans, and I felt like one of Jack's prize poodles. Glancing at the door, I saw all three dogs lift their heads and stare as if alerted by the opening of a can of Alpo.

Her money safely put away, Marm stopped shaking. Again able to stand alone, she took a step to my side and thrust out a wafer. She flashed a broad smile. "Credit where credit's due," she primly pronounced.

For a moment I stared, my brain unable to process fast enough to decide whether to accept Marm's drugged pastry in lieu of money, or again put my hands behind me. Then I fancied I heard an upbeat rhythm ringing in my ears and, from somewhere buried deep in my id, words surfaced:

Istanbul was Constantinople
Now it's Istanbul, not Constantinople
Been a long time gone, Constantinople
Now it's Turkish delight on a moonlit night.

The Deco-marred wall before me, otherwise uninspired—even bland—erupted like an undersea volcano, red lava pouring from its surface to release hissing streams of steam, and my eyes and brain cells forgot all about Marm and her pharmacopoeia.

"Not fair!" yelled Licia. Clad in her green-tinged jacket retrieved from Tonya, Licia leaped forward and snatched the wafer from Marm's hand—then shoved me.

My legs would not stay still. Somewhere between falling and walking, I lurched forward, either way, definitely tripping, not having time to put out even a protective arm.

For the first time, I danced the tango.

And what a tango it was. Mother Nature grabbed me by the ear and whined like a brat, complaining her diapers needed changing, then called 9-1-1 to report someone molesting her private parts. Whichever it was, she didn't like it one little bit. But, despite my clumsy molestation of Mother Nature's giblets, she passed the stone. I had time only to recall that the pin cushion was the wrong wall art, and that, thanks to Licia, I was passing through the wrong wall.

The last whine ended in the most improbable set of syllables I could have imagined: "By the vay, Pinky, nice suit."

CHAPTER 9

I stopped moving...my eyes opened. First insult was the realization that, far from appearing in some exotic port in an alien land full of three-breasted Tahitian babes, M&M's tango had landed me in a boring darkened room. From the clatter of my foot stumbling on some hard and noisy object, I gathered it was a broom closet. Even fancy-shmancy Frank Wright mansions in the mountains had to have a broom closet.

My head spun. For a moment I felt both giddy and nauseous—the effects of the first descent I experienced from M&M's Cloud Nine dance floor, due to Mother Nature's spiteful kick in the groin, maybe angry that I had ignored her welcome sign and committed the equivalent of a date-rape by molesting the wrong wall. Seconds passed and it gradually came to me that the darkness was not in my eyes—a moment's relief in that quarter—but was in the room itself.

It *was* a room: I felt the coldness of concrete through my worn shoes, the faint stubble of low-quality painted gypsum wall stretching in either direction, the molecules in the wall gradually returning back where they belonged. My little finger—the good one—found what felt like a light switch. I flicked it.

The effect reminded me of my yesteryear membership in a Masonic lodge in Brooklyn before I moved out West—'more light'. Suddenly all was clear—that is, as clear as mere photons could reveal. My eyes still downcast looking for the objects I had kicked, the second insult hit me—my shoes. The holes I had inflicted on the soles of my old footwear were matched by cuff-marks on the saddle. Elvis don't like dirt on his shoes. Or grit in his hair. Or dust on his suit. A quick glance showed I had gotten all three, courtesy of Mother Nature's outrage at my toying with her.

But my brain had no more time for important matters like

custom Canali fabric. The Goodship Marlowe had indeed stumbled into a broom closet, larger than any I had seen, Yours Truly having been raised in a dirt-poor home in Ireland before my parents moved to a just-as-small tenement in Brooklyn, and for a moment, a chill of relief shook me as I realized that hot water tanks the size of aircraft carriers flanked me on either side. One foot to the right or left, and my indexed universe would have been the inside of a vat of boiling water. I stepped clear—and again stumbled over wooden poles, falling backward. Brooms and mops and buckets scattered across the concrete floor, throwing more dust on my suit. Regaining my balance, I stepped carefully over the debris and looked around.

In truth, a closet it wasn't quite, but rather a full-sized room, the kind that might service a building or other lofty layout for big-shots, with steps leading downward to supposed cellars and the tanks that flanked me also descending downward through holes in the concrete. But my brain wouldn't wrap itself around 'broom-room', so it stayed a closet.

I penetrated the unknown by the light of the bare bulbs above, carefully stepping across the tangle of traffic caused by my entry and then it struck me... Where the hell was this? I knew better than to ransack my pockets for an instruction booklet written in pidgin facsimile since M&M had supplied no such helpful advice. All they had said was "Valk through". And I had valked. Or rather been pushed.

And puked—almost. I suppressed another burp as the indigestion digested.

A wide metal door took shape before me. A single glance showed it had no lock so I reached for the cold round knob. I turned it. Slowly. Carefully. Who knew what might be on the other side? Was I still in Marm Massolini's house in the Rockefeller wilds above Albuquerque? Was I even on planet Earth? A Multiverse sounded like more territory even than the Gadsden Purchase. I remembered my Papaw's old saw: *If something can go wrong—even if it can't—it will.* A Multiverse based on nothing but probabilities and a plastic button sure provided the gas for things to go wrong.

Very wrong.

The door swung wide.

Light from the next room flooded my peepers with more photons, eclipsing the pale glow from the broom closet behind. For a moment I paused as my ears picked up a stray vibe from behind and below, a distant sobbing, its echoes drifting up concrete steps. It stopped.

I stepped through the threshold into a cockpit. That's how it struck me. Not small, and with not much to strap my hiney into, but still a cockpit. On the floor were computer motherboards and what looked like Tesla coils piled in neat stacks. Along the walls were videocams suspended next to sound booms, sheltered by light blinds. In one corner of the spacious room were several dog beds with purple dog awards pinned above. Along the right wall was a wide glass window showing onto a square pool of sun-lit blue water fed by a moat.

I blinked. I was still in Marm's house. M&M had pulled it off. I had in fact simply 'valked through' as they had said. But I had arrived in the wrong suite of rooms. A glance at the still-quivering red button reminded me of the pink plastic sheath and, extracting it from my pant pocket, I slid it back on, re-contacting the O-ring. I smiled. Elvis might have to bolt for the border and this new finger, plastic or not, might come in handy.

At the center of the room, the cockpit drew me. I glimpsed a double bank of computer monitors arranged in a semi-circle, with two four-legged swivel chairs positioned at the center. The monitors were alive. If I could call what I saw on the monitors 'living'. Framed by the square pool in the window, the monitors showed distant landscapes, strange-colored sunsets, grey moon-like craters, what looked like video productions from Down South, and— strangest of all—human faces seemingly encased in white and blue ice, their cold eyes shut. Mentally I added a third M to M&M's Machiavellian penetrations of Nature's genitals: M&M&M, a lifeless frozen version of the shorter brand, one that would never melt, in one's mouth or otherwise.

Behind the double row of monitors were more stacks of electronic paraphernalia, merging into a minor warehouse of storage spaces and compartments, their back end shrouded in shadow. Who knew how many chambers—and levels—Marm's castle in the rough possessed? I recalled the downcast steps in the broom closet. Before my loopy grey matter could pop out a possible escape plan involving those steps, my eyes were sucked closer to home by a greyer and stranger construction at one end of the computers. Suspended beneath what looked like an old-timey—what were those dusty words I had once tripped over in seventh grade history?—*flying spandrel* of steel, was a metallic dome, small at the top and broadening to wide at the bottom.

I blinked. No decorations. No sign of method of manufacture or purpose. Plain-Jane as ever was.

A bell.

The bottom lip was just high enough for a napoleonic guy like myself to risk his neck by thrusting his curiosity-driven skull beneath to sample the darkness within. My memory cells remembering the odd experience of the bell in the adobe church, I could no longer control my curiosity and I peered inside, holding the clapper to preserve my ear-drums. A quiet ringing began—as if someone had phoned the Operator. It took on words.

"Mios Italianos...my love for you is as great as ever. When will you come for me and release me from this cold?" Again the Italian accent—and Italian language, straining my recollection of Berlitz.

I'm not one to give frenemies the satisfaction of seeing me sweat. Or humoring smug smiles from dippy detectives or insane kidnappers whose names begin with 'M'. But I don't mind scribbling into the cosmos' hologram that I got a repeat of the restless leg syndrome that had struck me in the bell tower at the Miracle of the Desert.

Snapping my head back—and banging it accidentally against the side of the bell—I stood straight.

Another burst of Italian quickly followed: *"You are there? Have you come for me, my friends? My beloved followers—is that you?"*

Who knows what more there was? My get-away-sticks had already flung me to the steel door that stood by the collection of poodle beds. I yanked off my magic digit, and on the chance that the doorknob failed to work due to being locked from the outside, I prepared to punch the button with my hitch digit once more, just to get the heck out of this Italiano madhouse.

I paused. I was clear of the bell, but somehow a human voice was still tickling my eardrums. Or more precisely human voices. Not as clear as from within the bell, which had gone silent, but clear enough to stick in the brain cells of my biological flash drive, and accompanied by multiple footsteps increasingly loud, and the pitter-patter of several sets of quadruple paws on a wooden floor.

"—how *could* you?"

"You raise a child. Who knows *what* she will do?"

"She could have set us back months, my dear Mrs. Massolini. *Months.*"

I could almost hear her shoulders shrug.

"You'll just have to manage, Mr. Muck. But she will certainly be punished, you may be sure of that. Come along, Licia. If anything has happened—"

From the far side of the massive door, keys jangled.

"Imagine it, dear Bob. Vhat vere the odds that our young lady friend here vould interfere in the indexing of the Multiverse at the exact moment that—"

"Odds. That's good, Jack. If I were a bettin' man."

Keys rattled inside the keyhole, began to turn.

"Vhy, he might even have reversed the indexing and attempted to come back the same vay..."

The key stopped.

"Don't even *think* that, Jack. You know what could happen."

"Yes, of course, dear Bob. The less said about that, the best—"

"The better," Bob said.

"The better," repeated Jack.

With a snap, the lock turned.

The door swung slowly open, coming to a full stop on the face of an adjacent old fashioned filing cabinet, the threshold to the rest of Marm's castle laid bare. Elvis, Pietro, Quinn and I stood with one elbow propped on top of a tall imitation-gold poodle award shaped like the Empire State Building—with me the big ape. Well, at least I had come up in the world from being dirt under Bob's fingernails. And all due to a finger—and not even the most important one.

My plastic finger reattached, and my fedora cocked on my

head, I let out a puff from my e-cig.

Smiled.

Bob stared hard, only outdone by Jack. Marm and Licia stood behind them, Andrew and Frankie gumming up the works in the none-too-wide hallway, a trio of poodles thrusting their inquisitive snouts between several sets of legs, waiting I supposed for the signal to turn their wet-nose-in-the-air tolerance into rip-this-trespasser's-throat ferocity. I counted nine. Stuffed the number in my habit-hole.

Licia had difficulty staring; her eyes kept wandering to the ceiling and blanking out as if under the effects of Marm's drug. I recalled her last grab and snatch and understood why. I fancied I could see crumbs from Marm's wafer still on Tonya's—that is, Licia's—green-fringed, red-spotted, black-feathered jacket. Somehow I just could not switch the jacket image from Green Eyes to her coughing, fist in face, sister.

On cue, Marm withdrew her nasty pipette and burned one end, sending a cloud of cherry ash hovering to blend with the fruity weather of my own flavor of the day. Licia swayed and coughed into her tight little fist. No more harsh a punishment could I imagine—Licia's was for life. It seemed there might be a little justice after all, even amidst the infinite tangle of 'verses that M&M had cooked up.

Jack jerked back in horror, matched by Bob's open mouth.

"No, no, no. Ve can have no smoke in the *Theater.*" I noticed Muck gave it an over-the-sea accent: tey-A-ter.

More confirmation, if I needed any, that his blood didn't bleed American red. I was starting to get fed up with all the aliens. I puffed a bigger one to get even. To my surprise, Jack and Bob didn't react to my e-cig. But when Marm expelled her own blast, they jumped.

"Ya gotta put it out, Miz Mass," Bob said.

"I must agree vith dear Bob, Mrs. Massolini," added Jack, "you know very vell that the *theater* is composed of the most delicate instruments—ve cannot allow contamination from tobacco in the room. I believe ve made that clear some time ago, dear lady."

A dry pinched expression settled on Marm's dry pinched face. For a moment she seemed about to object—some people (I glanced at Andrew) just can't hold their tongue—but she exhaled a curt breath and went bland. Turning, she yanked the cigarillo from the tip of her pipette and tossed it past several surprised faces into the hallway where it twirled on the polished wood floor like a whirligig. Andrew stomped it into submission. Frankie picked it up, holding it like an IED.

Marm again turned and, elbowing through Montez & Muck, strode clear across the Cockpit, clicking her heels past the banks of monitors and entered the broom closet, the door still open as I had left it, her last stream of smoke drifting behind her like a tugboat chimney.

What hold did M&M really have over Marm, I wondered? Did she fear a repeat of the Miracle of the Desert, with herself posing as the before-miracle picture? Was such a 'miracle' what happened to Americana Rick? I could not help but follow Marm's back as she disappeared in the closet's darkness, half-expecting to see Rick's disembodied hand fall from one of the buckets I had kicked.

M&M also stared at Marm's retreating form. I sent another blast from my e-cig into the ether, just to rub it in.

Jack looked at me, relaxed a trifle. "A little perfume from your mechanical blunderbuss...vell, that is not so serious a matter, dear Mr. Marlowe." Jack wasn't smiling, but Smiling Bob made up for it. "No harm, no vowel," Jack added.

"No foul, Jack."

"Oh, of course, dear Bob. No foul, I man to say."

"Not man. Mean."

"But vhy be mean? Vhatever for?"

"Man. Good enough, Jack. Good enough."

M&M parted and opened a path through the Red Sea, motioning me to walk between them out the door, Muck glancing once at his Empire trophy as if to inspect it for dirt. I walked. Both mean and foul lurked inside me—for all nine pins. All I needed was the right bowling ball.

Bob also glanced. At the phalanx of monitors—then back to me. I could almost swear I detected a hint of worry on his pale, white-crested face. This pair had chinks in their armor after all...somewhere. Too bad I was trussed up better than a Michigan stag on someone's hood by this business with Wendy. I fingered my plastic PI permit still snug in my Canali pocket to remind me that it read *detective* on the card.

Taking a step into the Red Sea, I suddenly stopped. From behind, from the direction of the broom closet drifted the same reverberations I had heard a minute earlier, echoes that sounded even more like sobbing. Somewhere a woman was crying. As I stood there in the middle of this kumbaya of Massolini misfits—now amounting to eight—I distinctly heard a second voice join the first. I could not make out the words, but the tone was clear enough: Marm was scolding someone and the tearful recipient, a woman, was arguing. It seemed Marm's castle had not just a moat and quicksand, but a dungeon.

My glare fell on Bob. He wasn't watching me, but like me, listened to the distant exchange from the broom closet, the expression on his face as readable as black-letter print on the front page of the 'Querque Gazette. His eyes focused on the bank of monitors, and I turned to follow his gaze—paused on one of a pair of rectangles that displayed frozen faces of what I supposed had once been humans, encased in blue and white ice, eyes shut in death, or what was close enough that the difference didn't amount to a mound of *hopalenos*. For one second, Jack shot his glance to me—I knew, and he knew that I knew. Hell, even the poodle pack understood and dropped their gaze to the floor in shame. Heck of a price to pay for seventy-five dollars. This family's trash was getting too deep even for a wholesale truck of trash bags.

"Now, if you please, Mr. Marlowe," Jack said. There was no shame there, just a scientist focused on his *vork*.

Andrew pulled out his piece to make clear it wasn't a suggestion.

"Ve still have a few more details to explain before you vill be ready to *take on the vorld*." The scientist's smile returned.

I walked into the hall, M&M behind me with Muck's poodles at their heels, Andrew and Frankie bringing up the rear.

Back in the main reception area, we halted. Jack again squatted his bulbous bulk on the white divan in front of the glass table, his poodles collecting around him, on and off the divan. Bob sat cattycorner on the other divan. I sat on the third, opposite Jack, while Andrew and Frankie stood behind, flanking me like the dogs flanked their master. Licia hovered at the back of the chamber, staring out a wide tall window in the hallway, watching the blue water of the outdoor pool shimmer in the New Mexico sun.

"Now, dear Mr. Marlowe. You have seen vhat this is all about." Next to him, Smiling Bob was already back in form and crossed his legs in relaxation. "Ve vant vhat you somevhat innocently call the Blarney Stone. Only you know vhere it is...or more precisely, only the Pope, but only you can get the Pope to reveal its location. Vonce you find the Stone, you vill pick it up and valk out."

I narrowed my eyes. There had to be more to it than that. "But the Vatican is like a jail, guys. There's walls everyvhere." I shook myself. Jack had *me* doing it.

"Do you still not understand, Pinky?" I guess Jack was taking my spoonerisms to heart and starting to get annoyed. "No jail can hold you! No vall is an obstacle to you anymore. Anything you put on your person or in your pocket or hold under your arm, even if wrapped in a blanket, vill transport vith you directly from the old universe into the von that the Indexer selects. Indeed everything in the new universe vill be precisely as it vas in the old von, including us."

"But..." I was starting to see the puzzle in all this. "Won't that mean that I will be leaving the pair of you in the old universe also?" Now I squinted, trying to force this into my grey cells.

"Yes, Pinky. Of course." Jack grinned. "But ve will also be in the *new* universe, including our complete consciousness-s-s, exact duplicates of us in the old universe, down to the last atom. Our observation vill entangle our consciousness-s-s-s," Jack stumbled again over the consonants, "ensuring that the transition, so to speak, vill be indetectable."

"Like magic." Bob nodded. "Might as well say it. Like magic."

"Yes." Jack's eyebrows climbed up his gleaming forehead. "You yourself, Pinky, just saw the infallibility of the technique. Do you see any difference betveen the Jack you met a few minutes ago and the Jack whom you are speaking vith now?"

I shifted uncomfortably in my seat. Two Jacks? Two Bobs? Two Mrs. Marms?

"I am not the same Jack Muck whom you met this morning at

the Convention Hall, I assure you, Pinky. Just as I assure you that this is not the same Bob Montez. Or the same poodles..."

I crossed my legs. "What happened to the old ones?"

"They are still there, Pinky! Still sitting in Mrs. Marm's house, vaiting for you to reappear. But you did not re-emerge in *their* universe, but in *ours*! Our little technique, you see, entangles our consciousness-s-s, vhich allows our consciousness-s to follow you and svitch to our doppelgangers in the new universe every time you press the red button. Ve vere there...and now ve are here. Absolutely everything about this universe is precisely the same as the other universe you just left, down to the smallest atom. Practically speaking, there is no difference. And that's all that matters."

Bob grinned. "You'll never be rid of us, Pinky. Never."

"Glad to oblige," I muttered. That notion I had briefly entertained of beaming into that three-breasted Tahitian babe universe and leaving these characters behind in their obsolete universe evaporated.

"Now, Pinky," continued Muck, "vhen you meet the Pope, and ve know he vill agree to meet you because he vill believe he is reuniting vith his old friend, your Uncle Flynn, you are to slip some of this into his coffee. Ve happen to know that this Pope loves his coffee. So it should be easy to do that."

Andrew stepped from behind my divan. Withdrawing a small glass vial from his pants pocket, he handed it to Bob before returning to resume guard duty at my shoulder.

So Andrew was not only the organ-grinder who had cranked bullets into Joe's head; he was also the Mickey in the Mickey Finn who put the Zen in my Zen Green Tea at Rick's Americana the other night.

Bob held the concoction up. Light glistened in its depths. "Okay, Player. A single drop of this little baby will put our good friend the Pope into la-la-land where he will be happy to spill the beans on anything at all."

I opened my mouth. "Spill his guts. If that's what you *man*."

"Don't get funny on us, Pinky. Just a turn of phrase. It's truth serum. Our own concoction."

"I think I've had a little more than a turn of phrase pumped into my veins, Montez."

Bob glanced at Jack.

"More than once," I added, remembering Andrew's injection the previous night.

Back to Bob. "Here's the dope, Pinky. One drop makes him talk. Two drops will get him a DWI in his pope-mobilc. Three drops will turn out the lights, enough to perform a little grand larceny, or even a little operation. It's up to you to decide how many drops, and when and where. But not to worry. It's perfectly safe no matter how many drops you give."

My eyes wandered to my left little finger where the pain, though less than earlier, had still not disappeared.

Ponytail Bob went on. "I guarantee, Pinky, that after you slip a drop of this into Ye Merry Olde Pope's drink, he'll be not just your friend for life, he'll be eager to do anything you ask, including take you to the Stone. Once there, he will go to sleep. That will be your chance. That's when you grab the rock and skedaddle. Now here's a map of the Vatican. Memorize where you should go and how to get there. Once you're through the last obstacle, we'll have a car on the street waiting. Our driver will whisk you to the promised land."

I rubbed my temple. I had to think.

No time. At the back of the room, Licia's shadow had split in two. One of them handed something to Licia to ease her quiet coughing, then moved toward our table. It stepped between the angled divans and deposited a tray on the glass table, on the tray several glass cups filled with liquid.

"Tank you, Diego."

El Salvador nodded and, before Andrew could toss a plastic menu at him from behind my shoulder, vamoosed. As part of my habit of scribbling everything I saw and heard into my memory banks, I counted one lime tequila and a red vino, which Diego had placed in front of Bob and Jack. Just like old times. To my relief, zilch for me.

A blip interrupted. My cell phone came to life—and damned if M&M weren't right about that universe crap, after all, since it was still turned on and with the exact same battery charge as before I stepped through the wall. There she was. Wendy's naked backside, as pretty as ever, swinging on her silver pole. I knew she had already bolted for Idaho, but that didn't make a Dutchman's Difference or give me a Chinaman's Chance given that M&M knew what was down with me, or more precisely up, concerning my favorite pole-dancer. They just had to rub it in—a little reminder of what was at stake should I wander off The Reservation.

Looking up I saw Jack grinning at me, his thumb on his cell phone. Touché. Or was he just touchy? While I watched, Jack reached for his wine glass and rubbed his finger around its rim. He smiled while the reverberations filled the room.

Just like a bell...

CHAPTER 10

J ust that little thing... Is that all they want? Why not ask for the sun and the moon and world peace? Those at least are real and part of this universe. But the crucial part of that slab of rock unearthed centuries ago—which was so marred by the lips of middle-aged Irish women losing faith in their child-bearing hips, and by old-aged Irish men losing the gab of their profit-bearing tongues, that the Stone's surface was smooth as glass—had been switched by Flynn a decade ago. And, given the extent of idol-hunger throughout a sterile and dying Europe, who knew what the heck Flynn had unloaded on the Pope? And who knew whether the Pope had the Stone anymore, or even remembered it?

But for Wendy's sake, I had to try. Not to mention the sobbing I had heard from Marm's dungeon. Whatever Green Eyes had done to me, she didn't deserve that...whatever 'that' was.

Two days later, I stood at the entrance to the Albuquerque airport as Andrew and Frankie watched me from the limo, like misers eyeing their investment. I wondered at the absurdity of having to spend twelve hours on a commercial jet when I had just traveled from one universe to another in twelve seconds. Surely M&M could do better than a round-trip ticket on New Guinea Airlines and a pocketful of lira. And not a full pocket, mind you. Just enough to keep me in meatball cannolis and Strawberry e-juice. Apparently, this business of inter-universe travel to save clients' reputations was not as lucrative as laymen might think, and, since Mrs. Mass was keeping her dough close to the breast as her part of the deal, that meant I was stuck with coach.

It seemed I was back to being dirt.

With Andrew and Frankie watching, I verified my belongings. Suit cleaned and pressed? Check. White shirt with pink tie? Check.

Shoes shined and sole repaired, including the usual extra height on the heels? Check. Grey-banded fedora dry-cleaned and propped on my head with affected nonchalance, tipped so as not to disturb my black-Irish Elvis wave? Check. With Loreto sunshades and Movado watch? Check. And gun returned comfortably under my left underarm? *Nyet*. Snake-boy and his sidekick would not allow one near me. But I didn't argue. No guns were allowed on board, and anyway who needs a gun when I have the keys to the universe embedded in my body? After my brief trip back to my cot at the cleaners, I had left the Colt .45 in my locker. For later.

Passport, cell phone, comb, electronic cigarette: check, check, check, and check. And an extra-wide suitcase in hand—the unreconstructed hand—not so much for personal needs, but to contain the Prize once I lifted it. And, most important, one tiny glass vial with faked medical prescription data too small for anyone with only two eyes to read plastered on its outside, delivered at the last moment by Andrew between thrusts of his pink appendage, the concoction that would ensure cooperation from the High Vicar of Christ.

Piece of cake. And not too far from a couple of odd jobs I had pulled off in the distant days of my Brooklyn youth, with legal consequences to match... Well, who are *you* to judge *me?*

I had wasted no time that morning, and, noticing a pause in the morning rush, I hurried into the main reception area for my shoe inspection, the Italian bros driving the limo away with parting upraised fingers in response to the angry glare from a minimum wage don't-even-think-about-parking-here attendant.

Once through the passenger line, my shoes passed with flying colors. As did my suitcase, cell phone, hat, and liquid vial—even my newly circumcised finger, which to my relief remained invisible to all but me. I stepped into the gyrating X-ray moon-viewer so the federal inspectorette could get a quick cheap thrill, and, stepping forward with hands over heads—another reminder of those distant *odd jobs* and their legal aftermath—I began to rotate like that Seattle tower eatery that likes to fill you up before making you dizzy enough to upchuck it into space.

The exit opened.

Sauntering out, I felt a surge of confidence. Funny how with human-types even the smallest test triggers a feeling of triumph once it's overcome, and, considering all the polls and samplings and surveys and questionnaires that litter the Internet like those finger-bones of saints that litter old world churches, perhaps explains the success of the entire Internet. In my book they were just as authentic.

I put my Canali jacket back on and picked up my bag and slipped into my freshly shined loafers, and re-pocketed my wallet—when someone tapped my shoulder. A blue-uniformed attendant with a downward vacant stare, one eye occasionally wavering at the wall clock as if counting the minutes till break. Stares are always downward in my case, though, as if every joker ever lived thought he was hot shit compared to *mio*. I gritted my teeth; with the taste of M&M in my mouth, this attitude was getting harder to take.

"Sir, can you come with me, please?"

Behind him a second cop identical to the first took a step, also staring down at me. And, yes, anyone in a blue uniform is still a cop to me, gun or no gun.

Quinn called for a swift kick to the gonads. Pietro focused on a female in a blue uniform, standing behind the two males, who filled out her blouse in complimentary fashion. But Pinky bit his lip and replied, "When? And how high?" There's a time and place for everything, and this wasn't it.

Following them aside a few steps, I paused as one of the cops poked a latex-gloved hand in my front pants pocket. He fished around before extracting a metal object. My e-cig.

"What's this?" Their politeness was fading.

"My personal charger, gentlemen. My Five Minute Energy injection. My sucka from another brotha." A Universal Indexer these clowns had no problem with—but for a run-of-the-mill e-cig they were ready to shut down the airport.

They exchanged puzzled glances.

"Once more, sir. What is this?"

"You got me, copper. My ticket to Cuba."

Worried glances now.

I wanted to strangle Quinn to make him keep his mouth shut. But Quinn, Pietro, Pinky and I were having too much fun. Finally I got to thrust back—and to people who deserved it.

"Don't you recognize a nicotine killer, gentlemen? It's a drug delivery system to get off the cancer sticks. Whadaya, live under a stone?" I almost blurted out 'Blarney', but managed to smack that smart-aleck Quinn down in time.

My back had been to the TSA merry-go-round at first, but now we shifted so that my gaze shot through the rotating chamber to the long line waiting to get the TSA treatment themselves. Something caught my eye.

"Killer?" The cop threw a glance at his partner.

"Drug delivery?" The other threw back.

Damn that Quinn.

A hand landed on my shoulder. "We would like you come with us, sir."

'No' wasn't an option.

But I no longer listened. Or watched. My eye had settled on a pair of figures shoving through the line of barefoot belt-less customers on the other side of the X-Ray Whirligig—the pair yelled and flashed badges at the TSA dicks.

Dorkman and Krupke.

I wasn't sure whether to grab and kiss them, hide under a bench, or make for the border.

The TSA cop released my shoulder and turned to see what was happening, and I could see from the shocked faces of the trio of blue-unif'd stooges standing beside me that the twin dicks' commotion had summoned in the TSA fears of attack by black-bearded Muslim hordes with suicide belts. Cupping my hands, I threw my voice to the other side of the Gyrator: "Allahu akbar!" which fit right into Krapke's round open mouth like a hot boudin. Then I thrust my hands in my pockets and whistled the Star-Spangled Banner.

That did it.

Next thing I knew, blue-shirted TSA cops sprouted from every angle like a fast-motion vegetation nature film and fell on the two 'Querque dicks in an avalanche. The happiness I felt at seeing the pair's surprised faces was only exceeded by the joy of watching their badges spin in the air and nosedive under a wall of passengers' travel bags, guaranteeing a long delay before anyone would believe their story, whatever the hell they thought they had on me.

But however much I enjoy watching Dork and Krapke get their comeuppance, I couldn't hang around to celebrate. Duty called. And this was probably my only chance.

I hoofed it. Cradling my suitcase to my chest, I ran through the boarding area.

More cops appeared and I slowed to a casual saunter, carrying the case properly while staring downward, just like hot-shit people.

The number of cops grew as more TSA swarmed. How could they reproduce so rapidly, I wondered? I decided there must be some alien queen farther up the hallway cranking them out, a giant blue-uniformed spider with a horse's head, drooling acid.

The desk for New Guinea Airlines loomed right behind this blue alien army. But to push my way through and subject myself to another inspection seemed not the greatest idea.

One of the cops touched a knob in his ear to listen to a private broadcast. He directed his gaze toward me. Scanned me with a glance as if matching my features to an invisible ID.

Whether it was Dork & Krapke's unicorn tale or the trio of TSA cops' boo-hoo'ing, it was again time to hoof it.

Behind me I heard a yell. I turned. The alien army was coming at me.

Beside me was an open door, or more precisely, a wide threshold of white tiles with brown perimeters, beneath a sign that read 'Hombres'. It's Albuquerque, after all—can't get away from the down-south signs.

In I dove. After running into a back stall, I clicked the privacy door lock and, still hugging the suitcase—just in case M&M's calculations might be a few centimeters off regarding personal items within the red button's shotgun scatter.

I plucked off the plastic tip of my left little finger. For a moment it slipped and I had to juggle it like a circus ball, almost dropping it into the toilet—but caught it in time. Just try doing that with nine fingers. I breathed out to regain control. M&M had better be right...it would be just my luck if the whole thing had been an April Fool's joke and the Massolini clan at this moment were rolling on their Frank Lloyd floor, laughing uproariously as I banged my nose on a solid bathroom stall, one foot flushing.

Footsteps behind me, the stall's back wall erupted in bubbling spume, volcano red swirling on its surface. A familiar musical lyric swirled in my brain, though my conscious mind realized it was only an inner ear interpretation of a high-pitched ringing. As hard-soled boots tramped across the tiled floor of the men's room and muscled arms banged open privacy door after privacy door—I stepped forward.

I wanted to wretch. It was a bit like a land-lubber deciding to go deep-sea fishing when he had never so much as dipped oars in a rowboat. But it passed quickly, more quickly this time. I found myself, complete with suitcase, hat, cell-phone, passport, and all of my other personal essentials, including even my e-cig, standing inside a stall. For a moment I panicked, thinking it didn't work. Then my eye noticed the stall was different, and that I was turned around. Cautiously pushing the stall door open, I noticed a lack of urinals, bigger mirrors. I was in the 'Señoras' restroom. Outside the door, the TSA still swarmed, their feet stampeding inside the men's room next door like elephants after they smelled lion.

The women's restroom was empty. No way could I walk out the front. After all, men can't go in there—that just isn't done. I walked quickly to the far wall. Punched the red button again.

Swirling spume—red volcanoes—red hair. Again the idiot lyrics about Turks in 'Stambul embedded in my brain. I couldn't separate the impressions...I stepped forward.

I emerged on the other side of the women's restroom wall not more than twenty feet from the entrance that led on board New Guinea Airlines. The ticketing booth was empty, both attendants, having ushered their passengers on board, hovering behind the army of cops outside the men's room, rubbernecking to see who was getting elephant-stomped.

No one had seen.

Across from the Airlines' booth, the airport's neon schedule signaled that boarding time was expiring.

All attention—of the few remaining airline passengers in the waiting area, and of the attendants and cops—was directed away. At the New Guinea desk I pilfered a boarding pass, then walked into the boarding chute.

Out of sight, I ran.

When the airplane's door came into view, I again walked.

The door was closing.

I ran again.

Banged.

The door reopened.

A surprised face appeared—pretty, dark. "Welcome, sir. Welcome aboard."

Seconds later I found my seat, threw my nearly empty suitcase into the overhead compartment, and sank into the seat's semi-plush depths. With a sly glance around to make sure no one was watching, I slipped the plastic tip back on my finger. It seemed Montez & Muck were right about this inter-universe travel. I gazed at the uplifted digit. Risked a smile. *Pinky...*a guy could get *used* to this.

***

I could not let it go. The green of Tonya's Green Eyes. The thick grass of the Emerald Isle, sucking every drop that the distant tropical current scattered over its rocky coast. The wind-blown clouds that allowed just the right amount of sunshine to bring the grass to life so they clung to the rocks like the feathers of Tonya's coat clung to its black leather: underneath, all Black Irish, but its fronds fringed in green. A perfect expression of Olde Éire. The place was in my blood.

As it must have been for my uncle. I was born there and had but distant memories. Despite traveling the world, Uncle Flynn had lived there his whole life. What Flynn could tell about those ancient stones, where they came from, what they were good for... In the tender years of my youth in rural Dungiven he had babbled stories in my ear, syllabic milk downed drop by drop, images and obsessions left to percolate in my soul as I grew. Dungiven. The Vatican. Italy. Ireland. He'd even taken me as a child with him a few times to visit Saint Peter's. Why did I care so much about a damned Italian suit with matching footwear? I glanced at the bottoms of my shoes, all that remained from an antediluvian Canali ensemble—for the first time in years, both sole and soul were in repair.

The plane rocketed onward.

My breath caught in my throat like a pit. I let it out—I could no longer fight it. Green fringes or not, her perfect face with its plum lips surfaced from the jungle of fronds, the volcano of swirling red. I was head over heels and knew it. I *felt* like a heel, and an elevated one, for leaving Green Eyes behind, at the mercy of this mafia gang. Sure, I knew it was wrong to go eighty miles an hour with a client, and more so when that client's bag of trash was mostly filled with family trouble, but Tonya's face drifted before my eyes with every cloud that floated past the airplane's window. Well, why not? I still cared for my Ex, Wendy, but she had given me walking papers— twice now. That page had turned. I was happy and free, free to buy my own ticket, to write my own book, to climb into any bag I chose. Funny how *freedom* works. As soon as a sidewalk joe gets emancipated, what does he do? Locks himself in the first jail he sees and throws away the key, then grins like he just won the Nobel Prize.

I breathed an honest breath.

Not only architects can make plans. First I had to get Wendy off the hook—for old times' sake. Then, as for Green Eyes...well, she'll have to be patient. This Joe don't need no stinkin' key. As Jack had said—*no jail can hold me.*

***

At the Rome airport I was left to fend for myself. Resisting the urge to walk through every wall I saw and collect extra lira as 'donations' from admiring, goggly-eyed spectators, and deciding it was too hot to trudge through the heat like a doughy-eyed tourist, I managed to flag a scarce taxi and, spouting the few lines of Italiano I still remembered, had the driver deliver me to a run-down hotel a few spits from Saint Peter's Basilica. The heart of the Vatican loomed so large that its upper levels were visible from my hotel's bottom-floor window. The Basilica must have seemed bigger than the moon in those distant caveman days when Rome was smaller and the Thingamajig had first been purloined and taken to Dublin. Allegedly. I tried not to think about the bottom line of the matter.

After a long rest, and the usual 'Continental breakfast' of Styrofoam and nuts, and a last-minute phone call to set up an interview with the world's most childless Father, who ironically was also the Father with the most children who ever lived if one counted Believers, I got my second wind and strode through the usual flocks of pigeons and herds of tourists. I wondered how 'Il Papa' avoided getting child-support orders from God for all his children, while I mentally measured the majestic height of Saint Peter's sky-high columns.

What secrets could they tell? The Church of Ages had stood for longer than even a private dick could count, and I already knew that the City of Rome's gun-toting gendarmes loitering in the plaza had no jurisdiction once they crossed from Plaza to street. When in Rome, do as the Romans. But once in the Vatican, you'd better watch your step. If Il Papa were to decide to keep humans in limbo and give pigeons a go-to-Heaven-free card in their stead, that's his get-out. Wouldn't be nothin' anyone could say about it. For a moment, I wondered at the wisdom of attempting to steal the sacred heart of this huge edifice and smuggling it out in the worn empty suitcase I lugged at my side.

At a bench I paused. Verified that the suitcase was working, opened and closed it, locked and unlocked it. I glanced at my watch. Yeah, I know. I had my cell. But mental habits are the hardest to break, and that includes how one tells time. Patterns of thought, unquestioned assumptions of what's real and what line of bull one should believe hold more souls in their jails than all the world's prisons ever built. Did I have a key to that? Where was the Red Button to escape from my obsession with Green Eyes? So far, I had been merely impressed with the showboating of Montez & Muck. Space-time travel? That's one thing. Let them come up with a get-out-of-love potion—then I would truly be awed.

Check, check, and check.

Including the GPS on my cell that would guarantee the appearance of M&M's getaway car at the precise point of exit once I blew this Vatican Alcatraz by dropping over its back fence with the Rock in stow.

Just one item was missing—the smock that would guarantee me entrance into Oz's castle. I couldn't walk in dressed like a private dick, and certainly not carrying an empty suitcase that looked designed to haul out treasure. Flynn, on the other palm, was a priest. He came and went like one because he looked like one.

An ancient memory stirred. Beyond the columns I knew a place that had once accommodated Flynn when I had accompanied him on one of our trips, a place that had repaired a tear in his smock.

In minutes, I found it.

Initially they gave me suspicious looks, not even my stylish Canali suit easing their attitude. A quick subtle transfer of lira changed their attitude, however. In half an hour—after ransacking their wardrobe for a size IV—they finally fitted me and even supplied a black ring around the collar for a tip. A happy *ciao* followed me out the door.

Back to my room to switch clothing, and I was on my way.

I again eased through the crowds. I noticed that my reception among the crowd was different this time. Before, the people had kept their distance and the pigeons came close as if expecting edible litter—now the pigeons avoided me while the people crowded close, smiling and nodding until it became difficult to make headway. For a moment, I wondered what sort of tidbit I could toss to distract them and avoid the endless entreaties to assist with photos and bless crying infants, despite the puzzled looks at what they must have thought was the shortest priest they had ever seen, strangely hauling a suitcase almost half his size.

But the hot-shit people finally cleared and I halted before the wide entrance to the Basilica. The rainbow Swiss guards parted like a cleft watermelon at my approach—not their job to interfere with anyone with a black collar, case or no case. In fact, *especially* if carrying a case.

My thoughts wandered back to those distant days, and I began to understand Uncle Flynn a bit better.

CHAPTER 11

From my phone conversation with Il Papa's secretary, I knew to go through the entrance and to the right. All the way to the right, right out of Saint Peter's, across the well-tended grounds and into the next building. It was confusing. My grandiose memories of those distant childhood visits I found were at times accurate, but at other times empty, tricking me down wrong paths.

I stumbled, and stumbled again.

A thin tall man (this describes just about everyone I saw in the Vatican) caught up with me, and smilingly took my arm and guided me out and back and into an air-conditioned hall until an open door loomed. Gently pushing me in, he shut the door from the outside and left me standing in a simple room bare of any more adornment than a small town retirement center. A set of dominoes lay spread across a square table as if a trio of Billy Bobs had just stepped out to attend to nature.

Yes, dominoes. The ancient memory stirred again. The Pope still played dominoes. But funny how I still could not remember his name. Only knew it was a variation of John, Paul, Benedict, or Francis. Despite my visits, Vatican affairs just aren't my thing. Best to call him 'Papa'—much better than 'Primate', which made me expect to see a gibbon swing into the room.

Enough thought about titles, though. My eyes were drawn to a second item on the table—a pot of coffee. And several cups. Il Papa must have been entertaining old friends with a game of dominoes and coffee until someone had reminded him of my appointment.

I glanced around. My smock was unfamiliar and pulled at my neck, and I was uncomfortable without my fedora, but the opportunity was too much to ignore. Verifying that no cameras were watching, I dropped the suitcase. I snatched the vial from a pocket and, unstopping the tiny cap, carefully, as if introducing matter to anti-matter, dripped one drop into the cup nearest the dominoes, figuring Il Papa must be the organizer of the game.

I put the vial away.

For a minute I stood alone in the room, pretending to whistle, rocking on my heels. I tried to put my hands on my hips akilter, but found the smock too entangling to permit this and I had to let my arms dangle helplessly by my sides.

I glanced again.

No one was coming.

I tried folding my arms, but that too failed to ease the tension.

My alarm began to grow. All my years of wrestling with murderers and addicts, and holding my nose at the stink that arose out of family problems, what with one spouse hiring me to spy on the other spouse, or parents asking me to track down the source of their teenage kids' drug supply, none of this had prepared me for how to play a smock-wearing priest trying to drug a pope so I could smuggle his Blarney Stone into a different dimension. Having earned an 'A' in 'Strange 101' as a PI in Albuquerque did not help.

I tried to pinch myself to purge my insanity—the thick smock didn't allow this either.

My eye lingered on the other half-empty cups. What if I was wrong about which cup was Il Papa's? I blinked. Again whipping out the vial, I hurriedly slipped one drop into each of the several cups, then for measure, let three more fall into the open mug half-filled with coffee—then three into a full jug of tea that was set alongside the coffee mug—just to make sure. This Papa wasn't going to escape paying Tonya's child-support.

All I needed now was to find the Stone. And 'Flynn' could do it—all I had to do was think like Flynn.

Behind me a grumble sounded. For a second I froze—had someone seen what I had just done? Slowly I turned. Stretched out on a pillow-strewn couch with his back to me lay a small man in white, mostly covered with cushions, which was why I had not seen him when I entered. Another groan and the pillows moved. The figure used his arms to push himself to a sitting position, and swung his legs slowly round till he sat up facing me. He reached for a pair of thick gold-rimmed spectacles from a small adjoining table and wrapped them around his ears.

He blinked twice. It took a moment but finally two grotesquely magnified brown retinas stared uncertainly at me as through mist, struggling to comprehend what I was doing there, who I was...perhaps who *he* was. The stare wandered around the room and consciousness seemed to return.

He breathed deep. He struggled to his feet, both arms assisting.

My heart tried to climb up my esophagus and slap me—*the One and Only*.

The Pope opened his mouth. Broken Italian came out, with a non-Italian accent that I couldn't place, maybe East European, maybe elsewhere.

"You may clear the table, now, Monseigneur. I guess our little friend from Dublin isn't going to show."

Isn't going to show? I glanced at my Movado—suddenly realized. The time zones had got me. My calculations were an hour off and I had missed my appointment. Mentally I promised to update my watch. Or maybe just squash it.

Faced with the prospect of M&M—and mine and Green Eyes'—project going down the tubes hardly before it began, I did the only thing I could. I stepped forward to grab Il Papa's full attention and enlarge my doppelganger self in his myopic eyeglass-covered eyes. Now that I was sure he had not seen my little deed, I felt braver. I was gettin' tired of being ignored and overlooked everyplace I went, and I made up my mind to no longer slouch toward Jerusalem, but to walk taller among its lofty columns.

I let loose a grin—the best I could muster. "Papa. I am hurt. I know it has been years, but do you not recognize your faithful Irish servant?" Inside, I let out a sigh of relief. I had never thought that acting was in my green Irish blood, but I believed I had passed the first test.

The spectacles focused, or rather the myopic orbs behind them. Il Papa took them off and immediately looked like a cave-blind Mexican salamander. He reached for a cloth and slowly, excruciatingly slowly, rubbed them with a circular motion. Putting them on, he focused again.

Stepping closer, he passed his gaze up and down my short body and fixed his errant stare on my face. Slowly, this time merely disappointingly slowly, he too grinned. Two arms out-spread. I cautiously stepped within them and he grabbed me and embraced me warmly, and we kissed each other's cheeks like the old friends we were, though I thought I sensed an odd sliding about of hands that reminded me of nothing so much as Dorkman's pat-down when I had first gotten my New Mexico PI license.

Stepping back, Papa held his enormous binoculars with thumb and forefinger, his inspection still continuing. But at least his gaze was now accompanied by a smile.

"Monseigneur Flynn, my dear old friend," Il Papa suddenly said, "What have I done to you to make you treat me so badly?" He arched his shoulders forward in that classic Italian don't-know-nothin' style.

Given the shaky state of my Italiano, I was relieved that he had switched to English, but the 'monseigneur' phrase made me nervous again despite the ease of the cheek-kissing. Had he seen, after all?

"Badly?" I feigned chagrin, mortification, shame... "Why, you are my oldest, dearest friend in all the world. *Papa mio*—*w*hy ever would you say such a thing? You know I would have come to you sooner if I could have freed myself."

His smile stumbled. He stepped back a half-step, oddly like before, leaving me to wonder if my memories of Papa's senility were true after all.

"You know, *Papa mío,* I have been tied up with my flock in Dungiven," that part was not a complete lie since my family had once been part of Flynn's flock, "and," I gave a hint of embarrassment, "I fell ill...for some time." I crossed my fingers, hoping this would work.

It did. Il Papa was clearly relieved, though I did not really understand why. If I were in his place, I wouldn't buy it. He embraced me again—without the kisses and pat-down—and still slowly, though less slowly than before, leaving me to conclude that Il Papa must finally be awake.

True, Il Papa also loomed a good half foot over me, just like hot-shit people, but for Green Eyes and the Ex's sake I slapped

Quinn down, farther, farther...until I was certain Quinn would not blurt out some crass comment to spoil things this time. Papa's thick spectacles aimed down at me like twin telescopes, huge and round, his pinkish eyes enlarging within, making me feel like an ant enduring a kid's inspection. Quinn hammered on the roof of his cellar where I had put him, thirsting to push back.

Then Papa became even odder.

He winked.

A sly, slow wink of one eye was followed by a half-smile on the opposite side of his face. More memories returned—it was the same wink and smile I remembered from my last visit when I was no longer a child, but rather older, when the Pope had encountered me alone in the Vatican halls without my uncle, his growing senility leading him to mistake me for Flynn, to share their little secret.

I'd succeeded!

He believed I was Flynn.

Another breath of relief, sincere, if not entirely honest.

The Pope turned his head to the right and gazed about, then to the left, and finally behind at the closed door. Yes, we were alone. He lurched to the little table strewn with dominoes. Shoving them aside without regard for his game, he motioned me to join him and take the opposite seat. Settled, he broke into a wide grin and leaned forward.

"My dear old friend," he whispered. "I must share something with you...a little secret." He peered around as if the Curia might have spies behind the curtains.

"You honor me, Papa. As always."

He waved my compliment aside with a short flick of his hand.

"I am joyous, my friend, that you could spare time from your work in Dublin to visit me. Joyous! The Rock... how fantastic it is. Our Lord Jesus speaks to me direct. As I said when you returned the Rock of our beloved Saint Peter to its proper place here in Saint Peter's own Basilica, I am eternally grateful." The grin lost some of its grandeur as frustration surfaced. "*Que lástima* that the world does not know of its existence." He shook his head. "Dear Flynn, you would be surprised if you knew just how limited are the options of a pope. I do not dare let the world know of this thing, this *cosa nostra*. The Curia is so convinced that the Rock is only a play on words for

Saint Peter—Saint 'Petros'—that they cannot allow themselves to imagine that it might be an *actual* stone."

I risked a comment. "On the QT, *Papa mío*. Like I said: On the QT." It was something Flynn might have said. Without waiting for an invitation, I poured myself a cup of coffee and made as if to drink. As I hoped, Il Papa took up the very cup that I had first guessed was his. To my chagrin, he paused and, without drinking, placed the cup back on the table.

"Yes, indeed. As you said before, Flynn, the Thing must never be revealed." He gave more sidelong glances. "If it were revealed, it would throw the entire Church into chaos. The world made upside down."

He leaned back. Again I lifted my cup of coffee—not forgetting that I had contaminated everything drinkable on the table, so I carefully refrained from actually tasting it. To my relief, Il Papa did the same, lifting his in response.

Again he paused, cup in air. "But," the Pope lowered his voice into an even quieter whisper, "there is something else I must discuss with you." Down went his cup, back in its place.

Locked in his cellar, Quinn groaned. Pietro laughed maniacally, his eyes on a picture of a curvy nun on the back wall, even her dull habit not killing Pietro's effervescent libido.

The Pope breathed deep. For a moment he held his breath, then forced it out as if attempting to master a deep concern. One magnified eye moved closer.

My eye remained on his hand where a thumb and forefinger still clutched his cup's handle. Would he ever drink?

"I hear *more*."

I twitched my eyelids. "More?"

"More." Taking no chances on the Curia spies, his voice reduced to even less than a whisper. I had to lean to hear. "Sometimes when Jesus is speaking to me through the Rock, I think I hear *other* things—*other* voices. It is hard to say, hard to be certain. My hearing is not what it used to be; perhaps I am not hearing Our Lord Jesus correctly."

"Correctly?" I leaned back and moved my cup to my mouth. Again Papa did the same, but once more, when I hesitated, he hesitated.

Back down went his cup.

Quinn fainted and lay flat on his cellar floor.

Again Il Papa leaned forward, tempting *mio* and Quinn. "But I hear *you* correctly, dear Flynn. And I *see* you as well."

"As well?" I didn't see how. I could barely see his cave-blind eyes through those pop-bottle bottoms.

"Some of the other voices," continued Il Papa, "I could almost swear are *not* that of Our Lord." His round eyes expanded like saucers in the double magnification. The pale retinas were spotted with pink, just like those amphibians forgotten for centuries in their lost little worlds. I wondered if they too awaited a sacred rock tuned to broadcasts from God.

I summoned the best mask of surprise I could. "But...that is impossible, *Papa mio*. You've heard the Miracle of the Rock of Saint Peter yourself." I risked a phrase from M&M, adding my own twist. Probability, I reminded myself—everything is, in the end, a roll of the dice. For the sake of Green Eyes and the Ex, I had to keep rolling. "Miracles don't appear from nowhere like a radio show."

"I know, Monseigneur. I know." He stopped smiling.

Il Papa made as if to rise from the table. Hurriedly, I raised my cup in a final attempt to get M&M's damn drug into Il Papa's system so I could finally interrogate him and I brought the rim close to my lip. "A toast, *Papa mio*. A toast. To our sacred Rock—and to Our Lord, Savior of us all, including Saint Peter himself." I was becoming desperate. I had seen that work once in a movie.

Shrugging, Papa took up his cup and raised it to his lips. Success! Almost. A sudden knock on the door, and like a spent rocket, the cup descended. A head thrust into the room. It was apparently the Monseigneur whom Il Papa had expected to see when he awoke.

"Papa," the priest said, "your guest has still not arrived. I think we should cancel the appointment and try again later." As I turned to look, his eyes fell on me. "Oh. Forgive me, Papa. I see Monseigneur Flint is here after all."

Il Papa smiled. "Flynn, Monseigneur, not Flint."

With a crinkled bow, the priest backed out of the room, closing the door.

"That is enough." Attempting to rise, Il Papa stumbled—his cup fell to the floor and broke.

It was all I could manage to keep the menagerie in my basement from bursting into tears all at once.

Brown liquid spread over wood parquetry.

Il Papa finally gained his balance. "Oh. What ill luck." He flipped a single domino, then walked toward the back of the little room. "Come with me, Monseigneur Flynn. I want you to help me. I want you to verify that everything is as it should be. We will go look at this little stone of yours—and test it out."

My chagrin over failing to drug Il Papa was only matched by my concern over what he meant by 'test it out'. What did I know about holy rocks? Did I carry a holy voltmeter in my pocket to measure the degree of Jesus-juice it might possess? Or a radio dial that detected speaking in tongues so we could tune to the right one? But I kicked myself. What was I worried about? Finding the Rock was the reason I had come, and the Pope was offering to lead me straight to it without the necessity of Montez & Muck's truth serum.

"Avant," I said, rising smartly.

Things were still on track.

Papa paused and turned back to me. "Don't forget your overnight bag, Monseigneur. You never know when you might need it."

A puzzling thing to say, but as we were up and moving, and as I was closer to my goal, I shrugged, ignoring the spilled coffee-bean soup on the floor.

CHAPTER 12

P apa did not head toward the door to the hallway through which I had entered, but in the opposite direction. Within a few steps, a deeply-carved rear door appeared, and Papa opened it and walked through, one hand motioning for me to follow.

Before us was a second, smaller room, either side hung with a vast accumulation of smocks and decorative gowns befitting the Pastor of Millions. At the end of this dressing closet, a smaller, narrower door came into view, hardly visible. Il Papa found a nondescript handle, brushing aside hangered gowns to do so. The door swung back and we entered a poorly lit corridor.

As bare of adornment as the public hallways were finely decorated, and lit by dully unimpressive electric lights, the hidden corridor stretched into shadowed distance.

Down its length we walked, turned a bend, and climbed a narrow flight of stairs. Another length followed, our footsteps echoing.

Stalking the halls as one long familiar with them, Papa's gait seemed to me odd, much like the oddness that hung about him in other ways, walking straight with both arms hanging stiffly vertical as if hewn from wood, his arms not swaying with his progress. His shuffling resounded off the bare undecorated walls, reminding me of a flight of locusts. Not once did he turn to ensure I followed, nor did he speak.

Was he still aware that I was with him? Had he forgotten me? I chalked it up to senility and braved on, clutching my case, and watching the shiny backs of his shoes, as unsoiled as if freshly out of a box. Shoes must be an Italian thing, I decided.

We came to another shut door. Il Papa fumbled with a set of keys—surprisingly few given the vastness of his Vatican estate. He inserted the longest one. With a creak the door swung open, the Pope waiting until I passed through to close and relock the door behind us.

Inside, I viewed a space as unimpressive as the bland corridors. Against one wall lay a simple bed with a crocheted quilt, gold crosses and cupid-like heads with golden sunbursts embroidered in the cloth. Big-shot saints, I assumed. Beside the bed stood a small round table surmounted by a dusty electric lamp with two decanters of hot coffee—I counted. And I smelled the coffee. Strangely, only one porcelain cup, on its side a sunny nature scene, a child skipping with a kite. Above the table and bed, a small wide cabinet was fixed to the wall, its flat panels shut.

The floor was composed of wooden slats that peeked out from the edges of a thin-piled carpet that showed more nature scenes that replicated across its warp and woof in unthinking did-not-compute patterns. The ceiling was high—the kind of height that society dames in Brooklyn pay *boocoop* rent for.

At right angles and opposite the bed was still another door, narrow and of cheap pine. To one side a fake window was painted on the wall with a pretend sun either dawning or setting. On the other, a pretend moon sailed aloft. The walls between doors and window and cabinet were of simple gypsum covered by dull, low-quality paint, cerulean, but faded with the years to simple pale pastel, several genuine jeweled golden crosses suspended, the only opulence in the room.

My eyes found another table, low and squat in the corner, where an old-fashioned long-play record player rested on a cloth, a small box of plastic platters stacked alongside. With better vision than Papa, and lower to the ground anyway, I managed to peep out 'Best of Al Jolson' on the label of the one recently played. So Il Papa was not just a man of the people, but a fan of the opera.

On the round table by his bed, next to the empty cup, was tossed a copy of the Vatican Gazette, some highfalutin paper I had seen elsewhere with a title in Latin very much like 'Apple Seed', though I didn't see what the legendary Johnny had to do with it. Close enough for a schmoe from 'Querque, though.

In the middle of the room, Papa halted. He turned to stare at me, and for a moment I got the impression that I was not a guest, but an intruder. Could the real Flynn have seen all this before, and my bad acting betrayed me as an impostor?

He broke into that blind-salamander smile and a second time threw me the casual hand invitation. *This way.* Turning, he bent over and dropped to his knees. Beside his little bed, he clasped his hands together and, resting them on the side of the bed, shut his eyes and began to utter a prayer—one I had heard Flynn often recite. Relieved that I still knew the words, I did not wait for an invitation, but promptly flung myself also to my knees and, alongside the Pope, spiritual ruler of half the world, clasped my hands and mumbled the same, my body hunched parallel to his.

At length, we finished. Without a glance at me, he slid his hands under the bed, which revealed itself to be hollow under the overhanging quilt. He grasped some large, bulky object.

Stunned, I could not help but leap to my feet and retreat. Did the Heir of Saint Peter, infallible Ruler to billions of people, really keep the secretive Rock under his lumpy bed as Uncle Flynn had once confided?

Out it came.

I wish I could say he kept it in a shoebox, but the Thingamajig of course was too large for that. In fact, Il Papa had a time dragging it out and across the carpet. The box was wood and looked like nothing so much as a grocery store pallet with raised sides, the kind used to display vegetables. Was that remnants of peppers and melon rind shriveled in one corner? He dragged it roughly across the shallow carpet and I glimpsed tracks permanently imprinted in its pile where he had done this before. Apparently Il Papa often called Heaven's Operator.

No cover lay on top of the stone. I didn't wonder at this. Who would believe this hunk of black basalt was anything more than a souvenir of Papa's vacation side-trip to Chile or Vesuvius anyway? Rock is rock.

Except this rock spoke.

Sitting by the Thingamajig, I waited for it to turn into a Gizmo, anticipating the crackling of a radio tuner finding its station. Papa sat up, and, pointing for me to assist, we lifted it onto his bed; Papa showed surprising strength for such an aged man. I confess the rock was heavy. For a moment I feared the fragile bed frame might snap. It gave a groan, then reluctantly settled.

Papa made as if he were about to turn the dial to his favorite station—unexpectedly he halted and gazed into my face.

"A toast indeed. To our Sacred Rock—our 'Petros'. The Rock on which our beloved saint was martyred in those long ago times at the beginning of the world, during the great drama that brought salvation to mankind."

"Indeed—a toast." I hurriedly agreed. My right hand fumbled casually in my right pocket, fingering the small vial of Rohypnol-derivative with plastic screw cap, Montez & Muck's special recipe. The next opportunity I would not miss.

Turning toward the table beside the groaning bed, he focused his spectacles on one coffee decanter and on the girl with kite cup and slowly poured one into the other. He straightened. Opening a cabinet panel above the table, a phalanx of similar cups were revealed, and Papa withdrew one and placed it on the table. He poured a second time.

The beverage wasn't hot—not that I gave a shambolean shit for the darn thing's temperature. I was so drilled on how to get a drop of M&M's happy juice into the old fart's body that I was almost ready to put the Pope in a full-nelson.

Full or even half became unnecessary, though. Smiling, Il Papa handed me the nearest cup and winked.

I hesitated. How to do the deed? Somehow I had to slip the mickey without Pointy-Hat seeing it. I decided to try my airport trick once more.

Sneezing to distract his attention, I watched while he placed his cup back down to reach for a tissue. My hand wandered to my face. "Allahu—" Just in time I caught myself...wrong channel. Again I threw my voice, deciding to merely crackle like static. After all, all radios broadcast static.

Crrrk.

It worked. Papa twisted in surprise, and like someone who had never heard a radio in his life, stared wonderingly at the lump of stone. He sidled closer. His hands reached out, wandered over its square surface smoothed by centuries of Irish lips and his eyes strove to focus, his mind entirely occupied.

The vial slipped out, one drop dripped into his cup. When Papa directed his expressive stunned face back to me, the sleepy-time potion was already in my smock, and my cup already at my lips.

"Our toast, *Papa mío.* Our Rock is preparing to speak. A toast to Our Lord, of Bolivia's finest brew to sharpen our sight and our hearing, the better to hear Our Lord's words."

For a moment he appeared confused. Glanced back at the stone, then at me. He seemed to be reflecting on the aged state of his own senses, and I felt I could read the doubt in his mind more clearly than the headline on the gazette, wondering whether he had heard anything at all, questioning his senses.

Again the don't-know-nothin' shrug with shoulders forward and palms up, and he took up his cup. No pausing this time—he drained the coffee in two gulps. Nothing like a sudden reminder of old age in doubting one's senses to make one clutch at youth serums.

The tension drained out of me—and the relief drained in with my own draft of brew.

All I need do now is wait.

The Item was literally within my reach, my hitch digit primed to launch. My cell GPS would guide me to the exact rendezvous point, and once I handed over the suitcase with the Thing inside, I would slide into that wide beautiful back seat and motor my way the heck out of Dodge, the mighty hunter come home with his kill to throw at the feet of his nubile young bride. Or, in my case, brides. Nothing wrong with a little old-fashioned harem dreaming, I supposed. Somehow, somewhere, in some part of the Multiverse, I believed that Quinn, Pietro, Pete and I were spelunking to our heart's content with a hundred harems, a thousand versions of Tonya and Wendy, each version more beautiful than the next. And they all had green eyes and snowy matterhorns.

Il Papa placed his cup with care on the round table alongside the bed and his eye went back to the squarish basaltic lump resting on the grocery palette. He no longer stared at me, relieving my concern that he may have seen my little maneuver. Instead he stared fixedly on the Stone, as if hearing static from the lump was the most normal thing in the world.

But he did not touch it.

Instead, Papa turned to me. He leaned close, again lowering his voice.

"Monseigneur, as I mentioned, there is a problem with this Rock. It is not just a miracle—it is too many miracles. Too many voices. Too many stations *on the dial*, as you say." He twitched his eyes. "Do you think...you could come closer...listen a bit," Papa paused to yawn, "see what you can hear from our Sacred Stone?"

I felt less confident, my previous doubts returning. Though hesitant, I stepped near. Papa made no move to stop me and I leaned and put my ear to its smooth face.

Nothing.

I listened again. Like a doctor listening to lungs, I pressed my ear against the surface in various places.

Still nothing.

I glanced up at Papa; his eyebrows rose expectantly.

Wishing I had a stethoscope, I picked the Rock up and with some effort shook it. Far from hearing a wide band of strange broadcasts, the thing stayed dumb—not a blip came from its heavy basaltic depths. Finally, I put it back in its vegetable stall bower.

Papa's eyebrows had sunk. I noticed what seemed like a dull expression cloud his magnified eyes and, internally, I rejoiced since Montez & Muck's Zen was clearly taking effect. All I had to do was keep *Papa mío* occupied for one more minute and then I could toss the Gizmo—which apparently had switched back to being an inert Thingamajig—into my suitcase and bug out.

I gave the forward shrug of my shoulders back at him and invited Papa to examine the Rock himself.

Papa lifted it. Shook it. Put it against his ear.

A quiet smile seemed to settle on his face, with a hint of... *schadenfreude*?

Suddenly, his eyes went blank and the life seemed to go out of his body and he fell backwards across his little bed into the only space not taken by the palette and its rock.

Done.

Relieved, I took my suitcase and opened it on the floor. Lifting the Rock with both hands, and, wishing it were not quite so heavy, I gave it one last shake and pressed my ear against its worthless hide. I was almost put out that it did not speak. What use was a sacred rock that didn't speak? Where was the sacred in being mute? Dumb rocks I had in plenty; why bother with another? Wasn't an Irishman good enough for an Irish rock? I made to drop it into my suitcase, and thought: Let Montez & Muck worry about it. I'm just the mule.

A hand gripped my arm.

Standing over my open suitcase, the Rock of Saint Peter aloft in both my hands, I halted. I could not have been more shocked if the dead had come back to life and called for a recount.

"What are you doing?" Il Papa sat up and leveled his magnified retinas at me. "What are you trying to do?"

He stood, my arm still caught in his tight grip. Surprise and anger were on him. "Why are you taking my Rock?" His hand squeezed my arm till I felt the pips squeak.

Wincing, I gave him another shoulder shrug: *Who, me?*

Papa released me. He grabbed the other end of the Rock. A look of sly triumph came over him and he shouted, again with more strength than I imagined the aged relic possessed. "I know you are not Flynn. I knew that the moment I saw you, '*monseigneur'*." Papa sneered when he pronounced the word. "You are no priest—just who are you? I think you are here to steal my Rock. Just like the real Flynn tried to do years ago, trying to steal it back after he himself gave it to me. But I fixed *him*. Yes, I took care of his little red cart."

Papa pulled back, snatching the Stone out of my hands, and I marveled at his surprising strength.

I tried to snatch it back. And I too could shout: "Okay, so I ain't Flynn. So now you know. But this ain't the Rock of Saint Peter either, it's the Sacred Stone of us Celts. Now let go of it, Mac. You don't need no Blarney in the House of Christ. Jesus ain't no Blarney. Oww—"

Papa swung the Stone, and like a pro wrestler slamming a referee, sent me prone on the floor. I managed to snap to my feet and clutch the Rock again. He wasn't going to get off that easy. This was no different from wrestling TV sets away from looters, and I had taken (and kept) many a set that way.

But I still failed to gauge Papa's strength. The old bird turned out to be wiry and slammed me down again.

"You may as well give it up, '*monseigneur*', whoever impostor you are." Papa's expression turned vindictive. He sneered. "This is not the Rock that Flynn brought me anyway. This is a fake. The real Flynn would have known that on first sight. I was just testing you with a shard I picked up from Vesuvius. I put the *real* Rock in a place where no one will find it. Not you. Not Flynn. Not anyone." His voice drifted into a childish whine.

Papa was slowing. He turned and dropped the Stone in its stall. Swaying once, then twice, he fell on the bed, where he lay with his eyes closed and his legs over the side still contacting the rug.

For a moment I could not decide what to do. Il Papa was passed out, but the Rock was a fake. This explained the ease with which he had led me to it and why it was silent. All was now clear. The Pope had 'made' me at first glance, and had only toyed with me to find out my motive.

On the bed, Il Papa gave a jerk. His legs twisted, then relaxed. Taking the Stone, I positioned it securely in its stall on the palette, and placed the palette on the floor. I slid it under his bed. I had no use for it. I spread Papa out lengthwise on his bed, which, thankfully, had not suffered from the weight of the rock. I meant Papa no evil; after all, even Brooklyn dicks still had a touch of the Irish and God's Holy Church in them, and that meant not leaving a pope with raspberries.

A blurb bubbled from Papa's lips. I leaned closer to hear. After all, I still had to find the *real* Rock of Saint Peter. His thin voice mumbled: "My petros has new shoes. My petros has new shoes." He burst into tears and his legs twisted more, then the vindictiveness vanished and the beatific smile that all Papas should have returned to his face and he lay still and quiet.

Dreamland.

Nice of him to notice the quality of my shoes, I thought. He has new shoes himself. Does 'petros' have something to do with that? I shook my head. No sense where there's nonsense, I reckoned.

Bong...

From outside the room, a loud series of chimes began to ring, and I felt sure it had nothing to do with time-pieces. Flitting a nervous look at Papa, I saw one hand had fallen off the bed where it rested on a panel embedded in the table. Diabolically clever! A hidden security alert.

In his last conscious moment, Il Papa had pressed it.

The ringing grew louder. Footsteps sounded from beyond the room's front door, and I heard an army of Swiss mercenaries marching behind.

I grabbed Papa's arm from the panel and draped it over his chest—the ringing stopped.

With cries of, "Papa! Papa! What is wrong?" assailing the room from the outside hallway, I stuffed my hand into Papa's pocket and withdrew his key ring. I quickly found the long key. As I leaned, something *tinged* on the table.

I could not wait to inquire. Fists were banging on the door and there was no time to interrogate Il Papa under the influence of Montez & Muck's truth serum as the door would give way under the pressure in seconds.

My skin had priority over any rock—even the Blarney Stone.

Abandoning my suitcase, with hands shaking I keyed open the back door—the one to the labyrinth of dull unadorned secret spaces—and diving within I vanished the way I had come, locking the door behind me just as a crew of actual frocked monseigneurs burst in.

Only after I had entered the dark empty corridor did I remember M&M's Universal Indexer. In all the confusion, I had forgotten the red button, but since I had no idea what lay on the other side of any of the walls of Il Papa's private residence anyway, it was not smart to use it. I remembered those boilers in Marm's castle. I'll take rematerializing in thin air over boiling water any day.

Down the corridor I ran. Down the stairs. Turned the corner, up one hallway, down another. I came to a door—or what looked like the back side of a secret entrance. It seemed familiar, but on reflection every few feet I saw similar doors. They all looked the same. Did I take the right stairway? The correct hall? There were so many infiltrating the Vatican's seemingly solid walls.

Softly, I tried it. Two rows of hangered vestments and gowns greeted me. By sheer luck I had found the correct room. I breathed again. Opening it, I stepped into Il Papa's private dressing closet where he kept his collection of public accoutrements, if my Cajun got the term right. Before me was the intricately-carved door opening into Il Papa's private reception chamber with his domino-strewn table and the pots of coffee and tea that I had laced a half-hour earlier with Montez & Muck's sleepy juice. The Pope and I had been absent at most thirty minutes. Now that I had accomplished the first part of my task, the tea-pots should be disposed of. But not to worry. It was reasonable to suppose that Papa's attendants had already removed this evidence.

My hand on the inner door, I paused.

The magnitude of my failure began to work on me. Not only had I failed to find the Rock of Saint Peter, and thus failed Tonya and the Ex, and not only had I lost my suitcase in the event I did find it, but I had learned that Uncle Flynn had returned years ago and attempted to steal the object back from the Pope and had disappeared in the process, which made me doubt the Stone itself. Could it be that every part of this cockamamie plan was wrong? That maybe I had just in fact kissed the actual Blarney Stone and discovered like so many others that it was a fake? That no rock ever talked to anyone, and that the Pope was nuttier than a pecan log? That Montez & Muck were even loonier than the Pope?

No, I assured myself. I had accomplished one thing at least—I had slipped the mickey to Il Papa. True, I had missed my chance to make off with the only Rock of Saint Peter that I had seen thus far, but Papa would sleep a long time, and this would give me many hours to wander the halls of the Vatican incognito, working undercover being another thing I had done in my past, like most PIs—and perhaps to find the real Blarney Stone, if such existed. Ireland deserved that much.

And when Papa finally awakes from his long sleep, he may feel so good that he might even send a prayer Heavenward in thanks that I, the mysterious almost-Flynn, had taken this huge weight of a confusing Rock with its tangle of miracles and messages from his stooped shoulders.

Yes, he may one day thank me for what I am trying to do, what I may yet pull off. If ever a thief could bring happiness to a victim, I was it.

I opened the heavy carved door leading to Papa's reception room.

Stepped through.

Seated around the square table where until recently the Pope himself had been playing dominoes, sat several men whom I took to be old friends and priests due to their combination of informal street and formal Vatican clothing. They lay pitched forward on their faces. Spilled cups lay beside them.

The outer door was flung wide and at the threshold stood several monseigneurs, a half-dozen rainbow-uniformed Vatican enforcers with pikes and pistols, and beside them two male attendants dressed in kitchen-white aprons who pointed trembling fingers at the obviously deceased corpses. No one looked happy.

One priest read from a small vial that he held in his hand, holding it gingerly like a loaded gun. Without looking at me, he said, "You are Peter Marlowe? You are the one who had an appointment with Il Papa in this room and who visited him in his private quarters a few moments ago?" He looked up. Not at me, but at the three bodies. His voice acquired the flat tone of an executioner. "Il Papa is dead. This vial contains cyanide. We found it in his apartment, and it has your name on it."

CHAPTER 13

I had always thought that an old medieval outfit like the Vatican would throw their criminals into some ancient crumbling dungeon with rancid water dripping from the walls and rats infesting its corners, then slam a rusted metal door shut to enclose them in complete darkness. Prior to having a nice barbecue when they got around to a celebratory auto-da-fé. I could picture the collegium of priests now, arm in arm singing kumbaya in Latin and roasting weenies in the fire that consumed my flesh. If now was ever the time for a return to the old ways, I thought with a chill, this was it—a minuscule spy had wormed his satanic ass into the heart of the citadel and killed Chief Pointy-Hat.

But as the monseigneurs and Swiss guardsmen strong-armed me down several stairways past open-mouthed tourists and stolid Sicilian janitors, they finally halted before a normal-looking door that reminded me of nothing so much as a room entrance at a Holiday Inn. Opening the door with an electronic key, they grumbled something like "Pope-killer" and thrust me inside. The door slammed behind me and locked.

For a moment I stood motionless. My mind conjured the most fantastic images of the revenge that the Curia would inflict on the assassin of their beloved leader. Dungeons and stakes were just the beginning. But the cell in which they had tossed me was anything but dire. Faux pictures of West Texas cattlemen decorated the walls. Twin single beds recently made and fluffed led to a kitchenette where instant coffee packets sat beside a Keurig. I tried the fridge. It had beer. And frozen pizza.

Scratching my head, I wondered where the hell I was. Could M&M's magical science have engineered something unimagined and unimaginable a few minutes earlier? My eyes lit on another picture beside the fridge, and Il Papa, complete with thick spectacles and white hair, stared back at me. No, there was no mistaking that I was still in the Vatican. And double-checking my pinky, I verified that I still had the red-buttoned Indexer in my little finger, and I knew that I had not pressed it since boarding the plane in Albuquerque, so I thought I could be reasonably certain that I had not been sidetracked to an alternate universe. An angry smock-framed face appeared in a small window set in the door, confirming there was no mistake. Il Papa was an ex-pope.

Helping myself to the pizza, I slid some in the stove and soon was relaxing with cold hops and hot pepperoni. Suddenly this business of accidentally assassinating popes didn't seem so bad. I started to relax a bit and the next time one of those smock-lovers stuck his ugly mug in the window to glare at me, Quinn emerged from the depths and I lifted a cheesy slice and grinned, and popped another can.

Here's to ya!

The face scowled and disappeared. Well, some people just can't be pleased.

I had just begun to turn my ginormous brainiac cells to the matter of why the hell Montez & Muck might have substituted cyanide for their usual Zen sleepy-time potion, when the door to my 'prison' swung open. The same crew of priests and guards crowded through the entrance. Grabbing me by both my arms, they dragged me forthwith from the suite, spilling pizza and beer on their freshly cleaned Howard Johnson rug.

One of them shoved his face into mine—another hot-shit holier-than-thou type. "Your card—it was-a declined-a," he muttered.

Well, I could have told them that if they had asked. Next thing I knew this gang had shanghaied me again and dragged me down yet another two stairwells into a much darker part of the Vatican, one that I began to think was unsuspected by the world at large. Electric lights were replaced by oil lamps, the floors were no longer polished imported wood, but concrete, and the doors were fewer and farther between.

We came to a rusted metal door encased in a badly shaped arch of crumbling stone and concrete. One of them produced an antique key and with it squeaked the ancient lock open. The door creaked inward. Another thrust a flashlight into the dark interior. Whadaya know? Dirty walls with rancid water dripping. A peep in one corner said infestation of rats. A third priest grumbled in my ear: "Killer of Christ!" With that, I was shoved down a well-worn stone step, and the door squealed shut behind me.

I thought the Christ part was a bit much—way above my pay grade, in fact. A pope or two I could handle. But a Son of God? I wouldn't know where to begin.

Feeling around like a blind man, I IDed what seemed like a corner and sank to a squat, not concerned with the dirt and grime of the cell's surfaces soiling my smock. So much for my reputation. Well, I wasn't planning on running for mayor this year *anyhoo*, though recycling block captain had crossed my mind once or twice. Now the only recycling I would ever do would be my ashes into dust.

I sighed. And sat.

Taking inventory seemed a good idea. No cell phone, no suit, no hat, no shades, no watch, no suitcase, wallet gone (a *contribution* to Vatican finances, no doubt), but I still had my new Canali shoes. And my passport—and real wallet, the one without the fake ID— were still in my hotel room. If I could ever get out of here... Well, thanks to M&M's Indexer, that would not be a problem. But not now. Not yet. Not only would the soldiers of Christ be watching my prison cell, but I still had to figure a way to take the Gizmo with me. The *real* Gizmo, not the fake Thingamajig under the late Pope's bed. And all I had for a clue to its whereabouts was an enigmatic death-bed utterance by the senile salamander. Okay, by 'Hiz Honor', the late Primate Vesuvius the Twenty-Fourth, or some such. I crossed myself to keep Quinn and Pietro, my reared-in-the-Church alter egos, happy.

Time passed and gradually my eyes adjusted. Slivers of light were finding their way through cracks in the masonry around the door and I found that my own eyes became like those of a blind salamander. Not much to see. Just the usual bones of a couple of forgotten wretches who must have offended Hiz Honor in the distant past. I touched one skeleton chained to the wall and it crumbled to dust. *Very* distant.

A chill passed through my spine and I cursed M&M. Montez & Muck had given me a way out, but it was they who had put me in this predicament to begin with. I sighed again, exhaling to give Quinn and Pietro a break from the tension. I decided to pull up a section of wall and get some shuteye.

A few minutes passed.

I was disturbed by a stray sound. From the corner farthest from the door, a rat rustled.

I reclosed my eyes. As long as they weren't biting me, they could be my guest.

Another minute; the rustling repeated—louder.

I stood and turned. My eyes had difficulty focusing since the slivers of light from the door barely penetrated to this far end of the cell, but finally I thought I managed to piece out a dark nob protruding from the wall about chest level. In no hurry to be introduced to what may be a troupe of rats holding a Balkan festival and folk dance, I watched, arms folded.

The nob pushed farther from the wall. It fell to the floor accompanied by a grinding sound. Something shiny poked through.

Rats I thought I understood—they squeak, they eat, they jump the bones of other rats, and that's about it. A quick ransacking of my memory cells found absolutely nothing to indicate that rats use metal spoons to scrape holes in the walls of medieval prison cells. The spoon scraped in a circle, enlarging the hole. Another minute passed to the sound of more grinding. My curiosity pinned down Quinn and Pietro in two simultaneous half-nelsons, and I moved closer.

A blue dot surrounded by white appeared.

The eye blinked.

What else could I do? I poked it.

"Jesus, Mary, and Joseph," spilled through the hole couched in an Irish brogue. "The devil take ye, whoever ye may be, ye ingrate!"

I sneered my upper lip like Bogie in an old black-and-white. "Ain't no room on this stretch of slab for claim-jumpers, Mac. And ain't no call to drag the Lord's name into it." I bent my elbows like Bogie did in imitation of a tough criminal who had long been stuck in solitaire, unable any longer to straighten them, just in case this claim-jumper was taller than four-foot-eleven.

"Well, whoop-de-do fer *you*. Fancy ye thinkin' ye're bein' so high and mighty when they've just given ye the heave-ho and thrown away the key." The eye returned. The orb resumed staring at me—a hot-shit eye just like hot-shit people—though with a bit more caution than before. "Now ye'll not be thinkin' ye'll be crawlin' outta this little holiday spot in time to take early retirement, do ye?"

Something wasn't right. I felt a sensation on the back of my neck like a combination of vaseline pain relief and crawling skin. Where had I heard that voice before?

"Now what do they be callin ye, Mr..." The eye wobbled. "Ah, ye bein a priest of our Lord Jesus, now I see."

My eyes widened. "I don't believe it."

The wobbling orb steadied. Focused. The Irish brogue resumed, "A priestly smock, a black collar... Well now, whatever in God's Heaven did ye do to make them treat ye like this, padre? Piss in their fountain? Beat the Pope at dominoes? Eat His Holiness's lunch?"

A broad smile crossed my face.

"Ah, so *that* was it." A laugh line appeared over the orb. "Ye sampled the Pope's fizz-water when the Old Bat wasn't lookin'. He has a fine likin' to his fizz-water. Best not to touch it. Aye, I learned that lesson the hard way. Never touch the Bat's fizz-water."

"*Had*," I corrected.

For a moment, immobility and silence.

The eye's brow arched, asking for more, but scared to get it.

"Yep," I nodded. "*Had*. As in former, no longer, erstwhile, expired, bit the grit, gone to his maker, fist-bumping Saint Peter, partying with seventy-two virgins, crossed the border on Come-To-Jesus getaway sticks."

The eye caught its breath. A long whistle followed. "Now that would *deed* be a bit beyond fizz-water and dominoes, ta be sure."

"Compliments of Mr. Present and Accounted For." If my prison cell had had a window, I would have stared quietly out of it like a lifer in Leavenworth. "Yep," I tapped one toe, "I'm *just* that kinda guy."

The eye blinked twice. He finally got it, too. "Well, I'll be... Jesus, Mary, and Joseph!"

"You win the pot, Uncle. Who the hell else?"

"Wait, Pete. Wait right there." As if I might be somewhere else. "I'll be breakin' these Roman bricks to bits and in a jiffy I'll be in there with ye, Nephew." The spoon began to scrape frantically. "Imagine that. After all this time—after all these years of loneliness..." Flynn's voice cracked with emotion as he worked to widen the hole. "Finally the Good Lord has given his poor servant a chance to exchange a few friendly words with another Christian soul. And who in all the world should appear? Praise be! Praise be to Jesus." Flynn paused to cross himself with his spoon. "Not to forget His late Holy Vicar on earth, God rest his soul."

Another chunk of brick protruded and dropped. I fell to helping him, and as the hole enlarged I managed to slip my fingers in and yank out a few fragments. More mortar crumbled and more ancient masonry came loose, and in a quarter hour the remaining obstacles burst out and strew the floor, sending the last rat scurrying.

I eyed the door. "Uncle, aren't you worried that our high-rent landlords might shove their mugs in here and say we're violating their lease?"

"Jest wait, Nephew. Jest wait."

Flynn squeezed through the hole and stood before me. By now my eyes had adjusted to the darkness and I realized the slivers of light by the door illuminated more than I had first thought. I had expected to see a bone-thin gulag vacationer who had not sent out for pizza since Y2K. Instead Uncle Flynn looked no different than the day he disappeared, the day we parted ten years earlier—except dirty, bearded, and buck naked.

He glanced down. "Sorry, Nephew, but several years of their hospitality will do this to a fellow, even the priestly sort. I'm afraid me Sistine Chapel vacation package didn't come with needle and thread." He briefly attempted to cover his privates, but soon ceased. "And if past history tells us anything, me lad, ye can forget their ever takin' an interest in ye again except to toss their version of an MRE through the door once a day—a pig in a blanket soaked in holy water. Without the pig."

I could not take my eyes off Flynn's face. While not quite staring in a mirror, I saw my future self. My last memory of the codger was when I was still young. Not that I'm old now, but ten years of wallowing in the dirt of the private dick business in my mind had made me old already, or at least more experienced than many twice my age. Flynn, on the other hand, who actually was twice my age, now looked truly old, and the several years' growth of white beard barely disguised the fact that he was the same size and had the same face as I. M&M's old picture of Flynn didn't lie and I no longer wondered at M&M's confidence that Papa the blind-as-a-bat salamander would confuse us.

Suddenly I understood why Il Papa had paused at our first meeting, why he had been thrown for a loop when I had said that I had 'freed myself'. Il Papa had known that the *real* Flynn was enjoying Hiz Honor's hospitality down below—or was supposed to be. And listening to Flynn's brogue, the flaw in M&M's plan suddenly became apparent. If Papa had not known that Flynn was already underground, he would have detected the difference as soon as he heard me speak. Ireland was in my soul—but not my larynx.

"But why, Uncle? Why did Il Papa do this to *you*? I know that bosses sometimes rat on their capos, but your Boss with the cross is supposed to be above that."

For the first time I thought I glimpsed a shade lowering in Flynn's eyes. I'd seen that look more often than I'd like to admit, usually in association with drug deals and pawn shop fences. As I recalled, fast-talking Flynn by rumor had been involved in both at one time or another.

He let out his breath. "I had it comin', dear boy. I had it comin'. After I delivered the Blarney Stone to the Pope, I had an attack of conscience."

"Well, you are a priest after all. Comes with the territory, Unc. Sight-a-God and all that."

His eyes brightened. "No, 'twas not that at all. Rather I came to feel that I had betrayed an even higher trust."

Now I was puzzled. "If not to Our Lord Jesus..."

"To *Ireland*, me boy. To Ireland—the Emerald Isle." Flynn sniffed back a tear. "It came to me one night that for mere money I had deprived me native home of its most precious relic, the most sacred stone of our Gaelic ancestors, and that I must do whatever I could to get it back." He breathed deep. "I knew it would'na be easy. I knew that the Pope would never willingly return it to Ireland, so I had ta find a way to get it back without his knowin'. So the last time I came to meet him—and after takin' ye back to yer home that last time we met ten years ago—I returned to Saint Peter's."

I listened as Flynn warmed up.

His voice lowered and his eyes flitted about guardedly again. "I penetrated its secret ways—Il Papa himself shewed me his secret door when I first smuggled the Rock into his private room." Flynn's eyes gleamed. "After takin' me leave of ye in Ireland, I returned to Rome and it was then I slipped into the Vatican's secret passageways."

Flynn leered.

I began to suspect there might be something behind those conman eyes that was not quite normal.

"I dressed me-self like a monk. For months I praised Jesus, Mary, and Jehovah by the hour, wandering alone in those secret passageways that wind through every structure in the Vatican like a labyrinth, connecting things in the most unexpected and amazin' ways."

He brightened. "The months stretched to years and I came to know the innards of Saint Peter's and its many buildings like no one else—not even the cardinals or the Pope himself." Triumph took hold of Flynn's wild eyes. "They're all connected, ye know! Every building, every hallway, all connected through the walls or underground. Though none pass under the walls to the outside, as I learnt. I could'na leave. Since all the Vatican's exits are guarded, once inside the labyrinth, ye canna escape without bein' discovered. Two years went by. Three. I fed me-self by stealin' out at night and raidin' their kitchens. And no one ever suspected. But finally, after communin' with Our Lord one night in me own special way, I finally whipped up the nerve to do what must be done. I decided to go for the Stone." The wildness in his eyes increased. "I felt me-self bold enough to sneak into the Pope's private chamber where I knew he kept the Rock, and, by the light of the moon and the sun..."

I thought back to the nature scenes painted on the Pope's private walls and wondered how mere paintings, which were not even of Elvis, could provide light to anyone.

"...by the light of the sun and the moon, I dragged out the wooden palette that I me-self had given him three years earlier. I lifted the Sacred Stone from its bower and I made for the secret door at the back of the Pope's private chamber."

The door came immediately to my mind, having used it that very morning during my unfortunate meeting with Hiz Honor.

"I opened it. Though burdened by the heavy Stone, I opened the secret door—*and there he was*. The Pope himself, standin' there, watchin' me, his giant eyes magnified by those thick coke-bottle glasses. No way fer me to deny it, no way to defend me act, no way to explain away the fact that his old friend Flynn was stealin' what Flynn himself had convinced the Pope three years past was the real Rock of Saint Peter, the foundation of the civilized world's entire Kirk, of Humanity itself."

Fast-talking Uncle Flynn still had the gift of gab. Down in his own basement, con-man Quinn nodded, comprehending the part about stealing.

Flynn shrugged. "What could I say? That it wasn't the Rock of Saint Peter after all? That I had lied about it all along? That I had taken the Old Bat's money, but that it was all jest blarney?" Flynn shook his bearded head and his voice cracked again. "Within the hour, Il Papa had tossed me bodily within the cell next door and condemned me to live out me life on a diet of wormwood and regret. And then he..." Flynn choked, "he excommunicated me from the bosom of the Kirk."

Overcome, Flynn dropped to the prison cell's floor. He grabbed the bottom of my priest's cassock and blubbered and sneezed and wiped his nose till I snatched it away, in no hurry to end up as dirty and naked as Flynn. I too had no needle and thread.

But I had something else.

"So the Blarney Stone is indeed in Saint Peter's?" I ventured.

"Deed it is," he said with a sniff. "I brought it in. What's in Ireland is a fake. I me-self did the switch."

Ask and ye shall be answered, I thought. That settles that.

"But," continued Flynn, "there be more to it, Nephew..."

My eyebrows crawled toward my ears, the better to hear with.

Flynn wiped his eyes and stood. He peered slyly about, then whispered. "More. The things I've seen. The things I've heard while skulkin' about in these walls. There be those inside the Curia *who desire to seize the Vatican.* They plan and they spy. I heard them, though not enough, not completely. And there be others. Folk inside the walls of Saint Peter to be sure ere workin' with folk on the outside."

The shades inside Flynn's eyes came down again and he peered at me strangely. His brows crossed. "But, Pete, me lad. Jest how did it happen that ye be here among the vicars of Christ? And how, me boy, can it be that ye of all people—a believin' Cath'lic, after all—could of done the awful deed that yer admittin' to? Not even in my lowest moments did I ever contemplate doin' in the head of God's Holy Kirk."

Quinn from his cellar noted that Flynn had not questioned my right to fake being a priest. Takes a con to know a con, I suppose. Maybe I was too much a skeptic about tears—Flynn's tears were good, but Quinn believed he had seen better. Anyway, it was time for my own shades to lower. Private dicks get information, they don't give it. At least not for free, not even to partners in Irish blood.

"Can't tell you all, Unc. Only that I was sent to bring the Blarney Stone back from Rome. And it seemed I almost had the ugly lump—till my sleepy-time potion proved to have more of a kick than I expected. I never planned to kill the Pope, only put him to sleep long enough to lift the Stone." I tapped my foot again. "*Someone* arranged an 'Italian solution' and played Yours Truly like a mouth harp."

"Ye don't say." The shades in Flynn's eyes flipped and rolled. He put his hands on his unwashed hips and rocked in what I supposed was his version of deep thought. Perhaps his hound-dog nose smelled out more than I was selling. But his brows crawled back down and he brightened again. "Still, Irish blood is Irish blood, Nephew. And this son of Old Éire is happy yer here, no matter." He embraced me, all-forgiving. "After all, old times is old times."

So that's where I got the phrase. Must be in the clover.

"I do say." I kicked at the fallen bricks, then looked up. "I still want the Stone, Uncle Flynn. So do you. We need to find it, steal it, and take it back to Ireland." This still wasn't the time to discuss my full plan. Flynn understood green isles; but, as a priest, he wouldn't understand my obsession with Green Eyes.

He wrinkled his forehead like an accordion. "'Need' ere the wrong word, Nephew. Dream, fancy, imagine...those are as close as ye'll ever get to the magical rock fer as long as yer stuck in here with me, which I fancy will be for the rest of both our lives." Using the spoon, which he still clutched in one hand, he crossed his chest again, and in the darkness his white eyes rolled up in a fair imitation of a corpse. His version of praying, I supposed.

It was my turn to lose heart. A fellow can only takes so much before the storm and dreck of daily life gets to him. I dropped my gaze. Sliding my hands halfway into my smock's shallow pockets, I nudged dirt with a toe, wishing for the first time that I wasn't that kinda guy. But I thought again about what Montez & Muck had done to me and how the next morning's papers might splatter my name and face as killer of the Pope, and my heart returned to its bower. Pietro Quinn Tiberias Marlowe—all four-foot-eleven inches of him—don't play *bi-atch* to no one.

Enough was enough.

I froze Flynn with a direct stare. "Two things, Unc. First: you and I—we're blowin' this joint. I got no time to waste spinning cobwebs in this Big House of P.T. Barnum reruns."

Flynn cricked his neck, puzzled.

"And we're doin' it by walkin' straight through that door. You and me together."

Amusement replaced puzzlement.

"Second—and here's where I need your help—we're takin' that lousy Stone with us. *If* you can find it. And it *ain't* that lump what's under Il Papa's bed."

His look reminded me of skeptical spectators when the skinny kid steps out of the crowd and announces he will pound the carnival sledgehammer and send the weight to the top of the pole. 'Do tell', he seemed to say.

"And third—"

"You said 'two things'."

"Well, I got a third." I tried to stand taller to keep my dignity, and was surprised when I gained a fraction over Flynn, who, since I had become a man, had always been the same height as me. "I have a date with a couple of...'compadres' at the north end of this funhouse at the crack of dawn tomorrow. Since I lost my GPS, it's too late to change the time. My compadres have a ticket to ride for one person—*if* I have the Holy Maloney. I'll get you past the gate. Once you're out of the Vatican, you can go to my hotel room, change into my clothes, and return to Ireland. I'll meet you in Dublin when I get there, and we can jaw then about how to finish your mission."

Flynn whistled again, perhaps getting the faith. "But—"

"Ain't no 'but' about it, Unc. You'll wait and you'll see. We gotta get some shuteye first. Just keep thinkin' about 'where'." I turned to look at the rusted metal entrance with the slivers of light seeping in around the edges. "I got the 'how' covered."

Tossing ourselves to the floor—not without a certain reluctance on my part in view of the dirt and grime littering the place—we soon were lost to sleep. Me quickly; Flynn while resting a skeptical gaze on my backside, perhaps suddenly seeing more insanity in me than I saw in him.

CHAPTER 14

y inside alarm clock kicked in and I nudged Flynn back to consciousness. I didn't know how much time we needed to find the Stone—or if we could find it at all. All I knew was that if I didn't locate the ugly Rock and get it to a certain stretch of north wall by dawn, the Vatican might have two ghosts roaming its labyrinths in limbo.

"Let's go, Unc. Ain't no sense in hangin' around this joint any longer than necessary."

Unc stretched himself awake and peed in the corner. I did the same, with the satisfaction of soaking a rat that had dissed me by becoming visible.

I tucked and faced the door. "Come on, Flynn. Get with the program. We're goin that a-way." I pointed.

He persisted in watching the rat in the corner squirm. "Now, yer not really takin' all this serious, ere ye, Neph?" He rocked with his hands on his dirty hips again. "That talk was before. This is now."

"Two things, Unc—"

"Aye, I know. Three things, really. You beat that horse down earlier, Pete, and smacked it through the floor. Let's move on to discussin' somethin' else."

I still had had enough. There was no point in talking further about where this streetcar was heading, and what stop I wanted, so like it or not Flynn was going with me. This streetcar couldn't run without him. Taking Flynn by an arm, I led him gently to the door. Turning round so he could not see the gory details of how to walk through walls—not that the dim light revealed much more than pale copies of ourselves anyway—I plucked off my pinky. Facing him, I grabbed him in a bear hug. For his orneriness, I again felt like making it a full-nelson, but we can't always get what we want outta life.

I pressed the red button.

Everything in the roughly forty-five degree angle that my pinky projected onto the door and its frame boiled in a Cajun broth, red and yellow spuming like the business end of Diablo Nuclear Plant. The dance floor changed—maybe due to the ancient concrete those cavemen Romans liked to play with.

Flynn's eyes locked on the nuclear bath. No longer resisting, all his energy vaped into a long little girl's scream. Right in my ear.

Five seconds passed.

Ten seconds.

Now that's motivation. Flynn in my ear, Green Eyes in my mind, my Ex in my...well, let's just say I finally gave Flynn a shove that sent the both of us, still entangled by our embrace, into that boiling inferno. Flynn's scream was replaced by the usual nonsensical whimsy of Istanbul, and I wondered what equivalent Mother Goose rhyme rang inside his head, and just as my brain settled on some delirium about six-pence and stiles which I thought I heard echoing off Nature's jumbled dimensions while we stumbled about, we soon were standing in the hallway on the far side of the still-locked door to the light of smoky oil lamps.

I released Flynn and clapped my hand over his mouth to finally stop his non-stop screech.

His terrorized eyes gazed into mine, and glazed.

I took my hand from his mouth. Silence returned, thank you, Jesus.

Again turning, I replaced my pinky ring. "We gotta move, Unc. I don't know when is the next feeding time, but we need to dive into that secret labyrinth that you keep jabberin' about before they find us gone."

He broke into a shake. Tremors rattled his body, gradually calming to a shiver. At length he recovered. To top it off he gave a repeat of his long, low whistle.

"Now that *deed* be a bit beyond ye old skeleton key, Pete. How—"

"Can't get into it now, Uncle." I glanced around.

From up the hall came a soft echo. Footfalls. Maybe looking

for the little girl who screamed.

Flynn spun on his heel. "This-a way, Nephew. Hurry yer arse. I be in no rush to spend the next seven years resumin' the company of Mother Nature's lower orders." He launched himself in the opposite direction from the echo.

For an old refugee from Galwey, he moved fast and I had a devil of a time keeping up. But at the end of the oil-lamp-lit hallway, and before that distant echo had a chance to become human, we arrived at an intersecting corridor that crossed to form a T.

Flynn turned left. Down we fled until we came to what appeared to be a dead end. The hall, with its corroded primitive cobbles beneath our feet intertwining with trickles of water, terminated in a semi-circle. With no exit.

I peered at Flynn.

He stared at an old plaque, originally of stout wood, but long eaten by worms and now barely holding its form. Across the front was a large X. Each quarter defined by the X held faded symbols that reminded me of pictures I had once seen in a book my father had owned about fancy knights. 'Heraldry' I think was the title. He was like that—though as tall as hot-shit people, father wanted to be even taller, and thought he could do that by claiming that some King Conk of Ireland was his ancestor. In Brooklyn I learned that a good judo-chop was worth more.

Flynn continued to stare.

From behind, the tinny echoes turned into foot clops. They were coming closer.

He reached out a hand. Grasping a barely visible hand-hold, he pulled. The stretch of brick-and-mortared wall spun on a hidden axis to reveal a slim doorway and Flynn yanked me through, then from inside pushed the secret door shut with a grind. It clicked. No one lacking a pinky ring would ever pass back through that door without Flynn's help.

By the glow of a distant but steady electric light, Flynn stood and stared at me in triumph, perhaps thinking he had regained some private advantage. He still didn't get the pinky thing.

He bowed. "This way, Nephew." Smiled. "Welcome to my world."

I wondered if Flynn's world was a nudist colony of excommunicated priests, but after traveling the length of several corridors and climbing two sets of straight stone stairways, we halted on a landing where the last stairway changed to a spiral. Corridors here intersected and stretched into darkness in several directions. Grand Central, I decided.

Around and behind one intersection, Flynn pulled aside a dusty wooden panel, and—after listening carefully for sounds from the adjoining corridors, and inspecting for signs of tampering during the seven years he was absent—we entered a hidden room.

Flynn's former base of operations, I assumed.

Food tins, utensils, bath articles, shaving razors, a mirror, spare cassocks and collars hung in a tent-closet, even a makeshift wet bar with a case of bottled wine, all lay about in close order, all under a soft florescent light that surprisingly still worked when he clicked it on. Everything one might need for an extended vacation.

For an insane person, that is. I could not imagine how Flynn survived in such exile for three solid years before Il Papa grabbed him. Or anyone.

Triumph returned to Flynn's eyes. Touching each of his sacred items in turn, he gloated as if the reins of power had returned to his hands.

I tapped my finger—one of the good ones—on my thigh. "Uncle, time is short. The fat lady is putting on her singing girdle."

He stared into his little mirror and, popping open several gallons of water which he poured into a tub, proceeded to give himself a sitz bath. "If ye want to keep to yer fancy ideas, me lad, that's fine with me. But if the stone in Papa's room ain't the right one, then ye need to be givin' me a bit more than 'Find the right rock' before I can help ye." All shyness gone, he rubbed and soaked.

I helped myself to a tin of artichokes. "Any ideas at your end, Flynn? After three years of wandering in this...uh, vacation paradise, you must have some idea where Il Papa might keep a heavy rock."

"The only rock I've seen is the one he kept handy in his private room. Yer the one sayin' different." A spit polish of armpits and elbows was followed by a shave.

I was impatient but I had to admit Flynn was quicker than a

Funk & Wagnall salesman who had just read that the Internet is coming. Soon he was done and powdered. Turning to his tent-closet, he carefully withdrew a cloth-covered set of clothing on a hanger. As I watched, he slipped off the cover to reveal—to my astonishment— an Italian Canali suit, fresh as the day it was made.

He grinned. "It's not fer now, Pete. It's fer when I finally locate the Grand Wazoo to return it to sacred Ireland." He kissed the suit's collar. Stepping to one corner of the flat, he lifted the hinged cover off a small wood casket to expose matching fedora hat and a pair of shoes, which, like a seven year itch, still gleamed from their last shine.

Full complement Italian suits must be in the blood too, I thought with envy, eyeing my boring priestly cassock, which was already torn and stained.

Flynn also kissed the hat and shoes before re-tenting the wardrobe, then withdrew another priest's cassock much like mine and draped it over his body.

"But fer now—Jesus calls. And as one of His most loyal servants, I'm obliged to dress like one." He dropped his smile. "Even if the ungrateful Bat did cut me off from the True Faith."

I caught my breath. Even more than before it seemed I was staring into a copy of myself, the only difference being Brooklyn versus Dublin. It was my turn to give a long, low whistle.

"Me feelin's exactly, Pete," Flynn said, looking up. "If ye did'na have the wrong name attached to ye, I might think that ye'd be me."

I shook off the trance. In *my* world, Brooklyn came first if only by a nose. *Has* to if you want to keep breathing.

Flynn dragged the wooden casket forward an inch and sat on it. "A thousand times in the past seven years I've wished I could get back here." He passed his gaze over the unkempt interior of his little domain. A tear fell. "A thousand times..." He stroked one wall lovingly. Pushing his face into his hands, he again sobbed, convincing even Quinn. But at least this time Flynn didn't blubber on my cassock.

After a moment, he dropped his hands. "Ah, yes. Funny what life does to ye." He sniveled. "How she brushes yer teeth one day—

then kicks ye in yer arse the next."

"If you say so, Unc." A bit odd, I thought, but each to his own.

Reflexively I glanced at my watch. Wearing none, I read two hairs past the first mole.

"I'm sure it's past midnight by now, Flynn. We have only a few hours left to ransack our brains and see if we can find our ticket to ride outta here."

He sniffed and stood on his feet. "Yer right, a course, Pete. Yer right. And I've been thinkin. Likely the best place to start would be the Old Bat's room. Excuse me, dear Lord, we should be thinkin' better of the dead...the Old Bird's room." He glanced ceiling-ward and crossed himself.

"It's your party, Flynn. Lead the way."

Dressed, cleaned up, and tears dabbed dry, Flynn stepped out of our little refuge. One foot out, he paused to listen. Hearing nothing beyond the usual rustles and creaks of a thousand-year-old castle, he led the way round the corner, and we traveled the length of one of the corridors. Turning once, twice, we climbed another well of stairs, and followed another hall for a hundred feet. I grew nervous and glanced at Flynn. Silently I thanked Jesus (and King Conk 'jest ta be sure'). Being fresh out of bread crumbs, I could never trace my way back alone.

Despite the tangle of corridors, the Vatican I noted was not really very large. The confusion lay in its multiple levels of secret passageways that joined the above-ground buildings in their several stories and in the many hidden levels that stretched deep underground. I gathered that Flynn's safe-house was just below ground. Having walked some hundreds of feet and climbed upward for several stories, I believed we must have arrived at one of the upper reaches of the several large administration buildings north of Saint Peter's Basilica.

I don't know if my guess was correct, but as we came to a halt at the end of the hallway I recognized the surroundings. In the light of a soft electric bulb that cast sufficient rays to negotiate most of the secret corridors, replacing the smoky oil lamps of the Vatican's dungeons, Flynn paused before another X-marked panel. This panel was not aged like the one near our cells, and the spaces around the X were blank but for the image of a domino. Flynn raised his brows at me and pulled another invisible hand-hold.

The door swung on its hidden axis.

We stepped through.

My eyes took in a thin-piled carpet, a simple bed with golden crocheted quilt, moon and sun illustrated inside pretend window frames painted on the walls, a round bed-table and electric lamp with cabinet attached to the opposite wall leading to a high fashionable ceiling.

Compulsively I peered at the bed—no, Il Papa's body was gone. To my great relief, we would not have to endure his cyanide-wracked grimace. And to the relief of a worried Pietro, who had inherited not only the family thirst for spelunking but also the Marlowe family's conscience, which Pietro perpetually insisted lurked somewhere down below among the discarded memories and boxed hopes.

Bereft of conscience or guilt, con-man Quinn however was more interested in the peculiar sound that repeated in the air. Flynn and I glanced at the far corner of the room where the long-play record-player still rested on the low-slung rectangular table. Someone had left the 'Best of Al Jolson' record in the player and it revolved steadily round and round under the needle, skipping repeatedly on one word:

"Mammy—Mammy—Mammy—"

Sinatra it wasn't. I lifted the needle to exorcise Papa's death chamber from the ghost of blackface.

When I looked up, Flynn had already dragged the grocery palette from under Papa's bed. No one had disturbed it. No one had removed it. And alongside the palette—my still empty suitcase, tucked beside the palette under Papa's bed.

The priests must have assumed the suitcase was his.

Progress.

Lifting the black lump from its slumber, Flynn briefly inspected the rock, and dropped it. He snorted. "Why, it be not even from Old Éire. A piece of Vesuvius, I reckon." With a scornful eye he glanced back at me. "Ye were right. What fool in all the world would be mistakin this piece of junk for our beautiful Blarney Stone? No

Irishman ever lived could make such a mistake."

I tried again to thrust my hands in my smock's pockets, but my hands' small sizes were too big for the cassock's tiny folds. "'Course not. What I thought when I first saw it." I broke eye contact and whistled.

"It cartainly be not what I was smugglin' out seven years ago when the Bat caught me, that much I know." Flynn straightened and began to pace, his hands intermurling. "Which means he still has it. Cartain it is that the Stone lies inside the Vatican. It can't be far. He must have hidden it after catchin' me in the act, jest in case more patriotic Irishmen shewed. Or common thieves." Flynn looked at me like he wasn't sure which I was.

I nodded. "We already knew that, Flynn. That's what Papa said. The question is *where*."

Flynn paused to think. "*Where* ta be sure, Nephew, *where* to be sure... But how do ye search forty-four acres near multiplied by eight levels?"

I folded my arms to project more confidence than I felt, a habit with me even older than counting. "A good way to begin a search is to trace a circle."

"Good beginning, Pete. But I don't see how we can search even a single acre before the sun comes up, circular or not."

"You got that right, Flynn. But there's a second-batter-up to this kind of game. It's to make someone squawk. Then you trace your circle around *him*."

"Ye mean make him *confess*?"

"Squawk, rat, gab, fink, squeal, flip, sell out, snitch, finger, sing a cappella, wear copper, spill the hopalenos, do the Chicago calypso—slip a shiv between his mother's angel wings."

Flynn's brows rose. People are always impressed by a professional at work. He nodded. "Well, ye won't find anyone in the world more willin to confess than a pope, Nephew, but if he's dead and gone to sip tea with the Lord, that's goin' to be a bit difficult."

"Not what I'm getting at, Flynn. Sure the old coot has gone to his reward, river-dancing with the heavenly host and what-not, but we can still make the Old Bat squawk. We don't search his room— we search his brainiac cells." To match my bent elbows, I faked a sneer of my upper lip, again like Bogie. "I mean maybe we can make the canary squawk from the grave."

"Another nice idea, Pete. And I'm willin' to kick it around. But me shoes have gone so soft I can't kick anything harder than an Orange pastor."

That was me to a T. I was still trying to project confidence, but, having no idea of how to actually do what I just said, I went silent, not even Quinn or Pietro offering to help.

"They're leavin' me speechless," added Flynn. "Maybe I be needin' work boots."

"Maybe they're just old." I looked down at the semi-slippers that the round-the-corner tailor had shod me with before I entered the Vatican. "Papa liked *new* shoes. Though I don't see what rocks have to do with them."

"Rocks?" Flynn looked up.

I shrugged. "'Petros' means rocks. Or so I've heard."

"'Rock', Nephew. Remember yer Greek. And I'm glad to see me efforts in bringin' ye to the Vatican when ye were a small lad weren't entirely wasted."

"Not entirely," I mumbled, no longer able even to spell Greek. Taking a breath I said, almost to myself, "'My petros has new shoes.'"

Flynn's brows rose again. "How's that?"

"New shoes."

"No, the other part."

"'Petros'?"

Flynn nodded.

"That's what the Pope said just before he crossed the border. A funny thing: 'My petros has new shoes.' Petros means rocks...or rock." I shrugged, a little annoyed at Flynn's persistence with the Pope's nonsense and his presumption that Greek meant any more to me than a sour cream gyros. "Shouldn't we focus on the task at hand, Unc?" I propped my hands on my hips, Flynn-fashion.

Flynn ignored me and stared at the framed sun as if the window were the real thing. He swayed on his heels repeating aloud, "'My petros has new shoes'... *Deed* that be a funny thing to say when the life be goin' out of ye."

He scratched his head. Crossing the room, Flynn opened a pair of cabinet doors above the table with the record-player. In one corner was a shoe box. He placed the shoe box on the quilted bed and removed the cardboard cover.

Inside was a pair of shiny new shoes. Black.

Flynn looked closer at the brand name on the box: the brand said 'Petros'. The previous scornful look returned to his face and he put the cardboard top back on the box.

"Well, now we both be knowin' beyond any doubt that this Papa was a whack-job." He nudged the wooden palette with his moccasins. "With his dyin' breath, the only thing on his mind was a new pair of his favorite brand of shoes." Flynn breathed deep. "Yer right, Neph. Il Papa had seven years to hide the blasted thing and, to find it, we'd need new shoes for both of us, plus another seven years to search."

Bogie took an elevator down to join Quinn. I didn't want either one of them to see my disappointment.

"You may be right, Unc. You may indeed be right."

I rubbed the back of my neck. Stepping closer, I took a turn inspecting Il Papa's pair of Petros shoes. Yeah, I know that pairs usually come in twos, but my PI soul demanded I count them anyway. I lifted the box-top and counted out loud: "One—Two." Raising them in the air, I admired their construction. They weren't Canali quality, but I had to admit Petros was giving my brand a run for their money.

"Hullo," said Flynn.

Inside the shoe box, formerly covered by the shoes, lay a soft pouch of purple fabric with gold threads. Gently Flynn picked it up. We heard something rattle. The pouch's neck was drawn close by a leather strip and Flynn stretched it open and poured its contents on the quilt where the golden aureoles surrounding the quilt's embroidered heads seemed to glow around the fragments of bone.

Human.

At the bottom of the box, formerly hidden by the pouch and shoes, was a scrap of paper on which were scrawled two words.

Flynn read the words aloud: 'Petros eni.'

We looked at each other. I was stumped. Flynn boosted my

confusion by translating the Greek: "'The Rock is here'."

Slowly, Flynn turned the shoe box over.

Nothing else.

Flynn scoured the box inside and out, and the shoes themselves in a search for more scraggly letters, while I examined every fragment of bone that lay spilled on the bed. I had some silly notion that maybe there was blood on the bones that could be typed.

Zilch.

Several minutes passed.

Finally I gave up and scraped the bone fragments into the pouch and Flynn sat on the bed alongside the box and shoes, bones and suitcase. Somehow I didn't think that Montez & Muck would be impressed if I returned with a case full of finger-bones, no matter how much faith Il Papa put in the relics. Clearly the Pope thought what he had in his possession were unannounced parts of Saint Peter, the 'Rock' of the Church, and had written himself a reminder in case of a sudden attack of senility. I might have believed it had I not been rather certain that St. Peter had possessed only ten fingers.

I wondered aloud: "Why did Papa speak of shoes when he bought his timeshare with Jesus, instead of his beloved 'Rock'? Who *does* that? And how in Limbo can a rock have shoes, new or otherwise?"

While I exhausted my brain, Flynn sat and thought on his own. He stood and resumed pacing. After a minute, just when I was ready to throw in the towel and call for Mighty Mick to take over my golden gloves training so something Rocky would finally be part of my life, Uncle stood straight and smiled. He put his hands on his hips, swayed in contemplation.

"Now *that* be somethin' to think about. Deed *somethin'* to think about."

"Spill it, Flynn. So far we're kayoed before we even made the first round."

"Ye spoke of searchin' the Old Bat's mind—ye may deed have stumbled on *somethin'* to think about."

Walking to the chamber's secret door to the Vatican's labyrinth, Flynn opened it and turned to me with a grin. "Nephew, we have an appointment in a cemetery." As I stood, he said, flashing his teeth,

"Don't fergit yer tote."

CHAPTER 15

As we walked, our shallow footsteps tippling the narrow light-subdued passage, I wondered at the strange fate that had confined me—a kid from the mean streets of upper New York—caught in this ancient labyrinth of religious despots. Latin Kings I had known on those mean streets. I had to admit Latin Popes had one up on the Kings.

Outside the labyrinth I had glimpsed the high class that the Vatican offered: the 'Sister's Chapel', the 'Rooms of Ralph', and 'Bogie's Apartment', not to mention the 'Room of the Incredible Deception'. It was almost more than a street kid could handle. I hadn't seen so much gold since I had been allowed to peek over Gimpy Gambino's shoulder as he counted Dutch Schultz's loot under a tree in Schenectady. And here I was, stuck in this cave with my loopy uncle like a termite in dirt, my extra-large suitcase making me lurch to avoid banging the unpainted stucco walls.

But I needed Flynn to navigate this low-way. I wasn't used to depending on other joes for anything in my life—hadn't since my old man threw in the towel, and my Russian-born mother, like Jolson's Mammy, had taken a powder back to her Moscow home before I reached the tender age of twenty-two. The thought of my early orphanage still choked me up.

As usual I could not follow the spirals and turns of the tunnels. Flynn, however, seemed to know them all. He strode on, the exact size as me, like a shadow eager to lead the way, preceding my every step and outraged at the notion that it should follow behind like the rest of the world's goyim.

That's right—I said it. Dutch Shultz was Jewish. We can give him that much in memoriam.

Ahead we walked in straight arrow for what seemed hundreds

of feet, though I doubted that could be possible, knowing the smallness of the Vatican's outside world. Again we turned and down we crawled through an improbably narrow stairwell, my suitcase scraping the wall with each step—at the noise Flynn more than once glanced back and up to glare at me as if it were all my fault.

Finally we came to a halt. Before Flynn was another of those mysterious X-marked panels which I had learned was a door, a door whose far side bore camouflage. I was confused not only about location, but about time. (Like always?) How could Flynn know whether the other side was guarded, or swept by a janitor, or swarmed by worshipers? Perhaps we were about to spring into the midst of the Vatican's humongous baldachinos, before Saint Peter's altar itself? That would take *splainin*.

The panel opened.

To my immediate left I sighted an unimpressive altar at the top of three marble steps, a silver goblet and two unlit candles on top barely visible in the half-light. We stood in a space that resembled a hallway, though not as narrow as the termite cave from which we had just emerged. A row of half-desks were each joined to a matching row of indented hollows, like closets but only two feet deep. We had stepped out of one such closet and behind us Flynn shut the door, which was so well camouflaged that, after it closed, I could not distinguish it from the other closets.

Flynn nodded to me. "Our blessed Clementine Chapel. Many a time I trudged me tired body here after dark to pray for Our Lord's guidance." He glanced at the chapel. "Now we be needin' His guidance more than ever." Flynn genuflected then stood up and led away down the hall.

I paused.

Overhead and strewn above each wall was such a profusion of hammered gold that it took my breath away, intertwined with sirulean...no, cerulean blue and sky white. I shook my head—the gold was not real, I realized, but only fancy artwork. It was a darn sight more happy to the eye, though, than that La Raza-ito graffiti under the I-40 overpass, which was the closest comparison I could come up with. My childhood wanderings in the Vatican had never brought me to this particular chapel.

We turned left. The path curved to the left yet again and we came to the entrance to another stairwell. This one was straight east-west, and descended to a platform before descending farther. At the bottom, which I gathered was two levels below the main tabernacle of Saint Peter, we turned right, stepped a few feet, then left. In front loomed a hole in the brickwork. With some difficulty Flynn and I climbed through and we found ourselves in a poorly lit space, small but just large enough for several people to stand—a full-sized closet. The tiny rooms and shoulder-squeezing walls were starting to remind me of the insect-paths of the secret labyrinth, and I again shuddered.

Flynn pointed up. "Ye be now in the Campus Petri, our blessed saint's original tomb directly under Saint Peter's altar and its twisted baldachinos."

I shrugged. Ain't no arguin' with a professional.

He pointed down. "See this white wall?"

I nodded.

"Now lower..."

I looked. A small repository lay gouged in the bottom of the white wall, chicken scratches marring its ancient surface.

Flynn's finger settled on one set of scratchings. "How's yer Greek again, Nephew?"

Staring closer by the dull rays of the electric midnight lights, I barely made out some words. "'P-e-t-r—eni'?"

"That's right, me boy. Sound familiar?"

Standing straight, I recited, "Petros eni." I shrugged.

"*The thing lies here,*" cited Flynn. He bent over. "Let's look inside."

Inside this jagged hole ripped into the lowest part of the white graffitied wall by true believers two thousand years ago, was a glass case resting on a small marble slab. Really small. The hole itself could not have been more than two feet in width. Flynn slid his hand up either side of the hole and found more marble, forming the insides of a box those true believers had installed in those days before even cavemen existed to hold the remains of their beloved Rock.

Suddenly I understood.

With a sly grin, as if all doubt had been removed much earlier and he had gone through the motions just for my benefit, Flynn stretched his hand past the glass case to feel the top of the repository. Grey fragments crumbled and he pulled the glass case entirely out of the hole to give himself more room. The glass case contained what appeared to be more finger bones of Saint Peter.

"This one's only replicas," he said, glancing upward, "the real finger bones of Our Saint lie two floors up in a bronze casket."

With the aperture clear, Flynn squatted on the floor and extended both hands inside the repository where he fumbled about a few moments before seizing on something. With a grunt, he extracted it from the ceiling. He slid it out.

Like Cagney, I scrunched my eyes. Like the Count of Monkey Crisco, I widened them to the max to take in the full rich scene.

Flynn placed the thing on the floor and we both sat and admired it—a hunk of night-black stone, one side smoothed from centuries of pilgrims' lips slobbering over its surface. Flynn recited: "'And I tell ye that ye are the rock, and on this rock I will build me church, and the gates of Hades will not overcome it. Matthew 16:18'." He read the graffiti again. "'*Petros eni. The Rock is here.*' But, Nephew, note the Egyptian ankh above the last word. That means these words can be read in an entirely different way: 'By this rock, eternal life is found.' Now *there* be a different take, Nephew. Maybe Papa was not bein' so crazy after all ta believe that 'petros' might be referrin' to an actual rock rather than to a person."

"Not sure I'm following all this, Unc."

"From this other point of view, Neph, Saint Peter has nothin' at all to do with the Church. The entire Saint Peter's Basilica, the anchor of the entire Vatican, would therefore be a fraud. Can ye imagine the reaction of the Curia if they discovered what Il Papa was up to? It was perhaps wise for him to be hidin' it here—in the last place the Curia would ever suspect."

"But you yourself sold the rock to him."

He shrugged. "'Twas in payment of a debt. Anyway—*caveat emptor*, Nephew. Above my pay grade."

I'd known enough con-men to realize that nothing I could say would change Flynn. Once a con, always a con. I added, "Maybe we should load it up in my tote and haul *case*, Flynn."

He paused. "One moment. We must be certain." Passing his

hands around the stone in linear fashion, Flynn mumbled, "Three feet by one foot by three inches." He nodded. "This is deed the Blarney Stone, all right. I'd recognize it even tossed in a quarry of shards."

I opened the suitcase, finally understanding why the case was so wide. Muck and Montez had known, as of course had Flynn. Why was I always the last to find things out? Together we lifted the Thingamajig—I was surprised at its lightness, I had expected something as heavy as the fake upstairs—and we easily lifted it inside the suitcase.

I froze.

Static had erupted—I dropped the rock.

"*Mios Italianos... your kiss is precious to me... have you come to let me out? Listen and I will grant you power over the world...*" Italian again, at least this time, inside the Vatican, it seemed more appropriate than it had in Albuquerque.

Flynn and I stood and swapped eye stares. Without a moment's delay, together we lifted the Thing into the case and I slammed the suitcase shut and flipped the clamps before more puzzles could emerge. Muffled noises drifted from within until finally falling quiet.

Yeah, I thought: *caveat emptor.*

Without waiting, I stood and lifted the case from the floor with both hands. Clumsy and bulky it was, much more so with the Gizmo within, but it was not too inconvenient to carry. I lurched for the exit like a kike hauling his Talmud and Flynn followed.

Explanations? *Fuggidaboudit.* My ride waited, and I had my ticket.

Back through the hole we climbed, then right, and right again. Up the two-level east-west stairway to the curving hall that led to the hidden door next to my darling Clementine's Chapel. Once again inside the insect-labyrinth, we hauled case—myself unable to keep the bulky trophy from gouging the unpainted walls every few steps, thus triggering more frowns from Flynn as if his years of skulking had put an ownership deed to these halls in his pocket.

At his direction and insistence, we returned to Grand Central and rested. Rather *I* rested. Flynn, having done little but gripe and whine, stuffed his oral orifice with canned artichokes and sardines, following them with the stalest crackers known to man before finally switching his clothes.

Odd, I thought, that he would choose this time to drape himself in his new Canali outfit right down to new shoes and fedora hat, which he had previously said were reserved for the final stage of his Resurrection, after he had returned the Thing to Ireland. I had already explained that that wasn't part of my immediate plans. But each to his own.

Soon he was done and—under my direction and insistence—we set out to make the north wall before dawn broke, very little time remaining to us, at least if Flynn's time-keeping was accurate. Glancing once through a narrow slit at a clock hanging outside, he indicated that five a.m. was close.

I turned to make hay while the moon shone, but Flynn kept staring through the slit. Suddenly he pressed a switch and another hidden panel opened. Through the wide-open doorway I glimpsed an upper floor of the Vatican Museum district, gorgeous paintings on walls and ceilings splayed before us along a hallway that paralleled our hidden passage.

Flynn glanced left and right, then stepped into the subdued night-lighting of the hall. He crossed to where the Vatican attendants had stretched a guide rope to corral visitors. Approaching the longest stretch of rope, he unhooked the thick cord from its stays and, swiftly wrapping its length around one shoulder like a mountain-climber, returned to my side.

He snapped the camouflaged door shut.

"Wings," was all he said.

I shrugged. Like I said, ain't no arguin' with a pro. Especially not when the clock is tocking and the moonshine wearing thin.

We hurried off, Flynn almost flying ahead of me and I had to strain to keep up while trying my best to keep my burden lengthwise with the passageway. Once more, I had no way to judge how far we had gone, or in what direction, though it seemed to me that the various lefts and rights added up to a northerly trend and that the various ups and downs totaled to two levels above ground.

Finally we came to an X-marked panel that had another eye-slit. Flynn allowed me to gaze through the slit—I was stunned. My eyes took in a row of apartment blocks across an open-air gulf and a wide empty street several lanes in width, all lit by the first rays of the dawning sun just visible above the eastern hills of Roma.

We had come to the end. The Vatican's *terminus ad queer*, if I recalled my community college rightly. We had but to swing wide this last panel and somehow drop the several stories to the ground below.

CHAPTER 16

My mouth opened in surprised respect of Flynn—thus the rope.

For a moment we stood there in the small passage, facing each other, me wondering how much closer we would have to be were the two of us 'normal' size. We barely fit in the tight space as it was. We breathed deep—once this last panel opened and we began our descent there would be no going back. I only hoped that my co-conspirators, meaning Montez & Muck, or Montez *or* Muck, or even one of their despicable henchmen, stood below with the ride they had promised me in that Albuquerque Frankly Right house, which seemed now a world away in time and space.

Clandestinely I felt my left little finger, rubbed the nerve-dead plastic of its final digit to assure myself I still had the ace in the hole, that, come what may, if all else flushed, I could at least pass through whatever obstacles those piebald Swiss credit card thieves with their pikes might attempt to place in my path.

Flynn interrupted my reverie by pulling the panel door. It opened inward, like the rest, and Flynn opened it to its full measure, pressing it against one side of the passage. I remained vague about how he planned to use the cord to get us down—Flynn took the cord and, coiling it over and under the panel's lower hinge and twisting it, it was soon apparent that he had made a solid connection.

Turning, Flynn tossed the remaining cord out the door's threshold where it uncoiled against the side of the Vatican's high wall like a wet noodle. Staring down its length, I noted that its lower end hung still some five feet off the ground. Not much to you maybe, but to the napoleonic-sized... Well, baby ducks jump farther before their wings work. I would just have to grow a pair.

"Let's hope, Nephew. I've never dared test the strength of the museum's guide ropes before."

I looked at Flynn, shrugged. Who first?

Before he could answer, a flash of light hit my face. Dawn! Involuntarily I peered into the gloom of the street below, which had formerly been obscured in darkness. I stiffened. A black object took shape—beside it stood a single upright figure.

More light crept. The street lit, showing a wide patio leading to a wide set of doors to my lower right, which I recognized as the entry to the Vatican's Museum halls. Before long, tickets would be offered for sale to a growing crowd of tourists. Our escape would then hardly be private. I was annoyed, not knowing who to blame for this needless risk—M&M or Flynn.

But, for the nonce, no crowd had yet appeared, just the single black object that was now clearly a black limousine, which comforted me since so far I had every reason in this crazy world to distrust that particular make of car. At least my ride had appeared, though.

I was further comforted by the fact that the upright object had materialized into someone I knew—a woman, in fact—who stood by the engine as if the car were stalled. Funny how when a joe goes abroad, even life-long enemies suddenly become treasured friends, as does anyone at all, provided one can just think of a familiar face.

No face was visible here, but she was dressed in a black pullover shirt and American style jeans, and she stared directly up at Flynn and me, not showing the least surprise at the appearance of this pair of odd-balls thrusting their heads out of a lone aperture where no opening should be, in an otherwise blank wall three stories high. A blond wig and dark glasses were accompanied by a green feather jacket, further assuring me of who the hell it was—*Licia*. And at the driver's seat a figure that could only be Frank. Even that evil-ass scumbag warmed my heart.

I grinned—thirty more feet and I would be free.

The grin faded. From inside a pocket, Flynn whipped out a pair of handcuffs, and in a single swift motion, cuffed my left wrist to the upper hinge of the door. Before I could react, he snatched the suitcase.

As if having held his breath for an hour, Flynn let it out in a huge sigh of relief. "Now don't be tellin' me, Nephew, that ye be surprised. Ye of all people should be knowin' how reluctant I are of returnin' to the hospitality of Saint Peter. I simply canna' pass up a ticket to ride. Dressed like ye in yer finest suit and haulin' yer case with the Stone, I s'pect I'll travel first class to whatever sweet destination yon car might be headed, lookin' exactly like ye as I do." He pulled his hat onto his head, hiding his white hair. "I have but to keep me mouth shut and do as I'm told to make them believe I'm ye."

Flynn gave me a flip of the hand to his forehead, grinned a leprechaun's grin, and climbed out the window. "Till next we meet, Pete. And I truly hope it won't be another seven year."

He slid down the rope.

No, I hadn't seen it coming. I usually pride myself in my ability to sniff out people's second natures and sort the Flugenheimers from the Goldbergs, but I had to admit that Flynn's betrayal was a surprise. For a slice of a moment I stood there with the golden sun bursting on my face, one hand cuffed to the panel's exposed hinge, stunned into total silence. Hell, my jaw even dropped—and I wouldn't have believed such a hackneyed expression if I had read it in any novel, but there it was, and there was I, mouth open like that fucking Hawaiian volcano that still won't heal, only surprised air coming from inside as my Mahi Mahi white-round eyes watched Flynn's grinning face sink over the edge, one hand on the rope and his other clutching my own enormous suitcase.

I felt... well, an even more unexpected emotion bubbled up— admiration. To think that my own flesh and blood had outwitted *me*—the private dick who was a veteran of a hundred foiled swindles in a dozen cities. My own genes, which meant in a way my own genius. It was I who was climbing down that thick rope in the cool morning of an April day in the lair of Romulus and Remus. I who had out-smarted my nephew, that smart-aleck street-wise muckraker from the streets of the New World named Pietro Quinn Tiberias Marlowe. From their basement, both Quinn and Pete heartily clapped.

I was proud of Flynn. *Deed* I was.

But frustrated. No, despite my love and admiration for my quarter-gene relative, no self-respecting dick could allow his reputation to be dissed in such a public manner. I stretched as far and as fast as I could manage, and, wrenching both arms, my right hand grabbed Flynn by his collar. Yeah, I know that was no way to treat a fine suit, but once in a while a shlomo has just got to prioritize. This was then.

Flynn hung, his feet dangling. He gave a kick to force me to lose my grip, swinging the suitcase to increase the pressure on my right arm. Finally he let go of the rope, clutching the suitcase with both hands and risking falling to his death, and the pain shot up my limb, zapped through my spine and did a little dance up my left arm to where my hand was still cuffed to the upper hinge of the panel—the metal of the handcuff stabbing my wrist like a knife. I felt like an automobile belt under maximized torsion, a rubber rudder stretched to point to heaven and hell at once as if that guinea Dante, so beloved inside the Vatican, had taken up residence in Limbo.

"Let me go, Nephew! It won't do ye any good by delayin' matters. I ain't got no key to the handcuffs, so ye cain't benefit from stoppin' me anyhow."

"Squawk, rat, gab, fink, squeal, flip, sell out, snitch, *finger.* See yesterday for the rest." I shouted down at him, hoping to burst his ear drum.

Again he kicked. More pain shot through me. I groaned. If I were to give in to the pain, not only would I lose the Blarney Stone, but Uncle Flynn himself would be dashed to pieces. Down below, people had begun to appear, and not the right ones. The limo was still parked and Licia still stared—she seemed to catch her breath and one hand covered her mouth—but with the arrival of dawn the day's customers for the Vatican's Museum tours were beginning to accumulate and they paused to stare at the spectacle of a man in a business suit hanging thirty feet up from a formerly hidden opening in the Vatican's blank wall, clutching a tan suitcase and kicking his feet, while a second stranger clung desperately to his collar with head out-thrust. Several women shrieked at the prospect of the man in the suit falling. Others hurriedly videoed, mentally counting Facebook Likes once they posted.

"Have it your way, Neph." Flynn looked up at me. He let loose yet another grin—in a flash I knew what he planned.

"Don't do it, Unc. You'll regret it."

"I think not, Pete. Ye be presumin' too much." He looked down—and dropped the case.

Twenty-five feet it fell—slammed the ground with a gigantic crack. Flynn hugged the rope with both hands for reassurance. We both stared down. By some miracle—an item apparently in plentiful supply around this ancient Etruscan hill—the suitcase had not opened. Split and twisted, yes, but still locked shut. Flynn and I did mental performances, as well, invisibly crossing ourselves in relief. Damn, I thought, I really gotta ask M&M about the manufacturer, if it wasn't they themselves.

But our time was up. Below, Licia rushed forward and snatched the suitcase, then turned back toward the limo. I thought this would become quite an octopus in Rome's woodpile if she were allowed to proceed.

I could delay no longer. I let Flynn go. With my now freed right hand, I plucked off the digit of my left little finger, and twisting my pinky so it aimed directly at the metal handcuff, my thumb punched the red button.

Heretofore I had had no call to use my pinky ray for anything but flat surfaces like walls, which to their misfortune had happened to block the progress of my life, and so far no difficulty had resulted. Never had I attempted to dissolve anything smaller than a sheet of wall board. Would it work? Would my frantic fanatic attempts to free myself to avoid the humiliation of being discovered by the Vatican's "guards of color" while chained to Vatican furniture and to pursue Flynn succeed?

Just in time I squinched my stomach to avoid the inevitable motion sickness. Smoke and fumes exploded from the handcuff and the metal dissolved into a spotted brown pretzel, the effect bypassing my wrist to encompass the hinge, a section of door, and a wide cone of plaster behind it. I wondered how far this violation of Nature would penetrate, but I had no time to observe. There was no time even to contemplate the musical fate of Constantinople when the heavy panel fell inward, its lower edge contacting the floor with a snap, the rope-wrapped lower hinge bent but still intact.

I yanked my hand free.

In another moment I was clambering down the guide rope with the eagerness of an ape in his forest-ville, hot on the track of that con-man to end all con-men, Benedict Arnold Flynn.

Below me he had already reached the end of the rope—he dropped the remaining few feet and landed on the thin strip of weeds that lined the bottom of the wall.

As fast as I could I followed down, but the priest's cassock slowed me, interfering with my judo-tuned acrobatics. Whoa there, don't be so skeptical. I can flip and toss with the best gymnast, I just don't like to show off. I didn't this time. So I reached the end in more dignified fashion.

Below, something was wrong—Flynn had stumbled. Barely gaining his feet when I dropped behind, I tackled him like a Black Lives linebacker does a white quarterback right after taking a knee. Together we rolled across the pavement. I hated to insult Mr. Canali, but bidness is bidness.

Two things interrupted our clan-bake. First, a horde of rainbow guards burst from the Museum entrance, ignoring the growing crowd of wide-eyed spectators, and goose-stepped toward us like spastic gazelles. Angry. No. Pissed. Very pissed.

Second, Licia arrived at the car and a darkened back door half-opened, and ignoring Flynn and me, she hustled the case inside. She paused and turned to stare as if awaiting the outcome of my and Flynn's tussle. An invisible driver gunned the limo's engine.

I couldn't waste no more time. Leaping to my feet, I lifted the cassock like Marie Antoinette and bolted for the limo. In the corner of one eye I glimpsed panic seize Flynn and saw him scramble back up the dangling rope like the misanthropian he was, while in the corner of the other I saw the horde of Swiss guards focus on me and break into a run. Only seconds remained.

No more than a few feet separated me from Licia. As I neared at a run, she removed her dark glasses—I nearly exploded from the shock. It was not Licia, but Tonya! Green Eyes. My true love herself stood there before me, offering me everything I needed in this world, most of all an open door to freedom. One more step and I would leap into that beautiful limo and it would purr and lurch away like God's chariot, leaving this mortal Vatican behind.

Tonya pulled a white slip of paper from a pocket and let it drop to the ground—almost in secret, as if afraid it might be seen by her comrades. She slipped in the limo's back seat.

This was odd, but okay—the door remained half open, though I still could not see who or what might be inside.

I neared.

I arrived.

I put my hand on the door.

Beside me, the pavement rattled with the boots of a dozen angry Swiss, armed with the latest in medieval weaponry.

Behind me, the escape rope was pulled up.

Before me, the back door pushed open. A man stepped out and stood full-height. A pink tongue shot out, once, twice. Andrew grinned.

"Not you, Pete," he guffawed. With a shove, Andrew pushed me to the ground. He reentered the car and slammed the door. The limo spun dirt and raced away.

I sat. Without resistance, I let the guards take me. One shock a joe can take—maybe two or even three—but the series of shocks that had tumbled on this schmoe as if Heaven had decided to empty all its prisons and municipal dumps on my head at once had had its effect. I was done. With a last forlorn act, almost like an autonomic motion, my hand took the slip of paper Tonya had dropped and I absent-mindedly stuffed it in my pocket. What else did I have to remind me of her?

Nothing.

Funny how even when a guy's true love betrays him, his mind still clings to her like a drowning man in a flood, even though he knows she's no good for him. As a half-dozen pairs of arms grabbed me and I was carried and dragged into the Museum entrance like muscled orcs dragging a dwarf, I still could not help but think of those beautiful lips, those haunting sloe eyes, that midnight black hair, always paired by her black jacket with black red-spotted feathers tinged with green at the tips. Red and green merged in my mind like a marriage of Ireland and everything Peter. My soul could fight no longer. I lived—and died—for her.

Mostly died.

The guards dragged me through the Vatican's halls like a pigeon who had missed a payment to his loan shark and down we went, level by level, until we arrived in the catacombs—no, *below*— in the lower-most level of this ancient castle, a level unknown to the world outside. The passages were illy lit, the air stank of smoke and rancid water. All familiar. We came to a wide thick door of oak and hammered metal. It swung open. Without ceremony, they shoved me inside, not even muttering 'Killer of Christ'.

As the door slammed shut and locked, I got slowly to my feet. For some reason I felt depressed. I sighed. Not even the realization that they had put me in Uncle Flynn's former cell, as was apparent from the Irish runes scribbled on the walls signed 'Flynn', brightened my mood. Seven years? I'll be lucky if I'm given only seventy. They had even plugged the hole that Flynn had scraped in the wall not twenty-four hours previous.

Oh well, I still had my insurance. As M&M had said, and experience had proved—no jail can hold me. I looked to my little finger and prepared myself mentally for yet another penetration of Mother Nature's privates. There was no point in waiting. I had no taste for a meal of white wafers and wine.

Plucking off the rubber tip, I started to point the finger at the door. Halted in mid-motion. *The red button was gone.* My mind sank into brain-freeze. I peeked, I inspected, I sniffed, I jabbed, I poked the stub of my finger—nothing happened. No volcano, no spume, no smoke, no weird tunes about the former capital of Greece.

My Universal Indexer was broke.

Which meant I was too. Well and truly imprisoned for the remainder of my life in this awful dungeon, at the mercy of a brotherhood known for their cruelty to schoolchildren's knuckles and anyone who works in masonry. As the assassin of their leader, and now a thief of something in their possession, whatever the heck it actually was, I was just about as *persona non grata* as the Vatican ever *grataed*.

As if that wasn't enough, a sound permeated the stone walls surrounding me, its cacophonous notes coalescing into a steady beat.

As fearful and maddening an assault as ever afflicted the eardrum of any unfortunate prisoner unable to escape its effects, hammering my sensibilities and degrading my ability to cling to a last remnant of civilization. My soul shrank before its evilness.

"Fiends," I yelled out in my pain and anger. "What could drive you to be so cruel? Have you no humanity?" No reply came. I jammed my fingers in my ears and cried in my sleeve, hoping my torturers could not hear my pathetic efforts to block the music of *Adelle*.

In mid-sob, an alien sound attracted my attention. Like a hiss, but more subdued, and accompanied by a strange change in the dull light that seeped in from the cracks around the door.

Void of hope, I looked up.

The door shifted and bulged like the overhead psychedelic display at a Jimi Hendrix concert. A volcano erupted at its center, spreading to its edges, pouring smoke.

There was no mistaking what I saw.

I stood.

Like a subject at a Mezmer demonstration, I walked forward till I was at the center of the swirl of Nature's terrifying energies. From the far side of the tunnel, which meant the far side of the Universe, a muffled voice sounded.

I needed no invitation. Into the center I stepped.

CHAPTER 17

I might have stepped over a cliff. I might have stepped into solid rock. Or magma erupting from the center of some tortured alien planet. No such luck. I was back in the familiar torch-lit basement beneath the Vatican.

Where was my benefactor? Glances up and down the passage revealed no one—a brief sound drifted from the far end where the passage turned a corner. I was able to glimpse no more than the heel of a black shoe disappearing around the edge. Then it was gone.

At my feet was a white kerchief with gold embroidery; on it rested a small red button.

I almost choked. Carefully releasing my breath, I picked the button up. The smoky interior hid much, but as near as I could tell, there was nothing the matter with it. Not that I knew a damned thing about the mechanics of quantum travel or universal indexers. But it had to be put here for a reason. Someone who knew more than he or she should know wanted me out of the Vatican's dungeons and, I could only suppose, to resume M&M's little game.

I shrugged. In my hotel room I still had a pocketful of lira and a fresh set of clothes. All I needed was to make sure my digit-al miracle still worked. Carefully I screwed it back in place. It must have fallen out when I wrestled with Flynn, and someone—Flynn himself?—had discovered it and returned it to me, perhaps even having used it to free me?

My brain jerked trying to figure it all out. Who? Why? What the hell for? If it was Flynn, how did he get out of the Vatican to retrieve the button, and if he had managed to escape, why would he return just to help me of all people, whom he had just tried to handcuff to a door? And how the hell would Flynn know the significance of a little red button dropped on the ground? I had never revealed that secret to my uncle. And whose kerchief was this? I had no memory of that either.

Well, I'm the last Juan Doe in the world to look a gift wop in the mouth, so I swallowed my confusion and hurried to the end of the hall. I turned to where I knew a stairwell lay. Up I climbed until I reached the catacombs.

No need to go into the gory details of how I escaped the Vatican a second time. The harrowing brushes with priests and guards, the hiding in dark recesses until night should fall, the silent borrowing of several choice items from nooks and corners, a quick visit to Il Papa's old apartment, and the blasting of several walls with my re-installed get-out-of-Saint-Peter's-free card. To my relief, the button worked as it should.

By midnight I was back in my hotel room, no longer enamored of the beautiful vista, in fact thankful that it was too dark to see it. All it reminded me of now was treachery and prison and I only hoped the new pope, whoever that might be, would be less devious and vengeful than the last. I found my e-cig and puffed till it glowed red.

Cleaning up, I grabbed some sleep, changed into my favorite clothes—complete with fedora, and after another continental breakfast of acorns and pizza dough, vanished among the many coffee shops before news of the escape of 'the maniac pope killer' could be broadcast.

After half a day of skulking, finally assured that no public announcement was forthcoming—due likely to the mysteries of Curia politics—I relaxed in a Roma coffee shop and spread two items on a table next to a piping hot cup. First was the kerchief. I turned it over—the words 'Bourbon Street Tailors' smacked me in the face. Green Eyes. She must have lost it when she leaped into the limo. Second, I unfolded the mysterious piece of white paper that Tonya—clearly unharmed by Marm's treatment—had deliberately dropped just before turning Benedictress on me *again* and diving away to leave me in the dirt.

Once before she had slipped me a piece of paper. On that paper had been a picture of a bell marked in rough pencil, which was still a puzzle. This paper had more. It was again a picture of a bell, but with more detail: the bell seemed suspended, as most real bells were, of course, but suspended not in a church steeple but held up by a dozen chains in the center of flying spandrels that supported each other at the top in a circular structure, reminding me of the spandrel I had seen in M&M's headquarters, along with the printed words: 'song of the bell' and 'MilkCow'.

When will these damned puzzles end? Isn't that just like a woman, fragile and all. Why can't Tonya just come out and tell me for once what the hell was going on, what M&M were up to? Why had they armed me with the key to the universe, then, after I did their job, shoved me in the dirt to rot? It was enough to make a private dick retire and go keep bees.

Then there was the *I'm not only dumb but I'm stupid* angle. It had finally sunk in that Jack & Bob wanted more than the Blarney Stone—and whatever was embedded inside it—they had *wanted* me to kill the Pope. That was their plan all along, at least in part.

I needed more information. But without my 'brain', my phone having been confiscated in partial payment for my little vacation in the Howard Johnson suite, I had no means of researching bells. Just how the heck would one do that anyway?

I glanced again at the kerchief. Maybe that would be more productive. Here I at least had a name. With barely enough lira remaining—including my most private reserve, which I had sewed in the ankle cuff of my pants—a trick I invented after my fifth rolling by Aztlan homies to examine the contents of my socks—I made my way to Rome's smallest airport to evade overzealous authorities and I booked a passage to Sardinia.

Once in Sardinia, I managed to book passage on an international flight and head back to the U.S.

My entire time in Italy I had been both dumb and stupid.

Now I was just dumb.

Progress.

I arrived in New Orleans exhausted but not broke—not yet anyway. I pawned a Picasso I had borrowed from a hallway of the Rome hotel and walked out with a Smith & Wesson Saturday Night Special, the kind that makes enough noise to scare old ladies and every backyard dog in a mile radius. The pawnbroker was excited to see a genuine Picasso. So was I. He had it in his shop window for sale before I left.

Picking up a burner cell phone, I located the right street and address and taxied my way to a side street. It had been a while since I visited the old French Quarter. Graves of a few Irish ancestors rested somewhere up Canal Street—accompanied by many Italian graves. Not many realize how many potato eaters and spaghetti stringers populated New Orleans in the old days. Many remain.

Up Bourbon Street I slouched, one hand keeping the brim of my fedora over my face as I carefully eyed addresses. Finally, there it was—'Bourbon Street Tailors'. With the usual narrow entrance for that corner of the city. Nothing strange about the place...but as every PI knows, not only *can* appearances be deceiving. They are—*always.*

Rather than stand in the open, I dove into an old book shop across the street.

The place was stuffy but comfortable. Books climbed stack upon stack fairly begging for a fire—my kind of place. For coffee that is. The proprietor brought some Guinea brew and I sat by the window and cracked a best seller, 'Poodle Springs'. It seemed appropriate. I pretended to read, keeping one eye glued to the 'Tailors' storefront, casually noticed the adjacent establishments: one a combo blues and strip joint named 'Gentleman Blues', in front of the other a sign that read: 'Rick's Cigar Lounge'.

I counted the people entering Tailors. A few early afternoon pedestrians strolled casually by, a few walking in, a few strolling out, mostly women, the men choosing the Lounge presumably while they waited for their class-climbing wives to conclude their high-nose shopping.

The clock spun.

I was in no hurry. I counted—and measured time—by watching their faces across the narrow one-lane street. That too is how PIs roll.

I emptied my cup. With a turn of the hand, I got my cup refilled by the stretch-black-shirt girl condemned to service total strangers by selling badly-sewed souvenirs. Her frown persuaded me to buy a raggedy dog but I continued to sit, sip, and stare. In this business that's mostly what one does.

And think...

Again I took out the kerchief. I could not explain why it took so long for me to get that it belonged to Tonya, that she had flashed it at our first meeting. Maybe because it lacked perfume, thus failing to trigger the instant memory response which smells bring to average josés. Maybe because my recent stumbling about in the Vatican had fried my memory cells. *That* she had delivered it to me deliberately, like the crumpled paper, I had no doubt, though it was not a high heel that I had glimpsed disappearing around the corner while in the catacombs. *Why* was a different matter—there must be a reason why she sent me here. Somewhere inside that women's clothing shop was another piece to M&M's puzzle. There had to be...

My e-cig in my pocket, I was tempted to step outside to crank up the lithium and inhale its life-giving vapor free of the contaminating dust that drifted from the books. My watering eyes settled on the Cigar sign and my brows rose. Why not? Mixing a little fun with business wouldn't hurt. I decided to light up the real thing for a change and maintain my vigil in a bit more comfort.

Dropping another fiver on the coffee table, I sauntered out without bothering to bring the book. I'd had enough of poodles. Making a beeline for Rick's Cigars, I crossed the one-horse lane and stepped into the joint. Not much to tell. Just the usual two lines of wall booths with two more lines down the center separated by a wall crowned by semi-see-through panes with imitation leaves of grass embedded in the glass. On the walls were a collection of the usual cigar lounge paraphernalia: giant neon ads, pictures of big-shots sporting huge lit cigars, and mirrors to make the place look bigger than it was.

Life in a nutshell.

I sat by the front where I could continue to see who was coming and going at the Tailors next door. On the wall above me was a blank spot where a picture had recently been removed, the edges stained by cigar smoke. Underneath on a plaque were the words 'Our Founder'. Apparently Mr. Founder, presumably Rick himself, had taken up membership in somebody's Lost & Found.

Towards the back of the lounge was a pair of pool tables where several characters hammered balls home with precision—I'd seen better—their formal jackets draped over more booths. I'd seen better jackets too.

Next to the pool tables stretched a bar where a young smuck with a Japanese hair knot sucked a Macanudo while he prepared highballs. A pair of waitresses trotted to meet the steady stream of men that wandered in. One took her time serving me, but finally got around to taking my order: a White Zombie and Rocky Patel blunt. I'm a creature of habit, there was no need for me to waste my time perusing the glass case of overpriced cigars behind the bar.

In the far back was another series of booths. The gloom was more than I had expected—due not just to the deep layout of the place and the poor lighting dimmed by the drift of cigar smoke, but to the dark stained wood of the booths. Suited me fine; I drooped the brim of my hat. I'd just as soon watch without being seen.

Halfway through my cancer stick, while I sat hunched in a corner of the hard dark wood of the booth, still savoring the gin and sweet fruit flavors of the Zombie, a pair approached off the street. The woman aimed at Tailors, while the man angled toward the lounge's entrance. Familiar? I didn't see the woman's face, but something about the man's face 'rung a bell'. Yeah, I couldn't get the phrase out of my head. It was, after all, why the hell I had come to New Orleans in the first place and why I sat here playing 007.

The man swung open the glass door and sauntered past, heading for the back bar. Before he made contact, I was up and sliding farther back, taking advantage of the central wall with the glass-enclosed green grass to stay hidden. Not too difficult actually for four-foot-eleven. One day I really would have to hang a picture of Napoleon in my future shotgun shack where I could sacrifice virgins in his honor. Connotation intended.

Frank of the Massolinis... I mouthed the words silently to myself while I maneuvered past the busy pool tables, trying to get closer to the bar without being seen. Beside back booths, I paused, pretending to mess with my burner, fedora hiding face and phone screen, but one eye still on Frank at the back bar. He seemed to mutter instructions to Mr. Snot-nosed Top-Knot.

I tried to edge closer without arousing suspicion. In the process I glimpsed another wall picture. In luxury framing stood two persons. I instantly recognized the first: the most famous mob boss in

New Orleans, Carlos Marcello, in his younger days. Almost as short as me, testifying as to what this glorious world has to offer to even the most minuscule. The Boss was handing a check to a young woman with too much makeup. I was slow to get her. Only when I read the caption did I comprehend: 'Mr. Marcello donates $100,000 to Mrs. Angelica Massolini's Truth Preservation non-profit.' Big grins on both. Especially on Marm.

Oh, *yes*, I nodded. None other. The picture showed Marm in her younger days before she hooked her children on dope, the family business.

I continued to speculate about Montez & Muck's hyperventilating and greedy partner, her image spreading over my brain like a scout tent in a storm when her face seemed to grow old and her smile faded into a permanent disapproving scowl.

Suddenly I realized the real thing had walked in.

Jerking her pipette out of her purse, Marm clicked her silver-plated lighter so it flared in the darkness like a Roman candle, and cherry tobacco added its rich aroma to the cloudy brine that filled the place. Behind her strode a pair of expensively suited unsmiling men one of whom carried a heavy bag. Together, Frankie and Marm stepped behind the bar and the man plopped the bag onto the alcohol-soaked platform, his partner persuading with a glare the only customer at the bar to relocate.

Without warning, the men and Frank made for my seat.

I could not let them see me. It was too late to make an escape via the front. Behind me was nothing but the establishment's restroom and a hallway, leading even farther back in the long-skinny establishment.

The Patel still in my mouth, I dove into the restroom, silently debating whether to leave the door open a crack to observe them or to lock it shut and stay alive and breathing. For a moment I fumbled with the lock—it refused to work.

Abandoning it, I rushed into a stall.

The outer restroom door banged open. Frankie and his partner stuck their heads inside the restroom and glared like junk-yard dogs that smelled cat. I couldn't see them, but I sensed it as clearly as any psychic sensed anything. Removing my jacket, I let it drape below the door to my stall, hoping it would calm their fears, and, without trying, puffed a cloud toward the ceiling.

A half-snort half-sigh of acknowledgment emanated from the restroom door and it squeaked semi-shut again as the pair withdrew, apparently satisfied that I was nobody of concern.

PIs don't learn much sitting on toilets. As soon as the door shut, I put on my jacket and hurried to peek into the hallway. Frankie was alone and unlocking a side door while struggling to hold a heavy bag in one hand. The door opened and Frankie pushed through.

Shielding the glow from my cigar, I was right behind.

A stairwell met my gaze—Frankie's footsteps sounded from below, distancing as he descended into what must have been several floors beneath the surface of New Orleans' French Quarter. I followed, quieter than him. I had a difficult time keeping my mind on the Massolini thug below me, and off the growing thought of what I should expect fifty feet below.

Smuggling dens? Slave quarters? An old state prison for punishing interracial marriages? What use could the corrupt and vicious Massolinis have for a hidden world beneath their seemingly legitimate above-ground businesses? What connection could it have to M&M and Tonya and to what had happened to me?

I listened and crept down.

As I rounded the last angle of the stairwell, my eye caught the back of Frank as he spun a wide captain's wheel with one hand, his other clutching the heavy bag. The wheel was set in an enormous solid steel door that seemed like an entrance to a bank vault.

As the door swung slowly open, I heard the unmistakable sound of coins jingle in the bag. I nodded. Rick's Cigar Lounge: HQ for the Massolini's drug operation and who knows what else? And suddenly I also got the missing picture: Rick Massolini, the guy who had started the Lounge and the ill-fated Americana venture in New Mexico and who had thus triggered the anger of his wife, Angelica Massolini. Missing Rick had inadvertently given his wife a pretext to boot him out and take everything he owned. By pre-existing plan?

Wouldn't be the first time. I'd seen it all and heard it all.

From my narrow vantage point, however, I could not see what Frankie was up to, or what lay inside the vault, but his sounds drifted to my ears, consisting mainly of stacks of paper flopping onto a table accompanied by the loud clanking of coins.

It was clear enough. As the sound of footsteps got louder and the door to the vault creaked shut, I retreated up the stairwell, and with a glance to make sure no one waited in the hallway, I entered the hall and again made for the restroom. I could think of no better place to become invisible while Frank walked past.

Quietly I walked to the door and pushed—I froze. The door was locked. Someone had succeeded in making the rusty door lock work from the inside, leaving me stuck in the hallway between Frankie on the one side and Marm on the other.

Pulling my brim down further, I skulked back to my seat, still hoping I would be overlooked. Behind me, the stair door swung open and Frankie strode in. He too pushed on the restroom door, and finding it locked as I did, he shrugged and walked toward the bar where he paused.

His eyes fell directly on me, taking in the empty drink glass, the still-smoking Rocky Patel, and in my mind measuring my small-package size with eyes like a measuring tape.

Without reacting, however, he walked, and a moment later had passed me by and halted next to Marm by the bar. He seemed to reply to a series of questions put to him rapid-fire by Marm, which, though not easy for me to make out in the semi-darkness, still seemed clear enough, given her obsession with money, which as I now understood was the only motor that made this *bi-atch* tick.

As one, they turned and looked...

CHAPTER 18

Marm emerged from behind the bar to join Frankie with two more thugs in tow and together they approached my seat—I was already in the stairwell racing downward, my right hand patting gun and pinky. I came to the solid steel door. I thirsted to discover what lay behind that bank-like gate. Once more images of the Count of Monkey Crisco floated before my eyes, an ape-like man inundated in ill-gotten jewels. Yours truly, fer sure, if only I could swing it.

The door would not swing for me, of course. That went without saying. But, just as I knew by now that no jail could hold me, the reverse was also true: no jail—or bank vault—could keep this ape out.

Steps pounding the stairs behind me, I plucked off the plastic like a race-horse paws the ground at the Preakness and aimed it at the ponderous structure. No other escape hatch existed.

I pressed the red button.

In an instant the metal of the wide door, half a foot thick sufficient to withstand the explosives of any safecracker, whatever his resume, melted like low-fat butter on raisin-toast. The bubbling commenced and, just as those footsteps hammered home on the last of the stairs, I rushed through, with the now comforting strains of Istanbul in my ears.

Once I was on the other side, the door rematerialized behind me—I staggered at the sight that met my eyes. The subdued light of a perpetual under-wattage electric bulb flickered off a thousand rare surfaces, gold and silver scattered in such profusion that I rubbed my eyes in disbelief. Not even the legendary greed of Angelica Massolini and her ancient thieving clan, positioned at the delta of the largest river basin in this quarter of the world and collecting a tithe from every illicit transaction that occurred, could account for this mountain of treasure. And not only coins, but folding money, most in bags and bands, but much just lying tossed about on the neglected floor like maple leaves in November, their green and gold inscriptions glowing a river-troll's gold.

Sounds penetrated the door; someone was twirling the ship's wheel.

What to do? Across the room, not small by any measure, but still a single chamber, I ran along a central path free of what must amount to centuries of theft, and came smack against a second steel door identical to the first. My pinky cap was still off. I could press the button any time—its energy was limitless, deriving from the Multiverse via its microwaved crystal of whatever-the-hell it was.

But what lay on the other side? The first door I knew opened onto a treasure room. But a second door? What the heck could a schlomo expect to find in *that* direction? Anything solid would be my grave. Even an open chamber could be my death if the air was poisoned.

It was too late to wrack my brain. The door at the front was opening. I heard high-pitched female voices giving harsh instructions to low-rumbling low-IQ enforcers. There seemed to be more than four people. More than four pretty much neutralized my karate-judo combo.

Again I pressed the button, overcoming the latest obstacle that a Loki-like fate had thrown before me, and I threw myself through the bubbling opening, the metal recomposing just in time for me to avoid detection by New Orleans' shadow government.

This time I had closed my eyes. Now I gradually opened them, knowing not what to expect, only that this place would contain no treasure. Like the latest chamber of Dante's stacked levels, I resigned myself to the worst. Hell, I thought, Hell itself had to be down here somewhere. I found myself sniffing the darkened air for traces of sulfur.

My eyes adjusted. This place too was lit by under-powered electric bulb, and not one, but many, stretching into the distance. In between, from cavernous wall to cavernous wall, stood rows of dull unresponsive monuments like gigantic termite mounds I had once glimpsed in a nature show. Except these monuments had see-through plastic masks fixed at face level on every mound.

I shuddered. A street joe sees a lot—and Oh Lawdy this joe has seen more than he ever wished—but nothing yet had frightened me so much that I was ready to retire to Sunnybrook Farm. Till now. I could not put my finger on it—not even my pinky—but something about this phalanx of silent monuments to the dead buried far below the surface of the oldest and most corrupt city on the Gulf made me shake to the marrow of my bones.

Still, I couldn't resist. Fight as I might, my feet dragged me forward to inspect the first stalagmite in the phalanx. Just below the plastic faceplate I spied a plaque and on the plaque were words. My hands grabbed my knees to keep them from knocking. Quinn and Pietro and even Elvis were glad that no one could see the act—a tough PI had a *rep* to maintain, and knocking knees did nothing for that rep.

'Carlos Marcello' read the plaque. Raising my gaze, I locked eyes on the plastic—staggered a step. Behind the plastic was a round face with eyes shut, a full body extending below into the case of the monument, blue and white ice-like crystals forming a backdrop like those godlike crowns of gold that priests love to paint around their favorite martyrs. I had to admit that the face I stared at bore a strong resemblance to the picture of Marcello I had just seen in the lounge.

Except I knew the former head of the New Orleans mob was dead.

Long dead.

I moved to the next monument and stared at the plaque. 'Lee Harvey Oswald'. Now I was not just frightened, but confused. How far did M&M's plans extend? Could their plans involve time as well as space? To the next monument I stepped. 'Chicago Bishop Paul Marcinkus'. His face, too, was frozen in death—or M&M's death-equivalence conjured up for their nefarious plans. From somewhere, perhaps a stray comment I had overheard once in the Vatican, my mind connected Marcinkus with the Vatican Bank, the biggest big-shot after the Pope.

And to the next. 'Licio Gelli'. Now I drew a blank. All I knew was that he had something to do with the Sicilian Mafia, which was no surprise given my current situation. A plaque reading 'Michelle Sindona' followed, which name was tied to Gelli. Another stray scrap of memory linked him to the Mafia and the Vatican Bank, his body allegedly found hanging from a London bridge.

The plaque that followed made me halt and stifle a cry: 'John F. Kennedy'. In the monument, his body seemed whole, no head wound visible. Peacefully sleeping. I tried to force my brain cells to think—there had to be some sense to the nonsense that M&M and their Mafia enforcers were up to. All I could figure was that they were all Catholic—or had killed a big-shot Catholic—and they all had some connection to the Vatican. I had seen them before: when I stumbled into Montez & Muck's operations room in Marm's castle in Albuquerque, these same faces had been visible on their closed-circuit monitor, though I had not recognized them at the time. No wonder Bob Montez had broken a sweat when he saw that I had seen them.

I felt I was getting closer to their secret.

For a moment I wanted to turn and wave at the camera I imagined was watching me. But there was no more time. Behind me, the second vault door was opening. Was there another exit like the second steel door that had enabled me to escape the vault? The cavern looked huge. And at least—as the Massolini gang began to search for me through the monuments—there were plenty of places for a small guy like me to hide.

In the semi-darkness I slipped from one monument to another, wondering at their number, the mounds stretching across the cavern like a forest, and I finally paused, cornered. A woman's voice echoed through the chamber interspersed with coughing.

"I don't see anyone. I wanna go back." Licia's voice.

An older deeper woman's voice answered. "No, you'll come along with the rest of us like I said. How many times do I have to tell you? You have not just privileges, but duties. Everyone has. Whether you like it or not."

"I don't care. I'm tired. My feet hurt."

"Maybe if you weren't so spoiled with things like new shoes every year or two, they wouldn't. Do you know how much I spend on your frivolous ways, child? Do you know how much?"

The gang spread farther into the cavern. Licia and her mother appeared almost in front of me. I slid deeper into shadow.

"No one at all is down here. Frankie made a mistake." Licia glanced at Frank who had his gun pulled while he peered behind an adjacent mound.

Frank replied. "I don't make that kind of mistake, Miss L. It was *him*, I tell you."

"Well...I didn't see him, but we have to be sure. We simply cannot take the chance that that little tramp has come back. You said that Andrew took care of him, didn't you, according to Mr. Muck's instructions?"

"Yes, ma'am. Those were Andy's words."

"Then that should be that." Marm puffed her cherry pipette with one hand and rubbed the pearls around her neck with the other, throwing nervous glances in the darkness. "But you did hear something in the vault—we all heard something in the vault. And *no one* enters my vault without my permission. *No one.*"

Licia halted. Another blast of smoke hit her and she coughed into her curled hand. "I don't want to do this anymore. I'm tired." She thrust her face into Marm's. "If you don't let me go back right now, I'm going to rip up every napkin in Daddy's lounge, and then I will go to Tailors and I'll rip up every blouse. I swear I will." Licia shouted into Marm's face.

"I'm warning you, child. As long as you're living under my roof, you'll do as you're told."

"No, I won't. And I don't care about you. I hate you! I hate you and I hate Andrew. And I hate Tonya and her problem. And I hate the Bell, and I hate what you did to Daddy, and everything else that you and Mr. Muck are doing in Poland."

Down came the hand and slapped Licia across her face. Marm raised her palm again and struck twice. Licia staggered—covered her face with her hands and I noticed that she no longer was the keeper of the purse with the wafers. Apparently Marm had spanked her for some offence.

"How many times, child? How many times? When-oh-when will you learn to keep your mouth shut?" Marm exhaled deeply as if the life had gone out of her. "Oh, hell. Here. Have another wafer.

Have two. And go back up to the lounge. You're of no help here."

Marm extracted one round thin wafer and offered it to her daughter. Licia snatched it and ate it greedily. Her conniption seemed to pass. I decided the whole scene was more act than real, designed to extract extra feel-good pills from Dr. Feel-Good Mother.

Licia retreated. As the eyes of the clan rested on her back, I sank deeper into the cavern.

A door appeared. Not a steel vault door—not that the type of dance floor mattered a whit to my Indexer—but a routine unassuming door. Of metal to be sure but not the kind of door to suggest that anything lay beyond but an exit.

Just what the inmate ordered. Except with the gangsters close behind, and the darkness so deep, using my get-out-of-jail card might attract the wrong kind of attention and trigger a bums' rush in my wake—I tried the knob.

It opened.

A quick inspection showed that the lock only functioned to prevent access from the outside. Finally, I thought, a ray of rationality in this monument to bedlam.

Up I raced, across two, three platforms intersecting the stairways. A last door loomed. I opened it and found myself in the storage area of a clothing shop, large spools of fabric lining the walls, stacks of piebald cloth piled among them.

Glancing behind for sounds of pursuit, I stepped into the main reception area.

The last thing I expected was to be greeted by a pink-tongued reptile.

To an explosion of light, I ran straight at Andrew. The tongue retracted; Andrew's eyes grew round and I knew I had caught him in total surprise. His hands extended to halt my onrush—at the last moment I grabbed them with both my own hands and slid over the slick storeroom tile between Andrew's legs. Yet another little maneuver that only the napoleonic dare execute. Beneath him, I dragged his arms with me, yanking his mug face-first onto the floor.

A dull thud resulted—I hoped to high Heaven his awful tongue was the first to be crushed.

I wasn't done yet. In the midst of a half-dozen young women

'manning' the storefront and tending to customers, shock and surprise on their faces, I released the reptile's hands and, with memories of his gun-to-the-head execution of Ugly Joe fresh in my mind, planted one foot in Andrew's rear, jamming his face even flatter against the tiles.

Damn that felt good.

A deep breath of satisfaction at revenge long-delayed, I stood straight and grinned with my hands on my hips. Not even the knowledge that some specks of dust must have attached to my Canali suit dimmed my joy.

I started. The back door banged open and Marm's Mob came spilling out. Their eyes found me.

With a shout they raced forward.

Now wasn't the time for pride. Sure I had more tricks up my sleeve, and sure I could have dropped the lot of them with a little Chinee judo and Okinawee karate, but priorities called.

My dead cigar was still locked in my jaw. Turning, I jumped onto an adjacent clothes display and whipped out a lighter previously set to flame-thrower throttle. Guessing my intent, the mob paused. With an even broader grin, I sparked up the lighter.

"Pete. No," Marm shouted.

"Oh yes." I shuddered with anticipation. Raising the lighter to one of the fire sensors, the sensor triggered, and an instant later an avalanche of water cascaded from the sprinklers crisscrossing the clothing store.

I leaped down and raced out the front door, beating even the crowd of employees and spectators hurrying to exit.

In the street I paused. There was really no point in trying to outrun Marm and her Mob. Their legs were a damn sight longer than mine and they knew the French Quarter a damn sight better than I, and, besides, it was a certainty that someone had already called the Po-Po and my face would soon be on the laptop screen of every cop in New Orleans.

Marm exited into sunlight. Upon seeing me, she took a few steps, then halted. She glanced around, puzzled. Why wasn't I fleeing? I was just standing in the middle of Bourbon Street with a contented smile on my face. I could read the confusion in her talcum-powdered visage now streaked with water: why wasn't this pipsqueak begging for mercy or running for his life like every other miscreant that she had ever sicced her dogs on? The rest of the clan exited behind her and collected on either side, waiting for her signal to attack, twitching their legs and sleeves to shake off the water.

I snapped out my Saturday Night Smith & Wesson and spun the chamber.

Everyone—even gawking bystanders—ducked.

I fired two shots in the air. Before I could lower the gun, police cars appeared all round and another avalanche, this time of blue uniforms, enveloped me, guns at the ready.

"Let it drop, asshole."

I let it drop.

"I hope you like jail food, creep, cause that's your new home!"

As they clamped me in handcuffs and stuffed me in the back of a cruiser, I smiled at Marm. *Jail*...just what the doctor ordered.

CHAPTER 19

I walk the streets of N'Orleans
With the girl of my dreams on my arm...

Jazz trumpets and horns drifted on my mind like snowflakes on the Catskills. Monuments, catacombs, dead wise guys, voices from nowhere swarmed my brain, looking for some pattern to fall into. In my jail cell, shared with a dozen drunks each hoping to be the next Lightnin Hopkins, I enjoyed the sensation of not having to pay rent for a night or two and having hot meals thrust under my schnoz for free. For some of the drunks, their time as guests of Uncle Huey Long, very late though the former Gov may be, earned them the only square meals they were likely to get. To them, jail was *deed* home.

Not to a guy in an Italian suit, however. And not when he had a nice set of vengeance to inflict on two self-appointed Menlo Park wannabes trying to take over the world. Yeah, I was pretty sure of that. That line of dope they fed me about 'repairing reputations' by 'fixing bloopers' was wearing thin.

Sitting between a couple of Angola Prison grads, I rubbed my forehead and nudged forward on the metal bench to avoid my suit making contact with their grubby work clothes. Of course, I myself had more than a few 'bloopers' that could use some fixing, for example my face being posted in the entrance to the Vatican as the assassin of the Vicar of Christ. I wouldn't mind switching to an alternate universe just to remove that Wanted poster.

But I had no leverage. Though I was head over heels for Tonya, I still could not allow Montez & Muck, not to mention their gutter-cat friends, the Massolini clan, to harm Wendy even though she must be lost somewhere in the white peaks of Idaho by now. Images of her own peaks shattered my concentration for a moment. I was sure there was no way I could find her now, but I was just as sure that the Massolinis could find her faster than an addict finds a vein if I went too far out of line.

So again I swallowed my anger, my resentment, my gall. Not forever, mind you. One day I would vomit it up and spew it right over M&M's big-shot mugs, with a few chunks reserved just for 'Angelica', that purple-wearing, pearl-wrapping, cherry tobacco puffing, child abusing, drug pushing wop who probably had no more valid citizenship than her dead hero Carlos.

I didn't push those thoughts too far, however. After all, my parents had brought me to Brooklyn *after* preschool in Ireland, making me damned lucky to even have a passport.

So there was nothing more to be done. I waited for night to fall, and just before dawn on the morning of my appointment with a judge, I wangled a visit to the nurse's station where I zapped the back wall. A corridor and another wall later and I stood in the humid night air of a New Orleans side lot.

I made a stopover to grab another burner. A quick refreshing pass through a women's locker room was next on the itinerary, which, though the sight of me sent the ladies scurrying, only made me think even more of Tonya, so the push-button venture was less happy than I had supposed.

Finally I managed to penetrate the back of a genuine bank vault off Canal Street where I relieved the groaning shelves of multiple stacks of Franklins, stuffing as many hundred dollar bundles in my suit as I could carry. Only temporarily, of course. I'll pay it back if it takes decades. I'm just that kinda guy.

Emerging on the far side of the bank's back wall, I stepped into a parking lot. The sun's last rays as it rushed to embrace America's Great Western Desert threw red shades on several faces. Nary a one smiled. In the pit of my stomach I felt a great weight like a kid just caught by Mommy with his hand in the cookie jar. I'd been a bad boy—a very bad boy.

Six mugs were waiting.

A swollen purple tongue extending from a bruised mouth was accented by rapid-fire winking of a right eye. Andrew's mug made me want to hurl chunks and sing hallelujah at the same time. Want some more? I thought. I kept my mouth shut, but I couldn't keep a smile from transforming my own mug. As soon as I recognized him, no one on planet earth was happier at that moment than I.

Frankie thrust his rat-faced mug forward. And four more mugs that I recognized from Marm's cigar lounge appeared.

How did they find me? I glanced at my burner cell. Yep, they don't call it a burner for nothing.

Before I had a chance to react, the gang jumped me. To my surprise, no one gave me the Oswald onceover before stuffing me into another limo. It couldn't be the same one I had missed in Rome, could it? Or could M&M even switch cars when changing universes?

Inside the car, no one pulled out the rubber hose, cop-style. They didn't even grab the cash that bulged in my pockets, making me look like a raggedy Pete doll. I almost said Raggedy Andy, but I felt so sorry for the purple-tongued wretch sitting shotgun with his damaged face glaring at mine, and his right eye flicking like an unplugged stoplight, that I almost couldn't bear to rub it in. Almost, I said? Nyet! The hallelujahs rolled and I kept grinning.

Over the cobblestones of old New Orleans we rattled. No speeding. No need. Frankie knew where he was driving, and though I was certain no cop would interfere with Massolini business, he seemed careful about attracting undesired attention. This is New Orleans, after all, where the people don't tolerate corruption—they *demand* it.

Were we heading back to *le Quartier Francais* and the ever-missing Rick of Rick's Cigar Lounge? The streets passed beneath our wheels once and again. We were nowhere near Bourbon or Canal St.

We hopped a freeway, turned till I got confused, then raced under gathering gray clouds. Sprinkles clouded our windows and finally we launched ourselves in a westward direction.

There's little to say about the trip. We chased the sun, madly pursuing the yellow orb as it melded into red and, after the disc had vanished over the horizon, still drove west. Ever west. All night we drove and all morning, pausing only once or twice to obey nature's needs under the close eye of my captors, then in late afternoon after endless miles of flatness the car plunged into winding hills. No one had called on me to help with driving—which was good because I would have selected the nearest ditch and wrecked the thing—so I'd had a long opportunity to rest and to sleep.

When we arrived at the familiar guard-gate, I snapped a smart salute at the sullen attendants. They ignored me and merely nodded at Andrew, who had taken the wheel from Frankie. Up the hill we drove until we came to a halt before the same Frank Lloyd Wrong monstrosity I had previously visited in the hills to the east of Albuquerque.

Before I could exit the limo with dignity, the gang dragged me out by my bent elbows and without ceremony pushed me into the house. Still no gators, I noticed. For a second, I thought I had escaped being paddled, but Papas One and Two came into view, shattering that illusion.

Bob Montez turned to face me. I had mistaken skinny Bob for a Greek pillar so had not noticed him at first.

"Pinky," called Jack Muck. He approached from across the foyer. Jack had abandoned his burgundy shorts for full-length burgundy pants but with similar white embroidery traveling up the side of each leg, making him appear even more like the mariachi player he had formerly reminded me of. He wore the same style white shirt, but these sleeves ended in scattered white French frills, his barrel chest overlaid oddly by blue suspenders. Jack smiled, his bald head and face still slathered with spray-on orange. Knowing a bit more by now about Jack and Bob's subtle calculations, I wondered if even the orange spray had some unspoken purpose.

Jack dropped his smile. He frowned like a father. "You disappoint me, Pinky. You vasted much time vith your playing around in Rome and New Orleans." He glanced at Bob who wore his usual light lavender jacket and pants with wide white lapels, his white ponytail swinging as he rocked from side to side, hands in pockets.

"Told ya so..." Bob withdrew his hands from his pockets and waved them both in the air, index fingers extended, his body swaying side to side like he was inventing a new doo-wop dance. He grinned with his usual schadenfreude.

"No, Bob. Our little man has much left to do for us. Ve still need him."

"If you think he can do the job. I wouldn't give Pinky the time of day after his flop in Italy."

Jack dropped his glance. "He tried, Bob." He looked back at me. "You did try, didn't you, Pinky? You tried your best."

I stared through half-closed eyes. I was starting to do a slow burn. If not for rat-boy on one side and Andrew the winking salamander on the other, I would have launched myself at both of these mad scientists and given them something more than purple tongues to complain about.

"You got your goddamn rock, didn't ya?" I said. "Isn't that all in this goddamn world that you care about?"

"Oh-oh-oh," responded Jack with a grin, casting a surprised look at Bob.

Bob smirked and stared at the floor.

"The bantam-veight little man again vants to throw his veight around. That von't vork, Pinky. You see, ve know all about your *little activities.*" Jack whispered, greatly amused: "Ve know *exactly* vhat you have done." Jack smiled even more broadly and Bob smiled back. Jack winked, ignoring the ugly frown from ever-winking Andrew. "Yes, ve do."

"Crack that whip, Jack. Pinky's been bad."

"I'm afraid so, Bob. That ve cannot allow."

Jack sat in his usual place on the divan with the square glass table by his knees. Bob continued to stand behind him.

I had no chance to sit. So far I had managed to keep the stacks of cash inside my suit, though I was painfully aware that my suit concealed nothing and, though my pockets still bulged with loot, Marm's thugs had so far made not the slightest attempt to deprive me of my bank-gotten gains. Now, at a signal from Jack, Andrew jumped me and, together with Frankie the Rat, ransacked my pockets, depriving me of every bill I had borrowed, leaving me more busted than Gypsy Rose Lee. I *vill* pay it back von day, I *svear.*

Andy and Frankie danced a little posy while holding up the wadded cash. At a glance from Bob, they calmed and stacked it all on a small side-table before returning to guard me with folded arms. Through all this time, including the long trip, Andy's compulsive winking and projecting purple tongue hadn't faltered.

Finally I sat, occupying my previous place on the divan across from Jack.

"You must never do that again, little man," scolded Jack. "You might throw things out of kilter, not to mention attract police attention to our Sirius Enterprises. Vhich is most *serious*, I assure you, Pinky."

"And don't get any big ideas, Pete," added Bob. "They may be police, but they're *our* police. If ya get my drift."

I got it, all right. I drifted right through the Gulf Stream all the way to Ireland before I came back to earth.

"So won't do nobody no good to go cryin' 'bout this to no one." Bob propped his hands in superior hot-shit style on his lavender hips.

Involuntarily, I nodded.

"And I also must varn you against...how to say?" Jack glanced at Bob.

"Dumpster diving?" suggested Bob with a shrug.

"Vell, that is von way to put it," Jack said.

"Sailing the light fantastic," Bob added.

I cocked my head at Bob's eloquence, knew he wasn't done yet.

"Looking up Joseph's technicolor coat."

"Wrong gender, *Bob*," I spat out, drawing out his nasty name.

"As long as you're gettin' the message, player. Don't play. That's the message. You don't walk into no more women's locker rooms cause we ain't lookin' to become Page One news. Ya *got* me?" Bob posed like George Raft and flipped an imaginary coin in the air, though his ponytail destroyed the illusion.

I nodded again. If only I were more than a bug squirming under M&M's thumb, I could finally do something about it. Even a bug deserves to play once in a while. But I breathed deeper. Now that my hiney was spanked, I let my gaze wander about the room and wondered if Marm had taken the poodles with her to N'Orleans. Letting a combination of the two diddle in my brain, I couldn't help but laugh, and my thoughts had even more fun when I threw missing Licia into the mix... But when Tonya stood next in line, I stopped smiling.

Playtime was over.

I looked back to the mad scientist Dr. Einstein-oppenheimer-burg and his sidekick Woodstock Bob. For some reason I didn't feel like reminding myself that old times is old times. I was ready for these times to end.

"So what's *left to do*?" I blew out my air, crinkled one corner of my mouth, and let my gaze settle on the floor.

"That is better, Pinky. You are so much better vhen you cooperate. You become...how to say? So much *bigger* in our estimation." Jack grinned another big one at Bob, who *cooperated* in their little joke, which, like all of their jokes, was at my expense.

"Mexico, player." Bob looked down his sharp nose at me. "How's your *espanol*, amigo?"

"Concerning mad scientists who use people up and throw them away?" I sniffed. "*De nada.*"

A giggle bubbled from Jack's stolid body. "Our Pinky has a sense of the humor, dear Bob. Oh, that adds so much entertainment to our potentially *boring* vork." He grinned back at me.

"Just like monkey gyms," Bob said.

I stepped suddenly back. Could M&M's police connections extend all the way to Albuquerque's Homicide Division, including Detectives Dorkman and Krupke? I shook the unpleasant thought away.

"Von of our dear Andrew's favorite phrases, Pinky. He spread it all over town—unfortunately now dear Andrew has difficulty saying anything at all." Jack displayed a sympathetic half-frown in Andy's direction, and Andy winked both eyes alternately like a boat with a stuck purple rudder. The spectacle was so revolting that Jack and I both shuddered and looked away. Had I ever seen Jack Muck show sympathy for anyone before this? Nein. And I doubted it would ever repeat. Caring for others just didn't seem in his makeup.

I couldn't resist. "*Tiempo pagar la rent. Solo una familia en el apartamento.*" I looked at Andrew. "*Señor Andrew, digame...el gato tiene tu lingua?*"

Montez & Muck burst out laughing. Andrew clearly got the drill and reacted as if electrocuted, biting down so hard on his swollen appendage that blood spurted.

As he writhed in pain, Jack said, "That vill do, Pinky. Your Spanish is good enough. In fact better than ours. Isn't that so, Bob?"

Bob was frowning. He was never happy when someone knew more than he did, unless it was the great Jack Muck.

Jack continued, "So much *left to do*. Oh yes, Pinky, there is *very* much that is *left to do*."

"What's on your dance card, Muck? And don't try to tell me it's all for charity." My empty pockets had put me in a foul mood— fouler even than what usually followed my abductions.

More giggles from the balding Czech. "And do not try to tell me that you don't dance, Pinky. In the end, despite yourself, you *vere* successful in Rome."

"I danced okay, Jack, including the tango. But it seems someone didn't go home with the date that brung him."

Jack glanced inquisitively at Bob.

"Little guy's still pissed that he missed the plane."

Mouth opening, Jack paused then added, "Yet another cute colloquial expression from our Pinky." He grinned broader. "But you found your vay back anyvay. I believed you vould. In fact, ve've been vaiting for you." He glanced at his watch. "I'm only disappointed that you took so long." Jack shrugged. "Oh vell. No matter. It's time to move on."

"Not so fast, Muck." It was my turn to point the big finger. "Why the hell didn't you tell me that your drug was poison?"

Jack's brows lifted an inch. "Vould you have administered it if you had known the truth?"

"But why, for God's sake? Don't you know you tricked me into *murdering the Pope*?"

"Only in *this* universe, Pinky, not in any other! You can sleep big and easy knowing that in all the others you killed no von."

Like that really helped. I slunk my gaze back to the floor. Where was the universe where I got to keep those bundles of cash?

"It vas necessary to eliminate this Pope in order to be certain that you vould recover the Stone. Ve did not vant to vorry you vhile you vere executing your task, so ve told you...a little vhite lie." Jack shrugged. "But don't vorry, Pinky. Ve have the Blarney Stone now, and ve have extracted the crystals that ve desired from its depths. And now that ve are through vith the Stone ve shall deliver it back to Ireland vhere it belongs, in von piece and vith no harm done." Muck stood there, the tips of each hand's fingers touching its counterparts. "Of course, it vill not speak to anyvon any more. But that is all that you need to know about this need-to-know subject. It is time to discuss your next assignment."

I pursed my lips. How long a dance card did these jokers have planned for me? While I listened, my mind thought about crystals: a crystal in my finger, crystals extracted from the Stone... What was this leading to?

"Near the city of Juarez, vhat the qvaint locals call I believe 'Ciudad Juarez', there is a place."

"Just in the outskirts," added Bob, serious.

"A shack on a hill. But the locals take this place *veery* seriously, Pinky. In order to find this place, ve must first contact two gentlemen named El Chapo and Mayor José Gonzalez. Vhen you find them...you vill *kill* them."

Now my own brows rose. "Say again?"

Jack smiled at me. "*Kill* them, Pinky." He pointed his finger. "Vith a gun." His biggest grin.

"Guys..." I shifted my feet. "I ain't no wise guy...or assassin. You really got the wrong joe to do all this."

"Nonsense, Pinky. You are exactly the man for this job. Despite Bob's doubts, I believe that you are *up* to the task."

That really hurt. I glanced at Bob who stared down at me with his usual bigger and better than thou frown with his arms folded across his white-lapeled chest while Jack stood there and smiled, his arms spread open in good salesman fashion.

"Won't work, gentlemen. I'm onto your good-cop bad-cop routine."

Bob frowned even more but he stopped folding his arms. He looked at Jack. "Told ya so, doubles. Maybe you should clue events to the Man in the Moon."

Far from being annoyed by Bob's comment, Jack replied with a bland expression and a straight face, "No, dear Bob. Ve still have our obligation, and now that ve have the means in hand, ve must fulfill it von way or another," Jack smiled back at me, "and I still have confidence in our little Pinky here that he shall come through and help us achieve our goals." He expanded, large as life. "You *vant* to help us, don't you, Pinky? You *vant* us to achieve our little Enterprise, do you not?"

With visions of quicksand, gators, angry poodles, a drug-pushing mafia queen, mad-hatter scientists, and a gang of hardened killers, all focused on murdering Wendy, not to mention myself, and capable of even worse regarding Tonya if I didn't cooperate...what could I say?

"Why the hell not?" I kicked at the floor.

Jack beamed. "There, dear Bob. You see? Your doubts are not justified. I know that our obligations to the Man in the Moon are behind us, and ve had thought that ve vere over that phase of our life, but vhy not try if the probabilities once more have...how to say...come home to roost."

"*Are in our court,*" Bob said.

"Ah, that is the expression. *Are in our court*, once more. Tank you, dear Bob."

"Just like Vegas. In the right universe, every game you play comes up cherries. And then you own the city."

"Yes, yes. Do you get it, my dear Pete? So long as ve have the capability of selecting the odds, there is nothing to vorry about. So find Chapo and José...and *shoot* them."

"If you think Pistol Pete has the nerve." Bob smirked.

"Vell, it never hurts to remind Pinky of the alternative to helping out." Jack took out his cell phone and punched it with his hammer fingers.

My burner came to life. I entered my secret code and immediately the old picture of myself firing a gun into Taxi Joe's head re-appeared, followed by a new one of Wendy walking in a snowy scene with Idaho mountains behind her. They had tracked her faster than I had feared. Even I didn't know what part of Idaho she had moved to.

"All done, then." Jack rose to his feet. "It is time to go to the plane. Grab your things. The von thing ve cannot replace gentlemen is *time.*"

The gang proceeded to race about, retrieving bags and stuffing them, while Frankie stood still and kept a level eye on me, one hand in his pocket. Jack and Bob briefly disappeared then returned with suitcases that, from Bob's less muscular effort, must have been packed full of clothes and—what else?—my cash, I was sure, that I had stolen fair and square and which had now gone into M&M's pockets. That is, discounting the notes that would end up with tobaccy-packin' Marm.

Left with almost nothing and warned not to 'borrow' more from local banks, and given no time to pack any of my own stuff, I tagged along as the Einstein Gang piled into the same limo as before and took off down the winding road.

A half-hour later we arrived at a tiny rural airfield with a half dozen private aircraft lined up on one side.

As we exited the limo, Bob sidled closer. "We're travelin' to Argentina, player, with a short stopover in Juarez. We want to check up on our office where we're doin' video shoots for the Big Fishes. You'll get further instructions when we get there."

Okay, I nodded. I was relieved to have a plane ride. Juarez wasn't too far from Albuquerque, but after my long car trip from New Orleans I wasn't eager to make my own way.

Andrew and the rest hauled their bags to a sleek mid-sized jet, the largest plane on the strip. Soon, they had their baggage loaded and mobile stairs positioned for boarding. Last in line with my own bags in hand, I realized that the few airport personnel had made no effort to inspect our items. Must have left their brains in another universe, I mused. Either that, or they too were beneficiaries of my bank heist.

Jack and Bob climbed the stairs in front of me and entered the plane, followed by the rest of the gang, and Frankie after he had parked the limo, and finally Andrew, with me bringing up the rear.

Andrew had improved a bit, despite my little joke, and was at last able to keep his tongue in his mouth on occasion with the result that he had recovered the power of speech. The old reptile tongue still darted out at inconvenient times, however, and his right eye still blinked, but it was less unappealing than before—I found I preferred reptiles to boats.

At the top of the mobile stairs, Andrew halted. Turning, he looked me in the eye. "Not you, Pete! Here's your bus ticket." Throwing the ticket in the air, he shoved me down the steps where I came to a stop at the bottom. Andrew waved at me with a grin, stepped inside the plane, and sealed the door.

The engine gushed.

Scrambling, I picked up my fedora and raced back to the limo before the exhaust consumed me. A movie-extra gangster still sat behind the wheel. Seeing me, he peeled rubber.

Alone, I stood on the tarmac staring as the jet climbed and turned south while the back of the limo shrank in the distance without me, my burner cell phone in pieces on the ground.

Some people fly. Some people drive. We all know what kind of people walk.

CHAPTER 20

In the beginning, God said The Word and created the Universe. What posterity missed was that he changed his mind in mid-sentence because he had uttered the wrong word. "Wait a minute, I really meant to say..." But it was too late. The Universe was done. And done with one lousy word, without even the usual common-sense conditioners and qualifiers that normally come with a complete thought.

So now we have a world filled with spades, chinks, spics, dagos, guineas, gippos, huns, jigaboos, wops, wogs, flips, frogs, gringos, gooks, goys, golliwogs, micks, crackers, rednecks, kaffirs, kikes, yids, shylocks, crips, bloods, zips, krauts, limeys, pakis, squaw-jumpers, fuzzy-wuzzies, and Congolese jungle bunnies from the remotest plantations of Tarzan-land. But who am I to judge? I'm just a Blarney-Stone-kissing, paddy-wagon riding, bad-check-writing, snowy-mountain-spelunking Irish-Amerikanski refugee from the jungles of Babylonian Brooklyn, the city that killed Cyrus and dug Swan, and spread dodgers and goombas over the rest of the country like Santa Claus with Ebola.

But hell if I would take a bus.

Andrew's bus ticket read: *One way – Ciudad Juarez.* I snorted. No way, Mayor José. I had my own transportation, and after a not-so-quick thumb ride from a couple of pill-hopped highwaymen who thought they were cruising the interstate from Mars to Jupiter, I was soon back in Oriental-land where the clothes dryers and chemical cleaners revolved with the certainty of the sun. Thank Thor the Queen of Cheena wasn't in, and with a smart crawl under the barbed wires of the DMZ, I managed to locate my locker and smuggle out the keys to my antique Oldsmobile and motor it away before I found myself in yet another ground war in Asia.

It was night, so why not? I paused at one of the Irish bars and threw back a White Zombie. This time I couldn't resist and followed it with a Singapore Sling, then a shot-glass of the wormiest Tequila the bar could find just to fortify me for wrestling with taco-goons south of the Big Ditch. Then, after removing my suit and folding it on the front seat, I stretched full-out on the back seat of my car and instantly entered a wonderland of bank vaults and women's changing rooms where no one could see the Invisible Man as I wandered open-eyed and smiling, except for the Chosen One who happily followed me to realms that were even more private.

The next morning, I came back to this universe and prepared for the task ahead. I had reluctantly picked up M&M's fucking bus ticket the day before and now, slowly and deliberately, I placed it under one wheel of my car. Slowly and deliberately, I drove over it.

I didn't stop until I was well out of Albuquerque, the afternoon sun glittering off the peeling green paint of my hood as I purred south in my 'rental' from Honest Juan, wondering suddenly how the hell I would cross the border without a passport. Then I remembered. Montez & Muck crossed borders from universe to universe and no one yet had stopped the exercise of my little red button to ask me for identification papers. That's another little detail that God forgot when he stammered over his Word: an inter-dimensional police force to stop galactic wetbacks and coyotes like Montez & Muck. A little thing like a DHS gumshoe to inspect universe border-jumpers apparently wasn't worth a second's thought.

Still, barreling an entire car through the cone of magic that the red button shined didn't seem like the greatest idea, and the prospect of sitting in an alternate-universe Mexico with only a seat and a steering wheel after a partial leap made me decide to go a bit more legit.

When I finally rolled into the outskirts of El Paso, having left Truth and Las Cruces behind, I stopped just short of the last bend in the road to the carefully selected Good Neighbor International Bridge. In the noon-day heat, parked by the side of the road, I leaned casually against my car and struck up my e-cig ('Fruitopia' brand juice), making sure to flash some green.

A car soon stopped. Two rancheros in straw hats stepped out

and between grunts and eye rolls it turned out that my Espanol was good enough to conclude the deal: they agreed to drive my car to the location I provided in Juarez and leave it by the curb—whether or not there was one—and not to fuck with the car because I'm tight with the Juarez Cartel, see?, and they'll have your names and faces if you cross me.

I flashed more cash and got photos of their faces and their Matricula permits before finally crossing their eager callused *palms* with green inked *coconuts*. Confused but suitably respectful, they drove the Olds across the Bridge, one ranchero driving my car, the other their own, both unconcerned that my car might contain drugs since no one smuggles *las drogas* southward.

That left me walking. In ten minutes I had reconnoitered the American customs station and found the best wall to walk through once darkness fell.

It did. Because that's what the Word said, and who was the Earth to disobey the command of the Holiest of Holy pronouncements that 'In The Beginning' reverberated and that still reverberates throughout the infinite universes that exist veiled and hidden all around us. Funny what a schmuck can learn just by opening his office door on a sunny day in May.

The wall, however, wasn't so much a wall as a corner metal door opening toward the Bridge, dense enough that no amount of force could break it. So at closing time, under cover of doused facility lights inside and twilight outside, my fedora and I wrapped in an abandoned Oaxacan wool overcoat, on the presumption that cameras were always watching, I zapped the selected private spot and prepared to walk through to...well, if not to freedom, at least to a universe further from the non-freedom in which I was caught.

Aiming my digit, I let fly—without warning, the door opened. The twilight revealed an American customs officer returning from his rounds inspecting the underside of the International Bridge, his power flashlight still lit.

I was already in movement, too late to stop. Once again Napoleon came to my rescue and I slid past the officer under his bright beam while he marched into the facility. Distracted by the image of red spume bubbling directly in front of him, the officer jerked to a halt. His mouth dropped. Then he became aware of a Oaxacan-wrapped *Mexicano* beside him and forgot all about the spume.

"What the hell, amigo?"

His two large hands grabbed me. Thank Jesús this officer was all gringo and knew less Espanol than me.

"*El tiempo bueno?*" I mumbled.

His large hands pushed me dutifully away from the open door and toward the Bridge.

"Not today, José. Crossing time is over. Come back mañana. Or go to another bridge."

I was tempted to let my eyes drop in disappointment and turn away. That's all that duty required. But suspended behind the officer and covering the open doorway remained that bubbling cauldron my finger had created, like a web lying in wait, about to bring a fate impossible to guess to this man. I had crossed into a universe IDed just for me, in which everything would be precisely the same. He had no such selection and was going the wrong way. What were the odds of everything being the same for him? I didn't need Montez or Muck to explain what was about to happen.

"Señor..." I faked my best fake Mexican accent, which would fool no one but an unschooled gringo, "...pleeze do not go through the door. I don' know how to splain myself, but beleeve me, you don' wan' to do that. You must wait here several *minutos*."

A look of disbelief came over the man. Staring down as from a great height, though of course from my point of view every height is great, at this insult from a mere Mexican peon, he let loose a laugh.

"What's that you say, little man?"

"Pleeze, sir, something very bad weell happen to you if you walk through that door. I beg you, Señor. Pleeze wait."

Another wave of laughter burst from his lungs. Indignantly, he shoved me away from the facility in the direction of the Bridge, and, drawing himself to full height as if to emphasize his hot-shit superiority, his eyes still on me, he walked straight through the cauldron. For one moment he seemed to pause, his eyes gazing around as if he saw things invisible to me, then he slammed the metal door shut and a rattle of keys from the inside marked his locking multiple locks.

A nightmare—a paradise—or the same universe as mine? I had no way of knowing what it was he encountered. And I never would. Whatever world the officer had entered, it was his alone and not for the prying eyes of others.

Slipping across the bridge in the darkness, walking past late or disappointed clients seeking entry into *Los Estados Unidos* one way or another, I suddenly realized that the Indexer had needed the metal door only to *create* the field, and that the field had remained at the threshold for a time even though the door itself had been moved. M&M might have mentioned this. What other secrets were they hiding?

In Juarez, I placed my fedora back on my head and walked the several blocks to the address M&M had given me. Despite being in Juarez, I was beginning to feel confident and sure. The confidence and sureness wasn't in *me*, however, it was in the power and terror of the local cartel, which I was certain no local would dare defy, and which the fact of my association with the two Mexican mules had likely spread.

And there was my car, peeling green paint and all, untouched. And the office. The corner street sign was half eroded, but the wooden sign erected over the little storefront was readable even in the growing darkness of the Juarez night: 'Videos Para Ti'.

Parked in front of the gleaming steel shutters that plated the front of the little commercial stall was another limo. Was I again dreaming? No, it was not the same limo, but an even fancier version, its black color tinged with magenta, my ancient heap taking up space behind it. I glanced up and down *la calle*.

Down the block, in the light of cell phones, locals dressed in a mix of traditional *camisas* and *pantalones* with Wal-Mart sunshades and orange sneakers carefully avoided eye contact and moved away from the suddenly popular stall with the picture of the videocam memorialized in painted pine above.

No one in Juarez wanted anything memorialized.

Yeah, I got that message.

Across the narrow street, almost blocking non-existent traffic were poised two more vehicles: a pair of Land Rovers. Spanking new. I detected two more faces hidden in the darkness, watching me from behind the Rovers. No orange shoes or *camisas* here, just black clothing to match the black of the Rovers, their thick shirts suggesting hidden side-pistols.

So much for arriving incognito.

The grey-steel shutters had been lowered over the front of the office, leaving no way to bang on the door, which was also made of steel. In the darkness I saw no videocam or other means to alert those inside to my presence. Do I knock shave-and-a-haircut? Or rattle merchandise like a vacuum salesman? Somehow neither seemed appropriate given the steady stare of *los buenos amigos*, the down-south good-fellas, watching in the growing darkness from across *la calle*.

My gaze settled on a series of color photos of underage Mexicanas advertising various sex acts pasted on an adjoining wall when, without warning, the shutters kicked into gear and glided noisily upward as some motor jumped. The noise of the motor cranking up the half-inch thick and heavy shutters must have been audible from one end of Juarez to the other. A lump of nervousness rose in my throat.

A door flung open—inward, to prevent being lifted from its hinges by strangers. From the suddenly exposed interior, light blazed and lit up the four vehicles parked in front of the office like it was Cinco de Mayo, and a swarm of voices shattered the silence, echoing up and down the street till even those distant observers with their glowing cell phones, formerly eager to make themselves scarce, paused to stare.

The two muchachos tending the Land Rovers came to life. Hurrying into the street, they swung the street-side doors of the Rovers open wide. Out of the office strode Jack Muck and Bob Montez, still clad in their same partial-Mexican attire, Jack poodle-less, Bob still waving his hot-shit nose in the air like a gun. Behind them walked Frankie the Rodent...and Andrew, Mr. Tongue-Action himself, his purple appendage finally having reverted to its former hunt-and-peck style, still no one but me seeming to take offense.

More to the point was the pair of new faces in the group exiting the shop. The first was light-skinned, stolid, and tall—that is, taller than me, which I guess doesn't say much—but from the way he kept repeating 'Argentina' in smooth musical tones, I gathered he was speaking Espanol with a South-South American accent, absent the more clipped delivery of local border-jumpers. Mr. Argentina wore a suit, though not much of one as I noticed in the glaring light flowing from the office's open door and windows. Well, we can't all have good taste.

The other muchacho was...no, he was not a muchacho. Focusing on his short size my first glance had missed his wide broom mustache. On closer inspection in the bright light I managed to make out a pockmarked face and skin far darker than the first fellow's and a Wal-Mart-special pullover aqua shirt. Jack put his arm around the short man's shoulders in friendly fashion and they headed for one of the Rovers. In the middle of the street, Jack bent over to hug him and they exchanged cheek-kisses, which led me to ponder if Muck was really of East European origin since that sort of thing I'm pretty sure isn't done there. To my surprise, Jack and the Argentine then did the same, followed by Bob with each. Cheek-kisses flew all around.

"*Mucha gracia, amigo. Coge los otros para mi.*"

Jack looked puzzled.

Bob translated. "Fuck 'em good, my friend."

In the glaring light, Jack grinned. "You may be certain that ve vill, Señor Chapo. Vithout exception."

Bob added, "*Y hasta luego*, José. We'll return soon from Buenos Aires."

The big Argentinean shook hands with Jack. "*Pronto*, Señor Muck. *Pronto.* We are the last Peronistas. It is up to us to bring your great plan to successful conclusion."

"*Mucha gracia,*" rang from every throat as the two visitors crossed to the Land Rovers. I watched as El Chapo—who else could it be?—slid into the back seat of the Rover. His driver jumped behind the wheel, gunned the engine, flicked on the lights, and lurched away.

Behind him, Señor José Gonzalez, the Mayor of La Ciudad de Juarez, as I instantly concluded, slid into the back seat of the other Rover. The other driver jumped behind the wheel, spun round, and took off in the opposite direction, presumably Juarez City Hall.

Oh, I got it, all right. Boy, did I ever. I tried to keep my knees from rattling as I contemplated the dwindling backsides of the cruelest mass murderers in Mexican history: El Chapo, and his chief protector in these here parts, ex-Argentinean Mayor José Gonzalez.

Before I could utter a word of fear—or surprise—Bob and Jack slid into the back seat of their black-magenta limo, and Frankie and Andrew, after performing their duties by shutting the limo's back doors, entered the front seat. The engine leaped to life and the limo banged over potholes in the direction of what I gathered must have been the closest airport to resume the flight of their private jet to Buenos Aires.

It was like standing on the tarmac again.

For a minute I stood there in semi-shadow, unnoticed *again*, given the backhand treatment *again*, left to stew in the juices of M&M's high-and-mighty kick-him-in-the-nuts and see-if-he-squeals attitude *again* since Jack and Bob must have known that I had been standing there watching, my car being parked *right the hell* behind their own.

Did I rate so low on their Richter Scale that they did not even bother to take thirty seconds to give me the gist of my assignment— the gist being *just how the hell am I supposed to kill El Chapo and Mayor José?* And why in hell didn't they tell me that they were the best of friends with their targets, as I just witnessed in this little kumbaya episode?

I blinked.

Maybe that was why...the less M&M notice me, the more plausible the outcome. That didn't explain their lack of objection to my parking my car in front of their own stall. But maybe my rancheros had parked it too late for M&M to object and M&M didn't want to endanger their plans by acknowledging me...okay, that made sense...so I swallowed my gall. Guessing *why* they treated me so badly, though, didn't make it go down any better.

I turned back to the entrance. The door remained open with the light glaring forth like a circus and I ventured into the full glare of its shine. As if expecting me, a diminutive Mexican woman stared without reaction from inside. Briefly she turned her head.

This way.

Relieved to finally find someone shorter than me, I stepped in.

Once I was inside, she pulled a lever and the heavy steel shutters came rattling down, cutting off the eternal darkness from the nourishing light. Mounting (with some difficulty) a high step positioned halfway through the foyer, where fancy *biznizmen* meet customers trudging in from the street, she led me around the show-counter with its loud posters advertising the shop's video services, which promised wildly successful *Quinceaneras* to happy fathers. We then walked past several side rooms filled with sound poles and backlight frames and green curtains into a partially lit back chamber—a small warehouse that had been converted into an observation room.

I'd seen this type of *cockpit* before.

A wooden bar spanned most of the width of the warehouse, mounted behind the bar a line of glowing monitors, the overheads dimmed to enhance the images. So this was where Montez & Muck shot videos for the cartel big-shots, meaning especially Chapo and José, and viewed them. Did they realize that M&M had actually set up this operation not to make money but rather to ease their victims' suspicions before somehow *killing* them?

Somehow...well, that was the issue, wasn't it?

In front of the wooden bar stood a pair of wooden stools, still slowly turning from where they had been recently occupied.

"*Los jefes se fueron,*" declared the cleaning woman with firmness, stating the obvious. Behind her, two monitors suddenly displayed horizontal voice patterns that responded to the volume of her speech, no other scenes appearing on the black screens. Around the corner of the bar, she pulled open a drawer and extracted a large envelope. Returning, she handed it to me.

"*Para ti.*"

It was sealed. As she took up a mop and wiped the floor, I broke the seal of the envelope and withdrew two large full-color photos. For a moment I thought it was more photos of underage Mexican girls and wondered if M&M had decided to go in for pimping child porn, and I turned the photos away from the cleaning woman's sight, but they were something else: two photos of Chapo and Mayor José respectively with guns aimed at their heads just like the one that M&M had sent me of my own hand firing a gun at Ugly Joe's mug, and again by digital magic what looked like *my* own hand doing the killing. M&M must be serious. More *bloopers* to destroy my reputation—in glorious print even.

Sliding the photos back into the envelope, I closed the flap. Offered the envelope to the Mexican munchkin. (Yes, I can be hot-shit and mighty, too.) She continued to mop the floor and wordlessly indicated the open drawer. I walked to the drawer to drop it in.

Paused.

Inside the drawer was a *third* color photo.

I picked it up, watching the cleaning woman from the corner of my eye. Focused and sullen, she pushed her out-sized mop. I inspected the picture. It showed a shrine of a peculiar little statue of a brown Mexican in a white suit and black necktie, perched on a table-stand, with gray rocks and stones piled behind, the kind that Mexican peasants toss on the bones of their saints for good luck.

Behind the statue on a wooden plaque was posted the words: "*Gracias a Dio y a Malverde por protegérme siempre.*" I knew just enough Español to translate: 'Thanks be to God and to Malverde for always protecting me.' Around the statue sprouted flowers and a line of lit candles. True to the name 'Malverde', no green was visible, green, or 'verde', being the color of misfortune among these ancient sun worshipers.

I blinked—hard.

Jes*ús* Malverde himself, the patron saint of drug traffickers, smugglers, and professional killers in Mexico. My knees rattled until, with effort and embarrassed for a weakness to be seen even by a cleaning woman, I summoned images of Humphrey Bogart, George Raft—and just to be sure, James Cagney, all guys bigger than Nature made them—till my knees finally calmed.

More could be seen. On the photo was traced in pen an arrow pointing to the lower part of the statue which was devoid of paint, revealing black raw stone. The arrow was clear, no mistaking it.

After a moment's hesitation, staring into the darkest corners of the warehouse ceiling as if the answers might lurk like cobwebs, I wordlessly slid the envelope into the drawer on top of the photo of the shrine, my knees back to normal.

Approaching the woman, I pointed at my Movado and she paused. She stepped to a back door and inserted a key in the massive steel door and slowly opened the heavy slab—also inward.

I walked into the night. I thought: I really ought to prepare an invoice. M&M's demands on my time as a professional killer were mounting. And after seeing that third photo of the *Mexicano* shrine, it may be time to demand a tip.

CHAPTER 21

I couldn't stop turning it over in my mind. As I headed for a late-night cantina, I tried to puzzle it out. Just why did M&M want Chapo and José dead? And why did they want *me* to do the job? They could recruit a pair of locals to do it, though maybe, given the power and intimidation of the cartel, that was not so easy. That might explain why they wanted me as the hit man. But that did not explain why they had such interest in a local religious icon.

The third photo kept coming back. Red... green... black... what did these have in common? My mind filled with images of these colors. Red for red volcanoes—not only the frightening eruptions that I stepped through every time I walked through walls, but other eruptions, other magma, other volcanoes such as the ones that cracked and steamed in Mexico, and that fiery Gaelic flag of *La Resistánce*, my red hair.

Green for Ireland—and not only the green of its luxurious grasslands and rocky peninsulas thrusting like thirsty tongues to lap up the generosity of the Atlantic Gulf Stream, but for luck, both good and bad, the luck of those ancient Gaelic Druids sacrificing to the gods of their woods and creeks to grant a good harvest and many young lambs, *gamboling* that the gods would hear and obey, pressing their pale ears to their ancient holy stone, hoping for some response, some voice however dim, to coach humans in their sacrifices, guide them in their struggles—struggles that perhaps were no different in other places, other hemispheres, other countries—and green for Tonya's green eyes, accentuated by the green fringes of her jacket.

Black for the color of the rest of her jacket, and for the Blarney Stone itself, the color of Hades and Chaos, the source of wisdom, the channel to the Above, the Ear of Dagda, the Mouth of Odin. Could there be another Ear, another Mouth, in another land, another Magic

Stone similarly black as night, similarly sought by these inter-galactic border jumpers, Muck & Montez, which they wished to obtain for similar though still mysterious purposes? I kept thinking even as I passed through the swinging door of the cantina and headed for a seat. The smoke inundated me, out-doing even the ever-present accumulus of the foyer at Suite Chicas. I sat as far in one corner as I could manage, far from the jumping-jack Juans and Josés who popped heavenward with every beat of Conjunto that blared through the interior, like polkafied reggae on steroids. I was in my element. Though my ear was not tuned to the back-beat (my taste being more for jazz and Sinatra) I could be myself, relax a trifle when in the company of undersized personas, whether Gaelic, Texmex, or Russki, conscious that neither the dancers nor the servers were likely to tower over me as was usually the case in the States.

My gaze passed over red sweat vests, Tijuana blue-jean knock-offs, Velcro Target sneakers, and the occasional huge sombrero on top that made the short people underneath seem even shorter. As their Lilliputian owners hopped, the sombreros flopped in the smoky air like extra-large jellyfish seeking the best plankton field.

There seemed a shortage of women. But I had heard of the...*how to say?*...'extra-legal' abductions in this part of Mexico. So many that the ratio of jeans to skirts was two to one, jeans flooding up from down south to grab their share of cartel money as fast as the skirts vanished, migrating either to El Norte or scrambling for El Este or even El Oeste, or to anywhere else on Este Earth, to avoid ending up *muerta-este*.

Pietro was so scared at the thought of ending up the same way, that he hid in the basement behind Quinn.

I could *deed* be next. Whatever the heck M&M had in mind at the end of their Double Indemnity San Fran streetcar, it seemed clear that my ticket here, just like the bus, was one-way only. Again I asked myself: Why the hell am I doing this? Wendy—okay, a good gal who deserved better than Yours Truly, threatened by these universe-hopping highwaymen who didn't care who they killed because it's *only in this universe, Pinky, and not in any other!*

But Wendy was the past—Tonya the future. They would not

kill Green Eyes, I was rather sure of that since she was a daughter of Frowny-Face Marm, and was once-a-nonce her favorite, but Marm herself seemed to have no compunction about taking her 'discipline' to unheard of levels. This put Green Eyes too in the danger zone.

And me? Okay, so I'd been framed for Ugly Joe and, if I refused to cooperate with M&M and Co., they would have copies of the picture of Joe with my gun at his head in the hands of Dorkman and Krupke in a Brooklyn minute. But prison is one thing; dead another. If I came anywhere near El Chapo or Mayor José with a gun in my hand, dead was a quick certainty—and probably in the most unpleasant way.

Yes, I had to go forward with M&M's plan.

I've put my life on the line before, had every day for the past ten years. But this was different. Killing El Chapo and Mayor José was simply too dangerous—my knees rattled again under the table as I contemplated the burn-barrels associated with their names, enclosing the bodies of their enemies, some not yet dead when dumped in. Could I arrange something with Chapo and José that would convince Montez & Muck that I had killed them, when in reality I had not?

My knees calmed. Yes, *that* was the way out, my only possible exit from M&M's streetcar to Nob Hill cemetery. If they were merely out of the way, then M&M could do whatever they wished with the Malverde shrine, and, if no gun were involved, El Chapo's gang could not blame me.

I would figure something...

First step, however, was to get introduced. I took out my e-cig, and its vapor joined the cloud of smoke that filled the bar's interior. Sure Juarez City Hall had prohibited smoking in bars in an effort to follow trends in the States, but, like everything else in Juarez, the real Power said different. Seeing nothing to indicate I had been noticed, I visited the establishment's restroom. Came out, passed by the attached kitchen where more evidence of gang-banger influence was visible through the open door—a poster of one man choking another. Big letters read: 'Choking Ahogo'. To this day I don't know what the heck Señor Ahogo did to offend so many people that they posted signs encouraging his choking throughout an entire continent.

But that's life.

Leaving Mr. Ahogo to his fate, I retreated to my car where I spent a more or less satisfactory night stretched out in the back seat of the Olds. I slept well, knowing that my alleged connections to the cartel must have spread through Juarez by this time. No one would dare touch so much as a hubcap.

The next morning, after a backseat shave and stop for a quick breakfast taco with *limonada*, I propped my hat and approached a teenage kid outside a convenience store. Refusing the usual offers of *drogas* and *las mas jovenas muchachas*, I communicated that what I really needed was not a new phone, which only seemed to bring bad news, but a *pistola*.

In half an hour he returned with an antique blue-steel Colt .45, and a pocketful of ammo and, after some negotiating, accepted a sloppy combination of dollars, pesos, and lira. Buying some black electrical tape, I returned to my green Olds where, pretending to inspect the tires, I taped the loaded gun inside the back bumper. Cheaper than State Farm, and a lot quicker.

Next I walked the several blocks to City Hall.

On the left was a potholed parking lot guarded by a large man sunk into the depths of a well-used metal chair, one good eye watching the cars between inspecting the drivers who came and went, sometimes demanding ID, other times satisfied with a subtle transfer of cash. I watched as a kid approached him and delivered a greasy bag and the gate-guard extracted a handful of tacos. The happy crunching that followed drifted all the way to my ears on the far side of the street.

On the right, City Hall rose three stories and occupied the remainder of the block, its neglected wood and adobe matching the aging buildings that surrounded it. Funny how once the bodies pile up, no one feels like painting anymore. Down the street, a bicyclist lay in the road, his face planted in the concrete, legs still tangled, unmoving. Pedestrians hurried past as if merely reporting the body might bring on them a similar fate. Even the Juarez police ignored it, driving into their station in the back of City Hall to deliver unfortunates to a back-lot jail.

Yep, I thought. I'm definitely in cartel-country. I wondered what a TV commercial might look like if El Chapo paraded guns instead of cigarettes: *Yes, it's a new day here in Cartel-Country. Just ask Chapo about his favorite brand.* Flash to Chapo shooting a pedestrian in the head. "When I want to reelax, I choose the Glock 41. It's smoooth." I made a mental note to tell Bob. He'll appreciate the idea for his next cartel video shoot.

Surprisingly, there was no gate-guard on the front double doors of the Hall. Well, after all, it was a public building manned by 'public servants'. I walked in and hovered about like a butterfly, casually wandering here, carefully observing there, knowing that in 'Mexico time' there is always a delay.

As I neared an elevator, an attractive young woman— correction: schoolgirl—finished folding paper airplanes or whatever the hell she had been distracted with, and whistled loud and rude to command my attention.

Behind her rose a single wide wooden stairway that divided sharply to either side at its second floor apex. No doubt leading to conference rooms. My eye lit on another stairway beyond, which reached the third floor, the entire building consisting of a single open interior that reached the two upper floors, where walkways like catwalks surrounded the interior space. A slight ding from the elevator carried as someone exited on the third floor and walked to a large door that bore an equally large sign reading: 'El Mayór'.

The schoolgirl blabbed something in Border-Mex. I got nary a word. A sharp stare followed as she took in my Canalis, that, as I intended, broadcast not just *gringo* but *rich gringo*. Before I could reply, a big guy in a suit came down the stairs faster than I would have thought possible, given his size and weight. Here I should add that PIs are not just given to counting, but to recognizing faces. And I recognized his—he appeared to be the twin of El Generalissimo outside, guarding the parking lot, even squinting strangely in the same eye, making me for the smallest moment wonder which was more real: astrology or genes.

"Señor Paco," he introduced himself. "I can help you?"

"If you can explain the likelihood of twin autistics, you can." Damn that Quinn. I thought he was put away in his basement, but he just couldn't resist a smart put-down at the worst possible moment.

Luckily, El Generalissimo of bad Mexican suits didn't *comprendo* my comment.

"Que?" he lapsed into his mother tongue.

"Not K," Quinn corrected, "but 'okay'."

Generalissimo was still puzzled, his autism or whatever it was apparently slowing both his memory and his computing banks. I decided to let the jolly tan giant off easy.

"Just kibbutzing, my friend. No need to make you do anything drastic. Like earn your keep." I glanced at little Miss paper-cutter. "Or Momma Maria over there."

I spoke fast since autistics are generally stuck on dial-up speed, therefore I only got more puzzled looks in return—as I intended.

I had seen enough.

"*Gracia por todo*," I murmured and headed for the exit.

A silent glare followed me—apparently he had gotten something from the dial-up.

As darkness fell, I found my way back to the previous night's cantina where I planted myself in the same corner. As my e-cig puffed its usual storm, I spent most of my last doubloons on Tequila and Dos Equis, watching, waiting. A plan had formed in my mind. As the long evening approached midnight and the crowd began to lessen, I perceived a pair of Tejanos in farm hats sitting silently at a side table. I shifted an elbow—their eyes moved.

Bingo.

I let my eyes rest on theirs for a fraction of a second longer than necessary, then rose and walked out of the cantina. In the parking area, apart from several couples striking late-hour biological bargains in remote corners, I waited, my e-cig expelling clouds into the darkness. Before long the two men exited and stood, looking about as if searching for someone.

I stepped forward.

They approached at a burro's pace.

The three of us stepped at the same time into the light of a suspended parking lamp. They lifted their straw hats and, as I saw their faces for the first time clear of smoke and vapor, my brows rose. It was the same two rancheros who had driven my car across the Ditch. For a moment I was non-something, whether non-plussed, non-multiplied, or non-divided. Painfully I recalled that I had boasted to them of my connections to the Juarez Cartel. It was suddenly clear that this pair had the connections which I pretended to possess.

One raised his face to the night and passed his gaze over the stars, the blackness of most of Juarez enabling the orbs to shine. I found myself wondering: Is this how civilizations collapse? When cities can no longer keep their lights on because the criminals outnumber the citizens?

"The night in Mexico is darker than in the United States," he said.

Imagine my surprise when I realized that he spoke English better than me and with almost no Spanish accent. Had he played dumb in El Paso just to jack up his price for transporting my Olds? I could just about bet... But I played his game. Scanning the sky under the brim of my fedora, I replied, "But brighter. If you count the stars." For a moment I had to restrain myself from trying to count those infinite points of light. Even PIs can't count that high.

"Si," immediately added his companion, a man only a trifle taller than me, but more muscular than I or his taller, thinner comrade, "but there ain't no star nowhere een the sky that can compare to El Sol." This ranchero had an odd combination of Spanish accent laid over Western drawl.

The first nodded agreement. He repositioned his hide-store boots, worn by use with cattle and dust. "What my friend is trying to say is *we love the sun*."

This seemed odd. I understood loving mountain peaks, loving a smooth engine, or loving a nicotine gush. But loving El Sol? There was something code-like in his talk and I was certain these two, when in Mexico, were doormen to El Chapo's Cartel Hotel. So I answered in code—omitting the obvious 'swordfish'.

"I'm lovin it myself, *compadres*. Gives me the juice to get through the day, and I don't mean orange."

They exchanged glances, as puzzled as Señor Paco had been in City Hall.

Did I get through? I sighted tiny gold circles buckling narrow short ties around both their necks. The pieces were falling into place.

I added: "Golden apple, my friends. The golden apple of the Sun." I squinted skyward as if the yellow disc were glaring down on us instead of black night. "Its juice nourishes my soul each and every day." I dropped my gaze back to them, staring as if correcting schoolchildren. "As it should *yours*."

They smothered their doubts.

"What do you want?" said the first one.

I put my hands on my hips, inwardly summoning more images of 1940s black-and-whites to bolster my courage, knowing that I could be making a date with a burn-barrel.

"I wanna meet El Chapo."

Immediately they exchanged wild—and apprehensive?—looks. The way they shifted their boots in the dirt made me conclude that I had said exactly the right thing.

The second one looked at me. "I don't see no camera."

"I'm not from Hollywood."

"And we don't need anyone to make meth for us in Albuquerque."

"I'm not a cook." It was easy to guess I was from Albuquerque.

"We don't need no one to distribute State-side neither."

"I don't own chicken restaurants or pizza joints."

They paused.

"Well, then, what the hell are you bothering us for?" They were getting testy. "Again."

I reached into my pocket and pulled out a small jeweled cross—straight from the private room of Il Papa. "Mis amigos, I can launder money like nobody's business." I handed them the cross. They inspected it in the soft glow of the streetlight, paying particular attention to the jewels. "I have an inside track to the most private private bank in the world, and I can get Chapo *inside*."

The first guy swallowed. He nodded and pocketed the cross. "We'll be in touch."

My turn to nod. "You know where to find me." I hoped they were not aware that I was sleeping in my car—big international financiers rarely sleep in their cars. But my goal was not to bring Chapo to the Vatican, but just to get him to City Hall with Mayor José.

I had a goddamn plan.

The next day I wandered about the city, wondering what to do with myself. For a large town—even a former large town—there were a surprising lack of children. But then, there was a surprising lack of women, so that explained that. Young men, though, seemed everywhere, soldiers or potential recruits for the local cartel, or a rival cartel if one decided to go indie and start hiring.

I found a small taqueria with outdoor tables and sat to enjoy another limonada. After a while, I was about to mosey off to while away the time until the cantina reopened, when a white bus came barreling into view. It parked in front of an *iglesia* part way down the block, a large neon cross looming over its roof—except the neon was ne-gone and the cross went dark at night.

Not that there was no activity inside. On the contrary, when the bus rolled up, scattering dust in the early summer heat, a portion of the adobe wall that surrounded the church slid to one side and four unsmiling men came out. More appeared from somewhere, and the bus's passengers exited and entered the church one at a time under the glare of the watchful men. Semi-automatics and pistols came into view, their business ends aimed at the passengers.

No mystery here, I thought. Just coyotes at work.

One of the coyotes seemed to be their leader, clean white button shirt with dark jacket and slacks, no tie. Yes, PIs notice clothes too. How else would I have such a nose for suits? My meandering came to a halt when a passenger exited the bus arguing loudly, I guessed continuing some complaint that he had been nursing on his long hot trip from the south. Between the bus's open door and the open entrance to the church, he halted and thrust his own unsmiling mug into the faces of two of the passengers' armed escorts, upsetting the flow of traffic into the combination safe house, prison, and school for border-crossers.

Gee, what did that remind me of? Memories of M&M's Albuquerque hills training ground came up like yesterday's gruel.

A brat of popping echoed through the street—the excited passenger crumpled.

My mind froze. Despite my effort to expel it, to keep it out of my memory banks, an image of the cartel leader standing over the passenger's body, gun barrel smoking, the passenger's face frozen in surprise as he lay in the dust, entered my mind and was filed away.

A fat man who for a moment seemed familiar to me dragged the corpse into the church. A moment later, the passengers resumed exiting the bus and entered the church, ignoring the blood.

My knees again shook. Knowing that it was just the cartel's coyotes giving a lesson on obedience to the sheep, and that this particular sheep would never cross this particular border, didn't help calm me. After all, I realized, I was a sheep too, and Ugly Joe had been my own lesson in obedience.

I sucked the *limonada* and breathed everything out—I had one chance to escape my own bus, my own 'safe house' which was guarded by the inter-universal coyotes Montez & Muck, no matter what I did, where I went, or *when*.

That night at the cantina, I sat alone. In the same place I squatted, like a gargoyle waiting for nothing, or a war-bride hoping her war-hero husband still lived, hoping for his return to make everything good and worth going forward.

The rancheros didn't show.

Finally I left and passed another night stretched in the back of my car, knowing that I could not do this much longer, that soon someone would overcome his fear of cartel business, and, attracted by the prospect of stripping my Olds, would begin taking it apart one night after the bright sun sank. And if I happened to be inside—*no problema*. What's one more body in a city littered with bodies?

Another day came and another evening at the cantina went by.

Another day of *limonada* and tacos followed, watching another bus arrive packed with humble compliant passengers from lands so distant I doubted even the Empress of China had heard of them, and as they exited to file into the church, the thug in slacks and clean shirt shot another passenger—this one seemingly for no reason—but to remind them that *this* airline's TSA tolerated no backtalk.

Into the cantina I wandered, beginning to wonder at the wisdom of it all. Perhaps my plan was not the best, perhaps it would not get off the ground. Perhaps my jeweled scepter of kingship had passed to another king and I was SOL.

They appeared.

At the door they halted, barely visible through the haze, both rancheros still wearing their straw farmhand hats though it was late in the night. I had to steel myself not to get excited or jump to my feet or display a smile. Unlike teaching in classrooms, in negotiations one has to come in weak and then grow strong. Unless, of course, one is truly weak. Then the opposite is best, but a double fake-out is the best insurance when one has no idea who else is in the game, or if there is a game. I only hoped that, if this was a game, that I could learn the rules before the game was up. Unlike life itself, where one never learns the rules until the game is done. Those goal posts 'don move for no one'.

With an exchange of looks, they turned and exited.

I waited a full minute to throw off casual observers, then rose and followed.

In the light of the same parking lamp we met. The taller ranchero was expressionless, his face lit eerily by the vertical rays.

"Cheche is ready. He doesn't like waiting, so we need to go now."

"I haven't paid for my tequila."

He glanced at his shorter compadre.

Compadre cricked his neck. "No problema. It's on the house."

My reaction of subtle surprise seemed to amuse them. I nodded. *Of course* the cartel owns the bar. This is Juarez, after all. The cartel owns the city and everything in it—including the people.

"My cross?" I nudged the dirt with one shoe as if a mere cross inlaid with rubies and amethyst was nothing to write home about.

"Cheche will return it to you." Number One shifted his jaw, exposing more skin to the ghost-light. "*If* you are what you say you are." Briefly he shook his head, barely noticeable. "And if not..."

Last chance.

With a blink, I exhaled.

"Let's go," said the taller ranchero. The pair walked into darkness. Out of range of the parking light, which started to seem like a life-float in a black sea, a Land Rover loomed. They beeped it open. Jorge indicated the front seat and I took it.

I made a move to buckle up then noticed that neither of my companions did, and I stopped. It was too small a matter to bother with given the life expectancy hereabouts.

To my surprise, we drove to City Hall.

Despite the late hour, the police access in the back was lit and, parking behind the building, we walked by a deserted alley strewn with clothes and the Styrofoam remains of lunches, an alley that opened on the City Hall's side parking area, fenced and topped with barbed wire. Only one corner was free of fencing and, walking through, we entered the brightly lit police intake office.

A drunk and a prostitute were the only customers. Swarthy police, two males and two females, were taking fingerprints with casual efficiency. We entered without comment from the police— bodies on the street, wranglers in the Precinct, and a near total lack of guests for a city this size. What else might this roll of the dice reveal?

Through a short hallway, we passed by a side electric door. From within I heard rapid Spanish and calls for 'agua'. Must be where the cells are located, I guessed. At the end of the hallway, we entered what must have been the back-est backroom in the place, and I straightened in surprise.

A tall, slender man with short trimmed beard and sporting pressed black slacks and white button shirt with dark jacket and no tie sat behind a well-ordered police desk. His feet were propped up. To my further surprise, he picked up an e-cig and sent a powerful puff reeling across the space between us.

"Officer Cheche." Number One Ranchero lowered his eyes and nodded his head, farm hat in hand.

Number Two Ranchero almost fell to the floor for evening prayers.

"This is the one." Number One looked at me.

I looked back under the brim of my fedora. Cheche...so Mr. Casual Killer from the bus at the church had a name. Silently I strangled Quinn to keep him from letting loose with his usual provocations, and simply gave Cheche—who apparently was the Juarez Chief of Police—a calm stare. Clearly he did not remember me from the breakfast bar across from the church where he executed passengers.

"Gracias, Jorge." The Chief flicked his eyes to the door.

"Thank you, Santo."

Beaming with Cheche's approval (or was it relief from escaping possible punishment?), the rancheros, whom I now knew as Jorge and Santo, left the room, sliding to one side to make room for a wide load entering.

Once inside, the huge man scraped up a four-legged chair and deposited his bulk, clinking a ring of keys. I instantly recognized him as the hombre who had confronted me on the stairs the previous week when I had visited City Hall via the front door—and who was also the fat man whom I had seen drag away Don Cheche's victims at the church. He still wore a suit, which struck me as odd since he carried keys, and keys in a police department, if I knew anything at all, had to do with jail cells. I gathered the suit, like Cheche's casual clothes, was due to the Department's 'extra-legal' activities.

"Paco, I would like you to meet our new friend."

To me, Cheche indicated an empty chair. I sat, trying to make as much noise as Paco, but some things just aren't possible. I raised my chin. Quinn, after all, wasn't really dead, just whipped into line.

"Pietro Quinn Tiberias Marlowe," I pronounced, letting one end of a lip twist. "You can call me Pete."

Fat Paco let loose a grin—the hot-shit kind. "A beeg name. Are you sure a man like you can carry a name that beeg?"

Cheche waved him quiet. I got the message that this Cheche was all business, and as if to prove it he immediately pulled out the cross.

Paco scraped his chair forward to see. "Oooh. Don Cheche!"

Don Cheche inspected the jewels in the light of overhead fluorescents, permitting a half smile. "I've already shown this to El Mayór. He would like to speak with you, get to know you better."

"Damn right he would." I folded my arms. It was time to take control of this situation, or at least of my third of the room.

Ignoring my body language, Cheche leaned across his desk, holding the cross higher, the better for me and Paco to see. "My colleagues tell me these jewels are valuable—very valuable. I know El Mayór will want to ask you himself, but may I ask...how you came by them?"

"Grace-a-God," I replied. "Can't say any more until I see *El*

Mayór and his *friend*."

Paco and Don Cheche glanced at each other as if I had spoken the name of the devil. They sat silently for a minute, watching, waiting to see if my inner demons would force me to blurt out more information, something they could use against me. They didn't know that by that time I had Quinn tied up in a corner, and that Pietro would continue to yawn unless one of those pretty muchachas in uniform that I had glimpsed in the intake room reappeared. I let my lip curl.

Finally Cheche allowed himself a brief nod and he and Paco rose to their feet, the latter struggling.

The Chief of Police offered me his hand. "Until mañana then, Señor Marlowe. Let's say around noon?"

"'Pete', I corrected, as I took his hand. "Noon will do."

"Pete." Cheche lifted his chin.

Paco had lost his smirk and stood aside to let me walk out first. That's better. A little *respeto* was definitely called for in this southron neck of the woods—Pete don't take no tacos from jailhouse Pacos.

Once outside, I realized that Cheche had not returned my cross, as Santo had said he would. Oh well, what use did I have for a cross, anyway? Sure, my doubloons were about gone, but for me time and space—and therefore money—had taken on a different meaning. For me there were always other realities, other universes. It was only a pair of female anchors that kept me in this one.

CHAPTER 22

Next day bright and early I strode in the direction of the pride of Ciudad Juarez. Across *la calle* from the building I paused to watch the wide double front doors. I had no worries—aside from the usual hesitation that anyone might have before walking unarmed into the lair of a dozen hardened killers who had a thing about gringos. But I had a job to do.

On the left side of the three-story building sat Taco King, still crushing his folding chair, still guarding the pothole-strewn parking lot with his one good eye. I decided not to approach the front doors directly, but to cross the street farther down to avoid him.

Down I walked. At the corner, a short drunk Mexican, his face covered by a sombrero, came out of nowhere and thrust out his chest. I gave this *borracho* puffed up with alcohol and *machismo* a wide berth, confident that his proximity to City Hall and *Los Policias* would soon bring him to a bad end without me, like the corpse on the busted bike that had finally been removed to the morgue.

Turning my back, I proceeded to cross the street, watching for heedless farm trucks and SUVs. On my left, my eye caught the back of a tan jacket worn by another short man as he hurried away from the Hall, apparently having exited the building's front doors while I was avoiding *el borracho*. I paused at the corner—two more figures were hurrying away up the side street, having exited City Hall via the back police entrance, a large man in a quiet imported suit alongside a short dark Mexican in secondhand clothes.

I shrugged. To each his own.

Arriving at City Hall's front doors, I swung them wide and paraded in, ignoring the indignant pretend outrage on the face of the girly receptionist, who apparently had not been told of my appointment.

"*De nuevo?*" she asked.

"Whatever," I answered, not bothering to doff my hat. Let her wave her drying nails or do whatever the heck else she wanted. I was here on bigger business.

Truth was, I was a half hour early. But I wanted another opportunity to scope out the place for the few seconds I would have before Miss Friday decided to do her job and challenge me. She decided more quickly than I expected.

Still, I could see enough. My eyes were fixed on the distant door on the third floor with sign posted above—the lair where *los bandidos* presumably met to plan their capers. Would El Chapo show? I had not seen him since that night outside M&M's shop. What if he didn't? I had little time left to execute my plan, with a shrinking stack of pesos to keep me in *cervezas* and *limonada*. What if Chapo had flown to Argentina with Montez & Muck? What if he was too busy happily chopping off heads to lay at the feet of his Malverde statue, wherever that might be? One player at a time was not on my schedule.

To my relief, a pair of black Land Rovers pulled up in front of the Hall. That's chutzpah, I thought. Not many secrets in this part of the woods when the chief criminal of the most murderous cartel in this part of old Mexico parks his car in the police chief's space.

Ignoring the catcalls of Miss Friday, I heard a ding. Before I turned to look, I already knew things were clicking into place and began to breathe easier. Down the stairs lurched jailhouse Paco, still in his bad Mexican suit, this time a few keys ringing at his side—I supposed a mini-ring version of the full thing. From the back door leading to the police intake came Cheche, the police chief himself, his jacket bulging over a shoulder strap that contained a tucked pistol, a Glock, my P-Eye noted.

La Secretaire went silent as the front door spat a pair of *chulos*, casually dressed in tan para-pants topped by blue and white Hawaiian *camisas,* their shirts also bulging with barely concealed *pistolas*, like an out-take from Scarface. They passed suspicious glances on either side while they held the door open for a stocky man of muscle—both his, *y los otros*—with a wide mustache. El Chapo. His clothes were also casual, though not as loud as his not-so-secret service, but chosen from the discount pile of the same store, to my mind.

Wandering in like another lost client looking for some clerk to whine to for assistance with a mis-signed form, two more Hawaiian clothes-horses entered the Hall behind Chapo and covered his rear. Like several others, I noticed they wore golden pendants about their necks like little suns.

Chapo's eyes lit on Paco and Cheche and a brief tick of acknowledgment passed among them. On their cue, Chapo turned his pockmarked face to me. I almost said 'upon me', but, as I noticed once more with something like relief, his height was the same as mine, and—could I believe it was so?—thought for a second that I detected the same relief in his eyes. Then his glance passed to the elevator where Mayor José was exiting, and the moment was gone.

With the gang gathering, they ignored my presence, exchanging a host of eye flicks and eyebrow raises, huddled like footballers using code to decide on a play, or pickpockets eyeing a prospect. When Mayor José Gonzalez joined, they paused for the obligatory cheek-kissing, the tall and light-skinned *Peronista Mayór* from Argentina hugging the Half-Mexican half-sized dark-skinned Chapo with the Pancho Villa mustache. Then Cheche kissed Chapo, then Chapo kissed Paco, then they were done. I began to breathe again, happy that no one had attempted to draft me into their circle of perverts.

As one, all eyes turned to *mío*. I can't explain exactly why, but I felt a swell of pride as if I had just been seconded in my bid to run for city dog-catcher, or recycling manager. But such things don't happen to society's rejects—even in Juarez—so I calmed and turned my thumb-in-your-eye personality back on.

Despite all the guards and watchful expressions, no one had as yet searched me for weapons, and at a flick of the brow from Chapo, his two foremost guards rushed to my side where they efficiently ran intrusive palms over every square inch of my epidermis, not neglecting socks and underwear, which provoked a moment of indignation from Quinn as they thrust hands into my pants. Thank god they left at least one cavity unmolested. The process was so quick I had little time to respond and I found myself thinking that the real government in these parts maybe wasn't so lazy and inefficient after all.

The onlookers watched with amusement, but once completed, the guard-dogs retreated and Mayor José and El Chapo approached, leaving Cheche and Paco and the rest where they stood.

"You know," said Chapo, his stare fixing mine, "I have to hand it to you, my freend. The others are not sure if you are jes' *loco*. But I theenk you have the biggest *cojones* this side of Tuscon. *En realidad*, basketballs of steel."

Yep, this hot-shit character too was staring at me like I was some barnyard rooster. And I didn't like it one bit. Though I could see Chapo's guards shift their feet in preparation for something drastic to follow, I made ready to unleash Quinn, whatever the consequences. Quinn was stopped at the gate by Mayor José.

To Chapo, José said, "Not steel, my friend. But *minerál*. Definitely *minerál*." José spoke with the same smooth South-South American accent I had heard the previous week outside Muck and Montez's video shop. There was no mistaking that Way Down South accent. Or his Across The Sea aristocratic attitude. Leaning in to Chapo so they spoke brow-to-brow, Mayor José cautiously slid the upper half of my cross decked out with the full assortment of jewels from the inside of his coat pocket, letting the jewels twinkle.

Chapo stared.

After a moment, José silently slid the cross back into his pocket.

It worked. Whatever doubt El Chapo may have had about the meeting evaporated, and he turned his wide broom lip to me. The chicken-shit look was gone. I was suddenly Somebody. Though Somebody without a cross, and, as it sank in that at least one of the gems had been pried off, certainly to disappear forever, it hardly mattered because I knew by this time that I would never regain possession of Il Papa's toy. Inwardly, I shrugged—cost of doing business.

Chapo turned on the charm. From hard-eyed executioner he became suddenly friendly Uncle Chap, and displayed a smile broader than his Uncle Joe mustache, taking my hand in both of his and shaking vigorously. His watchmen visibly relaxed and stopped sweeping the lobby with their eyes as if looking for possible quick exits. Chapo winked at me. I had to admit, when he wanted to be someone's friend, he could do it; even Quinn instantly warmed to Chapo's smiles and winks.

"Now, my freend. José tells me you have come from our beloved Padre's castle in Roma—"

"You got it, bud. José got it right."

Chapo still clung to my arm like a python. I finally shook it loose, but as gently as I could manage so as not to torpedo the negotiation.

A fast glance to his underlings and Chapo leaned to me for our own brow-to-brow and lowered his voice. "I like your leetle cross. Can you get more?"

I repositioned my feet. I knew this was coming. "Chapo, pal. Don't tell me you're carried away by small enchiladas like this." I almost said 'small potatoes', but this wasn't New York and I wasn't a Corleone. "Like I told *El Mayór*," I tossed this bone in José's direction so he wouldn't feel left out, and whispered, "this is about cleaning, not mining. I have an inside track to the biggest laundromat in the universe—the Keys to the Kingdom, my friend—and in *this* life, not the next."

They were suitably impressed. Even if I was not impressed by their suits, though I had to admit the golden suns hanging about their necks were flashy. José fingered Chapo, and the gangsters leaned away from me for another tit-to-tit. I heard the Mayor whisper even more quietly into his colleague's ear: "*Il Banco Vaticano.*"

Chapo's eyes sharpened. He got it too.

I nubbed the floor with a well-heeled toe. "Well, gentlemen? Should we talk where everyone can hear? Or go someplace private where we can get this *carnavale* on *la calle*?"

Watching José's face with care, I tossed a brief glance at the elevator, then followed by resting my eyes on Chapo. The *cartelista* gazed at the lengthy stairs with a hint of reluctance, while José looked at the elevator with a similar hint of longing, though neither seemed willing to show a sign of weakness in front of each other or their fawning awe-struck followers.

I suspected this—had a plan for it.

Putting one foot on the first step, I pretended to stumble. Looking up, I lay a steady gaze on the elevator that beckoned a scant twenty feet away.

Like a flock of birds, all immediately headed for the elevator. Paco rushed his bulk to be first to open the double-door. Behind him, Cheche held one arm wide for El Chapo as if escorting a guest at a Hollywood gala. Chapo's Don Ho look-alikes brought up the rear, still sweeping the interior of the Hall with their eyes for possible threats, now clouded by confusion as to how to fit nine people in a small size-four lift.

I forced the matter by getting there first and holding the open-door button, thus modestly assuming the job of operator, while Chapo and José happily perceived that I had accepted the role of servant. I could almost see the wheels turn in their minds as they smiled, thinking so much the better for *el negocio*.

But what goes around, comes around. I punched the close-door button, shutting everyone out but me, El Mayór, and Munchkintown's El Chapo. I even had the satisfaction of seeing the Luau sing *gone-baya* while Paco, Cheche, and the rest of the Hawaiian gang grew eyes big as goose-eggs as the elevator doors shut, knowing that their Little Caesars were suddenly bereft of their protection.

Phase One was accomplished.

As the metal box lurched upward, I pried off my fake digit, aimed the cone of science at the ceiling, and pressed the red button. On cue the ceiling began to bubble like Mount Kea, very appropriately given the plethora of Hawaiian shirts in the lobby. The elevator was opaque, not being the kind which I had seen in fancy-pansy places like San Fran or Phoenix where the doors (and the women's tops) were sometimes see-through. I could imagine the frustrated looks on the faces of the mercs stranded below.

I had no need to imagine the looks on the faces of José and Chapo. They seemed anxious—they sensed something was wrong. As usual, the lyrics of Istanbul swirled through my head, alerting me that the Thingamajob was working, that we were about to pass into a different dimension, a new world, where who-knew-what might happen, and *would* if Muck's guesstimates on the laws of probability were real.

How could the pair not see what was happening? I gazed up at the terrifying eruptions that exploded in the metal ceiling as the molecules burped and screeched in protest of being catalogued and molested by M&M's Indexer. What rhythm, what tones were being unleashed in the minds of the corrupt Argentinean politician and the vile Mexican executioner whose only strategy was to equate people with problems, and eliminate both? From somewhere I thought I perceived accordions and Mexican polka, their own Istanbul song.

Chapo tapped the side of his head to clear it. José cast a confused glance at Chapo, then at me, but failed to look up—not that it mattered. We were about to plunge literally head-first into Muck's void.

Ever since I had witnessed the DHS gate-guard walk through a soap-bubble veil after the door had opened, it had been slammed home in my mind that the Indexer only needs substance to create its Door to another universe. After the creating was done, that substance could be removed—a door could be opened—or the ceiling of an elevator rise above it.

Thus the three of us—me at the controls, and José and Chapo in front facing the door ready to exit—passed without event, almost calmly, into yet another of M&M's intersectionalized multiverses.

Of course, I had never seen any actual differences in any of the alternate universes that I had penetrated. And M&M had assured me there would be none—which the Indexer ensured. So I was confident that when we arrived at Floor Two, a simple push of Chapo and José from behind would expel them into that universe, while a return trip back down through the still-bubbling Door would return Yours Truly to my *original* universe...which would continue exactly as before, except for the convenient fact that Chapo and José would be *missing*. Gone AWOL. Hitched a thumb-ride with Easy Rider on the road to Uni-Vegas, and not coming back. Then Muck and Montez would be happy, Wendy and Tonya would be safe, and I would finally be released from M&M's servitude and could go back to singing happy songs about rain and birds in my little non-rent office. Most important of all, there would be no bodies—therefore, those henchmen in the lobby below would not intersectionalize *me* afterward.

The ceiling bubbled and spat wet sparks, drenching our clothes in confused electrons and protons that no longer knew what was expected of them, and José and Chapo did nothing but blink. They barely noticed. I felt like the boatman of legend taking souls across the River of Sticks to Hades, thankful that all I had to do to take this pair to their eternal reward was to punch Floor Two, since I had never learned to pilot watercraft.

The bubbling passed through our bodies and still they did not perceive that they were passing into another world, though I thought I saw Chapo tap his foot to lyrics that I could barely make out, something about *la vida* and *el corazón*. At the second floor, the ceiling jerked to a halt, the bubbling in the ceiling now positioned below our feet, still bubbling, still swirling, though now appearing more like a glistening rainbowed soap-bubble.

Phase Two had arrived.

The outer doors separated, not waiting for me to press the open-door button. At the first crack, I sensed something was skewed. Had I jumped forward in time? Or somehow backward and forward simultaneously? Chapo and José stood beside me in the elevator— there was no doubt of that. Their shoulders, especially José's, partially blocked my view of the new universe beyond the doors— but standing outside the elevator doors, opening swiftly, too swiftly for me to comprehend, were...Chapo and José, with myself behind them. Standing calmly, the three prepared to enter the elevator, which already contained Chapo and José and me.

All eyes met at once.

José stared at José. Chapo stared at Chapo. Pietro Quinn Tiberias Marlowe looked deep into the eyes of Pietro Quinn Tiberias Marlowe, and I was fairly confident that the other Pete had released evil Quinn and lusty Pietro, not to mention Elvis Himself, from the depths to join the crowd standing on the second floor fore-deck.

So much for Phase Two.

Almost on reflex, I punched the close-door button to get the heck out of whatever the hell had happened as fast as possible.

I had one more chance. City Hall of Juarez has three levels and we had visited only two. There was one left.

I pounded the elevator button for Floor Three. Pointing my pinky upward, I unleashed the torrent a second time.

While the doors closed on the shocked gazes of Chapo and José, cutting them off from their counterparts waiting to enter the elevator from the second floor, the two again stood passively beside me like wood, too stunned to react, too confused to comprehend, too astounded even to think of glancing up at the elevator ceiling, which once more had begun to erupt with lava.

"Huh." I shrugged. "Your people must have ordered a mirror and were trying to move it. Bad timing."

José and Chapo exchanged worried glances. Chapo shook his head and felt his churning stomach. "José," said Chapo. "If I ever buy street tacos again—shoot me."

"*Para mi*—no more brandy before lunch," José added.

Both felt their middles. They were suffering from the usual after-effects of 'verse-travel, I realized. It would wear off soon. Upward we lurched and, the pair still not noticing, we passed through the second Door to yet another universe, and arrived at the third floor. The swirling of confused atomic slices settled to a second rainbow soap-bubble around our feet. For a moment I contemplated the implications of passing through not *one*, but *two* doors to new universes, and what parts of my body I might lose if I failed to return to my own universe in time. Presumably my ass—I desperately hoped the original door was still active between the first and second floors below, because if it had already expired, then there would be no way that this Pinky would ever find his way back home, even if he cried waah, waah, waah all the way there. My Indexer had no 'back' button.

The doors parted.

Like a veil tearing open to reveal the secrets of nature, the twin portals moved oppositely on the third floor with a Star Trek swish, and again I froze. José and Chapo, having learned not to rush in where no gangster fears to go, also made no move, but remained in place, staring, searching for anything out of the ordinary on the third floor catwalk that surrounded the open interior of the Hall. Not ten feet away was José's luxurious office, with the garish 'El Mayór Gonzalez' sign over the door, the sign I had seen from the lobby below.

We stared at a pair of back-sides.

More precisely, Chapo and José stared at a pair of shoulders and backs that were turned away from us and toward José's office doors, while I peeked over and around Chapo and José's shoulders, at the second pair of shoulders as they walked past the elevator.

Muck—and Montez!

Dressed as they had been when I saw them cheek-kiss José and Chapo and head for their plane to Buenos Aires, their mariachi style still lacking only *guitarras* and sombreros.

M&M slowed to a halt. Slowly they turned...

CHAPTER 23

Frantically, I banged the close-door elevator button a second time, and without delay pounded the Floor One button to make sure.

My plan had failed: *big-time*. I had planned on pushing José and Chapo out the elevator door, which meant into an alternate universe where they would detect no difference, but which meant Montez & Muck would be rid of their arch-rivals in our own universe. With exactly the wrong people loitering around the elevator of these alter-verses, this was impossible.

But there was still the return trip.

I had brought José and Chapo into a second alternate universe—plainly I could not push them out any door now. I had to bring them back with me through both doors to our original universe where I would have to come up with another plan. This meant I must plunge downward back through the first soap-bubble door which, I hoped beyond hope, might still preserve its rainbow film in the location that had originally been the ceiling of this stupid metal box.

Down we lurched. I felt the need to blurt out another inane explanation, hoping my guests would not catch on that I was behind all the weirdness.

"Sorry, gentlemen. We're headed back down. I think there must be something the matter with your lift."

They weren't listening. José cast his eyes at Chapo: "*Jo pensé que nos amigos volaran a Argentina.*" "I thought our 'friends' had flown to Argentina," my brain translated.

Chapo wasn't listening to José either. "Sometheeng is veery much wrong here..." He made a move as if to search for a hidden blade.

Sweat beaded on my palms. As the elevator chugged

downward with the molasses-like slowness of a computer on reboot, I held my breath, not daring to speak, breathe, or twitch an eyebrow. At that moment all I wanted was to shrink into myself, go invisible, and I swore that once I got back—*if* I got back—I would hit up M&M for an upgrade to my Indexer, a second button that would let me go too skinny to see.

No elevator in any universe dropped slower than that damned box in Juarez City Hall as it ground its agonizing route back to Floor One, back to the universe where I could be sure of what it contained, the universe with Tonya and Wendy, with Uncle Flynn wandering his empire of tunnels, and Montez & Muck still in Argentina where they were supposed to be.

We left Floor Three behind. Slowly we dropped through the second soap-bubble, which rose around us like a breezy veil. José only sneezed.

Floor Two came into view, a vague shadow-play of light and dark seeping through the closed doors, alerting Quinn that our three counterparts still stood outside the elevator doors—perhaps the Pete in that universe was hoping to push his José and Chapo *into* the elevator just as I tried to push them *out*. Who knew, given the tangle of universes out there.

We left Floor Two behind.

Again the floor of the elevator beneath my feet glistened with soap bubbles, even as the layer of soap-bubbles overhead vanished. The rainbow sheen rose about my feet...

Traveled up my legs...

Up the legs of José and Chapo...

Climbed our torsos.

Engulfed our necks.

Our heads.

Finally rose back into place, coinciding with the ceiling, all with the agonizing slowness of a low-powered bathroom hand-dryer.

With a tiny pop, the bubble vanished. The door was gone. Presumably the second door invisible above us would also vanish in another instant.

But we were back—the first 'door' had lasted long enough for me to return, with Chapo and José beside me.

Slowly the elevator pulled aside (none too fast for me) and I felt free to move again, take in a breath, let my Elvis hair down. Stepping outside the lift, the three of us paused to rub our temples and shake our arms and legs as if we had run a marathon. I could not help but stare upward, and true to my suspicions, no counterparts to me or José or Chapo could be seen waiting on the second floor, or figures of Muck and Montez loitering on the third. Despite M&M's assurances that everything in alternate universes would be the same, they had existed only in those universes.

"You know," said Chapo, "I theenk today is not the day to do this."

"*Jo contigo*," José agreed.

With a look of disappointment that took every ounce of fakery in me, I nodded. All I wanted at that moment was to get away, sip more *limonada*, and try to figure out what the hell had happened, and how the heck I might reengineer a solution.

I spat out, "Looks like a tick got under the saddle, bros. We can always try again tomorrow."

Faint nods replied.

The Hawaiian Don Hos wrapped themselves around us like henchmen of Dr. No, motivated by the superior retirement packages that gangsters and henchmen always seem to have, eager to sacrifice themselves at the whim of their mad employers. In response to their masters' nods, however, the cartel gangsters parted and let me go.

Cheche and Paco were equally obedient to their master, *El Mayór*, and stood watching as I walked out the front door to Juarez's City Hall and stumbled toward my usual roadside bistro. Only a shot of hard *limonada* could make my knees stop rattling.

***

I never had time to finish my *limonada* or puff my e-cig before they came. Sitting on the front half-covered by palm fronds porch of the little bistro, I watched the daily bus scrape to a halt across *la calle* and begin expelling the next batch of 'logs' being made into lumber for the trip north.

Cheche and Paco were there, all right. But this time they didn't arrive by unmarked private car; rather in police cruisers with lights flashing, though they still wore their bus-service clothes rather than police uniforms, which only showed how quickly they had received their instructions. The cruisers braked at sharp angles aimed at the bistro and the pair stepped out and walked quickly to the porch, guns drawn, their eyes on me. Mexican police in regular uniforms stood behind.

"What's the news, bros?" I feebly protested, pushing my fedora back friendly-style. I tried to decipher what was up: was I being invited to another discussion of Vatican money laundering—this time via the stairway no doubt—or was I down for something else, like parking my Olds in a donkey cart loading zone for too long?

Don Cheche tapped his gun barrel on his clenched left hand. "Turn around, Señor Marlowe." The police chief covered me with the gun while Paco-jote, out of breath from climbing the measly two steps to the bistro's porch, holstered his weapon and took out metal handcuffs.

As I turned and offered my wrists from behind, Fat Paco grinned.

"Eh, leetle guy with the beeg name. *El Mayór* says he don' have no more time for you. And you did something bad, so you must come with us." The locks clicked over my wrists.

At least he was not El Chapo, I thought with some relief. In Mexico, capital punishment is the exclusive reserve of gangsters, and they don't like the government or mere policemen encroaching on their turf by killing people. So, as far as execution goes, that probably wasn't on Cheche's calendar, at least in his role as Chief Cop.

What, then?

Packing me into the back of a cruiser, we rolled leisurely through the few streets that separated the bistro and the little church with the high privacy walls from the three-story building that served as the City Hall and *El Departamento de La Policía de La Ciudad de Juarez*. To my amazement, the drunken young man whom I had carefully avoided an hour earlier still staggered about, confronting pedestrians to find a sparring partner, his fists punching air—and, even more surprising, the corpse on the bicycle, who had been face-down in the street for several days and, which having finally been removed, was back again, in the same place and on the same bike, face again to concrete. Perhaps the next of kin had failed to pay the pesos demanded by the mayor for collecting roadkill, so the city had put him back where they found him.

We wheeled into the parking area behind City Hall and parked. Cheche and Paco exited the cruiser and entered the Hall without a backward glance. Underlings pulled me out and dragged me after. This encouraged me. If they had so little interest that they couldn't be bothered to search or watch me, then the charges could not be serious. That is, if lying to El Mayór, El Chapo, and the Chief of Police about money laundering wasn't serious enough.

Inside, they did the obligatory intake: pants inspected, shirt rifled (this upset me most), my body examined right down to the last cavity (thank god the inspector was female)—and I realized that I had left my e-cig at the bistro. Damn the luck. I had been so engrossed with Paco and his *leetle* words that I had forgotten it. Next went the tie, then my belt. Okay, I got that part. They didn't want any 'accidents' to happen, except their own. And I got that they had to take my Movado watch—but my fedora hat? I sighted one of the guards trying it on for size down the hall as the policewoman temporarily released my handcuffs to take my fingerprints.

Then came my wallet.

For this, Cheche returned, and he and Paco went through it, card by card. My insurance plastic was tossed aside. As was my expired triple A card. Credit card—I owned none after the Pope's Swiss guard cut my last one up, which fact the *policia* didn't seem to believe, though repeated searches failed to find any. Grocery coupons stuck in the back provoked amused smiles; the coupons joined my insurance card in the trash. My plastic Starbucks coffee card went into the pocket of the policewoman doing the searching, while the few remaining pesos and dollars in my possession went into Paco's pocket (and the lira into the can). A blood donor card triggered laughter; it too went in the trash.

My New Mexico driver's license and PI License, along with my gun registration per License requirements, were of greater interest. Paco loomed his bulk over the smooth counter where he swept similar items belonging to similar suspects aside in order to examine mine, and Cheche strolled in, and together they read and nodded and read again until at last they seemed satisfied that they had found what they wanted. Amused smiles returned to their faces and Cheche and Paco motioned to the policewoman to take me down the hall.

The handcuffs went back on.

At the end of the short hallway, we came to a massive door where some invisible watcher popped a loud electric lock; the policewoman pulled the door open and pushed me through. Along either side of a long hall were several cells designed for a dozen inmates, and smaller ones designed for only a few—into one of these she guided me and shut the metal-barred door with a clang.

The noise jerked a half-dozen suspects to consciousness and they immediately hooted and called for *agua* and *molé*, or if those were lacking, *tequila* and *pussé*. A gentleman hates to be so blunt, but, when food and water proved to be in short supply, I later saw a skin-clad woman enter with a bottle of booze in her hand. I could almost hear the *policía* cash register ring up her charges through the metal door as the jail personnel extracted more *dinero* from its inmates.

It must have been hours that I sat there. Quietly. Lost in thought. One eye on the dirty drunk sprawled out on the only other bench in my little jail cell, lying in his vomit. He breathed, lost in some alien world of his own, where thank god snoring was outlawed.

No matter how I thought it through, my thoughts thunk the same—I was being played. That is, my arrest was fake—real enough, but still fake—it was part of Mayor José's negotiations, the usual treatment he meted out to brash gringos who had the balls to walk into his place as if they own it, and dare to treat him as an equal. He must have promised El Chapo that their best approach was to break me down before again meeting with me, to give themselves the best advantage in my Vatican laundering deal.

But why keep me in jail? Why take my wallet? Stealing one's money and *limonada* isn't usually considered negotiating in good faith.

At last the electric door popped.

The door swung wide and Cheche and Paco entered the

hallway. Calls and whistles from the other inmates were hushed by the policemen's warning glances, and they walked the length of the corridor and approached my cell. On the other side of the network of vertical and horizontal metal bars, they stopped. Both were still in their casual clothes, the same they had worn when I had first seen them execute troublemakers on the bus from *El Sud.*

Fat Paco still knew his place, too. He looked to Don Cheche before talking.

Cheche smoothed the white button shirt beneath his dark greyish jacket, *sans* tie, and cocked his short trimmed bearded head while he contemplated me. Maybe he also didn't quite get what had happened.

"Señor Marlowe. Have you ever been tested for...*aptitude* for professional occupations?"

"Huh?"

"Perhaps you have heard of this." The change in Cheche's face suggested doubt. "There is a test one can take that indicates, when a psychologist looks at the results, what line of work might be most suitable for one."

I smirked. "Do tell."

Cheche let a half-smile take a half-lip. "Let's say the results show an aptitude for dealing with people on an equal basis—or, on the contrary, an aptitude for not dealing with people at all."

"What's the bottom line, *Señor* Cheche?" Quinn had finally climbed up from his basement and he sneered the 'Señor' part. Quinn and I sensed more twisting of the knife coming in *El Mayor's* 'negotiation'. I added, "I got an appointment with Tony Robbins."

Paco snorted.

Cheche kept looking at *mío*. "Just this, my friend—"

The obese jailer Paco grinned.

"After you left your little meeting with Don Gonzalez and Don Chapo, it seems a couple of friends of yours got back to town. They called the station and asked to speak to the chief of police..."

Now Cheche and Paco both smiled—my smirk began to fade.

"Your friends had some very interesting things to say."

For the first time, I noted an accent *Espanol* break through Cheche's flawless English, made a mental note that no matter how many layers of deception we drape ourselves in, sooner or later our real nature will out.

"For instance?" I decided to be brave. No, bluff was more accurate.

"For instance, your friends have told me: First, that you have been to the Vatican, but that you have nothing to do with the Vatican Bank. Second, in case you didn't know—the Pope is *dead*—so he won't know you from Adam."

My brick wall of bluff showed a crack.

"Third, that since the Pope cannot confirm you, you cannot launder money through his Bank."

There was a flaw in his argument somewhere, but since he had clearly made up his mind, I decided it would be a waste of breath to point it out.

"Fourth, that you are not an international financier with Libor-bank connections, but just a small-time thief who is barely hanging on to his investigator's license issued by the City of Albuquerque in the state of New Mexico."

It was getting harder to find those flaws—except in the bricks of my wall of bluff, which were beginning to crumble.

"Fifth, that you are trying to infiltrate the Juarez Cartel in order to help the authorities in *Los Estados Unidos* track our *inmigración* operations. That is what your friends have said to me."

The wall crashed. All I could do at that moment was try to calm my knees by blowing smoke. Except I had no e-cig, so no smoke.

From one of his expansive pockets, Paco produced my PI license issued by Albuquerque along with my gun registration. My driver's license was there too but was hardly necessary to complete Cheche's bulldozing of what remained of my brick wall.

Cheche let loose a grand smile. "So it seems you are going to be our guest for a while, Señor Marlowe. A long, long while." He laughed aloud.

Joining in, Paco let loose a deep humorous rumble. He glanced once at Cheche, who blinked in response.

Paco turned his fat face back to me. "Your freends were veery talkative, Beeg-time Border Man. They say you have a former wife in Idaho who is veery enterested in what happens to 'Peenky'."

My 'friends' were M&M, all right.

Still laughing, Cheche turned and walked to the electric door. He let loose a sardonic look back at Paco.

With permission to keep speaking, Paco added, "We theenk it's about time for you to pay us for taking up so much of our time. And since you are a Yankee, we will let you have your one yankee phone call: to your ex-wife. Tell her to wire *El Departamento de Policía de Ciudad de Juarez* fifty-thousand dollars. By six o'clock. If she pays your fine, we have a nice clean bus to give you a ride back to Gringo-land." Paco stared harder. "If she does not...well...El Chapo has hees own appointment with you. And he is already on hees way." Paco let his hands fall to his sides with palms up in the Mexican equivalent of the Italian don'-know-nuthin', can't-help-that gesture.

At the electric door the lock popped.

I grabbed my metal bars. "It won't work, *Señor* Paco." Pressing my face between two bars, I almost shouted, "No jail can hold me!"

Hearing this, the pair paused at the electric door, Cheche holding it open with one hand, *El Mayór* Gonzalez himself visible through the gap, busy with a sheaf of papers. "We'll be right back with a phone," Cheche called.

Fat Paco grinned back at me. "*Dinero or die*, Peenky. As you Yankees like to say: that's all she wrote."

In another moment, Cheche and Paco walked out, leaving me, if not knee-deep in my cell companion's vomit, at least neck-deep in Muck & Montez's wasteland. For in my mind there was no mistaking who had done this. What, when, and how were easy enough. *Why* M&M would do this to me and wreck their own plans for having me infiltrate the cartel and kill Mayor Gonzalez and Chapo I could not imagine.

But I was going to find out.

I glanced down at my plastic digit and a new look of hardness froze my face. Outside the high small window I could see the sun begin to set. No one—not that pig jailer or his Don of a police chief who thinks he's playing a bit part in a Godfather movie—could stop me.

Facing the wall, I removed the tip of my little finger.

I pressed the red button.

CHAPTER 24

A nd so I walked...and I sneaked back to the video shop while the sun was setting...and I found Montez & Muck seated at the head of their own little HQ, watching and spying on everybody's private parts like hot-shit people, all smarmy and smart.

And I put my gun to Jack's bald head, sideways, gangsta-style.

I switched glares in turn between Bob and Jack. I could not resist one last jab.

"Who first, eh?" The barrel shifted between them, evoking streams of sweat down the neck of each. "Which will be easier to clean up? White on red?" I looked at Bob Montez with his white ponytail and out-of-fashion coral-colored jacket with the wide white lapels. "Or red on white?" I turned back to Jack Muck and his perpetually pale skin with spray-on orange tan and off-white tourist Polo shirt and shorts. Try as I might I could not wipe the triumphant grin off my face. Who was trying?

With a quick move I leveled the gun at Bob's chest and unleashed a roar that reverberated off the metal sheets covering the establishment's front and back. Tufts of white lapels and ponytail exploded—splatted on the floor streaked with scarlet. The ruin of what a moment earlier had been Bob Montez shuddered, but still refused to exit the swivel stool, remaining upright and gazing blankly back at me. Jack's eyes angled to stare at the ruin in horror.

A second blast erupted. Jack's pale and orange Czech skin exploded with crimson dots like a squid in love. Though his face went blank, his corpse, too, declined to abandon its bird-like perch and continued to face me as though nailed in place.

Unleashing the rest of the bullets, I emptied the gun into their chests just to make sure—no, because it felt good. I grinned. Danced my jig again. Finally paused. The bodies had still failed to fall off their stools and, as their eyes stared crookedly into the warehouse's gloomy corners, I sighted a detail that had somehow eluded me up to now in the semi-darkness of the interior. Jack's hands remained in place over his crotch, right over left, and I realized he had not moved his hands since I entered. I had thought he was frozen in terror. Now he was dead. Last I heard the dead don't scare.

I looked at Bob. Bob's hands were a copy of Jack's. Right over left. Both over crotch. Both frozen.

Inching forward, my suspicions aroused, I peered closer, taking care not to step in Muck's muck. Around Jack's wrists I glimpsed see-through plastic handcuffs linked to the rotating seat, the bar stool's legs bolted to the floor. A glance at Bob's hands revealed the same—more transparent loops prevented his escape.

My eyes peered. Rose to examine memory banks without interference from the here-and-now, which could always be fucked with. And someone had sure the hell fucked with this. Lowering my eyes, I gazed up at the monitors. Same as ever in M&M's control room... A strange glint where none should be triggered even more suspicion—I stepped around Bob Montez's mess and peered.

A plastic screen came into view, formerly invisible in the soft interior lights, and which I was certain had not been there when I had first visited, but which now clearly interceded between the doomed pair handcuffed to the stools and the row of monitors stretching behind. Gore dripped from the lower half of the transparent bullet-proof screen, leaving the expensive computer monitors squeaky clean. One monitor showed two graphs of voice patterns with two large red Xs superimposed. They did trigger a memory.

"No..." Sailing right through arguing, my third favorite activity after gloating and complaining, I arrived at my fourth favorite and launched right into whining. "God-dammit." I stamped a foot. "Don't tell me—"

"Then ve von't," rang a familiar voice from the door at my rear.

I turned, already spinning the Colt's chamber.

"But at least take our compliments, dear Pinky...for a job vell done."

The chamber stopped spinning and by force of habit I aimed the barrel at the twin nemeses standing in the doorway. But I knew I had shot my bolt, in my anger at the dead-namic duo, having fired all my bullets. There was no mistaking their identity as the lights brightened—only *they* would stoop so low.

The flab face grinned under its bald round head. The taller more gaunt figure smiled just as broadly beneath a shock of white hair gathered behind in a ponytail and drooped over a coral Mexican jacket with wide white lapels.

"Jack. And *Bob.*" I exhaled.

"Bob as ever was," smirked Ponytail. Despite his six feet of skinny, his voice was still a trifle lower than mine. This again put me off. At four-foot-eleven, mine should have been lower. But Nature screws who it pleases without even a polite Thank-ya Ma'am. That left the Thank-ya Very Muchs to Elvis and me.

"Then *who*—?" As Jack and Bob sauntered into the room in their usual smart manner with their squeegee-clean noses scraping the clouds, my gaze trailed to the corpses on the bar stools, still frozen in place. More plastic ties appeared in the growing light, fixing the corpses' elbows to the bar stools' wooden backs. Someone had made damned sure this pair would not escape—or talk, as I gathered from the red Xed-out voice prints visible on the monitor behind.

"No wonder they didn't move...or squeal," I said.

Approaching his look-alike, Bob raised one hand and punched obscure points on his palm and instantly the doppelganger corpse transformed. Losing the white hair and ponytail, the corpse assumed darker colors. I blinked. Still breathing deeply—dizzy from the ordeal of believing I had just executed Montez & Muck—I stared into the face of a light-skinned Argentine.

"José," I blurted. "*El Mayór* of Shitty Juarez."

Bob grinned.

Jack read the future in his own palm and leveled a five-fingered salute at his own deceased look-alike. A half-blood Mexican appeared, also tied and shot—the gang leader fallen victim to one of his own favorite methods of execution for those who crossed him.

"El Chapo," I blurted. Now I was more than shook up—I was terrified. My eyes spun round looking for the inevitable retribution from El Chapo's Bad News cohorts.

"Such a little man you are, Pinky," snorted Jack, in his usual faintly Czech accent. "You are so predictable."

"Heh," added Bob, smoothing his ponytail. "An open book."

I propped the empty Colt behind my belt and stepped back. I needed to get as far away from here as possible before the worst happened—if anything could be worse than killing the chief of Mexico's Sun God cult, who was known for taking bloody revenge on entire towns. "But what—?"

"Ve *knew* that you vould not go through with it, Pinky. You vere so terrified of Mr. Chapo that the only vay ve could get you to kill him vas if you thought you vere killing someone else. Same with the Mayor." Jack grinned.

"And who do you hate more than anyone else in the world?" Bob smiled at Jack.

I blinked. Gradually caught my breath. I got the hate part.

"And how?"

"Ve simply invited them back for a little emergency meeting vhen ve returned from Argentina. A nerve gas put them to sleep, along vith their drivers." Jack glanced at the back of the warehouse where I thought I glimpsed in the far corner two pairs of feet protruding from under canvas. The drivers. I wondered if the cleaning lady was due a raise as much as I was.

"But...but why kill them at all?"

Bob said, "Remember our talk about parallel slits?"

"Huh?"

"Heh," repeated Bob. "You still wouldn't understand, Pinky. But trust us. This was for the best."

Jack added "It has to do vith a certain object that El Chapo's gang has in their village in the mountains."

"So you flipped me to them...gave me up...knowing that I would walk through walls to escape and come here...and knowing that I would kill them instantly if I thought I was killing you."

Bob and Jack exchanged mirthful grins. "Pinky is catching on."

"A simple phone call to the police chief ensured that they vould put you in jail," said Jack, "vhich ensured that you vould come here."

There was something wrong. "But how could they get here before I even arrived? I just left Mayor José at City Hall, and El

Chapo is right now driving to City Hall to kill me..." My eyes indicated the transparent plastic ties that still held the two bleeding bodies to the bar stools.

Jack and Bob exchanged glances—for the first time I saw hesitation. Yes, something was *deed* wrong.

A loud bang reverberated through the office.

The grins faded.

Voices rose outside. Angry voices.

Bob looked at me, face like wood. "Pinky—*what* did you do?"

Bob, Jack, and Your Stoolie strode quickly to the little shop's main reception area as more bangs resounded on the metal sheaves. Voices traveled from the back of the shop, where another metal plate covered a back door. Cobalt-plated grinders popped into gear and ripped into the metal sheaves, tearing strips off the front of the building. The noise meant nothing. Though half of Juarez could hear it, by morning the City would remember only silence.

Bob glanced at Jack. "They'll be guarding the back."

Jack nodded. "Big fish vaiting for little fish."

Bob looked back at me. He spoke normally, but his face was still like wood. "Pinky, have you ever volunteered for anything?"

"What do you mean, *Bob*?" I squinted. "You know I never volunteered for nothin'—and especially not for this."

The front door grew thinner as more strips of metal ripped away. The wooden panels underneath the metal sheaves began to splinter.

"Just thought you might be interested in learning how volunteering works. I mean, it's never too late to learn, is it, player? Even for you."

My suspicions even more aroused, if that were possible after what I had just witnessed, I stared hard at Jack and Bob. They stood beside me in silence, one on either side, their backs to the wall that separated their little video shop from the neighboring stall—the same tiny shop I had traversed just minutes ago to access their video production office.

The door exploded.

A stream of stern-faced thugs poured into the anteroom, sporting AR-15s and Glocks, two black Land Rovers and part of a green Oldsmobile visible through the gap in the growing twilight.

I glanced at Bob and Jack. If anyone could save themselves, and get me out at the same time, it was the Founders of Sirius Enterprises. With quiet smiles, each took a step backward. Merging into the wall, they vanished.

No volcano.

"*El pendejo aqui.*" Two of the intruders sprang to my sides and gripped my arms. Taller than your average Mexican, they towered above me, their grip unbreakable. My eyes focused on the smashed entrance where two more figures stepped through the still-smoking gap. Their harsh glares poured over me like anti-sauce on anti-pasto. The light-skinned one was European heritage, South-South American, while the darker of the two was almost my size and bore a wide broom mustache with pockmarked cheeks. The other gang members parted before them with the fear and respect of pizza delivery boys for a four-star chef.

Another voice shouted from the adjoining room. "*Venga aqui! Mira!*"

The pair followed the voice while their acolytes dragged me limply behind. They halted.

"*Coge El Dios...*"

Before their wide stares sat the two bodies tied to bar stools, chests turned to mashed potatoes—with red gravy. Without Bob and Jack to weave their magic, there was no obscuring the identity of the two corpses. *El Generalissimo* of potholes lumbered forward to get a better look with his one good eye, and Fat Paco, his *Moronista* twin, right behind. "Chapo... José... These bodies—they are *you.*"

The two chiefs paled and crossed themselves. They kissed discs of the Sun God hanging around their necks.

Their gang stared. "You have been *fucked.*"

El Chapo and José turned and looked at the shortest *pendejo* in the room.

Another thug grabbed the still warm Colt from my belt. "And this is the *pistola* that did the fucking."

"So this is how you 'negotiate', Señor Marlowe?" Mayor José hissed. "I think that now I will make time for you. I hope your Vatican story is not entirely false—for your sake."

El Chapo raised one arm. In the light of blue screens of death that suddenly appeared on the computer monitors behind the corpses—doubtless an auto-destruct triggered by M&M before they left—my face barely had time to turn paler than its natural gringo skin when a blackjack kept a rendezvous with my skull, mercifully exchanging the here-and-now for a black void of there-and-then.

Quantum Marlowe

CHAPTER 25

I awoke in the back of an SUV to twin moons swaying against a glorious painted backdrop of blue sky and white streaks of cotton. The moons swayed in unison like jazz horns in the Coconut Grove. For a moment I was lost in imagined jazz riffs, then I realized my own gaze was swaying in time with the moons, and a sudden stab of pain made me remember that I had a skull, and inside the skull a brain—a brain that throbbed with an unaccustomed rush of blood and pain from a savage lump.

A bump jolted me to full consciousness.

I'd been given The Treatment by El Chapo.

As my eyes focused, a chill descended my spine, the kind that follows when a Gambino hugs you and calls you 'brudda'. The moons were round but closer than they should be, and as my peepers settled on their fullness, it suddenly came to me like yesterday's lasagna that, instead of nipples, which my mind kept trying to insert, these moons had eyes. And one had a mustache.

"I theenk *el pendejo* has finally joined us."

The SUV hit a pothole and sent another electric jolt through my legs and head. A mirror image of the moon with the mustache swiveled in his perch in the back seat next to the gangster who had spoken. I could feel his gaze on the back of my head, sense who it was.

"*Bueno*." Cheche's voice.

A hand gripped my forelock from behind and shook me hard, disrespecting Elvis. "You are awake now, *pendejo*?" It was Chapo's hand. He shook me again. "Take a good look, you leettle sheet. *Mira* what you did."

I stared hard ahead and glimpsed an upside-down landscape. With an effort I reorganized my mind and realized that the moons

~241~

were the faces of the Chapo and José whom I had just drilled in M&M's video shop, and who had been tied head-down over the open back of the SUV so their dead eyes would stare into mine, and that I myself was hanging upside-down by my knees to face them, my arms, like the two other corpses, tied behind me vertically to my feet, while my body hung by the knees over the first of the SUV's two roll-bars.

"How do you like your seat, little pig?" called Mayor José from his position in the back seat of the SUV next to Chapo, where he could reach back and touch me. "Just a little thing we cooked up. We thought you might appreciate flying *first-class*. Since you are such a big-shot international financier." From the second row of the double-seated SUV, José and Chapo chuckled, their voices distinct in my ears though my eyes could see nothing but their doppelganger corpses swaying against the blue sky, dripping blood on the vehicle's loading floor. I secretly exulted that I had shot their twins—wished I could get the real thing in my sights as well.

More scenery came into view. By the side of the dusty pitted track, rough crosses loomed, wooden sticks stuck in small piles of rocks by relatives to mourn the handiwork of those who now had me in their sights and, on occasion, from my upside-down position I saw bodies sprawled uncomfortably on the shoulder, bodies that relatives had not yet discovered. Behind the SUV motored a black Land Rover packed with thugs toting more AR-15s and Uzis, the car's outline edging from behind the moons only to be eclipsed again. From the sound of more motors I concluded a third vehicle must brave the way somewhere in front of our little caravan.

The driver swerved—deliberately hit the next pothole. The pain jolted my knees and spine and laughter rose from four throats. "*Bueno*, Cheche. Who says *El Gobernador* does not care about our roads? We have potholes right where we want them." They laughed hard.

The road began to curve and climb, enabling the third SUV to escape the lunar eclipses to reveal a clutch of unshaven, long-haired gangsters in their now-familiar Hawaiian shirts, their weapons perched nonchalantly. My brain still reorganizing, I glimpsed behind them a two-tone car bringing up the rear, driven by dark uniforms and tri-color flags on their shoulders, expanding our caravan to four vehicles. Were *Federales* escorting El Chapo, or was El Chapo escorting *Los Federales*?

Desert surrounded us, but as the road turned it opened onto an oasis of greenery set in a little valley among hills that climbed to a range of mountains. How many more such oases lurked among those ridges? The road evened out, the potholes filled, and dirty adobe huts sprouted, expanding into a shantytown as we entered the high valley.

The valley was dominated by a hill, and the closer we came, happily with fewer bumps, I noticed through the haze of blood over-saturating my brain and the swaying pair of slaughtered corpses propped in front of my face that the hill was larger than I had supposed, almost mountainous, and that our caravan had turned a sharp corner. We drove up an incline, the expanse visible to the left below and a blank slope climbing on the right.

Up we drove until we took a hard left onto smooth level pavement suggesting that the asphalt of the village had given way to concrete, seemingly out of place for such a remote locale, though welcome after the many potholes.

More adobe walls appeared. We jerked to a halt.

At last a knife cut my bonds. My arms tried to fold backwards, evidently as confused as my brain after having been suspended upside-down for hours, but after a pained moment or two I managed to grip the SUV's roll-bar and send chemical signals to my legs to climb down. In time they might again become getaway sticks—for now they were just sticks.

"The leetle sheet is trying to move." El Chapo again.

"I'll help him," said Mayor José. From the back row of seats José turned and with a swift movement shoved my feet, sending my heels overhead, and the moons dropped below the horizon. I landed on my backside in the blood pooled in the flatbed of the SUV.

Howls of glee came from outside the car.

At a bark from Chapo they grew quiet. "Don' forget. Thees *pendejo* believed he was shooting *me* a while ago. In his mind, he did. And in my mind, that is *my* blood on him."

Hands dragged me out. With a tingling rush, blood returned to my legs. I stumbled, finally managing to catch my breath and stand, the dizziness slowly receding. Not much remained of my new Canali suit. By chance it had been buttoned when they clubbed me and it was still on and still fit, but the stains and dirt and blood had accumulated so swiftly that I could scarcely be distinguished from the growing crowd of peons who had climbed the long ramp behind the caravan and now gawked at the arrival of their leader, El Chapo.

We had parked before a row of houses that extended left and right. Behind me, the road led down to the shantytown. I turned and—surprisingly, after my ordeal—saw that at the far left end of the row of houses the road hooked right to disappear around the west side of the mountain. The hill, I realized, was not natural, but was a huge three-stepped pyramid, the result of enormous labor which had terra-formed the rockface and dirt from what must have originally been a natural formation. A smaller, shorter level loomed far above us, not accessible by the road. The back of the pyramid, I supposed, merged with a ridge of smaller hills visible on either side and eventually rose to join the range of peaks I had glimpsed in the distance when entering the valley.

The pyramid dominated the village and from its top I well imagined one could see anyone approaching from all points of the valley. From my position on the pyramid's first level, I could not see the top, but a wide stone stairway plainly climbed the pyramid from some point above us, pausing only briefly at the second level. As I stared up, my gaze climbing the stone tiers, I was more than surprised—I knew next to zilch about piles of stone built by ancient corn-eaters—but I was ready to bet the pot that El Chapo's pile was the biggest ever built by anyone, even King Toot and his Mommies.

My eyes finally dropped, and I saw directly before me a large luxurious house carved into the side of the pyramid, a forest of well-watered fronds waving around its garden-sheltered entrance, and I realized with a start that what I had thought was a long row of houses was actually a single wide structure, presumably the home of *El Caudillo*, the village's Big Man, El Chapo himself.

A cloud of dust drifted past, and the caravan expelled a dozen or so thugs who posed and cocked their guns for effect in front of the growing crowd of peons.

Cheche ignored them and gripped my jacket. He yanked it off.

I removed my stained shirt and tossed it after the jacket. I felt my hair. At least Elvis still stood tall.

"*Look* at thees, José," said Chapo.

The Mayor of Juarez glanced at the bloody pile of clothing and at the two corpses lying alongside, another thug attempting clumsily to cover them to disguise their identity from the growing crowd of onlookers. Squeegeeing a finger in my ear, I could sense a reprimand coming.

"You know what causes thees?" While José and Police Chief Cheche stared at El Chapo, the others cast their gazes down out of respect—or out of something else? "Turning a blind ear to beesiness. That is what causes thees." Chapo, who was my height but more solid than me, moved his bulk with the ease of an alley cat. He approached the corpses. "Thees is the result. Remember what they said in that movie which I told all of you to watch: blood...she is a beeg expense."

Cheche cocked his head. "'Blind ear', Chapo? I think you mean to say *blind eye*. Or *deaf ear*."

Halting in mid-step, Chapo turned to look at Cheche. The other thugs quieted. Chapo squinted. Smiling, he passed his gaze over the gang. "So, Cheche, you theenk that El Chapo is mean? You are not happy working for El Chapo?"

Paling, Cheche stepped backward. At a glance from Chapo, his compadres grabbed Cheche as I had been grabbed in M&M's video shop.

Chapo stepped near. Faster than a Chicago loan shark doubles his interest, he whipped out a stilleto and plunged it in Cheche's eye. Whipping it out, he followed up by drilling it into Cheche's ear. He wiped it clean of blood on my tossed jacket while Cheche dropped to the ground, struggling to keep from howling.

"When Chapo says *blind ear*, that is what you should hear. But just so you don' be confused no more, you can have a blind eye *and* a deaf ear. Are you still confused, mi amigo?"

Cheche shook his head, covering his orifices with his hands trying to stem the bleeding. José exchanged guarded glances with the *Federales* as they watched Cheche wallow.

José frowned.

Ignoring him, Chapo breathed deep. "It feels good to be mean. I theenk I like it."

A straggler among the peons finally made it up the incline and stood alongside the crowd. He was old and slow in dropping his gaze.

Chapo turned and stared at the fellow. Chapo pointed.

With a rush, his thugs grabbed the old man and dragged him away from the crowd. They dragged him to the pyramid's sloping wall where a thin concrete-lined ditch served to drain excess rain water away from Chapo's roofed residence.

Two AR-15s perped.

His blood flowed into the ditch. When his eyes glazed, the thugs picked up his corpse and dragged it to the far corner of the pyramid, which, from the position of the sun, I could tell was the pyramid's eastern slope. Chapo and his thugs and the crowd of peasants followed—and me, alternately pushed and dragged by two more thugs, while Cheche staggered feebly after, trying to cover his injured eye and ear with one hand.

When all had arrived at the edge of the pyramid, the gangsters tossed the old man's body down the side where it rolled until finally coming to rest below on a bloody heap. I saw with a shock that the heap was composed of other bodies, other victims, layer upon layer.

"Ay!" Happy shouts rang out all round. Guns popped in the air in celebration, golden neck pendants of the Sun God flashing, grilled teeth grinning.

Chapo waved. His followers grew silent. "Bring the fucked ones inside. I want an answer from this gringo as to how he found another Mexicano as handsome as me...and why he did what he did to such a handsome man." He turned to José, who had been silent during the execution. "And maybe he can even tell us who took our chopper."

As the bodies of Chapo and José, whom I had shot in Montez & Muck's shop, were dragged inside El Chapo's mansion, a single muscular thug picked me up with one arm and carried me in. The thought crossed my mind: I think El Chapo means to be mean. Perhaps it's best to leave jokes at the door.

I had expected the interior of Chapo's pyramid HQ to be long and thin like the two halves of a Georgia shotgun house rearranged lengthwise. But such was not the case. The two wings of his fairytale castle *deed* extended to left and right away into darkness, but the main structure was directly in front, and up, its inside wide and tall as Grand Central, extending deep into the pyramid. How far? No way to tell. But at least one corner faded into distant darkness just like the wings.

Wide skylights like a Silicon Valley mogul's solar panels drenched the structure's opening in sunbeams, and as a slight breeze entered through the open front portals, a cloud of golden disks suspended from rafters by cords flashed as they twirled, like sharpened flakes of snow.

Several sets of self-assembled blond Ikea guest combos littered the entrance 'vestibule' I guess is the word, if the 'Querque Gazette knows word-smithing. Servants appeared from either direction out of the darkness, dressed in what seemed to me Bed & Bath one hundred percent cotton bathroom pullovers, top-knots on their heads pierced by what could only be Wal-Mart volume-packed turkey feathers. But maybe I've spent too much time discount shopping instead of geographic exploring. At any rate, my eye began to look for Cortés on a horse to complete the history-book picture.

The servants laid out a large canvas. Here were placed ever-so-gently the bodies of Mayor José and His Worshipful Highness, El Chapo—'Señor Donatello Sylvester'—as his servants addressed him, or, in my mind, Don *Don* for short, pun intended. Must be part *New* Mexican, I thought. Which makes Don *Don* the first 'mixed' Mexican I'd ever met: half 'Old' Mexico and half 'New'. But still purer Indian than Benito Juarez himself, the very image of those angry swarthy malcontents whom, for half-a-millennium, the priests had failed to convert in the pizza oven desert on the road to Las Cruces.

A kick in the small of my back alerted me that my presence was required. I pitched and almost fell but managed to recover my balance. A pissed-off Quinn came out of his basement like a Dr. McCoy defying my Spock super-ego.

Two long-haired thugs propped me in front of Don Don while he leaned against an Ikea chair's silvery metal arm. I was shirtless. It was mighty strange to stand there in half a Canali in front of Chapo with Chapo's own blood still on my chest. At that moment, I was closer to meeting Saint Patrick than I had ever been...or meeting his snake, depending I suppose on my subsequent direction after my time in limbo.

"I have a leetle question for you, mi amigo."

I still had trouble with the blood reoccupying my legs. For some reason it seemed to regard my sticks as alien territory. Swaying, I noticed Big Man José Gonzalez standing not far from Don Chapo Donatello. Most of the thugs gathered around me, their eyes on Chapo. But a few stood closer to Don José including the half-dozen Federales in their dark brown uniforms and badges, AR-15s at their sides. Neither the Federales nor Don José was smiling.

Don Don, on the other hand, could not stop smiling. His smiles were matched by the enthusiastic expressions of his gang, who were better armed than the Federales, a few possessing military-issue grenades on their belts to match their Uzis.

To my surprise, Don Don pulled my jeweled cross—that is, the cross formerly mine—from his jacket. In the flood of sunlight, he admired its construction. Now that he was on home territory, his secretiveness was gone. I noticed that several more jewels had flaked off, presumably by Chapo. After all, it takes a lot of cash to fund the kind of retirement and medical plans that true gangsters demand. Just mention 'union' to your local city council.

I finally stopped swaying. Chapo—that is, Don Don—still leaning against his Ikea armchair, bent forward to stare into my eyes, his aqua-colored shirt reminding me of squid fishing in the Gulf of Cortés. I suspected I would shortly end up as squidbait as surely as Carlos Marcello's enemies in New Orleans had ended as gatorbait.

Chapo's eyes grew big. "Do you theenk that canvas works as well as tinfoil?"

My eyebrows crawled oppositely. Just like my mind. "Come again?"

"To get more power, to increese, as you say, the power you get from the shape."

I still didn't get it.

Don Don Chapo the Great snapped stubby fingers and all the

thugs with their Uzis and blue Hawaiian shirts and Mets caps and the Federales with their dark brown uniforms and AR-15s exited the palace. Several swarthy half-nude male and female Mayan-looking attendants with feathered top-knots—no, they were slaves I decided—appeared and hurried to Chapo's side, one bringing a length of bulging cloth and metal, while several others labored to bring a huge rolled-up item of what looked to be thick carpet. In the middle of the palace's huge interior they unrolled the large item. It wasn't carpet, but similar, thick-knapped to at least three inches, resembling the pad that floor installers put under real carpet, except it was ten times as thick, and sticky so it stayed on the floor where it was put.

While Chapo watched, his slaves drove the metal rods into the pad, which apparently served as ersatz dirt, and stretched the length of cloth over the rods. In seconds the items became a small camping tent—pyramid-shaped. The tent was accessed by an oval opening in the front, and Chapo pulled the opaque screen to one side and invited me to enter.

"I theenk it is important to have as leetle metal as possible in one's pyramid." I noticed he could not help but pronounce his *e's* long, so he really said *peeramid*. Taking Chapo at his 'word', so to speak, I entered. Not because I trusted someone who had just mutilated a close friend and executed a loyal follower, but because this Irishman had no choice.

Chapo crawled into the tent behind me. Together we sat cross-legged in the empty space formed by the pyramid's canvas and stared at each other. My imagination wandered to marshmallow toasting and singing Greensleeves, but I was pretty sure that El Chapo had something else in mind than Scouting reveries. I only hoped it didn't involve 'you show me yours'. There must be plenty of closets in Don Don's mansion where he could play games with his naked slaves without resorting to meeting strangers in portable tents.

He leaned closer, making me nervous. "I know that the shape of the *pyramid* gives power—and you, Señor Marlowe, you are from *Los Estados Unidos*, the home of beeg power and beeg technology. You know that pyramids give power to whoever masters them. I also know that how you *build* them is important."

My eyes began to wander away from Señor Madman's pockmarked face, no longer content that he was my size, and wishing there were pictures in the tent that I could look at.

His hand grabbed my elbow and shook it. "Meester Marlowe, you are a gringo, that means you have *teotl,* beeg power, so you know about the power of pyramids. My question for you is...is cloth as good as tinfoil? Or should I cover the outside of my leetle tent with Reynolds Wrap to increese its power? What do you theenk, *leetle shee*—" He halted himself, then: "What do you theenk, Meester Marlowe?"

Did I dare? I had no choice. Despite my frantic efforts to control Quinn, he jumped into the fray.

"I'm afraid I left my tinfoil at home, Chapo buddy, along with my silver bullets. But if I were you, I would start covering my hats and my tents as soon as possible to keep the negative *kumbaya* energy away. That stuff can be a real killer when you're trying to feed Old Quetzal his evening blood-feast. Believe me. I know."

Chapo's mouth dropped. He leaned back then slowly nodded.

"I knew it. That is exactly what I have been saying to that stupid José and his stupid Federales. But they never wan to leesten to me. In their pig eyes, thees leetle Mexicano is jus a leetle brown man from the desert. Like El Presidente Juarez himself." Chapo stuck out his chest. "Don Don Chapo—El Chapo Magnifico—perhaps soon: Chapo El Magnifico, El Presidente of all Mexico...if everytheeng goes right. I'll have to theenk about this, what you said, this 'negative kumbaya energy'."

What did I unleash? With a savage swipe, I sent Quinn back to his basement along with Pietro and Elvis before they got us all killed.

Chapo pointed to the front screen. Time to go. As I pulled the screen aside and scrambled out, I heard him make a happy sound. "And let those ceety boys theenk about what I jus deed to them. Next time they get a phone call from our Special Friends, maybe they will tell El Chapo instead of trying to keep it to themselves. And maybe they won't complain so much when Chapo says we should theenk about putting *las drogas* inside our leetle statues to send them north." Chapo frowned.

I got it. There was more to this *blind ear* matter than I had thought, and Cheche wasn't just a poor slob in the wrong place at the wrong time. Not that a coldblooded executioner of helpless bus passengers can be anyone's poor slob.

We stood before the tent. Chapo's slaves dismantled the canvas until their leader should want it again. At a nod from him, they promptly produced reams of Reynolds Wrap. Someone brought in a collection of sombreros and rancher hats, which they also began to cover with tinfoil. I had to hand it to Quinn; single-handedly he had launched a whole new clothing style.

Chapo turned again to me. "We 'technologists' have to steeck together. The rest of thees peons round here don know notheeng 'bout pyramid power. Not like you and me. Now, Meester Marlowe, you must go weeth my Indio compadres. They will help you get ready for when we mus' talk again."

Into the darkness they took me, the darkness that led under El Gran Pyramid itself, like that Italian job Dante who the Vatican loved to depict in its highfalutin paintings, a street slob who for Cruach-knows-why chose to dive into the lowest levels of hell. The cloud of sparkling crystals was left behind as four half-naked Mayan girls, two shorter than me, which surprised me even more than seeing Mets hats on long-haired cartel *asesinos*, led me gently but firmly down a wide hallway and around a corner into a candlelit spacious room in the center of which rested a broad ceramic bathtub. Already filled. I dipped a toe: hot to luke-warm.

Two more darky elfs appeared at the door, bearing gifts. And who cared if it was from Greeks or not? It was food. Not what I was used to, consisting of corn tortillas, corn soup, corn grits, and, you guessed it, corn on the cob. Not a potato to be seen. But there were bits of something edible in this maize-orama: slices of meat, though whether the meat came from raccoon, turkey, or 'long pig', I couldn't tell. I stuffed it down promptly, meat addict that I am.

Turning, I noticed that all four munchkin-itas still stood by the tub. One poured in liquid soap. Another perfume. The last two held in their hands what could only be scrub sponges.

Here's where my culture started to clash with the locals—I'm not used to bathing with others, not *with* underaged naked females, and certainly not *by* underaged naked females, whatever the hell that damned Pietro might fancy in his dreams. Two pulled out their turkey feathers and let their top-knots down. Waves of shimmering hair glittered in the candlelight, framing full breasts and pretty faces.

Well, there went that. Pietro came to life like an unpaid speeding ticket and I dropped my pants. As erect as satyrs on a Greek vase I stepped into the bath and let the black angels hover over me, scrubbing and washing, perfuming and massaging, and taking me with a smile all the way to full Thai Madame treatment. Without even charging my credit card. My ex-card, that is.

At last, when all was done—and done and done again—I had nothing left to discharge or wash, and like good geishas they finally helped me out of the bath. An additional surprise awaited. Two more Indian slaves entered holding a new Canali suit. My size. Therefore, a suit which could only have been brought from my rented locker in Queen of Cheeba's clothes-cleaning Oriental-land since I was rather sure there were no other Canalis anywhere between El Chapo's pyramid and Albuquerque, and I was absolutely sure there were no other such suits my size anywhere in North America. A third slave held up my fedora, again my size. Dressed to the ninety-nines, complete with pink shirt, pink tie, checkered-banded fedora, new Canali shoes, imitation golden Rolex (my Movado stolen in Juarez City Jail), and to touch off my status as the resident 'sapeur', a pink kerchief tucked into my coat breast pocket, gratis by Chapo, I strode out of that room with the confidence of a man who had not just kissed the Blarney Stone but made fucking love to the lump of rock for days on end. To complete the ensemble, I hooked one of the flowers over my right breast—also pink, like a carnation.

Back in the main ballroom, Chapo was waiting. Seeing my decked-out apparition, he smiled.

"How—?" I began.

"Like I tol' you, Meester Marlowe. You have *teotl*—beeg power." Chapo folded his arms as if getting back to business. "When I heard you wanted to meet me and my compadre José to talk about laundering money for us, and when I saw your leetle Jesus cross, I knew I was dealing with someone special. So, before we met, I tol' my friends in Albuquerque to bring you your other suit. I hope you like it."

In Albuquerque? 'Friends'? Just how far did El Chapo's empire run? And how did they know my place at the laundromat where I kept my last suit. And how did they bring it so quickly across the border, complete with my showy extras? And why had he hung me upside down in the back of his SUV if he planned to deck me out afterward?

I had no time to think about all this, however.

The three-inch thick astro-turf laid down for the canvas pyramid-tent was still there. Next to it had been laid carefully (lovingly?) on another mat the bodies of Mayor José and Don Chapo as if they had been the subject of careful inspection while I relaxed in the bath. Both bodies were stripped bare. Eyes staring skyward. Chests punctured like melons—proof that I was a pretty good shot with a .45.

Chapo was still puzzled while staring at his double. José seemed uninterested. José's gaze wandered between me, Chapo, Chapo's doppelganger, his own doppelganger, and the door, where his Federales lingered in the late afternoon sun just past the threshold. The threshold itself was occupied by Chapo's Hawaiian-shirted thugs, while in the sparkling shower of sunlight in the chamber behind us stood a half-dozen male and female Mayan slaves, like voiceless pawns awaiting their fate.

"Damned good-looking hombre," said Don Don, peering at his likeness on the floor. To me, or to the cosmos, or to no one. One bullet as it turned out had split José's skull, making him a tad less identifiable than Chapo's corpse. Not that it mattered. At length, Don Don sat in one of his ultra-modern Ikea chairs and placed his hands on its bare steel arms. He didn't look relaxed. The aqua of his Wal-Mart cotton shirt clashed with the growing dark-red of his chin-line, his neck starting to look as dark and mysterious as the deep interior of his Gran Pyramid that stretched into blankness behind him like an ancient cave full of sacred mysteries.

"Can you tell me their names?" Don Don still gazed at the bodies, his thugs almost out of earshot. I had to admit Chapo had some *beeg* cajones to sit there all alone and interrogate me when I was well rested and could have taken him down a notch with my King Chong karate training. But I didn't. Maybe he had me pegged better than I had him.

I glanced at the bodies and snapped: "Señor Donatello 'El Chapo' Sylvester—and his compadre: José 'El Mayór' Gonzalez." I thrust out my chest like a kid who had did a good thing.

Chapo's redness swelled. I hadn't seen him get truly angry yet; I had a feeling I was about to—that is, if I couldn't keep Quinn in his god-damn basement.

Suddenly Chapo laughed. He slid back in his chair. "That is funny, mi amigo." He let loose a smile. "You know how to get a party started, that is for sure. And you are clearly *un brave hombre*." Chapo glanced through the entrance where Cheche could be seen loitering morosely—he had found a black patch to put over his ruined eye. "Un very brave hombre. Or...maybe something else." He leaned forward in his chair. "Yes, maybe something *very* else."

"Like how else?" I clipped, barely managing to keep Quinn's sarcasm under control. But I couldn't keep him from spitting on the floor. Quinn spat a big one. Bath or no bath, this big-shot Donatello who belonged back in his maize fields with his slavish peons wasn't going to get the best of QT Marlowe, the best—and the best-dressed—PI in America's Southwest.

Chapo stared at me. "Like how maybe somebody put a lot of effort into finding guys who look jus' like me and José. Like how maybe somebody paid mucho money to a private investigator to come here and hang around a certain cantina to get us to meet weeth him. Like how maybe somebody wanted to get me in an elevator so he could switch me with that guy on the floor who looks jus' like me—but how Chapo was too smart for that to happen, so somebody had to kill that *fake* Chapo before the *real* Chapo, me, found out *somebody's* plan." Chapo tipped his head to one side. "Am I getting closer to the truth, Senór Private Investigator?"

I sniffed. "Don't know what to tell you, Chapo bud. I don't know any more than you do. Last I heard one elevator is just like another. And *yes*, I do have connections in the Vatican good enough to launder money, no matter what anyone else has said. In fact, everything I told you is true...every last word." I looked up, thinking of Flynn still wandering the Vatican's empty corridors, with access to every office and safe and who could certainly get me into the Vatican

Bank's offices. But there was something else about that City Hall elevator that began to seep into my mind—something that didn't bear stating out loud.

Chapo snorted. "I theenk it is time to drop the lies, Meester Marlowe." He slid farther in my direction, now on the edge of his Ikea seat. "Look at my face, gringo." I looked at the dead face on the floor, the more pleasant of the two.

Chapo waved his hand. "*Here*, gringo. Look here."

I looked up.

"Do I look like a fool to you? Do you see 'fool' written on my cheeks? On my forehead? Maybe tattooed on my neck?" Chapo unbuttoned the top buttons of his aqua Acapulco vacation shirt and pulled the lapels apart to make his point.

I looked closer but saw only the letters 'MS 13' tattooed on his upper chest. Yep, that really helped. Now even Quinn was trembling. I tried to calm my knees but noticed that my pants legs were shaking as in a breeze. But Quinn was getting even more riled.

"Don't matter t'all, Don Sylvester." I stepped a full foot closer and looked right into the dirty Don's face, fixing his eyes with mine. "Look here, Don *Don*...I don't know nothin' 'bout body-snatcher doubles, or Manchurian candidates, or seed-pods from Mars, or whatever loco idea you may have in your head. Or fancy-pants palace coups in the middle of your damned Chihuahuan desert, like anybody in their right mind would give a gnat's ass to be part of your pile of shantytown bricks. Nobody cares, Chapo! I'm just a private dick who wants to get his cross back so I can take my money laundering business down the road. I have an inside track in the Vatican, and it won't wait till your *mañana* gets here." For emphasis, I reached into the pocket of my suit and, extracting a match from where I had left it a month earlier, scratched it alight with my thumbnail. Too bad I had no cigar.

At this, Chapo calmed. He scooted back in his chair a foot. Put one hand to his chin. "But you are meestaken, Meester Marlowe. Somebody *does* care. Somebody does care about these 'shantytown bricks'." He again glanced at the bodies. "Thees blood is no accident. It was planned...and planned well. I theenk maybe not by you, but I theenk I know by who. And *why*. In fact, I am very happy they were killed. Because that means that those naughty boys' plan has failed, and it is clear that *you* made it fail. And because that beeg gringo movie I tol you 'bout is wrong. Blood is *not* bad for beesiness, Meester Marlowe. Blood is *good* for beesiness. *Very* good! Especially the blood of traitors."

My mind instantly traveled to Muck and Montez. Who else could have engineered this little fiasco? It had their fingerprints all over it, though for what reason I could not imagine, nor could I imagine how the heck they could repair this, their *own* reputation. It seemed Chapo had M&M's necks in mind for his chop suey, and it would take more than yellow nightmares or flashbacks to alternate realities to fix a mess this size. I only wanted to keep out of it.

Chapo tapped a finger on his steel chair-arm. "Jus' one more thing, Señor."

What now? I was not going to finger M&M, although they deserved it, though my mission to shoot Chapo and José had plainly failed.

"What did you do with my helicopter? It was very deeficult for my compadres to bring your extra suit by car."

Now Chapo really had me confused. "Heli-*what*?"

"My helicopter which I keep parked on the hill behind my Gran Pyramid. What do you know about my missing helicopter? You...or *somebody*—took it."

Quinn leaped up. "What the *hell*, Chapo?" I rubbed my hands over my suit, patting myself down. "Do I look like I have 'hijacker' written on *my* cheeks? Do you see 'hijacker' tattooed on *my* forehead? Do you see keys hiding in my pocket? I can't even spell helicopter, and I certainly can't fly one. Even if I could, how could I when I was upside-down the whole time you drove me to this *leetle* fun-house park of yours?" Yep, I couldn't keep Quinn from snapping out a *leetle* sarcasm of his own.

The Don slid back again, which I concluded always meant he was less suspicious. "There is one more matchstick in your pocket, Señor. But you have no key. Thees I know."

Even Quinn was quelled. At this point, I suspected Chapo knew my sperm count.

"I beleeve you, Señor Marlowe. My mind tells me I shouldn't, that I should be wary of your *teotl*, but I beleeve you." Chapo stood. On this signal, his Hawaiian gangsters approached in a mass from the threshold and surrounded me. Chapo turned. "Now it is time for us to go."

Go where? I listened for motors starting up outside but heard only silence in the late afternoon, not even the usual calls of nature drifting up the side of the pyramid. The Federales, led by Cheche and José, entered the chamber behind Chapo's men. They reminded me more and more of frustrated business partners who knew they were being screwed but could do nothing about it. Pietro and Elvis sent hopeful signals from their basement that maybe I was about to be patted on the back and sent on my way with a hearty handshake from El Chapo and many heartfelt *lo sientos*.

I shut them up. I knew better.

CHAPTER 26

I hate always being right.

Yes, we strode out the front entrance to Don Donatello's Shangri La mansion, but then I was marched into the garden to where a stone-stepped flight of stairs led over the mansion and at an angle up the side of the pyramid. Four more half-naked Mayan slaves led the way, carrying two large baskets containing sheaves of cornstalk and yellow and pink flowers, which they placed on the steps before us. Next came the Hawaiian-shirted thugs, me in the center, followed by Mayor José, Police Chief Cheche with his still-bleeding patched eye, which he paused on occasion to wipe clean, and several of José's Federales. All armed. None smiling but Don Don.

Once we reached the top of the mansion, the stone stairway angled left and up where I saw another flight of steps leading up from the far side of Chapo's mansion, matching the stairs we had just climbed. Both staircases merged into one wide flight of stone steps that arched dizzily above us up the sheer face of that vast pyramid, the stairs which I had glimpsed from the village when I first arrived.

Up the wide staircase we climbed.

The ascent was sharp; the steps were high and difficult enough for the full-size hot-shit gangsters around me. For me, the climb was nightmarish. Poorly gifted for climbing normal steps, I could barely make it up a single stair of this damned pile of rocks using my legs alone. The others paused to watch me in surprise, they had not thought this far ahead, it had not occurred to them that visitors might have a problem with size. It never does.

After a hundred or so steps, with my legs wearing out, one of the larger thugs offered to carry me, but my harsh glare put the goon in his place, and I managed the rest of the way using my hands for help and pausing to rest every ten steps. Sure, I slowed everyone down, but I was darned sure not going to ruin my last suit, and I tugged my fedora onto my skull to keep from losing it to the breeze that grew with the altitude. I frowned when the pink flower on my right breast decided to take a flight. Once I almost slipped on a maize sheaf laid down by one of the slaves. She paled and looked at me and then Chapo, but Chapo said nothing, his own climb clearly tiring him. Who were the flowers and sheaves for? Surely this was not usual procedure; there were no flowers on the steps from prior visits, though I did see a few shriveled cornstalks, indicating we were not the first to make this trip.

As we climbed, the sun lay farther and farther in the west where in distant regions it shone down on the Gulf of Cortés and Baja in its journey into evening. What was it about my escort that so many pairs of eyes glanced at the descending disc with strange expressions? Concern? Lack of confidence? I was pretty good at reading expressions due to all those years of dealing with desperadoes—both clients and back-alley bums. These compadres were clearly nervous.

We soon reached the second level of the stepped pyramid. From below I had speculated that Chapo had built a second mansion higher up, which similarly penetrated the mountain's depths. But here was only a ragged hut. Shanty came to mind.

The entire party rested a minute. Unlike the others, I refused to sit and continued to stand to spare my last Canali suit even though my knees were aching from the climb. Again, I stared upward. Behind the little hut, the stairs resumed their vast, world-spanning ascent. Around us, for miles in every direction, the world fell away, leaving the entire valley exposed, the adobe village at its base shrinking to toy-size.

The hut's door opened.

For an instant I couldn't breathe—as shocking a face as I'd seen in my life thrust into the sunlight. Framed by a jaguar's jaw and capped by a dark mantle with many folds, his eyes were covered by a pair of large sunglasses. The mantle covered the man's arms, leaving his chest bare, and descended to his legs to overlay trousers that sprouted a forest of white feathers. A thin fiber rope served as belt.

As my eyes followed the mantle to its extremes, I experienced another shock: the mantle terminated in fingers and toes—the mantle was skin. Whose?

Quinn, Elvis, and Pietro stared from their basement with eyes and mouth wide open. The dark pigment was not just due to melanin, but to something wetter, something redder. I had smelled blood before; not often had I smelled it weeks old and left to dry.

More surprises: on his chest and the portions of his face not hidden by the sunglasses, lay intricate tattoos, including deeply cut black-dyed scars across his breasts that read 'Mara', and below, 'Salvatrucha'. My eyes focused on the sunglasses. So that's what happened to my Loreto rose gold frames. They were imitation, of course, bought in a Bangkok counterfeit stall, but they were mine, and I didn't appreciate this repellent monkey wearing them like they were his.

But this time not even Quinn was willing to object as the creature pulled off his shades and daggered a fierce glare at me. Around his eyes sprayed circles of black tears, the kind that gangsters in the Big House tattoo on their faces to indicate they were 'made men'. I barely had time to contemplate what this meant when I focused on another series of bizarre tattoos: blue ridges like those of a Mandrill baboon had been scarred onto the man's cheeks while the bridge of his nose and the nose itself were tattooed red. He must have got that from reruns of Wild Kingdom.

The only thing that allowed me to keep my sanity while staring at this Hellish image was the fact that the apparition kept its tongue in its head. I thought too soon—out came the appendage, which had been split in two. At least sticking out his forked tongue was not compulsive with this guy, and unlike Andrew he was able to keep it in his mouth. As the tongue retreated, the shaman—as I concluded he was—shook a feathered rattle in my face.

I glanced at my companions. Not only I was intimidated by the hut's inhabitant, the others stepped back as well, their palms and faces glistening with nervous sweat.

Only El Chapo seemed unaffected. Don Donatello stepped closer to the shaman and spoke. My Spanish failed me, but the gist was clearly "Lead the way" because the witch doctor promptly turned and headed up the final flight of steps leading to the summit, the rest of our party following. The flower girls ignored Dr. Feathers and continued to strew stalks and flowers only before me, making my already difficult climb a bit more difficult. But hell if I would ever tell. I climbed like I was born to it. Except for the crawling part, which continued to evoke snide stares from those around me better endowed in the leg department.

Finally, after a last agonizing effort of at least twenty minutes, we made the high summit.

To cool myself after the strenuous climb I removed my hat. While a steady wind blew my red Irish hair, I gazed upon what first struck me as a strip shopping mall, bent in an L-shape of equal lengths, and I blinked to reassure my crowded interior alter egos that I was still awake, still living, although too exhausted even to pinch myself.

An open square of finely ground cobblestones at least 100 feet long and 100 feet wide was bordered on the north—directly opposite from where our little party mounted the final step—by a wide hut similar to the one in which the shaman resided on the pyramid's lower level. Yes, I would call this too a shanty. But wider. And stranger by far. Feathered hides hung over the front, hides of what or whom I dared not guess. Beads and wind chimes were suspended from a long overhang of a tightly secured thatch roof. Upon closer approach behind the shaman, who seemed eager to get to the wispy curtains that served as a door, I thought the beads looked more like pearls, and the chimes more like bones, of what or whom I preferred to stay ignorant. Streaks of dark red stained the white feathers in places. Red also stained the ground before the curtained entrance, as redness stained large areas of the plaza itself.

On the west, forming the other arm of the L as long as the first arm, was a wide, low-slung structure of what I could only call a cage. Vertical iron bars covered the top and front of this structure. I could almost imagine a sheriff's desk and 'Wanted' posters, but there was nowhere to put such—except perhaps on the wooden panel that lined the west side of the cage. Or at the southern end of the cage where a good twenty feet or so of the structure was walled in on all sides, presumably a storage shed, though, like the cage, its outer door bore a bicycle lock, also I assumed from the nearest Wal-Mart.

The southern edge of the plaza accessed by the wide steps was plain enough; there was nothing there at all, not even a half-grating to prevent accidental stumbles over the edge, which, if such occurred, could only mean tumbling the entire face of the enormous pyramid down to the priest's shanty on the second level, and perhaps all the way to Don Don's mansion on the first, not even the stone steps capable of halting such a lethal plunge.

The most disturbing of the four directions, however, lay in the east. The eastern edge of the little plaza also had no grating and no shanty-hut. And no cage. Instead, a small stone dais was topped by what appeared to be an ancient corroded stone altar, dais and altar permanently stained dark red, with deep channels carved into the plaza itself to channel fluid over the east edge and down the pyramid's eastern slope. I had already seen the eastern slope of Don Don's *gran* pyramid—it alone had no intermediate levels to interrupt whatever may tumble down its red-stained slope until reaching the pile of corpses at its foot.

I was starting to really miss Quinn's imagined pat on the back. I began to get the feeling that something very different than a pat may be planned. When the shaman reached the curtained entrance, he pulled the curtains aside and turned to stare. At *mío*... Suddenly my little bath episode with the nude maidens and the quick fetching of my entire fancy wardrobe from Albuquerque took on new significance. The rest of the group turned to look at me as well. So, this is what it means to be the life of the party.

A moan carried from somewhere. At first I thought it was the wind that steadily caressed the plaza and kept the bone-chimes ringing. Then I saw movement in the corner of my eye and realized the iron cage had an inhabitant. The sun was falling rapidly and would soon sink in a blood-red dust. The prisoner, dressed in silk and a gorgeous feather-topped headdress, stood within the cage and suddenly the prisoner's head was surrounded by a glorious solar halo as if the gods themselves had selected the 'fortunate' one to join them in the sky.

The halo quickly extinguished as the sun sank behind the cage's western wall, and Chapo motioned to his followers to take the prisoner out. The shaman hurried to the cage, produced a heavy key, and unlocked a small gate. Two refugees from Oahu's beaches stepped in, grabbed the prisoner and half carried, half walked it out. I say *it*, but by the time the prisoner was escorted past me toward the altar, 'it' became a woman.

I would be lying if I said that I was not a tiny bit relieved. But for what was about to happen—which only the least observant could fail to predict—I felt outrage. This was hardly playing fair, even for El Chapo. Two sets of hands grabbed me and held me in place. Clearly even Chapo and José sensed that chivalry was not *deed* dead and prevented me from intervening.

The others in the little group watched attentively, eyes bright, hands half aloft as if anticipating a celebration. How long had such pantomimes gone on? How many generations of barely disguised local beliefs been acted out in a circus of violence covered with a veneer of crosses and saints? Was this the real source of three centuries of resistance to the padres of Albuquerque, the priests recognizing that the Indians would always cling to their own beliefs, their own customs, their own symbols, which only the fires of an even more merciless faith could kill?

There was no mercy here.

Whatever her offense may have been, if any, the young woman was destined for the sky. First came the preliminaries. Dressed in her white robe and headdress, they led her—without any protest from her, mind you—to the altar where the Hawaiian-shirted thugs ripped the robe and decorations from her body and tossed them over the eastern edge of the plaza. They laid her face-up and nude across the stone altar itself, each gripping one of her limbs.

Next came the priest. Shaking his feathered rattle in her face—and with an occasional evil glance in my direction—he ran his hands over her exposed body, taking possession as it were. The goal seemed to be to inspire terror in the poor woman. She did not cry out, or cry, and in another moment, she had no opportunity because the shaman placed a stretch of white tape over her mouth to keep her silent. I would not have guessed the shaman's next move.

Leaping onto the altar, he stood over his victim and raised his face toward the setting sun. He shouted "*El Sol tiene hambre! Dio, eat your food!*" A combo meal of Spanish and English, to my surprise, mixed with a thick accent of alien sauce, an accent that didn't seem Spanish to me. He removed his feathered white pants and exposed his masculinity. Not for sex, as I soon saw. Removing from his discarded pants his fiber rope that served as a belt, and producing an obsidian knife, he cut sideways through his genitals and through the septum of his nostrils and ran the fiber rope through the cuts. Only one result could follow—an avalanche of blood—the shaman's own blood spilled onto the woman's exposed body. Quinn remarked from below and I had to repeat it; they really seemed to have a thing going with the blood bit. It was already dripping into the stone channels around the altar.

The shaman wasn't done. Stepping off the altar (Chapo and his gang stepped back to avoid splashes, while still stretching the woman's limbs out), the shaman went to business on his victim. Down went the knife, opening her up from stem to stern. In went his hands, cutting out her heart. He tossed the heart into a hollow at the end of the altar where one of the thugs sprayed dimestore lighter fluid and lit it, sending smoke into the evening sky. The woman was plainly dead. Without uttering a sound, she went to wherever the heck pointlessly sacrificed victims go, and her blood joined the shaman's, filling the stone channels and spilling over the edge of the pyramid like a river.

If I had thought the shaman's awful deed was complete, I was wrong. He went to work with his savage knife and performed the next step in his sacrilege—removing the skin from her corpse. No need to describe the gory details. When he was finished, he had a copy of the skin-mantle he was wearing, and only then did he direct the Hawaiian Don Ho look-alikes to carry what was left of her corpse to the side of the pyramid where they tossed it casually down the already-bloody slope. From where I stood in the center of the plaza I could not see the result, only imagine it, for which fact I was glad.

Ignoring the blood still flowing down his chest from his nose, the shaman tied his genitals with a bloody strip of cloth to stem the bleeding and pulled on his feathered pants, then returned to the altar, where, needless to say, no one bothered to wash anything. Clean wasn't the idea. Anyway, I had little time to contemplate the hygiene of crazed blood-thirsty killers as all eyes settled on me.

Far in the west, the rim of the sun disappeared behind the hills.

Dr. Feathers shook his rattle.

All of a sudden it was quitting time; time to punch the clock. The shaman hurried to his curtained sanctuary on the northern edge of the plaza, and the clang of a metallic bell rang from inside the structure—its deafening waves passed through us on their way to the ears of the cult members of the shantytown below and beyond. Did they respond? For a moment I thought I heard joyful cries from the village far below—overlaid by the louder joyful cries of Chapo's thugs. "Ay! Ay-ay!" They danced and waved and sprayed bullets in the sky from their guns. The flower girls threw their white flowers on the bloodied altar, then the girls hurried to toss the rest at me.

The shaman returned. I noticed that he continued to look at Chapo in a strange way. At first, I had thought it was just the shaman being a shaman, but now, in the midst of my compulsive observing, I was certain I detected something more. Concern? Fear? No, it was not fear, but more a stare of confused curiosity as if Chapo had done something out of character that could not be explained. The shaman's suspicious look repeated—now at José El Mayór Gonzalez. But maybe it was just astigmatism.

The shaman approached El Chapo. He muttered something, to my surprise this time in broken English, as if his own language was alien even to speakers of Spanish, which forced their conversation into pidgin Engla-franca. His voice was broken, guttural.

"You, O Don Sylvester. You want I should put the white man in the jail?"

Chapo leveled a respectful, but firm glance on the shaman. "Of course. Yes."

"With...the other?"

Glancing at the jail, Chapo shrugged his shoulders. "Other?"

"Like yesterday...the other."

"We are done with the other. It's the gringo's time."

"But...the other?" Dr. Feathers seemed to have difficulty making himself understood. He resorted to weak Spanish. "Y el otro?" he kept repeating, "El otro..?"

"Si," responded Chapo impatiently. "The other is done. Now is time for el gringo. *Mañana.*"

The shaman paused, still puzzled. Finally he nodded, and the shaman glanced at José as if looking for confirmation, then turned to me.

José meanwhile had walked to the northern edge of the plaza and entered the curtained sanctuary alone. He soon emerged and returned to our little group. A barely perceptible nod to Cheche, then Cheche also entered the curtained temple and a moment later also emerged, both happening while the shaman was distracted attempting to communicate with El Chapo.

Cheche and José exchanged guarded glances.

When the shaman looked to José, *El Mayór* José fixed a glare on him.

Yet again the mysterious stares, this time El Chapo was staring at José with precisely the same suspicious look. There it was...I was now certain that something was going on behind the scenes. What, I could not tell due to the dying light that cast increasing darkness over their faces.

Chapo had not missed José and Cheche's quick dive into the sanctuary. With a curt wave of his hand, he started the whole group moving toward the curtained entrance. Ringed by the Hawaiian thugs, I tagged along, though for the moment it seemed that I had been forgotten.

The shaman rushed to pull the entrance curtain aside to let the others enter the sanctuary, the only time I saw him rush to do anything. Apparently, he had no confusion as to who signed his paycheck, though from my point of view it could be either Mayor José or Don Chapo.

I thought I had seen the limit of horrors, but with the curtains pulled clear, I entered a place that had no right to be closer to God, but should have been, by all rights, lower, closer to His opposite. The interior walls of the structure were covered with more curtains, the heavy curtains themselves strewn with white feathers, beaded pearls, flayed skins of prior victims—even more than the heavy curtains that draped the outside—and bloodstains that could only have been deliberately smeared by the shaman or his slaves. The bone-chimes shimmered in the wind, and the shaman lit several large candles that, protected from the constant breeze by the heavy shifting curtains, cast weird shadows over the frightful chamber.

In the center, however, was what I should have expected, but somehow had not—the shrine to Jesús Malverde himself, on a stepped platform of daises, the highest dais itself consisting of the black stone that had imprinted itself firmly in my mind since I glimpsed the photo in M&M's video shop.

Here was Malverde in all 'His' horror—I was tempted to think 'glory' but how could there be glory in what I had just witnessed? White shirt, ruffled sleeves (what did that remind me of?), black necktie, behind the little statue a plaque of wood with words inscribed: "*Gracias a Dio y a Malverde por protegérme siempre.*" 'Thanks be to God and to Malverde for always protecting me'. Then and there I realized that the black stone was not merely propping the statue, but was the statue itself—a single lump of stone that had been carved and painted by some patient artisan into the Malverde idol that stood before me.

On the layered platforms beneath the little idol lay white flowers to match the white feathers on the walls. Around and behind the plaque were piled gray rocks and stones—good luck charms that Chapo and his cohorts had apparently donated to their little blood-thirsty god to protect them in their drug and migrant enterprises. Red, gray, white loomed through the smoke and fading light. Of green, there was none. Not a trace of the blessed Emerald Isle could be found in that hideous place.

On the right, the back curtained wall was bare of decoration. Here Chapo approached. The curtain on the back wall had been pulled aside, and Chapo gazed through the breezy opening. Several thugs followed his gaze, and, almost lost in the darkness, I peeked a look also, realizing that we saw what José and Cheche had seen a minute earlier.

We gazed on the back of the pyramid, its northern face. As I had earlier supposed, the ridge of hills—one of which had been shaped into the pyramid itself—spread behind us, a high ridge connecting the hills to the pyramid and forming a land bridge from the pyramid's plaza to another spot almost as high as the plaza.

Beyond, the ridge continued into the maze of hills and ridges stretching farther north.

The surface of the bridge was faced with carefully placed stones, each joined together like cobbles, the far end of the bridge terminating in a wider circle of similar stones, flat and to my surprise bordered by what looked like electrical equipment and a gas pump, lit by bright bulbs in the dying light. On the circular clearing someone had carefully painted a large X in white paint, large enough to be visible from the air. I had seen such elsewhere—a helicopter station.

No helicopter was present.

José and Chapo looked at each other, their mutual mistrust plain on their faces, and they moved subtly back from the open window and apart from each other. I recalled Chapo's accusation that someone, perhaps me, had stolen his helicopter—clearly his suspicion now focused on his partner, José. Just when I thought the tension must break, the shaman rang a second time a large church bell suspended on a wooden frame in a corner. As the loud chime slowly drifted into the ether, there being nothing in that stick and linen shanty to produce an echo, the gang stood back and watched. The shaman stepped forward and kneeled before the statue of Jesús Malverde and placed his forehead on the base of the statue and mumbled. In a day of surprises, perhaps the greatest now happened.

The statue of Malverde spoke:

"Mios Italianos, always remember our blood is sacred. The blood of our people will pave the way for a new age."

Each word was echoed by the large bell, the cast metal serving as an amplifier to the statue's mysterious words, like a Mexican wrestling announcer barking into a microphone on high reverb. And, yes, like the other divine messages I had heard, this one too spoke in Italian.

Ecstasy seized the shaman. Leaping to his feet, his jaw opened and his eyes rolled up, his mortal efforts to aid the gods in obtaining their hoped-for reward. Stepping back, he danced around the chamber, rattling his rattle and blurting out bad imitations of what Malverde had just said. I gathered from his confused garbles that the shaman had never visited Italy or read Dante.

Chapo also had a look of surprise, though it seemed far from ecstatic. Rather more like a railroad conductor when he hears the train's engineer blow its horn—all in a day's work. José, on the other hand, seemed more guarded than ever, laying mistrustful looks on both El Chapo and Dr. Feathers.

I glanced about. Used to sensing their masters' moods, it was clear to me that their followers were picking up on their expressions and retreating quietly into separate groups, the Federales with Cheche in one corner, the Hawaiians in the other, as if the Mexican wrestling match were about to begin for real.

Italian being close to Spanish, I concluded Chapo had understood some of the message. I understood a more—the statue itself was clearly another stone coveted by Muck & Montez—and probably for the same reason they wanted the Blarney Stone—and therefore must be why M&M had wanted me to kill Mayor José and Don Chapo in the first place, apparently not believing that I would be capable of stealing the statue itself, even with the Indexer. M&M had mentioned extracting a certain something that was inside the Blarney Stone. Could this 'something' be what was responsible for transmitting the messages? Messages that were transmitted by an Italian? I still didn't get it. Who, from where, and why, I could not explain.

José, however, seemed not to be puzzled—but triumphant. He knew more, I concluded. Perhaps more than me.

Upon a grunt from Don Chapo, everyone filed out of the sanctuary and walked to the middle of the plaza, the Federales and Cheche keeping separate from the Hawaiians. The latter tied my hands with another length of fiber rope and ushered me into the same cage that had minutes earlier held the unfortunate woman, and they closed and locked the gate with another bicycle lock. A Schlage, matching the Schlage that locked the little boarded-up room that my cage adjoined. Even in these direst of circumstances, the PI in me could not help but ID details and count things: twelve people remained on the plaza, excluding what remained of the murdered woman.

As the light died, I sat inside my cage on a short drum-like stool and tried to relax. I'm not one for worrying. But if someone had offered bets that a pale Irish skin would be decorating the side of Dr. Feathers' curtained shanty sanctuary the next day, I decided the odds-on-favorite would be too high even for me to count.

CHAPTER 27

Among clouds I drifted. Above the highest canopy of the oasis that watered the sheltered shanty-town, above the peculiar T-shaped mansion of Donatello 'El Chapo' Sylvester, above the wretched soul of the shaman doubtless resting in his rustic hut on the pyramid's second level after his hard day's work of massacres and drug runs, above any corresponding structure or hill within thousands of feet, I was perched in my little cage like an ivory-colored black-shoed canary, leaning my back against the wood-paneled side, sitting on a little drum-stool, my hands in my lap tied with fiber rope, my fedora still pulled tightly on my head. Images of what could be done with that rope crowded my mind. I shut them out. At least I was not destined to have rope ripped through my genitals. That little privilege was reserved for the master of ceremonies. They had other plans for me. And my *teotl*.

On the east side and ceiling, my cage had just iron bars. Through these bars I stared, my eyes searching the moon-lit night for answers, for clues...no, I'll be plain—for a way out. Even if I punched the Universal Indexer and danced the tango and escaped my cage, I had nowhere to go. The steps were certainly guarded by thugs with guns at every level below and on every road out of town, even if I could somehow commandeer keys to a vehicle and evade *El Gobernador's* potholes in the dark, and even if I somehow made it across the land bridge to the helicopter pad, how long could I survive in the tangled wilds beyond with Chapo's thugs after me?

And—as always—I felt responsible for what may happen to Wendy and Tonya—especially Tonya—Green Eyes. All my fantasies and unspoken wishes welled up like a torrent, her magic gaze fixing me like an insect pinned in a butterfly collection. Muck & Montez had only said to kill José and Chapo, but I was certain M&M's

ultimate goal was to seize the Malverde statue, which had spoken just like the stone in the Vatican.

In Rome, I had refused to listen to the stone. Here I had had no choice and had heard the same bizarre utterances in Italian-tongue that I had heard weeks earlier in an adobe church outside 'Querque, the site of M&M's 'Miracle of the desert', and then again in M&M's secret lab.

Who spoke through these stones? What connection did Muck & Montez have to this mysterious broadcaster? Why did José react so strangely to the words of Jesús Malverde, as if he knew what to expect? It was plain that Dr. Feathers and El Chapo had no conception of the power of their stone, believing that their dirty little idol had truly spoken. It was also plain that M&M, cowards that they were, had sent me to Juarez to do their dirty work of removing the chiefs of both gangs so that M&M might get one step closer to stealing the statue for themselves.

Lost in my midnight contemplations of motives and goals and strategies I thought of the iron bars that composed the eastern side and ceiling of my little cage. Wooden panels had been fixed to the west, perhaps to keep hope from living in the hearts of the condemned if they could watch the setting of the sun, which meant quitting time. The wooden panels behind my back, which leaned against the northern side of my cage, composed the wall between the cage and the shaman's curtained sanctuary. Opposite me, toward the south, still more wooden panels separated me from the enclosed storage room—a cage within a cage, its interior invisible.

I yawned.

A slight scratch sounded.

In my half-sleep musings, I was not sure if it had come from the storage room to my south, from the sanctuary behind me, or from the wooden wall to my west.

From where had the scratching come?

It scratched again—it came from behind the wooden panel to my right, which bordered the western side of my little cage. The western wall must overlook a catwalk that promised a quick death to anyone who missed their step and tumbled down the west side of the immense pyramid. Damned brave, whoever this was. Or damned stupid to take such a chance. Or, perhaps, just damned determined.

"Here, gringo..."

I blinked myself awake—this wasn't part of Chapo's Plan.

"Over here. If you want to live." The voice was a hiss, combined with a low and rough tongue as if the speaker were trying to camouflage his voice.

Pietro Quinn Tiberias Marlowe may be slow in body, and he may be slow in mind, but he sure the hell ain't slow to live. Now fully awake, I flung myself to the spot from where the voice had grunted and pressed my ear against the wooden wall.

"Ya got me, Mac. I'm all ears. And toes. And Canalis. What's your story?"

"Turn around, little man. But move slowly. People may be watching."

At first unsure what he meant, I stood and looked to my left across the plaza. I saw no one in the moonlit expanse.

"No. Sit down. Bring your hands to me."

In the shadows cast by the falling moon, my eyes finally adjusted to a darker patch, and with a barely audible creak, a portion of the wall was lifted outward. That was it—I sat and placed my bound hands close to the open patch. Moonlight seeped through the small gap and revealed a masked face. The face of a full-sized hot-shit human perched precariously on the narrow catwalk, clinging to the side of my cage.

A sharp blade glinted. Never had I imagined that I would welcome the sight of a blade aimed in my direction—I was overjoyed. Contacting my roped hands, the blade snipped them free.

Stupidly, I hissed: "Why?"

"Shut up. Take this." A soft metallic clink sounded. A larger object was thrust through the gap directly into my freed hands, followed by a thick leather belt stuffed with metal tubes. "Give a good account of yourself, gringo. That is the best one can hope for in this life. There lies glory."

With that, the wooden panel slid back into place, and a quiet rustling drifted as the masked man retreated back along the catwalk into darkness, having accomplished his purpose.

I glanced at what had been placed in my lap.

My Colt .45—with a hip-belt of bullets.

"That's the crank." I could not help but echo Andrew's favorite quip. Quietly, of course. I had no interest in attracting the attention of whoever guarded the plaza, assuming my new beneficiary was right in that matter. Carefully I turned the drum of the gun, which I had formerly used to correct the behavior of many an offender in Albuquerque—a collectible 1911 pearl-handled double-action Colt revolver, which every pawnbroker in Querque thirsted to get his hands on. The chambers were loaded. My 'friend' wanted action, all right—the kind that comes from a steel barrel.

A new day had dawned. Or rather a new hope on this increasingly moonless night. As the moon pursued the sun into ever deeper shadows, a plan sprang to mind, a way to get even with those smarmy hot-shit guys who thought I wasn't worth the dirt beneath their fingernails.

Rising, I took advantage of the growing darkness and stood. No point in delaying. I aimed my pinky at the northern wall of my cage—the side that bordered Dr. Feathers' holy sanctuary.

I punched the red button.

Just as the wall erupted into a dark red volcano and the familiar tunes about the Turkish conquest of a certain Greek metropolis rang in my inner ear, I thought I saw in the corner of my eye a shadow scurry across the plaza—it was headed for the sanctuary. Too late to pause, I stepped through the wall, hoping the shadow had been too preoccupied from fifty feet away to watch my Mount Kea erupt. As the last of the bubbles burst behind me, I hid behind the curtain that hung inside the sanctuary.

To watch. And listen.

Sure enough, the shadow entered via the front entrance, intent on its own business. No candles remained lit, all had guttered. But the shadow pulled aside one end of the curtains that lined the back of the little rectangular slaughterhouse, the direction that led to the helicopter pad, allowing traces of fading moonlight to enter.

I sucked a breath—the light revealed the face of Argentina's gift to Ciudad Juarez, its mayor: José Gonzalez. His face was strained, nervous. Several times he looked back through the entrance as though he feared discovery.

José crossed to the center of the chamber. Halted before the little green-less, red-fed, white-as-death statue of Jesús Malverde, the most recent embodiment of Dr. Feathers' ancient gods. So spake Pietro, and I had to admit Pietro was right about that. Grabbing the statue from its perch as the centerpiece of the shaman's place of worship, José carried the statue to the back of the hut and stared north again to the copter pad.

Pietro could almost read his mind: disappointment, concern, anger. The helicopter was still AWOL.

Finally, José turned and hurried the length of the sanctuary, skirting the very spot where I hid silently behind the curtain. When he arrived at the sanctuary's narrow west end, he lifted its curtain to expose a wall of wood panels much like the paneled wall that lined the western side of my cage, installed perhaps to minimize the effects of the constant breeze on the sanctuary itself and make it more stable. His hammer kick loosened one of the panels and with great care he placed the little statue of Jesús Malverde outside the sanctuary on the narrow catwalk along its western side. Returning the panel to its original position, José dropped the curtain back into place and walked to the front entrance.

In an instant, he was gone.

I waited, unsure what this meant—what it might mean for me. For a full minute I stood behind the curtain, thinking, pondering. Finally I decided to continue to execute my own little plan.

From the sanctuary's far end, a new shadow appeared.

I froze as I realized that this shadow had been hiding inside the sanctuary behind curtains just as I, and apparently had been there for most of the night, waiting and watching. I watched, still behind my curtain. Like the previous visitor, this shadow walked to the shaman's shrine to Malverde where it paused and stared at the empty space where the statue had been. After a moment, the shadow moved to the back window and, like the other, pulled aside the curtains to gaze upon the empty helicopter pad.

The face of Don 'El Chapo' Sylvester was framed in the bare moonlight. There was no disappointment here. Or concern. Or anger. Only *triumph*.

Walking to the west end of the sanctuary, El Chapo passed by my hiding place as closely as had José and stopped before the narrow wall of wood. Carefully, he loosened the board that Jose had kicked loose and gazed upon the statue of Malverde perched upon the catwalk. A knowing smile grew. Retrieving the statue, Chapo turned, passed by me a second time, and returned to the shaman's shrine where he put the Malverde statue back where it had been, but *reversed*.

He exited the sanctuary. I listened as his shoes made quiet progress toward the stairs leading off the plaza.

Only one thing I knew—Malverde must be mine.

Like a ghost I slid into the chamber. Stepping to the shrine, I abducted the filthy little statue and hurried to the west wall. I too pushed the panel loose. But I did more: kicking half its length, I took a chance and loosened the entire board, then knocked loose its neighbor, then slipped entirely through the gap until I stood on the narrow catwalk. The black-haired Malverde stared up at me as if to ask 'What did I do to deserve this indignity?' If it had been human, I would have strangled it and rolled it down the slope. Instead, I carried it south perhaps sixty feet along the catwalk until I stood behind the wood paneling that bordered the enclosed room bordering my cage—the storage room intended for Dr. Feathers' sacrificial items.

Off came my digit—as Mount Kea flamed and bubbled, I thrust the statue of Jesús Malverde through the wall into the storage room, and into another dimension. I wondered what insomniac residents of the village below might think of the repeated red flares erupting on top of their sacred plaza that night; then I realized that no one cared about their thoughts, least of all they themselves. In less than a minute, the tango was done and this time, not having stepped through the gap into a new universe, I remained perched on the catwalk in *this* universe.

I could have left the plaza at that moment and taken the high road to the north with my Colt holstered at my side and disappeared into the tangle of hills and ridges that led away from this nightmare valley. I could have. I had undermined the plans of both José and El Chapo. But Quinn wouldn't let me. Or Pietro. Or Elvis. Every inhabitant of my cellar banged on the ceiling with their brooms for me to take revenge on the cartel's parade of death, to use the equalizer that Providence had given me—to make the bastards pay. Why José had hidden the little statue and why Chapo had returned it reversed, I had no idea—and did not care, though that it was a trap for someone seemed certain.

Perhaps me.

But I had had enough. Prying loose the board my masked visitor had loosened twenty minutes earlier, and also its neighbor, I re-entered my cage from the catwalk, propped the boards back into place, and sat on the drum-stool to await what the morrow would bring. Before the sun reached noon, my equalizer would speak its mind. Finally sleep overtook me and I descended into dreams of shadows scurrying through dark curtained rooms, hiding who knows what from each other for who knows why.

CHAPTER 28

I awoke to the sound of clanking feet on the pavement of the stone plaza. Someone walked calmly, legs firm. Another walked quickly, propelled by nervous energy. While a third danced about as if on a fence between them. Opening my eyes, I saw what I expected to see in the late-morning sun: El Mayór José with his Federales bristling with guns, José himself carrying a Glock in his belt, a six-round nine millimeter; Don Don Sylvester with his clutch of Hawaiians as if on break from vacationing in Acapulco, the Don's mini-holsters displaying new twin Luger Mark IIIs with six-inch barrels, the mere sight of which was enough to intimidate; two maidens with baskets of white and pink flowers; and, not to be missed, Dr. Feathers prancing in his eagerness to commence his bloody work on the helpless gringo, his antique bloody obsidian knife sheathed in his rope belt, his face still framed by the skull of a jaguar. Hawaiians and Federales both carried a variety of Uzis, Glocks, and Smith-Wessons.

Was all this for me? Within my cage I continued to feign sleep, leaning back against the wall, sitting on the little drum, hat pulled down. But my eyes and ears were open. Would this army of executioners come first to my cage or enter the sanctuary to kneel before their blood-thirsty statuette?

Neither.

In the middle of the plaza, the group came to a halt. I lifted my hat to get a better look. José's Federales had separated from the rest and stood beside him, clearly in response to some signal from José. El Mayór shifted his weight from one foot to the other, his being the nervous energy. Don Don Sylvester watched without reaction, hands folded, he the calm one, Dr. Feathers standing by his side. Only the shaman looked confused, more than yesterday.

A second signal from José—a rubbing of his finger and thumb together, as my PI training detected—and the Federales lifted their guns and aimed them at Chapo and his Hawaiian-shirted thugs. I had to admit the coup was a surprise. It caught both me and the locals unprepared, and the latter looked to Chapo for support.

"Please do not move, Don Sylvester. My men are nervous...*very* nervous. Our safeties are off and even a small movement might make this day end in disaster." José took a deep breath; Chapo still had not reacted. "But," continued José, "there is no need for anything bad to happen to anyone. That is..." José glanced up at the sun that climbed steadily toward its apex. "Almost anyone."

Whoa, did that ever explain things. At that moment I understood what José's scurrying in the dark had been about. He was springing his trap.

"My friends...mis amigos," José said, mixing Engla-franca with local Espanol, some of Chapo's followers not completely familiar with any but local Indian dialects, "before you judge me too severely, I ask you to consider something."

With no choice, the gang of Hawaiian thugs listened.

"This man, this *hombre* whom you have given all your loyalty to: Who does he work for?" José was ever the educated diplomat, I noticed, and I wondered why he had joined this outfit.

The thugs exchanged puzzled glances.

José pointed at his partner in crime, Chapo. "This man, whom you and all your people down below in your village, whom you have given so much of your lives to serve, to whom you have given most of the money that *our* efforts have made and brought to *our* enterprise...have you ever asked yourselves: Who does *he* serve?"

The Hawaiians blinked.

"Who does he give *his* life to? What does *he* do with the money that you give to *him*? The money which, after all, belongs not to any one individual, but to *you...all* of you."

I had to admit, José knew how to give a speech.

"Have you ever wondered where your leader, Don Donatello Sylvester, *El Chapo*, puts his *own* loyalties, whose interests he himself is serving...since it is clearly not with *you*?" For the first time, José pronounced 'El Chapo' with scorn, as if to emphasize, 'this is just a little man', almost evoking empathy from Yours Truly. Only almost.

Quiet grumbles sounded from among the thugs. It was plain that similar thoughts had passed through their heads.

"My friends...mis amigos...I have a confession to make."

Ears perked even higher.

"Last night, during the darkest part of the night, I came up the stairs and stood upon this plaza."

Here it comes, I thought.

"I watched and I waited, for I knew that something would happen, ever since our friend Cheche was so badly treated by *this hombre* who stands before you now."

Yep, that had *deed* been the start of something bigger, as Chapo had told me the day before—I then noticed that Cheche was missing, apparently no longer able bodied enough for today's confrontation.

"I knew that something would happen. So I waited, and I watched. And our beloved Jesús Malverde, whose glory we all serve every day of our lives, rewarded me with luck, rewarded me by the sight of someone sneaking up the sacred stairs, hurrying in the darkness across the sacred plaza, and entering our holy sanctuary without our holy shaman and...when he thought there was no one around to see what he did..."

The thugs became more nervous, shifted their feet like José still shifted his.

"He entered our holy temple, mis amigos, and committed a sacrilege." José pointed a finger at his Cartel partner. "Don Sylvester, *El Chapo,* stole the idol of our beloved Jesús Malverde. Taking it from its holy shrine inside our sanctuary, Chapo took it away and hid it."

Everyone knew what this meant—even I who was not a member of the cult. José drove the point home anyway.

"He has stolen the source of our good luck and left us without a guide, without our charm, without any god to keep us alive in the dangerous business which our Cartel pursues." José looked more sharply at Chapo. "By his selfishness, this man has put all our heads and hearts on the altar. For without our Jesús Malverde, we are dead.

Somos todos muertos."

No more needed to be said. It was a good con job, I confessed. One of the best I had seen. As I stared from my cage—entirely forgotten—the several Hawaiian-shirted gangsters with their pistols and guns moved slowly away from Don Sylvester. Not quite in the direction of his accuser and now *former* business partner, José Gonzalez, Mayor of La Ciudad de Juarez, but clearly away from Chapo, even the maidens and Dr. Feathers stepping back. Whether they were entirely convinced by José's speech, I could not tell, but no one wanted to be in the way of a firing squad of Federales directed at El Boss.

I also had to hand it to El Chapo, though. The same calm stance and smile remained on his Benito Indian face. One would think he had just received an invitation to down tequila with his buddies instead of to dance under the impact of federal bullets.

Chapo spoke. "You know sometheeng, José, my freend, I had thought yesterday that no one in the world had bigger cajones than that leetle sheet over there in his cage."

Finally I had been remembered, but no one cared enough to glance my way, a fact which Quinn for some reason took personally.

"Now I theenk I have found someone with even bigger cajones, maybe the biggest in *el mundo*." Chapo crossed his arms more tightly, his every move causing subtle shifts to ripple through everyone on the plaza.

"Si, my followers let me have most of their money. But they do not do this because they love me, *Señor Mayór...*"

He threw the sarcasm right back at José.

"If they loved me, I would theenk that sometheeng beeg is wrong. For a good leader of men cannot lead through love, but only through *respeto*." The gangsters exchanged glances again, blinking at every word. "And if I did not reequire that they geeve me most of their money and if I did not kill someone in the village every so often then they would not theenk of me with *respeto*. They would have no respect for me at all."

A couple of nods were visible among the thugs. They got the death and respect part.

"And there ees another reason why mis amigos obey me, and

why they will never theenk of *you*—Señor Gonzalez, *el hombre grande* de Buenos Aires—as their leader. For I come from their own people. I am not part gringo like you, like all of you people from Argentina. I may come from both sides of El Rio Grande, but I am one hundred percent los Indios, los Aztecas, los Mayas. Those are all my people. My customs are their customs. My beliefs are their beliefs."

Chapo finally moved his own feet. Slowly he let his arms drop to his sides. More shifts rippled through the plaza.

"Now, my freend." Chapo stared harder at José. "I have something else to say. For you see, I too climbed the sacred stairs last night."

José stopped smiling. His feet no longer shifted.

"I too crossed the sacred plaza." Chapo raised a finger and pointed up. "I too waited in the darkness and watched. And I also saw someone enter our holy sanctuary."

Everyone's eyes grew big at this news.

"And while hiding at one end of the sanctuary I saw what that someone did."

Sweat appeared on José's face—not from the growing glare of the sun.

"That someone who took our beloved statue Jesús Malverde, our God who gives us our luck and keeps bad things from happening to us when we conduct our business. That someone, Señor Gonzalez, was *you*. You did not see me. You did not know that after I watched you steal our beloved Malverde and hide Him behind the west wall of the temple that I went there and brought it back before bad luck could fall on us, and I put Him back where He belongs in our holy shrine, so we can continue to benefit from Hees presence."

José breathed deep. "And proof? How can you prove the lie that you speak?"

The biggest smile crossed Chapo's face. "By the fact, *my freend*, that I turned our beloved Malverde around so that He would turn His back to *you*. And by the fact that the west wall now has boards that have been loosened. Loosened by your steenking foot when you keecked it open."

Chapo put his hands on his pistols. "And if I need any more

proof, I need only point to our helicopter pad, which you and I do not own, but which our entire Cartel owns, and which is only to be used in the service of our common beesiness, and wheech no one in the world has the keys to start its engine, mi amigo, except you and me, keys wheech somebody took two days ago and still has not brought back. I theenk your plan will not work, *Gran Alcalde José*. You will never take Malverde to Buenos Aires using *my people's* helicopter."

The Federales, seeming immune to Chapo's arguments, drifted into a line to face Chapo's Hawaiians.

The Mayor of Juarez put a hand on his own pistol. "I took no helicopter, Chapo. Rather it is *you* who took it, just like it is *you* who has been taking all the money from our business. *You* who do not respect anything or anyone. When our helicopter disappeared, along with *mucho dinero*, I told myself that was the last time that I would ever trust the great *El Chapo* with anything. And I say that your smuggling plan also will not work, Chapo. Oh yes, I know about that too. You will never smuggle *las drogas* across the border with the helicopter by hiding them inside little Malverdes."

While this exchange went on, Dr. Feathers stood between Chapo and José, more confused than ever, if I could read his dark Indian face half-hidden beneath his jaguar headgear and gory mantle of human skin. So far his eyes had been on the hands resting on gun handles, afraid to make a move. Now the dam burst and the shaman rushed into his sanctuary, clearly to verify one story or the other.

Like a housewife whose child had been kidnapped, a moment later he emerged, and, hands shaking, yanked the heavy curtains with the flayed human skins and gory stains to either side—almost ripping them from their stays. Sunlight burst into the evil chamber to fall full upon the little shrine of rocks and candles where the statue of Jesús Malverde resided, the little god's home away from Heaven.

Gone.

Tears streaming down Feathers' face, the Pope of gore pointed to the gap that existed where the statue had been.

Quinn climbed his stairs—I smirked and inwardly crowed as I watched plan after plan of my enemies, the enemies of humanity, crash into oblivion.

Chapo and José separated and led their followers apart into two distinct clumps: Chapo and five Hawaiian-clad thugs retreating to the east side of the plaza; José and three Federales to the west side, fortunately not directly by me—fortunately I say in view of what followed.

Like a prize fighter in his corner, Chapo halted, not even blinking as the flower girls ran for the stairs and disappeared, as those onlookers in orange sneakers had done weeks earlier when they caught sight of cartelistas outside M&M's video shop.

"Mi amigo, José. Do you know what it means when a man carries two pistols?"

José said nothing, but glanced north and south, at the shaman who continued to stand stricken with his eyes on the empty shrine, and at the backs of the flower girls vanishing down the stairs.

Slowly Chapo withdrew both of his Ruger Mark IIIs with the six-inch barrels. His thugs imitated his move and lifted their weapons.

"A man with *one* gun in his hand can still do something else with his other hand. He can build his house, he can fuck his women, he can even take a *sheet*. Life can go on."

The Federales and José formed a line, their own guns out.

"But a man with *two* guns in his hands can do only one theeng. If he wants to go back to leeving his life, he must use his guns for what he brought them for. He must fight!"

Before Chapo finished his last word, his twin-pistoled hands were in motion.

A phalanx of steel barrels lifted—*rattled*.

The opposing phalanx of guns from the Federal police erupted in fire and smoke, the bullets zipping across the plaza—the cloud of hail from both sides so thick that surely some must collide in air.

Bodies tumbled.

Screams pealed.

But the suspicion I had nursed since José had first spoken proved right—at the first movement, Chapo and José had both gone to ground—as the cleverest gunfighters always do before the first bullets fly—both huddled behind the bodies of their former supporters, who fell dead or injured.

Neither Chapo nor José had fired a shot.

Slowly José rose to one knee.

Twenty feet off, Chapo did the same.

Around both lay a slaughterhouse of blue-and-white shirted and brown-with-gold-badges chulos and Juarez wannabes, their blood seeping toward the altar, the ever-present monument to their god's lust for death. Glad to oblige, I thought. My eye passed over the results of their little incest quarrel. I smiled.

Chapo and José stood. They paused amidst the dead and dying—only the two leaders remaining uninjured, their faces showing their surprise at the outcome.

But each also realized that their dispute was not settled. It must play to the end.

José backed toward the sanctuary, avoiding direct sun in his eyes, his nine millimeter Glock still holding its six rounds, as was clear to me from the lack of smoke at the end of the barrel.

Chapo backed toward the south side of the altar, the better to frame his enemy against the backdrop of the shaman's chapel, his own pair of Rugers with the six-inch barrels waving evilly in the sunlight.

Dr. Feathers had retreated into the sanctuary and dove behind a curtain. Now he ventured to peek around a corner—yep, I knew he would be a coward. No one who has others hold down his victims while he kills them could be anything else.

Enough was enough.

I had the happiness of seeing the looks on the faces of all three when the iron bars on the front of my cage glowed red and yellow and spat bubbles in a waterfall of lava, the 'lava' falling up into the sky to vanish to the quiet background tune of a Turkish takeover of an ancient Greek city.

I stepped through and replaced the plastic tip of my pinky back on my finger. Up to now, the gangsters had been so distracted by their plans and their plots and their conspiracies against each other that no one had taken note of the fact that I now had a belt of cartridges around my waist, comfortably tucked under my ivory Canali jacket, and a blue-steel Colt .45 with rotating drum, the kind that whispers death when used by a pro.

That's what I am—The Pro.

Glenn Lazar Roberts

Walking toward José and Chapo as deliberately as a taxman in April and as confident as an undertaker when war is declared, marrying death and taxes as closely as two legs, I watched the two gangsters even out the space between them until we formed a triangle. A triangle of horror and revenge. Of a kind not even that blood-soaked plaza had seen.

From somewhere I fancied I heard Mexican trumpets, loud and pushy, their chorus rising to the inevitable climax, Chapo's surprised gaze flitting between me and José, José's eyes squinting in shock at me and back to Chapo, my own baby blues piercing through the smoke and fire that now completely evaporated from the open square to reveal our three-way duel of justice.

Justice, I said. That's all I wanted, all I ever wanted, and was determined to get. Of course in my book, I looked up that word under the R's: the first letter of 'revenge.' Somebody once said that people scare best when they're dying. In my experience, justice comes best with vengeance. And they're ain't no better veng-ustice than a Colt .45 saying its peace.

Easy to say—hard to live.

Slow as medium rare and hardcore as midnight porn, my piece rose and spat. José made the error of shooting Chapo first—I knew he could not control his hate, so José got my first shot of lead.

Chapo made the mistake of trying to pull his gymnastic trick a second time. I got him before he hit the ground, his own shots missing both me and José.

Before they gurgled their last, my gunsight sought out Dr. Feathers. Vanished. Either he had bolted for the stairs or was hiding in his sanctuary.

I thought of hunting him down, and of putting more bullets in El Mayór and Don Sylvester to make sure they were dead...correction: because I wanted to. I had to say that to keep peace with Quinn.

But I paused as something crawled into my line of sight—or rather hovered like an evil crow—a white crow. With multiple wings.

The sound had been growing in my ears for half a minute—I had been as oblivious of it as the cartelistas had been oblivious of me. Now the sound had grown too loud to ignore.

The white crow filled my vision.

A helicopter descended, its motor already slowing. Rubber wheels touched the plaza just beyond the piles of bodies, a final lurch and it came to a rest, the pilot, whoever it might be, knowing his craft. The rotors stopped turning and two side doors slid open. A pair of figures dropped to the cobblestones. They walked toward the center of the plaza, picking their way carefully over the bodies until they arrived midway between me and the sanctuary.

I had thought I had known confusion—this was new.

Having exited the helicopter, El Chapo and José stood before me, stared at the mass of bodies before exchanging looks. They looked at me. José was José, there was no doubt about it. The mayor of La Ciudad de Juarez wore his same suit and had the same Mark III pistol in his hand as the other José lying dead on the plaza. Don Donatello 'Chapo' Sylvester standing beside José was identical to the Chapo who lay dead as well, complete with a brace of Ruger six-inch guns stuffed in his belt. The jaws of both men hung open—they were as surprised at the scene as I was.

At this point Dr. Feathers found his courage. Thrusting his wide-eyed face out of the sanctuary, he hurried forward to Chapo and José, coughing and blubbering.

"El otro! El otro!" The shaman pointed his finger like a gun and popped invisible bullets into the corpses at his feet. He pointed his other forefinger at me. Well, that's one way to fix blame. Feathers then rushed back to his shanty and ripped wide the curtains from the entrance to let the sun shine direct into his shrine and demonstrate that their tiny godling was gone. Again he pointed at me.

That did the trick. Chapo glanced again at his doppelganger body on the ground—the second doppelganger of at least three, I now realized—and the spirit of his religion grabbed him.

"Our sacred Jesús Malverde has worked a meeracle, José. Malverde has brought us back from the hereafter to save our idol. Mira! That gringo in the white suit—that leetle sheet who we brought here yesterday in the helicopter and put in the storage room to stop his loud gringo mouth from talking so much—he has escaped and stolen our sacred Malverde."

"Si, Don Sylvester," said José. "Somehow this Señor Marlowe

has twisted everything in his favor. But Malverde will see us through to victory."

Chapo pulled out his twin Ruger pistols.

José aimed the barrel of his Mark III.

The reel ran a second time. Don't tell me how I knew what would happen next—there can't be that many universes in the multiverse similar to ours. Or can there?

Chapo aimed his pistols at José and pretended to fall—

—José shot Chapo before he hit the ground—

—I daggered two shots into José before he could turn his weapon on me, then put another bullet in Chapo to make sure.

Maybe this time he would stay dead. I scanned the skies and the stairs in case more white crows with doppelgangers came rushing into view and crossed myself with my pinky.

Something was wrong.

Staring down at my chest, I saw the lava had returned. Except this time it was red, only red. And it flowed down, not up or in circles.

One of their bullets, either Chapo's or José's, had found their mark.

Ten feet away, the shaman saw the flow of blood from my chest and broke into a sly grin. On a day of blood saturating his gore-soaked plaza, yet one more gallon was joining the queue, to the pleasure of the king of gore. Jerking into a dance, he slid out his obsidian blade and edged toward me. Finally, deciding I was too badly injured to defend myself, he rushed at me, waving his razored blade in the air, his jaguar headdress bobbing with each thrust of a naked foot on the stone floor. A horrid shriek filled the air as he called on his god to accept one more pain-wrenched life into his embrace.

My bullet caught him dead center.

Jerking like a puppet recalled by Gepetto, the shaman seemed to float in air for a moment, the reel playing its movie, the motion still slowed. He collapsed.

Staggering forward, I took the creature by his fouled hands and dragged him to the side of the pyramid, determined, whatever the cost, to rid the world of the parasite. I rolled him over; his eyes, still quivering, stared back with insane joy—he too would get to experience the sacred embrace. Let him. It was time to start anew. I glanced at the dead Federales sprawled on the stones of the plaza, and from the cellar came Quinn's newsy quip: 'I shot the shaman, but I didn't shoot the deputies.'

Quipped and done, all I could think of was breaking into the storage room to retrieve Malverde, and take the helicopter. I had no keys to either and did not know how to fly, but it was time to take a powder. After all, it was just a matter of time before more gangsters climbed the stairs, and a new hombre took control of the superstitious village, and a new priest was found. Habits of thought, habits of action. Can people really change either?

I stumbled. Falling to my knees, I could feel more, feel the blood draining from my brain, from my limbs, from my legs, to join the ever-growing stream that seemed eager to add its contents to the bloody lake spreading over the plaza, spreading east, toward the still rising sun, toward the edge where all of Malverde's bloody corpses end, where Chapo and José themselves and all their people would eventually follow.

Curious how the godling floated before my vision even now. Behind it I suddenly noticed a circle of flame like the cauldron of a tiny volcano ripping apart the front of the sealed storage chamber, out of which emerged the idol itself. Coming full into view, Malverde floated closer and I saw more: it was carried by a small man dressed in white...no, off-white, the ivory of a Canali suit, on top perched a white fedora hat with jagged grey band.

The strange little man placed the Malverde statue beside me. He knelt over me as I collapsed full-length on the plaza cobblestones. The gap between universes flaming on the wall of the storage shed behind him, I stared into his eyes. From somewhere came a distant memory: observation *is* entanglement.

I blinked.

***

Solemnly I stared down. Pietro Quinn Tiberias Marlowe lay before me on the plaza, dead, gunned down by the cartelistas. The same gangster leaders whom I had consulted three days ago in City

Hall and who had rejected my proposal to launder money through the Vatican. The same gangsters who had abducted me on *la calle* one block from City Hall just after I had barely managed to avoid meeting my second self when he was delayed entering the building—my second self who now lay dead before me. The same Chapo and José who had three days earlier flown me to this plaza in their helicopter and introduced me to the shaman as his next circus act, then, since the cage was occupied by the woman, imprisoned me in the shaman's storage room to await my gory end before they helicoptered away on their brief trip to the U.S.

It had taken quite an effort for me to stay hidden in the storage room and only watch, without giving in to sympathy and rushing to the aid of my other self in his hour of greatest need.

CHAPTER 29

O n a bright happy morning of an increasingly hot Chihuahuan day, I stood on the plaza HQ of Chapo and José's Cartel. I had once thought that passing through a wall into another universe was upsetting; passing through and returning the same way turned out to be as stomach wrenching as seasickness. And I had returned through not *one*, but *two* universes.

Which meant that coming back down the elevator in Juarez City Hall had produced not just one copy of Chapo and José, but two copies—three in all. Thank Malverde, all three copies of those terrible gangsters now rested peacefully on or under the plaza.

Welcome home, guys. Please stay dead.

At last I understood Jack and Bob's odd comments when I had been in their observation room in the hills above Albuquerque in what seemed an age ago: "Vhy, he might even have reversed the indexing and attempted to come back the same vay." "Don't even *think* that, Jack. You know what could happen."

Now I knew. You don't just come back—you come back *before you left*. That means there are henceforth *two* of you—in the same universe. And if you run through the turn-style again, you make another copy, who exited even earlier. And the earlier copy knew the most, remembered all...

No wonder Jack zipped his lips. No wonder Bob had been worried.

Silently I gazed at my tiny plastic digit...the power of not just one, but multiple universes residing in a tiny red button. And in any order I chose.

A creak sounded from the direction of the stone stairs leading down to the village.

I turned.

Cautiously a single head emerged over the edge. With one eye.

Throughout the gunfight I had spared only a brief thought to the absence of the police chief, Cheche, speculating that he had chosen to stay below due to his injuries, which had made him vulnerable in a gun battle. Here he was.

He held his hands in the air—no gun. He was alone.

Cheche walked toward me, hands raised, smiling, but still cautious.

My dead self resting on the plaza was armed with my favorite Colt, but my live self had no weapon of any kind, unless one wanted to call the small black and white idol I clutched to my chest a weapon.

"Don Marlowe," began Cheche, with *respeto*. He still had his eye patch covering one eye—and yes, it was still the same eye, as suspicious Quinn verified—and red-stained cotton stuffed in one ear. Still in his casual semi-suit, he turned his head the better to hear. "Don Marlowe, I can only imagine what you think of me. But know this before you judge." Cheche let his good eye wander over the more than dozen corpses littering the plaza, the worst of the Bad News Club. "Know that I did not plan for this, nor did I want any of this to happen."

My nasty expression put him off.

"Yes, I know I have done many bad things, Señor Marlowe. I have done many things that a good person should be ashamed of. Evil things. And I am sorry for that."

I let my expression relax a bit.

"I have had enough of this life," continued Cheche. "I do not want to kill anymore. I am sick of killing. Sick of causing bad things to happen. Mr. Marlowe, I am an educated man, you must know that everything I have learned says that all of this we see before us today is wrong and that we must not participate in such evil. This evil is what led to this." He pointed at his ear and eye.

My eyes widened. From pity? Or relief that he was unarmed?

"I wish to convert, Mr. Marlowe. I want to become a true Catholic, a Christian, and no longer be one of these fallen souls. I want my soul to go elsewhere." He glanced toward the east where the shaman's victims had been rolled down the slope. "I want to go to your Vatican, the home of Jesús, the true God, that place where you have been," his gaze rose heavenward, "and ask the Holy Church to save me. Can you take me there?"

Now I blinked. I had seen last-minute conversions, but this was a new one.

"I want to confess, Mr. Marlowe, to cleanse my soul."

"Don't let me stop you." I couldn't forget his hi-tone attitude when I was stuck in his Juarez jail. "So long as it doesn't include taking Jesús Malverde. I stole it fair and square. It's mine."

"I would not have given you your gun if I cared what you did with it."

It was my turn to be surprised. "*You..?*"

Cheche shrugged. "Malverde was going to disappear anyway. José planned to take the idol to Buenos Aires and use its messages to make himself into a new Peron—the newest Peron, that is. Dictator for life. From the beginning, that is what José wanted; he was only using Chapo until he could take Malverde for himself. He recruited me to help him."

"How could Malverde help with that? Last I heard, they don't worship idols in Argentina. Not even you Peronistas."

His eye brightened. "Oh, but *this* idol...this idol speaks in a language they understand. It speaks of Wenceslaus...and Milk-cow, the sacred site in Poland." Cheche let his eyes wander over the doppelgangers strewn about the plaza. "And José claimed that Malverde has even other powers...powers that could help him make his own Bell."

I started to nod: Italian... through the Malverde idol... Peronistas... And I recalled Licia's pouty accusation to Marm, which I had overheard when hiding below their store in New Orleans: 'I hate the Bell, and I hate what you did to Daddy, and everything else that you're doing with those people in Poland.' At the time I didn't understand. But something was starting to click.

Cheche sighed. "All José's big talk about his Mason friends in Argentina and Roma did not save him in the end."

Each time I thought I might have it all figured out, that Gordian knot kept coming again into view. "Masons? In Rome?"

Cheche nodded. "He said they have members even in the

Vatican. José had a name for them...I cannot recall."

"Try, Chech. This could be important."

Cheche glanced toward the stairs. "We don't have much time before the crowds lose their cowardice and come looking."

"Once more, Chech. Try."

His eye flitted. "P-2." He shrugged.

Like the rest, it meant nothing to me. I blinked blandly.

Cheche looked at the helicopter and pointed. "I don't know its meaning either. But I know we should not be here when the villagers arrive."

As if on cue, several faces peeked over the southern edge of the plaza. Frowning, angry faces. Machetes rose beside them.

As cries of outrage rose behind us, I yelled to Cheche, "I will take you to Rome—but our first stop is Albuquerque. I have an errand to run before we see Il Papa. And don't forget: Malverde is mine."

Needing no prompting, Cheche snatched keys from Chapo's corpse (the second one) and in another moment we were airborne, headed south. With no time to grab my favorite Colt, I was lucky to get my wallet from Chapo and just happy to get the fuck out of drudge before that angry crowd with their machetes reached us.

***

Our flight to Albuquerque was uneventful. That is to say no bullets or hurricanes or fighter jets ordering us to land *pronto*. We flew across the border and descended at the same small airfield where not so long before Andrew had pushed me down the mobile steps and thrown a bus ticket in my face.

Since I still didn't know how to fly a helicopter, I let Cheche keep the keys, and, after a brief encounter with the local inspectorate, Cheche took a cab to Albuquerque's international airport to inquire about international flights. Funny how the worst people always seem to have the best IDs, enabling them to travel anywhere they wish to commit their crimes.

I grabbed a different taxi and made for my old downtown office, unsure whether the former criminal Cheche would actually wait for me—nyet...his crimes meant that the word 'former' could never apply to Cheche.

My guess that my locker in Oriental-land had been cleaned out by the cartel's step-and-fetch-its meant that my office was the safer ground. I never did trust that Queen of Cheena. Therefore I was not surprised when, upon sliding into my still unlocked office and sidling up to my old desk under the classy stare of my velvet Elvis perched on the wall behind it (Tonya's sexy bared knees leapt to mind), I popped the secret slot and pulled out another gem-crusted cross borrowed from Il Papa's private apartment after his demise, along with an original Modigliani painting. For a moment I paused, thinking I had miscounted. I thought I had brought three. Was one missing?

I had no time to waste, however, in counting artwork. I had to spend a few moments online to try to answer some questions. I looked again at a certain paper, not the first one Tonya had given me, but the one she tossed at my feet in Rome just before she leapt into Andrew's limo and was driven away, the one with a picture of a large bell surrounded by a kind of Stonehenge with the words 'song of the bell' and 'MilkCow' scribbled. Once again I wished I had paid more attention in high school geography class, but thanks to Cheche's gabbing it came to mind like yesterday's chili: the word 'MilkCow' had nothing to do with cows or milk, but was a place in the 'stan of Poland. Tonya had just spelled it wrong.

Consulting the global brain-net, I soon located a little town in Poland called Milkow not far from Czech-land, the place where I had mentally put Jack Muck's home turf. Even more, I discovered that there was an old poem called 'Song of the Bell' by some kraut named Ferd Schiller, or some such moniker. Not as good as Rat's Ass Rudy or Lucky the Gimp, and too bad the translation was only English and not Gaelic, but like they say Ya gotta run with the ball they pass ya.

So I slowly recited half-aloud to myself as I read this period piece about how to construct a bell, picturing José as the bell maker and wondering how far I should carry this charade.

I ran across a funny phrase in Ferd's old-fashion poem: 'I call out to the living. I mourn the dead. I break lightning.' Damned if that didn't seem to cover what I had seen in the deserted Alamo and the

Aztec pyramid.

Next I read: 'If the bell is to rise from the ground, the form has to break apart.' Nothing clicked there, but I added it to my growing pile of memories in Quinn and Pietro's basement for later access. Finally I noted that Herr Schiller's friends dumped him after he wrote his little poem, pointing out that he had failed to mention a 'clapper' in his description of how to make a bell. They thought he forgot it.

A sneaky thought surfaced: What if he left the clapper out *on purpose*? What if this Ferd character (and therefore José) knew a lot more about channeling odd messages than did his friends? Like, maybe having kissed the Blarney he had heard things, or after he had stuck his head in large bells in the biggest churches after removing the clapper? Could he have known this about bells and their mystery voices *From The Beyond*, and his true purpose in writing his poem had been to try to give his ignorant buds a hint?

Then there was the Wenceslaus angle. After Cheche's comment, all I could think of was the Christmas carol, 'Good King Wenceslaus'. I listened to so many versions of that crazy tune online that it made my ears bleed, and I went over Cheche's stray comment in my head till it too made me crazy.

So MilkCow had nothing to do with milk or cows, but was a place in Poland named Milkow, which Tonya had either not understood, or had simply misspelled because of the name's similarity to MilkCow. But where the hell does a schnapps-drinking king of Czechistan come in regarding freaking bells, ancient Stonehenges, and forgettable towns in Poland? I couldn't figure it out.

To not lose Tonya's paper, I slid it back into the hem of my fedora.

Running back out to my still-motoring taxi, the dull speechless driver who looked like a refugee from Bal'more took me to my favorite pawn shop, and, after the usual dickering over dobbin, I came to an understanding with the broker, who placed the jeweled cross and Modigliani painting lovingly in his window on consignment (next to the Picasso which had not yet made the broker rich, but which eventually must) and advanced me enough folding money to fill my Canali's pockets before handing me another Colt .45. The shop being unfortunately out of my favorite blue-steel versions, not even another blank throw-down, I was forced to settle for grey. But the drum rolled as good as ever and was filled with *plomos*.

I had wrapped Malverde in paper and plastic and carried it with me—it really would not do to let anyone in Albuquerque know I possessed the unluckiest good luck charm that ever existed, glaring his bow-tie greenless glare at every superstitious *chulo* and *chicano* who happened by. Not even my rainbow belt in karate could save my white Irish ass then.

At this point I wasn't actually sure of every detail of my plan: an overnight plane to Rome, aim Cheche toward St. Peter's, then I would fly alone to Poland to find Mr. Wenceslaus in the city of MilkCow, or Milkow, or wherever the heck that was, but where I was fairly sure something big was going to happen, though exactly what and why, I still could not guess. But I would arrive with a gun, plenty of cash, a strange drawing, and the worst attitude that ever crossed a cross-eyed son of Éire—along with the angriest angry red button that had ever been loosed on all creation. Let Jack and Bob dicker with my dobbin then.

My next stop was, I had to admit, playtime. Having dipped into my gem-encrusted reserves for a pocketful of lira, I taxied to Honest Juan's fancy-schmancy wreck-it-yourself used car lot. No, I did not expect my same-old same-Olds to be back on the lot, as it always was before. That relic of a former time must still be parked in front of Muck & Montez's ersatz video shop in Juarez, by now totally stripped. Imagine my surprise when I walked into Honest Juan's and saw my same rusted green Olds back in its spot. I had to hand it to Juan; he sure knew how to repossess.

But this time I was the guy in charge and I sauntered into Juan's big-ass-fan office like a banker foreclosing on unpaid rent. His expression was priceless when I dumped the biggest wad of Uncle Sam's foreclosure notices that he had ever guessed existed onto his desk. And before the half-hour was up, I rode off his lot in the newest used Oldsmobile he had in stock, this time blue. It even had a vintage eight-track tape player, and I persuaded Juan, still open-mouthed, to toss in his *personal* collection of Creedence Clearwater and Elvis eight-tracks.

Not that I needed the wheels. Cheche must be waiting for me at the international airport. But wouldn't you want a few minutes of fun if you had just been tricked by universe-jumpers, hung upside down by killers, put in a cage, and forced to murder two of Mexico's most vicious cartelistas—three times over? Yeah, I needed to feel the wind in my red Irish hair—so I barreled eighty miles an hour on the interstate through specks of petrified forest, listening to The King's 1957 version of Lawdy Miss Clawdy. Smoooth.

My last pit stop—after combing my Elvis wave back into place and re-tapping my fedora on top—was to tank up and buy an international-enabled phone for use once I arrived in Italy with Cheche, and whatever country I ended up in. Too busy being relieved at not having become a decoration on Dr. Feathers' curtained sanctuary, drying in the Chihuahuan sun, I let the master of ceremonies—a teenage Mexican clerk whose English was better than mine (more annoyance)—turn it on and configure it.

I headed back.

In minutes I was in front of the Queen of Mean's cleaning establishment, parked in the same corroded wheelchair-only space as before, the only space where she would allow me to park, which meant never-for-free. If I had entertained the thought that I might sidle in and clear out my stuff in order to find better lodgings elsewhere, I was soon forced to drop that notion.

Here she was, in all her diminutive presence. Which meant *my size.*

"Where you be, Marlowe?" she frowned. "You no pay rent. Again."

I omitted mentioning that she had allowed gangsters to ransack my belongings in my absence, which I was sure she also had not allowed for free, and just to tick her off I let my hand wander to my wallet.

A smile broke out on her face. "Yes, Marlowe. You pay now. You pay rent. You pay late fee. You pay late fee on late fee."

I withdrew my hand and folded both arms across my chest. That had worked in Juarez.

Not this time.

Queeny shouted and at her back appeared the usual bevy of miraculously round dark-skinned laundro-listas from even farther south than Chihuahua, taking their cue from the Queen, smiling when she smiled, frowning when she frowned. Today they shouted. Too bad rainbow karate from Tierra del Fuego doesn't work on bowling balls. Mexican cartels are one thing; a crowd of cruel bi-hatches with grips hardened by decades of squeezing wet linen are quite another—I reached into a front pocket and resignedly counted out enough money for not one month's rent, but two. And another sum for 'late fee on late fee.'

She smiled. Though her eyes still frowned. So I laid still another salad leaf on the pile of dough in her open greedy hands and her entire face finally hung together like Oaxacan tapestry, all happiness with her *Chinee* luck. She stepped aside and motioned to the nine-pin of bowling balls to allow me through.

It didn't take long for me to retrieve my shit. Someone had pried open my locker with a crowbar and taken everything. I almost added 'of value', but that really didn't cover my situation. My cot was also broken, its wooden spats snapped in two, so I folded up what remained, took my only valise, and walked out.

When I came to my car, someone had stolen a tire. It's a good thing I don't speak Chinee, which I don't speak even better than Queeny don't speak English. At least I had had the sense a half-hour earlier to demand an spare tire from Juan, and, in a few minutes, after verifying that Malverde was still locked in the trunk, I had screwed on the extra, and was ready to get back on the road.

Did Cheche still wait? If our roles were reversed, I would not be. But then, I ain't no cold-blooded criminal, just a cold-blooded PI who deals with such. So I was the better guy. Still, I thought it might be the smart thing to do, before driving all the way to the airport, to call ahead and page Cheche to verify that this killer-turned-saint had not decided to fly to Rome without me, or return to his drug-smuggling, peasant-executing ways. Besides, I needed more answers than I could find online and only Cheche could give them to me.

Behind the wheel, I turned on my new phone.

Sometimes I have to wonder about myself. True, I had braved

Chapo and José in their lair where they were surrounded by thugs and killers, and I had ventured up the elevator with them, and, true I had come back down and exited earlier-in-time so that I had stood hidden in one corner of Juarez City Hall and watched while another version of myself entered the Hall and renegotiated what I had just finished negotiating. And I had been tricked into executing the very same Chapo and José, then hung upside-down for most of a day, and finally watched a massacre on the top of a hidden Aztec pyramid in the mountains of Sierra Madre.

In other words, I had done it all and seen it all.

So why was I surprised at what happened next?

My new phone beeped and a picture popped into view: Cheche sitting in a taxicab with his head blown off—and a still-smoking Colt .45 beside it. My new .45. How the hell did M&M manage to get my hand in the picture? That they were a helluva lot better at photoshopping than I was, there was no denying.

The sound of my back tire erupting air was almost an anti-climax. I power-buttoned down all my windows to get a better look at the bulk that rose up behind my car and glimpsed a short knife in his hand.

A big grin settled on the fat, strawberry face. "Welcome back, Pete. How was the wedding?"

On the other side of the Olds appeared a second bulk.

"How-de-do, Detective Dorkman," I greeted.

The first bulk put his knife away and leaned on my passenger window sill. "What's the matter? Didn't the purple undies fit?" Detective Krupke smirked as he gave the inside of my new-old car the once-over. "You still don't look happy, Pete. Victoria's Secret didn't have your size for your wedding night?"

At my elbow, Dorkman pulled my door open. "Outta the car, Marlowe. We've got a bone to pick with you."

As casual as an invitation to a dinner date, I climbed out (and yes I do mean climbed, which is the fate of all napoleons) and stood as tall as I might to face Dorkman's chest. Krupke came around and halted by my side, leaning over me like the Leaning Tower of Pizza.

I didn't have to think long and hard about how they happened to get here so quick. Or, come to think of it, why my locker had been ripped open when a common set of bolt-cutters would have done the trick. Was I wrong after all in thinking that Cheche and Co. had done it?

"Nice to see you too, Dorkman. Where's your season's greetings? Having a bad day?" No one but no one could have had a day to match *my* past few days, but hell if I would give these two gumshoes the satisfaction.

"Any day I have to look at you, Marlowe." Dorkman spat upwind, the spray hitting my Canali shoe. Quinn got restless: he noticed the usual plastic fork sticking out of Krupke's black polyester suit chest pocket and couldn't resist. "I see you're still fishin' for shrimp at Losers' Wharf, Krapke. Haven't you heard of sharing? Your partner looks hungrified."

Fuming, Krupke took a step—Dorkman stopped him with one arm. For a second, Dorkman stared as if weighing whether to kick me or just run me over. He took a breath. "You caused us a bit of a problem, Marlowe. A real take-out box of trouble."

One half-lip smiled. "Glad to oblige, gentlemen. That's my specialty." Too bad Dork didn't turn around so I could again stuff imaginary shrimp in my mouth while grinning at Krup. But sometimes ya gotta roll with the road.

Dork glanced down the line of parking spaces, where for the first time I noticed their usual government-issue white sedan parked behind several cars, hiding. I was starting to get the drift.

"This way, Pete. We're gonna take a little ride, you and me."

"You're not sayin' you're gonna finger me, are ya Dorkman? Cause we both know that ain't in your rule book." I squinted at Krupke. "Though maybe Krapke don't know that since he's still workin on his ABC."

Krupke squeezed and unsqueezed one fist. "That's GDE!" he shouted. "I mean GED!"

I grinned. Maybe if I kept up the zingers I could get his ventricles to squeeze shut.

Reaching into my car, Dorkman popped the lock on the trunk.

I wasn't happy with this. "Where's your procedure book, Dork?"

"Shut up."

Without waiting for a signal, Krupke walked to the trunk and began rummaging through...except there was nothing to rummage through but one item. He emerged with a paper and plastic-wrapped figurine.

I was very not happy at this.

"We got orders to bring you in, Marlowe. You and whatever the hell else you got on you." Dork watched while Krupke slammed the trunk shut then walked behind me and pinned my arms.

"Watch out, Krapke. There's laws against false arrest, too."

Krup squeezed my arms tighter. "Shut up," he added, his dirty round face grinning his flabby cheeks like a tent on two poles. "I've been waitin' for this, Pete. Been waitin' a long time."

While Krup held me, Dork did what I least expected—suckered me a good one in the gut. When I recovered and straightened up again, he traded places with Krupke—a second punch landed on the first.

Wheezing, I got out, "Administrative Procedure Act straight down the line, huh, guys?"

"Shut up," they both suggested. Two more blows landed: front and back.

Finally they let up and I felt their grubby paws and snouts feel and sniff every one of my pockets, taking out and inspecting and stuffing into their own pockets everything I had just put into mine: wallet, Colt .45, burner cell phone, and not to be missed a bucket-load of Franklins that I had fairly stuffed into every pant and side pocket on my person.

Their eyes barely registered as they transferred all the bills into their own pockets. I guess they were used to playing Robbing Hood. They didn't bother handcuffing me, just dragged me like a rag doll until we got to their car and shoved me into the back seat where Detective Krupke joined, one hand on a bulging barrel in his right pocket. At least he didn't stick out his tongue every ten seconds like another thug who had recently taken me for a ride.

Dorkman gunned the motor and peeled out of Oriental-land. I noticed my new-old Olds was left open and with the windows down. Not that it mattered at this point. Rain was impossible and I felt sure that even Queenie would have no interest in a stack of eight-track

Elvis tapes. Malverde sat in the front seat of the cop car opposite Dorkman. Dork seemed to have some idea of what was up, which made me wonder what had gone down during my absence from Albuquerque.

A few minutes and we were stuck in downtown traffic; a few more and we were on Cartagena Road around behind the airport and heading for the hills.

To my surprise, we passed the very adobe church where I had heard the Italian god speak to me in tongues weeks earlier, passing up—then down—the same hill. Rick's Americana was still gone, the new pavement still transformed magically into crushed shell. Whatever was happening must have been recent because they didn't seem to know the shortest route to where I suspected they were taking me—I guessed why when Krupke glanced behind once to stare at a car in the distance, and exchanged looks with Dorkman. As trained detectives, they were just being careful.

I was not under arrest—that was clear enough. No "Do you understand your rights?" or "We have to tell you about Carmen Miranda," or anything like that. But Krupke still glared silently at me, his hand on his gun.

We weren't going to any police station.

Sure enough, as the sun crawled past three o'clock, and the heat reached peak, we plunged into the desolate tangle of hills east of Querque, our little car entering darkened stretches of road and exiting from them like tunnels.

Finally we arrived at a stolid outhouse with an electrified gate and a pair of gate-guards whose stares were equally electric. Dorkman flashed some obscure signal—my PI training failed me and I missed it. The guard didn't, and after he raised the gate, we rumbled through.

The narrow road twisted like a pretzel but just as the sun touched the western horizon to kiss the first of many hills, we braked to a stop in the mini-circle path at the front entrance of Marm's country castle.

CHAPTER 30

D ork and Krapke wasted no time. One on each arm, they dragged me out of their bland government issue Dodge, though I had to admit that the narrow running boards did happily remind me of old Bogie flicks, and for a moment everything went black and white. It was only the transition from dusk to twilight.

But the sharp angles of the monument to Frank Lloyd Wrong and its blind-artist devotion to a colorless interior fit in with everything Bogie. I even bent my elbows once more in imitation of a convict just released from The Hole in the Slammer and wrinkled one end of my lip as the twin glass doors drew inward.

We crossed the threshold. And there they were—not that I expected any different. The pieces were starting to come together; only I didn't like how the puzzle was shaping up. Jack Muck looked up from rubbing the heads of his hysterically happy three-pack of poodles, their pink tongues slobbering all over a nice new suit. At least I assumed that's what it was. I hadn't seen this outfit before: it was brown bordering on grey, almost field-grey, with pockets on each thigh, which made him look fatter than he actually was, and a jacket of the same, with more pockets on his chest, and strangely several medals and ribbons attached over his breast.

No more the lonely mariachi.

Bob Montez stood behind Jack, dressed much the same. More field-grey, brown boots, and decorations on his chest—though fewer ribbons than Jack, I noticed, and no medals. Both had floppy caps on their heads of the same make.

Jack stared at me without expression.

Bob frowned.

From their posture it was clear that my arrival was a surprise. A suitcase lay on the couch beside Jack, open to the world, and inside I glimpsed a half-covered dark lump: the Blarney Stone. They still had it, but they looked prepared to leave and were about to take it with them. As if for protection, Muck & Montez glanced at their enforcer, Andrew, who emerged from behind one glass door where he had obscured himself, watching me, one hand clutching a gun.

Dork and Krapke walked up to Muck & Montez and halted—pushed me forward another foot—and released me. I tried to stand straight but the continued pain of their pig-knuckle blankets in my gut made me lean forward.

Bob cricked his neck at the two dicks. "What the fuck, fellows? We gave at the office...and we didn't order Italian."

The two gumshoes crossed glances.

"Uh," Dorkman stumbled, "we *found* him...Pete...he was running around Miz Tam's place." Dorkman lay a disapproving look on me. "Sticking his nose in *again*—where it don't belong." He smiled like all was now explained.

Krupke nodded agreement. "And Pete has a new car," he spluttered. Krupke and Dorkman widened their eyes in amazement at this fact, which seemed to be my worst offense.

"So?" sneered Bob. "What's he supposed to do, take a taxi? He's a joe just like the rest of us." Bob glanced at Jack and I thought I detected a daily combo of knowing half-grins and sarcasm. His reminder of Ugly Joe didn't help my mood, though.

The low-dollar streetwalkers looked again at each other.

"We didn't know what else to do with him," blurted Dorkman.

The Dork moved a finger and, taking the cue, Krupke emptied his pockets of everything he had taken from me: wallet, gun, IDs (real and fake), fedora hat, Movado watch, and—biggest surprise—my entire bucketful of Jacksons, which the two of them dumped on the marbled floor like litter, not attempting to keep any. I had taken it for granted that their vacuums were built to suck up dough permanently.

I nodded to myself. They must really be scared. This puzzle piece now made sense: Dork and Krapke may have looted my locker for the Cartel, but they had really been working for Montez & Muck all along—if not sooner.

Glenn Lazar Roberts

"Qvuin! Qvuin!" bellowed Jack, senselessly. "Pietro Qvuinn Marlowe," he shouted.

What was up with him?

"'*Tiberias* Marlowe', Jack," Bob put in. Again.

"Yah. Pietro Qvuin *Tiberias* Marlowe." Jack Muck pointed a large fat finger at an object that Dorkman had placed on the floor beside him, half hidden by one leg. Bob dropped his own glance onto Jack, then onto the object.

Both their eyes grew.

"Oh," Dorkman added, "and Pete had this too, locked in the trunk of his *new car.*" The Dork couldn't seem to get past my transportation upgrade. While Dorkman stood with his mouth open, Krupke picked up the plastic-wrapped idol of Malverde and stepped forward.

Andrew intervened. As he pulled his barrel out of his pocket, Krupke halted. Under cover of Andrew's gun and his rapid-fire tongue thrusts, which seemed to have shrunk to normal, Bob came forward and took the idol from Krupke's hands.

Bob placed it on the couch next to the open suitcase holding the Blarney Stone and ripped off the plastic.

Immediately, a high whine enveloped the room like reverberating feedback. Bob pulled the idol away and held it up while Jack stared, his large form shaking from a subdued excitement that he was unable to completely master.

Jack looked at Bob. "It is assured. Project Hexenhammer now cannot fail. Our Sirius Enterprises is now a complete success."

It was time to jump in. I managed to stand up straight. "Not from where I'm sitting, jokers." I threw a dirty look at Dork and Krapke, who stood there taking it from M&M like a couple of dollar-a-day ditch-diggers. "These two clowns, in the course of their *devotion to duty* worked me over before stealing everything I own, including that statue. And you two Einsteinians have made me popular not only with the Vatican but probly with Interpol. I need a Valium—and a little of that famous reputation-repair juice you like to talk so much about."

Jack acted like he hadn't heard a thing. Joining Bob, he examined the idol in detail, turning it over and over in the air. Last time I saw such casual treatment of china, the kids dropped and broke it.

With a gasp from the two dicks, Malverde fell and shattered on the floor. I too caught my breath. What the hell had I sacrificed my time and risked my life for? I stared unbelieving as Bob and Jack together lifted the idol again into the air then deliberately smashed it, the pieces skidding like beach-shells across the marbled floor. What would Marm think, I wondered, when she returned from New Orleans and found her floor scarred?

Then, again together, they raised what remained of Malverde back into the air. A great grey stone. To match the Blarney Stone in the suitcase.

I got it.

Could there be more? How many of these little miracle nubs of hardness existed in the world? How many did M&M need for the success of their Enterprise? And what the hell was the jackpot to their game?

Returning to the couches, M&M carefully placed the Malverde stone on the couch catty-corner from the Blarney Stone, some ten feet away. Bob disappeared down the hall and in seconds marched out with a second suitcase, smaller than the first, which he laid open on the second couch.

Jack wrapped the Malverde Stone again in the plastic and closed the case. He turned to Bob. "Oh, ye of the little faith."

"Yep, I gotta mit. He done did it."

"Teetus, dear Bob?"

"Teetus to the max, Jack. The turnip truck is loaded, the handle is cranked, and the sign is in the steeple."

"Mi ne frego?"

"Mi ne frego."

Jack pulled out his cellphone and stabbed it with his blunt fingers. In a moment, a tinny voice answered. Jack spouted, "Jorge? Is that you, my dear friend?"

The tinny voice rattled.

"Where are you? You are okay? Santo too?"

More rattles.

"Oh, that is good, that is good. But listen now to me: Ve know

now vhy you cannot find the object on top of the pyramid. Because it is here. Yes, ve have it. So there is no longer any need for you to risk yourselves. Our operation has been a complete success. The var broke out just as ve planned, and ve obtained the object just as ve vanted. Please to return, now, please. Tank you, my friend."

With that, Jack hung up.

He wasn't done. Jack hammered the phone again. He eyed me as he rang the other end, plainly not concerned that he might be revealing Sirius secrets.

Someone answered.

"Yes, Frankie, is that you?"

Buzzing answered.

"Oh, that is good, my friend. Yes, I am fine and so is Bob. You are okay? And how is Buenos Aires?"

Another buzz.

"So to speak, Frankie, I am calling you to tell you that ve have canceled Plan X due to the fact that ve have obtained the object. You are now to go to Destination Y. Ve are flying there ourselves in the jet. Ve shall meet you there in a few hours and then ve shall execute Plan Z."

More buzzes.

"Tank you again, dear friend. Please to hurry. The political situation is peculiarly good at the moment. But things change vith the stars, as it were, my friend, so ve must not delay."

Jack hung up.

Looking back at me, Jack rubbed his temple. I had not seen that little tell before—something was up, all right.

Bob took a deep breath as he and Jack stared at me.

"Ah, now to the...how do ve say...the *crux* of the matter."

"You said it right, Jack. You said it right." Bob nodded approval.

Jack rubbed his temple again with his right hand. "Vhat do to vith Pinky?"

Bob kept nodding. "To do, it is. To do, it is."

Muck looked at the two dicks, Dorkman and Krupke, and with a turn of his head indicated the front doors. "Please to vatch the grounds of Miz Massolini's beautiful house, my friends. Ve shall have to complete a little operation here, and maybe I think you vill prefer for to maintain...how to say...plausible deniability."

"You said it right, Jack. No denyin' that."

Dorkman and Krupke exchanged knowing looks. "Thank you, Mr. Muck. We really appreciate how you always think of us."

With a peculiarly nasty glance from Krupke in my direction, the pair walked to the front glass doors, pulled one door open, and disappeared into the waving gardens that surrounded Marm's castle.

Back to me.

Jack stared, hesitating. I didn't need any third-party joker to tell me what was up in M&M's brains regarding my future. I'd seen those expressions on the faces of more back-alley executioners and murderers-for-hire than I could count.

It came.

"Pinky...my dear Pinky—ve have a little problem."

I eyed Andrew. If I punched my red button, how much time would I have before his gun blasted me into the next universe? What kind of life awaited if I crawled through a wormhole with a hail of bullets in me? What fate awaited me in *this* one?

"Too bad about Cheche," added Bob. "He was a good spy. The bullet to the head was supposed to warn you off, Pinky. To keep you away. Now..." Bob rubbed his own temple in imitation of Jack. Whatever the verdict was, the jury was unanimous.

"Yeah," blurted Andrew, "and too bad about José. He wanted to go with us to Wenceslaus Mine."

Jack threw his glare on Andrew.

The sudden harsh stare silenced the purple-tongued gunman. Andrew swallowed, nervous. Even his tongue paused in its constant tasting of air. He switched hands on his gun and aimed it at my chest, taking refuge in his one ace card. Apparently he had spilled some *hopalenos*: the location of Destination Y, which I concluded was close to Milkow.

"And please not to speak any more, Andrew," uttered Jack. His grey eyes slashed and stabbed till his gun-toting henchman visibly shook, the three poodles rising to attention, adding their harsh glares to Jack's.

"Ouch," observed Bob.

"Pinky, my boy," said Jack, "it seems that vhen ve sent you on your vay to Juarez, you did something *wrong* vith your Universal Indexer. Something that has the potential to disrupt not only our plans but to bring instability to a much greater framevork."

"Greater framework. That's good, Jack."

With Andrew back in line, Bob stared at me.

"First is first." Jack pointed to Andrew.

The thug, eager to get back into his pack leader's good graces, pocketed his gun and walked up and grabbed both my arms. With Montez & Muck watching, I decided it was best not to react and in a few seconds Andrew had slapped metal cuffs on me. But my hands were cuffed in front. What was the point? Everyone knew I could still press the red thingamajig.

Jack pointed again—at the thingamajig. Now I got it. Andrew stretched out my left hand, my right hand dragging along, and Bob approached. Quickly, almost frantically, he plucked off the plastic end-of-digit and in another moment had unscrewed the red button. It was like being back in the Vatican cell, helpless. I guess I was lucky that Bob had not attempted to extract the rest of the device embedded in my flesh.

I could read the tells like a book; Muck and Montez were relieved. Somehow I had placed a bur under their saddle. Something I had done in Juarez—

"Second is second," continued Jack. "The problem is this: if ve liqvidate you in a...uh, so to say terminal fashion, there vill remain the possibility that another *you* currently residing in a different universe shall appear in *this* universe. But if ve let you continue to live—"

"I do have a few plans for tomorrow evening, including a reservation at the Tropicana."

"If ve let you continue to, how to say...exist...then you present a danger to our plans in Destination Y." Jack shot Andrew a remnant of his former glare.

"You did the deed, player. You got the big Magoo," Bob added.

"Yah," echoed Jack, "and by getting the idol of Malverde and bringing it to us, you thereby made yourself into a problem."

"You weren't supposed to succeed, player. You were supposed

to get the gangs to blast each other. Then leave." Bob shrugged. "That is, if you were still alive and kicking."

"You vere supposed to make sure that all of the gangsters vere dead, including Mayor José and Chapo Sylvester."

"Especially José and Chapo."

"And then, our rancheros, Jorgé and Santo, vere supposed to climb the Aztec pyramid, kill the priest, and take the Malverde statue."

It was time for me to speak. "And kill *me*...if I had survived."

Jack and Bob looked at each other. They didn't have to say the obvious.

"They vere then supposed to bring the Malverde statue to us so ve could retrieve the crystals inside the stone."

I glanced at the shattered terra cotta littering the floor.

"But something vent wrong," continued Jack.

"Yep. Somethin' sure did," Bob added.

They stared hard at me.

"Don't know what all the squawk is about, gentlemen. I just pulled old Crassus out of his holster and let em have my gift from god. I eased them into the next life, and I think they were pretty glad to go."

"Except for von thing, Pinky."

"Yeah?"

"You died."

I swallowed. I didn't want the conversation to go this way.

"Yet you are alive," said Bob, cricking his neck.

"Dead...but alive," said Jack.

"Living...but dead," Bob confirmed.

"Jorgé and Santo said clearly that they found your body on the pyramid along vith the rest of the gangsters." Jack held up his phone. "They have even sent us clear photos of your corpse."

"It's all clear, player. Clear as constant 'e'."

"So now ve must resort to something that ve had not contemplated for you, my dear Pinky. Something that ve have never done before."

"But we have the answer. We know what to do."

Still standing before me, Jack folded his muscular arms. At his feet, the poodles went into pre-attack mode, half-rising to all fours, their eyes and ears focused on me. I sniffed. I could have dealt with Andrew, and maybe even Jack and Bob. But a clutch of attack poodles? I hesitated...

"Right now, in this universe you are being both alive and dead. Ve are going to have to change this, my dear Pinky, so that you are...how to say...*neither alive nor dead*."

"That's the crank!" blurted Andrew, then fell silent again under his masters' glares.

"Ve are going to have to put you somevhere vhere you shall be neither alive, nor dead, for a very long time. This is not easy to accomplish, my little friend."

"But we've thought it through, bub."

"Yes, ve have thought it out. Ve have decided that ve shall put you in a box."

"Not big. Not little."

"An average size box. Vith padding and metal sides so you vill not be able to communicate vith the outside vorld."

"Not any part of this universe, player."

"Then you vill be subjected to a certain amount of the gas that ve have used to put our friendly *assistants* to sleep."

"Yep, we know all about your little adventure in New Orleans, player. We know you went through our inventory under Miz Massolini's dress shop."

I stayed silent. No point in arguin' with facts.

"Vhen ve put you in the box, you vill be alive. But after ve close the lid—"

"And lock it—"

"Ve vill then put the box in a very safe place that vill never ever be disturbed."

It was time to protest. "But that means...I'll die. I'll suffocate!"

"No, Pinky. You vill *not* die. But you vill also not live. In fact, ve vill not know vhich vill happen to you. And that is exactly the point." Jack smiled a happy smile, the kind that mad scientists let loose when they arrive at their maddest conclusions. "No von in this universe can know vhether you live or die, and therefore ve can go on vith our plans vithout you...and vith you, so to speak, at the same time. You vill be neither alive nor dead...for the rest of your life."

"The rest of his life. That's a good one, Jack. Another zinger."

"Ve vill, however, be free of your...implications."

"That's how to put it, Jack."

"So ve vill put your box...how they say: *on the shelf.*"

"We can't bury it. We can't do anything that we know will kill you."

"And ve cannot open it. Ve cannot do anything that vill tell us that you are still alive."

I blew out a deep breath. "So I guess this is how you winners say goodbye. No card or a kiss on the cheek." I stood straighter and glared. "And don't think of trying."

"As you please, Pinky." Jack smiled. No parting sadness there.

"It's been a hoot, bub. Now it's time to go into limbo. Maybe we'll see you...and maybe not." Bob too grinned.

"So it's the *crew de gas*, eh Jack?

Jack frowned. "Please to bring the box, Andrew."

Andrew paused, staring at the pile of personal possessions that Dorkman and Krupke had yanked from my pockets. Funny, he didn't seem to like the cash so much as my Movado watch placed carefully on top.

Jack nodded. "Yes, Andrew, you may have Pinky's vatch...*after* you finish your vork."

Andrew returned to his task with renewed energy. From one corner, he dragged over what looked like a heavy metal coffin shaped plainly for some other task, now being re-purposed. Inside was the kind of padding that might have cushioned delicate porcelain. Thick and soundproof. Andrew rolled in a full-sized dolly. Laying the dolly flat, he positioned the box on top.

"Oh, and Andrew, be sure of vhat I tell you now: after you take the box to the cellar and after you lock the top of the box, do not ever *ever* look inside. Do you understand me, Andrew?"

Andrew paused, his tongue darting.

"I repeat, dear Andrew. You must not ever open the lid of the box to look inside. For the rest of your life. You must not look inside. Not you. Not us. Not anyvon."

Finally Andrew nodded, his tongue for once behaving. "Don't

look inside," he repeated.

"Ve understand each other now."

Another nod.

"Please to continue. Now take Pinky to the cellar."

Turning to me, Andrew pointed at the box.

I really didn't know what to do. So I let out the best sucker punch I ever let out at Andrew's belly. Okay, it may sound great to always fall back on one's instincts, especially in times of trouble. But it doesn't always work.

Moments later, I was stretched inside the box. The lid slammed shut, and the last sound I heard was Andrew gloating between tongue-darts. "By the way, Pete. Nice watch." The dolly's wheels took me to Marm's dark dungeon. At least Andrew knew what time it was.

CHAPTER 31

I heard nothing more. No wheels. No snarky comments from Andrew. No elaborate explanations from Jack Muck and Bob Montez on why I had to die—or not die—whichever way their fancy explanations put it. I had a feeling it would be all the same to me. No light penetrated the box. The sides were padded, all right. Thick enough to block any cries for help that I may decide to cast into the darkness. I, of course, would not give my enemies the satisfaction of crying for help; Pietro did enough of that on his own down in the basement. 'Qvuinn' let him have five across the eyes to shut him up. I needed quiet...and time to think.

Time...but that was the whole point, wasn't it? In here I had time—all the time in the world. If M&M were right, I would be here till the end of time. But wouldn't I die and thus ruin M&M's plans for universe-domination, or whatever the hell Plan Z was? From a pair of holes in one end, a thin gas began to fill the chamber. The interior was wider than my waist and longer than my height, and twice as thick as my middle, so I was able to squirm about a bit, enough to place one hand against the holes and feel the impact of the inrushing gas.

My mind swirled. The gas that suspended people in frozen animation was being applied to *mío*. My body would therefore be frozen, and...my mind as well? A suspicion surfaced—amplified by the fact that Jack had said I would be only half-frozen. Suspended, yes, but therefore only half-suspended. Half-suspended between time and space. Half-frozen. Alive—yet dead. For how long? Did time still apply? What the hell sense did it even make for M&M to say that I would be both alive and dead?

For the tenth time I felt the place where the red button had been; for the tenth time I confirmed that it was gone; for the tenth time missed having it. In truth, it had become part of me, and losing it was like losing more than a finger. It was like losing a hand. Or more.

I had to hand it to M&M. This time they had *deed* given me the finger.

A scrape sounded.

Jerking upright, I banged my forehead on the padded lid. I blinked. I wasn't supposed to hear anything. The padded box was supposed to be so insulated that no one inside could ever see anything or hear anything outside the box.

Except in one event.

Slowly...the lid rose.

An avalanche of light slammed my eyes, forcing me to cover them. As I gradually adjusted, I stared upward into another set of eyes—and I recoiled in shock.

I could have sworn that just a few minutes earlier Andrew had punched me in the gullet, put me inside the box, closed and locked the lid and rolled me downstairs into Marm's dungeon. The face that stared down into mine while I lay in the box was *Andrew's*—but he had changed. Several days' growth of beard scraggled his face. His eyes were ringed with red stains as if wracked with sleeplessness and worry. His hair was stringy and lay limply across his pale forehead, neglected, uncombed. And longer. Sweat stained his neck and armpits, showing through a loosely buttoned filthy shirt. His tongue...well, if I was forced to take bets, I would have given ten-to-one that its huge swollen mass was primed to shed its skin.

For a long second Andrew stood and stared, his eyes impacting mine, as if some great puzzle of the universe like the Gordian Knot had just been solved, a look of triumph mixed with rage overcoming him.

Slamming the lid on its back to expose me fully to the light shining from a phalanx of harsh high-wattage bulbs, positioned like cameras in Marm's interrogation room, Andrew stepped back.

One hand clinging to the side, I rose like a vampire from its grave.

I climbed out.

A third shadow fell between us.

Andrew looked first—a gunshot rang, its echoes reverberating off the hardwood walls of the dungeon. Andy collapsed. His blood pouring out of a hole the size of my fist—no, of a larger person's fist. He died.

I looked up—lowered my gaze to someone my size, in my suit, with my gun, my Colt .45.

'Someone' wasn't finished. As I stared, the barrel moved from Andrew to me...

Suddenly I 'got it'.

As the blast ripped a hole in me the size of Andrew's, I too collapsed on the floor. My life-blood pouring out and mingling with Andrew's, the stranger stepped close and fixed his eyes on mine. A familiar phrase passed with my passing. Observation *is* entanglement.

***

I holstered my Colt and sighed. Killing Andrew had been easy—fun, in fact—but killing myself was not so easy. At least this had been easier than when I had been forced to patiently watch the cartelistas shoot me on the plaza without intervening. Of course, the version of me that had been in the storage room on the Aztec pyramid had not known that a third version of me existed—a version that knew everything, had all the memories of both versions of me that were now deceased. Just as the second Pete who had watched the cartelistas kill the first Pete on the plaza had possessed the first Pete's memories.

Like a flash of lightning, the memories welled up. How I had exited the elevator on the second floor of Juarez City Hall early in the morning before anyone had arrived for work, and, skulking in the street across from the Hall, had watched as Pete number two exited the elevator and the City Hall and hurried down the street to avoid being noticed by José and Chapo and their thugs, and how I had watched as our doppelganger, 'first' Pete, had then arrived to join José and Chapo.

It was not easy to avoid Pete number two, since he had also skulked and watched. I even had to throw on some dirty street clothes to do what I felt had to be done...I changed clothes and approached Pete number one and, pretending to be a drunken Mexican consumed with machismo, I had attempted to distract him, block him from entering, to keep everything that has happened since from happening.

But I failed. Ignoring me, Pete number one had walked into the building—while Pete number two watched from a distance. And while I, Pete number three, stood on the corner pretending to be drunk as I helplessly watched it all unfold.

But there was still a way out, a way to make it work, a way to victory.

For I—Pete number three—*had the red button.*

Exiting Marm's dungeon, I managed to push my way through the junk of a storage chamber next to the dungeon's wall and, turning, plucked off the plastic end.

I aimed the button and pressed it.

Close as I was to the wall as it erupted, I feared the effects might rip me apart, but in moments, the process of slicing nature into infinitely small units and transforming the units into waves of probability took on a familiar course as the Indexer processed infinite possibilities using the energy of the Multi-verse before finally settling on the one universe that had entangled me. With the strains of Constantinople in the background, now mixed with Good King Wenceslaus, I plunged into the lava.

What I had expected, I am not really sure.

What I found was more of a surprise than I could have guessed.

Before me stood...Andrew, leaning over a box that was absolutely identical in every respect to the box in the room, which I just had left in another universe moments earlier.

He turned his head—faced me. We both blinked in surprise. I don't know whose surprise was the greater. His face was scraggled with several days' growth of beard, his neck was dirty and stained with sweat, his forehead pale and covered with unkempt hair, his eyes rimmed red. Identical to the Andrew whom I had just shot dead in the other universe—yet here he was.

And what was in the box?

As I advanced with my Colt pointed at his chest, Andrew stepped back. I glanced inside the box. Inside lay a small man in an ivory-colored suit, his fedora hat still on his head, shined shoes still on his feet. Pete number two—the Pete who had hurried out of City Hall to avoid discovery by Pete number one, and who had been put in the storage room on the Aztec pyramid and finally emerged to murder Pete number one on the plaza—the Pete from whom M&M had removed the red button—*lay dead*. Scrape marks of his fingernails on padding inside the box testified that he had suffocated within minutes of being interred, before being gassed.

All was now clear.

Andrew, left to guard the box for the duration of whatever M&M had planned to happen in Poland, had lived a life of hell for almost a week. Unable to sleep, unable to eat, unable to think of anything except: *Was Pete alive or dead?* Andrew finally had given in and defied M&M's final order 'Don't look inside the box.' His curiosity propelled by his schizoid obsessions, he had at last approached the box, unlocked it, and lifted the lid.

At that moment, I—that is, Pete number two—died. Or rather I died a week before Andrew looked, within minutes of my being sealed in the box, and when Andrew finally lifted the lid, my death in that box had triggered life in another box, in another universe, and when the Andrew in *that* universe lifted the lid, I was *alive* and had been alive for a week and I crawled out, the retroactive death in one triggering retroactive life in the other.

Which the entangling Indexer had enabled me to detect. I had driven back to Albuquerque in my own blue Olds that Petes One and Two had left in Juarez, then, after paying a bribe to the Queen of Cheena, I, Pete Three, hung about, and when Dorkman and Krupke showed up and kidnapped me (Pete number Two), I leaped into my new Olds and, ignoring the slashed tire, drove frantically in the wake of Dorkman's white car to Marm's castle, where the Olds finally gave out just off the main road, the wheel coming off as I parked the Olds in a hidden grove. I then managed to sneak undetected onto the grounds of the castle, enter from the pool patio and hide in the stairwell, stepping into the broom closet in time to see Andrew descend into the dungeon, rolling his box.

It had been close.

But the Andrew in *that* universe was dead.

And I turned to the Andrew who was *here*, in *this* universe, the universe where everything and everyone I cared about still existed, still lived in ways I knew and loved.

"Crank this," Bogie sneered—and my gun spoke its piece.

Piece for Andrew; peace for me.

As *this* Andrew's blood ran on the floor of Marm's dungeon, I had only time for a single glimpse at the one lonely bed that inhabited the room—where what seemed an eon ago Marm had confined her daughter Tonya, and I wondered at the extravagance of my imagination that had supposed a dungeon filled with torture devices.

Retrieving my classic Movado from Andrew's corpse, I ran out.

In the custodian's room at the top of the stairs, I again passed the scattered buckets and brooms—a dim light seeping up from the stairs to light my way—and I noticed the door was open, the door that led to Montez & Muck's cockpit, their central HQ in Marm's castle where they observed everything, everyone, everywhere. Slowly I peeked through the gap, allowing only one eye to risk discovery.

Though lit, the room was empty. The same computer screens set up in phalanx on two broad tables, reminding me of their observation setup in Juarez, though the Juarez setup was smaller. Here was the grand play, the 'Coliseum', dim glows coming from the rows of screens, and, to the right, the same long window that opened onto the square pool of blue that I had seen the first time I used the red button, and that I had passed a week earlier when I followed Dorkman and Krupke after they abducted the 'second me' from Queeny's washing palace. Beyond all was night, the pool patio lit by glitzy light poles.

Sure I wanted to escape, but there were still too many missing pieces to the puzzle. I prepared to open the metal door and enter to examine the mysterious scenes I knew the computers would show and to attempt to communicate with the bell—which I was certain lay at the center of the mystery—when suddenly the room's overhead lights came on.

I retreated back into the broom room.

At the other end of HQ, Jack Muck and Bob Montez sauntered

in from the hallway that led to the rest of Marm's house, Jack's three poodles prancing behind. Dressed in the same field-grey uniforms as before, now sporting feathers in their floppy caps, M&M each carried two large suitcases. Ignoring the piles of discarded (and I'm sure carefully catalogued) computer parts and Tesla-like devices and the large metallic bell still suspended on its steel spandrels, they proceeded to a table beside the window and placed the suitcases on top.

I recognized one—it was my suitcase from my trip to the Vatican. And the other suitcase I knew contained what was left of Malverde. The other two were similar traveling cases, and M&M opened them flat and proceeded to extract a variety of clothes and objects from somewhere below the table and put them inside the open suitcases. Mutts one, two, and three sat on their haunches inside their doggie beds, all round puffiness and brows arched with curiosity. They wagged tails like they understood that a trip was in the works.

Bob and Jack mumbled. I could not hear what they said, they were too absorbed by their task of preparing to leave. Why the delay? I had been dead for a week. Andrew had been left to guard my box for that length of time, and the torn-up state of that gip Andrew told me as clear as Jolson's Mammy that a week had *deed* passed. Before they put me in the box, I had seen M&M already packing, rushing to fly off to 'Destination Y', which, thanks to Tonya, Cheche, and Andrew, I now knew was a place near the town of Milkow in Poland, in order to meet Frankie and the rest of their thugs, and complete 'Plan Z'.

My hand slipped, making the door creak.

Immediately the poodles jumped alert. In response, Bob and Jack stopped packing and looked at the dogs. Then at the door.

"Pinky. Is that you?" Jack stepped toward me, abandoning his suitcase packing.

Bob turned and glared. "If I were a bettin' man..."

I let the door swing open and stood in the threshold.

"My, my, Pinky, but you are becoming something of a nuisance."

"His specialty, Jack. His specialty."

They exchanged glances.

"But ve cannot let you interfere, Pinky. You know that you are no longer velcome in our little abode."

"Abode it is, Jack. An *adobe* abode. With no room at the inn for Pinky."

At the same time they both looked at the hallway at the other end of their headquarters, where the door to the hall remained opened wide. Loud noises rang down the hall. Ear-splitting loud. Exactly what was coming, I could not tell, but that it had to do with exploding cannons, knights on horseback, elephants, and jet planes seemed certain. Voices erupted.

"Goombas on our turf!"

"Someone's tryin' to piss on us!"

"Hurry, Frankie! Jack and Bob need us!"

The dogs jumped to all fours. Setting their beady poodle eyes on me, they launched into a frenzy of barking, adding their noise to the racket coming from the hallway.

Enough of that.

While Bob and Jack calmly turned to look at me, I ran back to the stairwell, where another door exited onto the patio. Exiting the way I had entered, I paused on the patio next to the blue pool. The barking followed—now echoing in the stairwell behind me.

Down the length of the pool I rushed; the last thing I needed was to tangle with M&M's well-trained guard poodles. Wouldn't do a thing for my Canali suit.

The shoes, I decided, I could sacrifice and I belted into the lush gardens behind the pool, attempting to follow the same path I had followed earlier that evening—but which apparently had become a week ago—and hurried through the darkness, strange constellations of stars showering down to light my way through acapia and sagebrush, huge willows snagging me.

All the while, the ferocious barking followed.

In the brush, I heard the padding of feet. Doglegs scurrying closer, heavy panting mixed with growls and barks.

Up ahead—I faintly recalled a swampy section. (Due to leaks from the pool? Or deliberately created to snare trespassers?) As I neared and the wet surface suddenly broke into the moon and starlight and revealed scattered broken sticks and leaves with an open stretch of prickly pear cacti and drier country beyond...

I slipped.

In an instant, one of the attack poodles rushed from the darkness—straight at me it hurled itself—two more snarling animals launching themselves immediately after.

There was no escape.

Half sitting amid a carpet of leaves, I raised my arms, shielded my face, braced myself for the inevitable rending and tearing, knowing that no rainbow belt in Okinawa-ráte could save me from what must follow.

A hint of wind brushed my cheek.

Nothing.

My eyes squeezed shut, my arms raised, I stayed braced. Seconds passed...a minute passed.

The barking had stopped, as had the snarling and growling. Slowly I ventured to open my eyes and look.

I stared.

Moonlight played with starlight across the calmly rippling carpet of leaves around me, carrying gently forward to the swamp.

The poodles were gone.

I was more than confused. Rising to my feet, I stared as deeply into the surrounding gardens as I could without giving myself away, in case the vicious beasts still lurked, still hunted. But no sign of them could be seen. With some nervousness, I ventured back, walked softly in the direction of the pool, Marm's house was brightly lit behind the dense trees like a lighthouse in a forest.

Within a minute, I returned to the pool—nothing seemed out of the ordinary. The terrifying sounds that had made me flee into the gardens had stopped, and in another minute I had sneaked the length of the huge pool and arrived once more at its end. The end that bordered on the wide glass window that looked into M&M's computerized headquarters.

I pressed my face against the glass. Inside, the lights still shined, the computers still hummed, and—strangest of all—Jack and Bob still stood by the table beside the window, placing shirts and personal items into the two open suitcases. They ignored my face on the glass.

Something was wrong—very wrong.

I hurried back inside, rushed through the broom closet once more, and arrived at the metal door that opened onto the HQ. Inside, Jack's three poodles sat on their haunches in their beds, contentedly watching Jack and Bob with their packing.

I stepped into the room.

Instantly the three dogs jumped to all fours. Bob and Jack paused to look at the dogs.

Jack turned to me. "Pinky, is that you?" He stepped toward me.

Bob turned and glared. "If I were a bettin' man..."

"My, my, Pinky, but you are becoming something of a nuisance."

"His specialty, Jack. His specialty."

Bob and Jack exchanged glances.

I let the scene play itself to the end.

"But ve cannot let you interfere, Pinky. You know that you are no longer velcome in our little abode."

"Abode it is, Jack. An *adobe* abode. With no room at the inn for Pinky."

Both of them turned toward the hallway door, where a thundering wave of threats and calls echoed as if every Gambino in the Bronx were rushing to attack, backed up by Hannibal with his elephants and a fleet of F-35s, the trio of poodles breaking into growls and snarls to add to the rising decibels.

I ignored it.

By M&M's side, I noticed waves coursing on several computer scenes. I had seen these programs before—audio waves—in the warehouse in Juarez where M&M had kept their second headquarters. And where I had been tricked into killing José and El Chapo just so M&M could keep their hands clean.

Walking over to the computer banks, I flipped the power switch on the ginormous power strip that fed them.

The noise stopped. The dogs vanished. Montez & Muck—as if sad that I had seen through their little game of fucking over the here-and-now, gave a little shrug—then too disappeared.

Gone. Gone to Poland a week past.

I was far behind them...but at least I still breathed. Thanks to a series of accidents, and to me, myself, and I, otherwise known as Petes One, Two, and Three. This cat had lost two lives so far, but I still had one left: Pete Three. I remembered everything that Me and Myself had done. And I had more. I had my Colt, my Elvis wave, my Universal Indexer, and I was still the best-dressed PI in Albuquerque.

Now I understood clearly that, by descending back through the elevator in Juarez City Hall, I had not just triplicated José and Chapo—I had triplicated *mío*. And that is what had Muck & Montez so worried, and what they had warned against when I first overheard them in the hallway.

What I needed now was to get the hell out of this castle and follow M&M to Poland. And I still had Tonya's mysterious paper that she had tossed me before jumping into the limo in Rome and vamoosing out of my life. Removing my hat, I extracted the little paper from the inside hem and once again perused the images: a large metal bell suspended between what looked like concrete pillars and the word 'Milkow', which I had learned was a town in Poland, and the words 'song of the bell', which came from Herr Schiller but which I now knew—thanks to Andrew—had nothing to do with Good King Wenceslaus, but referred rather to a place close to Milkow called the Wenceslaus Mine.

Progress. Only one way to deal with mugs who get off dissing you. Make sure you piss on their diss right back.

CHAPTER 32

B ut I still had a problem. I was stuck in Marm's castle and I had to assume that M&M's gate-guards still manned the entrance sentry box. I had to get past them and back to civilization.

I walked to the front door. Peering carefully out one corner, lights raised on poles established that M&M's limo was gone, which I confirmed by entering the room on the corner that opened onto the side drive where Frankie had once parked. No limo anywhere. There seemed to be no guards watching the front of the house, but the PI in me would not allow me to step into the open in case guards loitered in the front garden.

Only one way seemed safe—back the way I had come—via the blue pool and the lush backyard gardens. My plan wasn't clear. Even if I could bypass the gate-guards and find the private road that wound its way down to the public road, how could I make it back to my office in Albuquerque? My Olds was wrecked. I had no phone. I supposed I might catch a ride with some trucker-type for the final leg, but there was a lot of territory between Marm's pool and the public road. At least a mile.

So I steeled myself, or rather called on Quinn to whip Pietro and Elvis into shape for what was needed. Together (and doesn't every person truly have a whole city dwelling within?) we found the path which I was now trekking for the third time that night, and, amid the towering trees that were little more than ghostly images barely moving in the hot dry breeze, I managed to negotiate halfway around the house, back in the vicinity of where Muck's phantom dogs had caught me.

The memory of those growling, snapping beasts eager to tear my flesh stayed in mind. The darkened trees leaning like ancient guardians aroused within me wild imaginings of spirits of the petrified forest seeking revenge on careless trespassers.

A snap sounded.

From one side, it was quickly followed by a series of snaps and cricks from the other.

This was no phantom poodle—it was something real.

The whole gang: Pietro, Quinn, Elvis, and myself, jerked to a halt in front of the same leaf-strewn patch of swampy ground where my mind had previously been tricked by M&M's illusions. Turning, I strained to focus...two images, large tan trench coats, one with a plastic fork thrust out of a breast pocket.

"Say it ain't true, Detective Dorkman," the fork said.

"Not in my wildest dreams, Detective Krupke," answered his companion.

The two dicks emerged from the shadows and halted in a circle of moonlight, their pale faces like two round melons, too mismatched to suggest hotties. They stared down at me from their hot-shit heights with arms folded, though I glimpsed bulges in their pockets indicating loaded peacemakers.

"If it isn't my favorite dead-namic duo." My smirk out-smirked theirs.

Dorkman snorted. "I think we just won the lottery, Krupke. Too bad PIs named Marlowe ain't eligible to play."

His partner stepped closer. "And play we shall. Whadaya think, Dorkman...the head? Or the stomach?"

"I vote for both." Dorkman curled one half-lip. "Too bad, all right. Ya shoulda stayed put, Pete. Ya shoulda done what you were told by Mr. Muck and Mr. Montez. It mighta turned out better for ya." He shook his head. "Now, we're gonna do it *our* way."

"Ain't no choice no more," added Krupke. "And no escape. No way, no how."

"But I'm sure the hell gonna enjoy it. Like a birthday gift."

"An anniversary from the wife."

"A birthaversay from the family."

"An Octoberbirthaversaryfest, from me to me."

I narrowed my eyes and finally interrupted the two dicks' little exchange. "Think well, guys. You may not really want to go that way."

They pulled their government-issue pistols out of their government-issue suits and pointed them, one at my head, the other at my stomach. I could not help but tense. I realized I could not step backward for fear of what I knew in my bones lay beneath the carpet of leaves behind me—movie lot quicksand obscured by a towering thicket of brush.

What happened next I could not comprehend.

The chests of both Dorkman and Krupke turned red. Like a star becoming white hot, their fronts went through a rainbow of colors: red, pink, purple, green, orange, white. Lava erupted. Springing from their hearts, the fleshy rainbow flowed out and down and encompassed their uniformed legs to form a puddle of ruined flesh about their ankles. Strangely, the two dicks seemed not to notice but continued staring ahead, their beadle eyes focused on mine, hate and smugnicity triumphant in their pupils, their arms still thrust out, their hands clutching their loaded guns. Why didn't they pull the triggers?

The entire front façade of the pair now glowed, their flesh circling in a vortex that steadily grew till it swallowed every part. Strains of Istanbul rang.

In the vortex appeared an ivory-colored backside. Enlarging, the backside grew until it became an entire Canali suit. It stepped free of the vortex and turned.

"Don't step back," it called.

For a moment all I could do was stare. True, I me-self had just spent a week watching Pete as he watched another Pete struggle and plot, and true, I recalled being that Pete as he punched the red button and emerged from the storage shed on the Aztec plaza and shot the first Pete. But that was mere memory—this was here and now. Yet another Pete had emerged from some elastic universe right in front of my eyes...to do what?

"That's quicksand behind you." He turned and looked at Dorkman and Krupke; the vortex no longer swirled. The music stopped. Pete grinned. "I've been waitin' for this little development for longer than a famine in Cork."

A Colt .45 appeared—Pete aimed it at the two detectives, whose flesh was reassembling like a film run in reverse. In seconds, their molecules would be back where they had been before Pete zapped them from the other universe. Already a new level of hate glowed in the dicks' eyes.

The puzzle came together. Dorkman breathed deep, like a diver replenishing oxygen after surfacing too quick; Krupke heaved, the seasickness I knew so well from inter-universe trips affecting him. For a second he choked, then swallowed it down—no surprise there. He straightened up, his ever-present fork still in his pocket like a sacred charm, guarding against an attack of rap-sheet rutabagas, I supposed.

"My, my, my," Pete said, extending the Colt.

"What they hell," I protested. "You're not going to do it, are you, Pete? You can't. They're cops."

A devilish laugh came from Pete—I knew the true source, however: Quinn was in the saddle.

"You can't," repeated the Dork, desperation in his voice. "Like he said: we're cops!"

"Like Pete said," sputtered Krapke, "but *which* Pete? There's Pete...and there's Pete."

"You dicks thought you had trouble with one of us? Try two on for size."

"Uh, Pete, I think we can work this out." Dork flitted his eyes between both of us Petes. "Whichever of you is the real one."

"We both are, Dork. Haven't you got that through your brainiac cranium yet?"

"Both? But that's nonsense. You on a three-day high, Pete? You prepped on meth? PCP? Corner store Spice?"

"He's got a twin brother!" shouted Krupke. He looked at Dorkman. "Pete's got a twin brother—and we never knew!"

Dorkman shook his head. "No. It's somethin' else. That damned Montez & Muck...they did somethin'. This is somethin' else."

Pete cocked the hammer.

Krupke blanched.

Dorkman recited calmly with a touch of anguish: "cask of Amontillado."

The bullets slammed into and through them, lodging with dull thuds in the thin tree trunks beyond. In surprise, the two detectives looked down, briefly considered the fist-sized holes that had just appeared. Their eyes rolled up and they fell to their knees. They collapsed.

I knew that the tango was different on different dance floors. But I never suspected that one of those dance floors would one day be the bodies of Dorkman and Krupke. Inwardly, I danced.

Pete turned to me. "We need to put them in their car. It's the only way back."

I nodded, my fedora still on my head—and on his. Together we sneaked through the trees until we found their white sedan parked midway between the house and the gate-box where a pair of M&M's thugs still watched. Returning to the dead detectives, I pulled my hat tighter on my skull (as did Pete) and together we dragged Dorkman's body through the brush and heaved it into the front seat passenger side. Going back once more, we dragged Krupke's body to the car and placed it in the back seat, driver's side. Then we carefully re-arranged their coats to hide the fact that each had a pair of two-inch holes drilled in them.

Soundlessly, to avoid discovery by the gate-guards down the winding drive, we closed the sedan's doors and stood facing each other. Pete to Pete. Quinn to Quinn. Elvis to Elvis.

Pete quietly breathed. "You know what has to be done."

I breathed with him. "I was afraid you'd say that."

"No one never complished nothin' by stayin' comfortable."

"I was afraid you'd say that too."

"You mean...you knew."

"Yep. Like a lost twin who loves twice-baked *colcannon*. There ain't no secrets 'tween us."

"Not a one, Pete. Not a one."

Turning, I strode dutifully through the trees to the same leaf-covered watery swamp where my other self had just given Dorkman and Krupke their comeuppance and where earlier I had almost been consumed by three vicious phantom poodles.

I gave Pete a last solemn look. Without a word, I walked into the quicksand. I slowly sank. Now that be the strangest of all sensations, *deed* it do—to drown an inch at a time while you yourself stand on the bank in safety watching, knowing that you yourself are the one going under.

Just before my face disappeared for the last time beneath the surface of the dirt-sprinkled liquid grave, Pete on the bank aimed his naked pinky at me, then blasted me with his .45 to universe-come, my mind, as our eyes observed each other in my last rites, merging with his.

***

As the body sank, I stood on the bank and observed. Now I understood. Now I remembered. I remembered how, when I had been in Rome, in the dark cell beneath the Vatican, attempting to persuade Uncle Flynn to hold me tight while I propelled the pair of us through the erupting lava of the tomb's door, and how he struggled, and how for a moment we had stepped back over the threshold before pushing forward into the corridor.

At the time we had gone on, proceeded as if nothing out of the ordinary had occurred, never guessing that I had just duplicated myself, that a second version (actually a fourth version) of myself had exited a day earlier and waited until I and Flynn rushed to Flynn's little center of operations hidden on the upper floor.

Of course, after we found the Blarney Stone, and after Tonya tossed me the paper with the picture of Stonehenge and the words 'song of the bell' and 'MilkCow' written on it, and the limo had driven away without us, I had again been imprisoned by the Vatican's Swiss guards.

It was then that my mysterious benefactor had intervened by zapping the tomb's door again and placing the fragment of red button on Tonya's kerchief in the middle of the floor of the corridor. That was *mio*. Strange indeed to have not just one set of memories, but a second set overlying the first—and, in my case, a third and a fourth.

I myself watched the limo from the upper window of the Vatican wall after Pete and Flynn had descended. I myself watched Pete and Flynn struggle over the suitcase at the foot of the rope. I myself saw the limo drive away and the troop of Swiss guards seize Pete. I myself, who, after letting Flynn climb back up and pull up his rope behind him and disappear back into the Vatican's labyrinth, had myself then run down from the roof, exited through the Museum entrance, found the red button and Tonya's kerchief, followed Pete as the Swiss guards put him in the catacombs, waited for the guards to leave, and finally zapped the door open to free me.

And it was I who made certain that Pete found the red button and kerchief, and I who had disappeared around the corner so that Pete glimpsed only the heel of my Petros shoe, avoiding our meeting in case the earlier Pete might decide to abandon M&M's project.

Finally I myself had flown back to Albuquerque alone, too late to follow my other self when he drove to Juarez, so I was forced to wait in Albuquerque until I returned from Mexico, hoping that my earlier self would work things out, would survive in Juarez.

Which he did.

But now all the Petes are gone. Entombed, shot, or buried in quicksand. Leaving only one Pete, *mío*—but with the memories of four Petes impressed in my mind. What with Elvis, Quinn, and Pietro stuffed in the cellar and banging the ceiling with broom poles, it was getting crowded in here. But I was determined to make it work.

I had to.

Walking back to the car—with a glance overhead to make sure that I had plenty of darkness remaining—I fished out Dorkman's keys, purred the engine, and motored down the winding road toward the gate-guards. Dodge too made smooooth cars.

A single lonesome light appeared, suspended on a pole. Rolling slowly closer, I eased alongside the open stand where I sighted a guard leaning sleepily, one ear pasted to a chirping cell phone. Surely my luck won't last, I thought. One more second and he'll catch onto my jailbreak. Would I have to employ my ace-in-the-digit one more time? How could I do that confined in a car with two corpses?

Just out of the glare of the lamp, I halted the wheels. I squeezed myself into the driver's door, then pulled Dorkman's body halfway behind the wheel so that he seemed to be driving, my own body hidden by his. Another advantage of the vertically and horizontally challenged. I slid my right arm under his left arm. As the guard leaned out to look, I raised Dorkman's arm in a half-jerk to signal 'all clear'.

"You done, Dorkman?" The guard blinked, glanced at Krupke

in the back. "That quick? Mr. Muck said he don't want any poodle-doo left in the garden."

I should've known those jerks' moonlighting would be something like this. Poodle-scoopers.

I brought Dorkman's arm up to his forehead. "Manure's my middle name," I grunted in my best imitation Dorkman. "It's a crappy job, but..."

He bought it. The gate board raised and the guard twitched his head—you're outta here.

Wasting no more time, I gunned the engine and soon found my way to the main road, after pushing Dorkman back into the driver passenger seat. I had thought to pause by the wreck of my new Olds, which I had left with its bottom ground into dirt in a secluded off-road patch. But I couldn't find it. Reversing, I rolled slowly again past the location where I could have sworn I left it.

Nothing.

So I drove miles farther, and left the hills and canyons to break onto the open road.

I needed a hint of what to do next. I had a picture, a name, and a location. But not a *why*. And no one to give the screws to make them squawk—except one single joe. That 'joe' was made of iron. But at least he talked.

I drove to the adobe church. Sure enough the church was still there. I half feared that Rick's Americana Cafe would reappear, that Marm and Co. would suddenly start fighting over dollars in the fresh new parking lot while Montez & Muck's backsides materialized out of the boulders.

But all was quiet. Behind the boulders—there being still no sign of life in this remote memorial to atheism—I decided to unload. Correction, since all I had seen and witnessed testified clear as a wine glass that there ain't no such thing as non-belief, only crusades of some versus crusades of others, usually reducing to one against all or all against one as each victory transformed into Frankenwright castles, and average people like *mío* got somebody's heretic label pasted on their brows.

Heretic to the core, I paused to pull the two dicks' bodies out of the car—victims of their own kind of crusade—which I had just rendered unfashionable, and I left the pair lying lengthwise behind a petrified rock. The piss-ant kind.

There was no time to dance on their grave.

Entering the little alamo by its back entrance, still unguarded, I climbed the narrow rusted stairway, still unnoticed, and found the enormous bell, the 'iron joe', which somehow, someway, Marm's own crusade to Christianize the natives had ensured was installed along with the adobe church itself, passing the ancient pictures that reminded me more than before of the pictures of those godfathers I had seen in Marm's New Orleans bar, and I thought of the phalanx of frozen Catholics brooding in her basement. Truth marches on; or rather sleeps on, planning, dreaming. What does time mean to true believers? Or the fact that their churches might remain empty? Stand they must; or dream like sleeper cells, as fate deals its hand.

I was ready. I wanted more this time. Starting with name, rank, and serial number, but then dates, plans, and money trails. I wanted the whole song—

I rang the bell.

Someone cleared his throat. The reception was particularly good today, I thought. With a human at the other end, I had no more urges to flee like Versace Tarzan.

A high whine was followed by a flurry of rapid Italian. *"You are there, my friends? My dear Arditi, have you come for me? For so long I have been waiting, for so long I have suffered in this cold. I am lonely, my friends, lonely."*

I knew better than to interrupt a Mac when he's spilling his guts. "I'm here," I mumbled.

He, whoever 'he' was, took the bait. *"My beloved followers, you must speak louder. You are there? You are in Milkow? You are at the Henge? The Glocke is ready with the new crystals? You can at last bring me back? Our friends in the Vatican are calling for their leader. Our Mason friends in Roma have been patient. But they will not wait forever."*

I didn't get it, only the part about somebody doing something in the Vatican and Rome and getting tired of shuffling their shoes, in Italian lingo.

"You...you are not answering—"

Time to interrupt. I banged the bell. "Listen, Mac. I've had just about enough of your whining. What I wanna know is What the hell is this Glocke thingamagork? And why does it need crystals? And I'm pretty sure I know where your damned crystals came from—the ones I twice risked my life to get." And for which I lost my life thrice, I thought, but did not say aloud.

The god in the bell sucked a breath. *"Are you one of my people? You speak clearly and do not mumble about suns and sacrifices, which I never understand. You do not kiss me and ask how to make friends and influence people. This too is hard to understand because they speak in strange accents, though I try to help. And you do not ask about Saint Peter and ask strange things like What is Heaven like? And you are not like the many others who interrupt my sleep, asking me other strange things. Again I do not understand, but I try to help. I always try to help. My love is great for ordinary people with ordinary problems. Are you one of these people, my friend? An ordinary person with an ordinary problem?"*

Pietro almost burst into tears. For a second I felt the logic of the god pass through me, and suddenly I understood how generations of "ordinary people" could speak into grey stones and obey whatever the hell came back in reply. Because somebody up there cared. And that was all that mattered.

But Truth matters too.

Again I banged the bell, hoping to hurt God's ears. God needed to make more sense, help His people with more than just a few semi-helpful grunts. He needed to redo his Creation—this time with a complete rational sentence instead of a mere 'Let the world be.'

"The Glocke, Your Bellness. What is the Glocke?"

After the vibrating ceased, God said, *"Oh, that is the Secret! The secret of how I became God. From my humble beginnings to the most lofty position in Heaven, I watch and listen and advise. But you...I know now that you are not of my followers. Your motives are not pure. Your soul cannot be converted, you cannot be saved. The place of my creation is not for such as you!"*

"Not so fast, Mac!" Desperately I slammed the bell again, and again...but God did not return.

After wasting a few more minutes hoping the Operator would

reconnect me, I finally gave up and walked back down to the twin dicks' government car. One quick glance to make sure the pair had not come back to life as part of a zombie apocalypse, and I got into the car and drove.

I knew what was next. Returning to my office, I went to my desk—the hidden one locked in the back—and extracted a wallet (my third, special reserve wallet); another painting by Modigliani (Pete number one had brought two crosses and two paintings, but I had followed behind and looted Il Papa's room and surrounding halls for everything that remained); another e-cig heater (with ample supply of Wild Strawberry nicotine juice); my last Loreto sunglasses and Movado watch; more IDs (all PIs have lots of spares); and my *genuine* passport (the previous one being a masterful forgery).

Traveling to my favorite pawn broker's shop, I traded the Modigliani for yet more oodles of cash and another Colt .45, then headed to Honest Juan's. I didn't need another car, but I wanted one. Since I had the cash—why not?

To my surprise, I found not only my old-Olds for sale, which Honest Juan had found behind Miz Tam's place, but next to it my new-Olds, which he had already found and dragged back from the hills near Miz Marm's castle and repaired. Fancy that. Apparently I had failed to pay some kinda tax, and "pursuant" to our sales contract, he had repossessed.

Say la vino. That's life with the wife.

So I bought both cars—no habit like an old habit—and I drove one to the airport while Juan drove the new car all the way to...well, I gave Juan a fanny pack filled with Franklins and a phone that I had stolen from Marm's castle with an IP location that pinpointed a spot in Idaho via GPS. For Wendy. None happier than a guy like Juan when I walk in. Between us, old times is still old times.

And it was time I talked to God face-to-face.

At the airport, it was all too easy to slip past inspections using the button, and once on the plane I settled into first class. Now that's a habit a guy can get used to. Though the Polish and Italian phrase books didn't help much. The only phrase that stuck was '*Mi ne frego*'—'I don't give a damn'.

CHAPTER 33

I landed in Prague like a lost albatross, rain from the previous night soaking the airport's landing strip, and soaking the forests we flew over, and everything in between. It was harder to get past the international inspections in Czechistan, but apparently they also have walls, so I managed to hide the Colt, present my docs, then retrieve it. Hell, I could've smuggled in a battleship with 16-inch guns.

Outside, I tried the only phrase I knew and promptly got the middle-finger salute from a local taxi driver. I saluted right back—barely keeping Quinn in line. Quinn was ready to zap the towel-head back to whatever immigrant universe he came from.

But I wasn't here to pick a fight. I needed a ride. So I corralled the crowd of personalities lurking in my basement and flashed some green at the next taxi. This towel-head did not even glance at my feet for the missing luggage but simply threw open his car's back door. He grinned. Nothing says I Love You like silver and gold. Even if the funny money we usually toss around is only Christmas tree ornaments for children and fuels-gold for fools.

With hesitation, I took Tonya's scribbled picture out of my hat and showed it to the driver. Hardly a second passed before he nodded and jerked the taxi into gear. Into the traffic we launched as he tossed, "Yah, 'Die Glocke'. This way, sir."

More progress. I had already found the translation online via my cell phone that 'Die Glocke' meant 'The Bell'. And I had a feeling that it sang like a Chicago choir.

"Poland. Across the border."

I glanced at the driver's picture and read his name. "Go for it, Ahmed."

We soon left the lights of Prague behind. As we plunged onto a damp Czech autobahn at lightning speed, I got to wondering how many passengers Ahmed had already taken there. Where exactly? I was fairly sure that the pieces were falling into place, but I asked to make sure.

"Milkow?"

His eyes glued to a curve in the road growing darker as the sun plunged behind us, the driver nodded. "Yah. Milkow. Teeny village. By 'The Giant'."

At my puzzled look, he repeated in way of explanation, "Die Henge. You know. Like, ah...you Englisher 'Stonehenge'."

A silent explosion rocked my brain. Tonya's picture of the 12 concrete columns joined together was *deed* like Stonehenge, and it was tied to Die Glocke, or The Bell, which sang without a clapper.

"Irish, not English, Mac. But it don't matter."

Ahmed just shrugged. His eyes followed the road as we raced eastward toward the Polish border, where Jack Muck and Bob Montez and Tonya Massolini and everything else that had become important in my life I felt certain were involved in creating some event of multi-versal importance.

Less than an hour passed. I was surprised at how quickly we got to the Polish border, had to remind myself that we weren't in the Great Southwest anymore, that here in the 'Stans of central *Europa* countries were smaller, fences bigger, palaver more mixed. Racing quickly over the Czechistan mountains (how the heck did they carve such straight roads out of such high hills?), I could see from my cell phone map that the border was approaching fast.

The driver didn't slow.

"Schengen," he muttered. We flew straight through. Well, straight as the gently curving road could take us, a picture of an owl on a road sign looming out of the night suggesting we had entered Poland's Owl Mountains. No customs. No cops. Who could ask for more?

Another twenty minutes and we flipped left. A few more and he finally slowed and out of the blackness of the wet night, jagged clouds rushing overhead, we lurched to an angry stop. A flash of lightning from the east—a monstrous set of pillars, concrete-grey, angling their lego-structure into the rain-soaked sky, throwing shadows over the blue and white checkerboard of the cab.

I breathed deep. I had hoped I would be better prepared, that the crowd in my cellar could control themselves. As my eyes stretched skyward to take in the full size of the ring, the sheer height of the twelve joined pillars (yes, I counted them), made me feel small. Smaller than usual, that is.

Nothing was happening.

No Muck. No Montez. Not no one.

Ahmed pointed through a line of trees to where a crumbling building stood near newer modern-day buildings. "Museum," he muttered. As if I needed his comment to know where I was, he nodded back at the pillars. "Henge." An overhead sign boasted 'Ludwigsdorf Riese', which I already gathered meant 'The Giant of Milkow'.

I wasn't here for visiting hours, though. Whatever was happening, or was scheduled to happen, I was certain was already in the works, just not here, not in the open. I looked again at Ahmed. For the first time he blinked. More than once.

I knew such blinks...

"My friend," for a change I tried the butter-up technique, "we found Milkow, we found the Henge, but now..." I took out my wallet and dramatically fanned a stack of one hundred dollar American bills. "Now I need..." On a hunch, I hummed the first stanza to Good King Wenceslaus.

A storm of blinking followed.

Smiling, I sent word downstairs to Quinn and Pietro, and everybody else waiting on hooks for the final word from the Great Outdoors. "You got it, Mac," I said. "I don't care if I'm your first ride, or your last. Take me to the Wenceslaus Mine."

His hand reached out—

"Uh-uh." I pocketed the dough. "The Mine first."

More blinks. Ahmed powered down his driver-side window and pointed hesitantly at a worn sign on a rise close to the Henge, two dull metal doors underneath. The sign read 'Wencelas Grobe' and had a couple of pictures of a hammer and pick. Dummy loading carts on pretend rails rusted in front.

I shouted. "Do I look like an idiot, Ahmed? I ain't no tourist.

Take me to the *real* mine—the *real* Komplex Milkow." For some reason he was resisting me, and I smelled the influence of Montez & Muck and their Peronista buddies. I brought out a hundred dollar bill and waved it; then I slipped my other hand into my pants pocket and made sure Señor Ahmed could see the barrel of my Colt. Good cop, bad cop works best when it's paired with hospital, cemetery.

He gulped.

The cab lurched again into the night. Ahmed found a side track and, exiting the main road, angled north-eastward into foothills that rose rapidly before us, all wet, the rain picking up to throw a low blanket over everything, Ahmed squeaking his wipers on full.

Deeper into the depths of the Owl Mountains we climbed, often slowing to avoid rocks or holes in the road. Suddenly a wide low bulk appeared in the dark. Like a black hole at the center of a galaxy, no light shone to relieve my eye.

But from somewhere I felt a subtle vibration, as if a power plant resided just over the horizon.

Ground zero.

Ahmed trembled—not from the vibration. He was past nervous and plainly frightened. Well, let him. I was done with his puppy dog fear. Throwing a couple of hundreds in his lap, I snatched the towel from his head and used it to wipe my face. Stepping out of the cab, I draped the towel over my hat-covered Elvis wave and slammed the door. Lives were on the line. I had no more patience for cowards, though I did wonder who else he might have recently brought here, and why he was so scared to bring more.

Before I could turn, Ahmed spun mud and lurched back down the road. He had gotten his tip; the fate of an ex-passenger was now as far from his mind as the fate of a dodo. I only hoped I had not set myself up to be just as extinct.

Lightning flashed. In the glow, a gaping hole in the side of the mountain appeared, a ring of blacker black inside shadowy black, two concrete posts on either side propping up a concrete lintel like a giant's mantelpiece from the dawn of time. Everything around here seemed built for fuller-sized hot-shit humans; no wonder they called this area Die Riese, 'The Giant'.

A narrow gauge rail led into the hole. On the mantelpiece hung a neglected sign reading 'Dinamit Nobel AG'.

"Yeah, that's the crank," I whispered. "Those *Nazzis*," I hissed the word like Churchill, with a long z, "must have used the dynamite to make their tunnels." I sniffed. "How did M&M get mixed up with *this* crowd?"

The rain had paused and I used the gap to slowly approach the entrance. Somewhere far inside gleamed a point of light. Just what the doctor prescribed. Throwing fear aside—but keeping caution in my pocket—I entered, pausing only to straighten my rain-dampened fedora and towel the water off my fancy watch, Elvis cufflinks, and Canali shoes. A filthy tunnel in Polandia was hardly the locale to win first place in anybody's *sapeur* contest.

For a distance I followed the twin metal tracks, once having to step around an ancient barricade placed by some big-shot authority to keep people like me out of their precious mine, and twice stepped around rusty metal carts still perched on rusty rails. The light coming from far ahead gave just enough photons to keep me from falling into more movie-lot quicksand—or whatever the heck the open holes that I occasionally bypassed in the dirt-strewn ground led to.

The light turned out to be a weak florescent fed by a small electric cable hung on the wall. Somebody had installed a recent upgrade. I kept going, toward the next point of light.

I don't know how far I went, or how long it took. For a time it seemed I was back in the tunnels inside the Vatican, and wondered—even out-Quinning Quinn's usual suspicions—whether these tunnels somehow connected with those. No, I decided, not even all the resources of the Giants who built this place could dig an underground railroad all the way from Poland to Rome, though it would explain many disappearances when the saints had come marching in in 1945.

I kept stumbling forward. I followed the next set of elusive photons, listening to the background hum which grew steadily louder, staying alert for ambushes and snipers and...yes, even for the sounds of happy dwarves, pounding and picking in their underground world.

This was the strangest part. I could swear I even heard carts moving on the narrow rail line, and, when I arrived several times at cross-tunnels, it seemed distant echoes reached my ears as if this mine were active and not neglected and dead after all. Though if dirt was being moved, why was nothing being hauled to the surface? No rock being carted to the entrance for dumping? And something else reached me. In the immortal words of His Immortal Mason-ness, Alberto Pike: more light.

I arrived at a larger space in the tunnel, a twenty-foot wide room that boasted smooth walls, overhead fluorescents, and larger power cables. The cables hummed.

Just when I felt I could no longer march forward, no longer push a path through the dirt-crumbled floor of this spider's labyrinth, my eyes found a gush of light so strong it almost blinded me. At the same time, the hum became deafening and I slowed my progress to a measured, careful red-Indian pace. I wanted to discover the authors of the upgrade before they discovered me.

Following the reflection of light off the smooth wall of the corridor, I risked a peek with one eye around the corridor's end. I thought I had been prepared. I thought I was steeled for what Montez & Muck were up to. Not even life with the wife, however, could keep this hubby on the farm.

It was a wide and open cavern, its sides still rough with live stone, stretching half a stadium before me, steel girders propping up a concrete reinforced roof, more concrete composing the floor. Close by buzzed a giant's dynamo, thick cables of steel crawling outward in a dozen directions to entangle a slew of devices that defied my or Quinn's, or even Pietro's description. At the opposite end, an elevator descended, an overhead sign reading 'Museum'. I suddenly understood that the taxi driver had deliberately taken me far from the true focus of the night's events, which were *under* the Museum, to protect himself from punishment by the Conspiracy by dumping me in the middle of Wlodyka Mountain, not realizing that he had provided me with a back entrance by which I could discreetly view The Show.

And The Show had verily begun.

In the center of the cavern, perched stately on top of a twenty-foot wide circular iron platform, was a large bell, nondescript I had to call it, the bell lacking even the monotonous decorations of your usual holier-than-thou church bell. I was willing to bet my right Canali shoe that it was also lacking a clapper. I knew in my bones that this bell sang without one, and in barbershop harmony.

I had found Die Glocke.

At least nine feet wide and twelve feet in height, the Glocke was not suspended, but rested on several girders, which in turn rested on the platform. A web of cables and rubber gaskets held the Thing in a tight unbreakable ring, and, most peculiar, twelve massive chains were attached to its upper reach and lay flat down its sides, trailing across the platform. What their purpose might be escaped my best guess.

Another feature further confused me—a hole had been punched high up the side of the Bell. Through this square gap glowed a blueish-white oblong that surrounded a whitened human face, encased by a background landscape of ice. I had seen this before— on M&M's computer monitors inside Marm's Querque mansion and in M&M's video shop in Juarez, and again a phalanx of the real things below Marm's New Orleans clothes shop, lines of corpses frozen inside upright capsules stretching into the distance for who the hell knew why?

The elevator jerked to a stop.

For a moment I thought I had been drafted and inwardly celebrated the prospect of meeting Elvis in person until I remembered the year, the locale, the fact of the King's death long after his military discharge.

Out of the elevator spilled a clutch of uniforms. Mighty pretty they were too. Two wore white with white nautical caps, reminding me of admirals, though not from the American Navy. Two wore civilian suits—and good ones, as good as anything Canali made. Peering at their faces, I was surprised to realize that I recognized them. Not by name, but I had seen their faces on Italian TV. They were the top two politicians in Italy. Behind them lurked more: three men in brown uniforms with what looked like dinner salad spilled on their chests, which I gathered were military decorations, labeling these hot-shots as army generals. One even wore jodhpurs, his hips thrust out like a Baltic peasant woman.

Together they approached the Bell.

The highest military and political leaders of modern Italy had come. I knew that Montez & Muck had connections, but the fact that they could summon the elite of an entire country to their coffee klatch was a shock.

What was next? What was the point of the Big Show that had brought the brass here?

A curtain pulled to one side. Yep, now we're getting somewhere—another loop of computer monitors just like in Juarez and Querque, with two figures sitting before them, staring, watching for errors and tracking the Show's next Act. No, they were not M&M, but I recognized them: Rat-Face Frankie and a small figure whom I had last seen delivering drinks in Rick's Cafe: Diego the short-order bartender, apparently moonlighting for the overtime, and pausing on occasion to mop or fix drinks. With José and Andrew and Andrew's cops all MIA, I guessed Muck and Montez were growing short of flunkies to order about.

A noise erupted from the Bell, overshadowing the buzz of the dynamo—a pair of what looked like circular iron plates in the bottom jerked to life. They spun in opposite directions, one clockwise, the other counterclockwise. For a moment a band around the base of the bell glowed red, then purple, then faded back to red. The spinning stopped. I stared hard at the Roman legion of Italian big-shots accumulated a dozen feet from the Bell. Had they each acquired a tan? I was ready to bet my left Canali that their faces had deepened a shade. Maybe hiding around a corner of live rock was the better part of value, I thought, inspecting my forearms for possible radiation damage.

Why would these characters need such a device? And why did they each look like they had attended Italy's version of a West Point graduation ceremony? And why did they stare at the Glocke with such heavy-lidded skeptical eyes?

A clanking resounded through the cavern. At first I could not see who was responsible for making the noise—then a portion of the Glocke slid aside to reveal an interior chamber and a pair of figures emerged backward out of the Bell, hunched over, stepping with care over the many cables and chains until they came to the Bell's front as the door slid back into place.

The pair turned to face the audience.

Jack Muck and Bob Montez—in the flesh. And still dressed in their trench-brown combat pants from yester-wars, now with loose black shirts. Their own editions of salad were pinned on their black satin chests, and they still wore little black hats with black tassels down the sides. Back in the computer camp, I detected wagging tails and realized that Jack's poodle pack were lying among the monitors, happy to be near their master.

I could barely keep Quinn and Pietro in their basement. They jumped up with eagerness to take vengeance on the two mad scientists, but we-all hesitated when M&M pulled their next trick.

Whipping out small square aprons, they draped the aprons around the front of their waists and tied two strings behind their backs. The military expedition standing a foot or two below the platform exchanged mutual glances, still with the expressions of skepticism, then slowly pulled out their own white aprons.

Masons! What did that remind me of? Could there be a Masonic Italian West Point? A combination West Point and Annapolis 'lodge' in Rome? I recalled Cheche's reply on our helicopter flight to my question about masonic lodges in the Vatican: 'P-2' he had said. I had not understood what he meant.

A strong voice echoed...

"My dear *Propaganda Due*. Velcome to our Maximal Session."

Jack always did have a thing with speeches, and the voice to speech with.

'Propaganda Due', I thought, 'P-2'. Recalling them from Italian news sometime back, that explained a lot.

Jack thrust out his hand in a Roman salute. He peered at the military brass. "I, state-your-name, do hereby svear this meeting of *Il Propaganda Due* to secrecy upon pain of the death."

The generals and admirals thrust out their own hands and, as one, repeated, "I, state-your-name..."

"No, brothers, no," interrupted Bob.

They shuffled their booted feet in embarrassment and said, "I," they then each recited their own name, though in the confusion I heard nothing distinct, "do hereby swear this meeting of Il Propaganda Due to secrecy upon pain of the death."

They lowered their right arms.

One of the Generals stepped forward. "Brother Muck," he said in a thick Italian accent as if unused to bridging their language gap with English, "we appreciate the many sacrifices that you and Brother Montez have made investigating the Lodge's legend about our absent leader, and how you have left no stone unturned in your attempts to fulfill the words of the legend."

The General threw side gazes at his army and politician comrades. "And we appreciate your invitation to attend this maximal session of Propaganda Due in this...very special place."

The gathering let their gazes wander about the cavern, clearly as unfamiliar with the Giant's tunnels as I was.

I withdrew my eye around the corner of the connecting tunnel until they returned their attention to Montez & Muck.

"But your invitation was less than precise, Brother Muck. 'Veni, vidi, duce' does not explain much. Only the intervention of the leader of our Lodge, who *unfortunate-mente* is not here, persuaded us to honor your invitation."

"And ve thank you, Brother Moschin, for making the space—"

"Taking the time, Jack," corrected Bob, standing alongside.

"Oh, tank you, dear Bob," said Jack. "Taking the time."

"That's 'thanks', Jack."

"You are velcome, Bob."

Bob shrugged. He stared down at the lodge members.

"So, Brother *mío* Muck. Can you give us, if you don' mind, a little more to, how do say, 'go on' as regards your invitation? Can you give us the point?"

"Get *to* the point," corrected Bob.

The General glared, and Bob closed his mouth. "Tough crowd," he muttered.

Muck took a breath and grinned—I got the point. Jack was in his element.

"My dear, dear, *dear* lodge brothers."

Way to begin, Jack, I thought. That's pure Muck.

"Please to being patient...very patient. And I promise that you shall be revarded...very vell revarted..." Muck stumbled over the difficult words. "My brothers, I believe I must 'take the time' to...how to say...let you in on a little secret...fill you in on some information...bring you up to speed."

"That's the way to put it, Jack." Bob smiled. "You got it right."

The brass directed nasty looks at Bob, who looked up and quietly whistled.

"As you must know," Jack continued, "our beloved movement, born in the fires of var, and devoted to the glory of Greater Italia, vas vonce graced vith an eqvually beloved leader who led our movement to success after success, our country to victory upon victory, just like the mightiest empire of all time...Eternal Roma."

The brass breathed deeply at this reminder of wonderful memories. A few raised their right arms briefly again in the Roman salute, though through my little eye-spy from the tunnel I still wondered what the heck this was all about. Why would M&M give a history lesson when they can jump borders of the multi-verse?

"My beloved brothers. In the year 1945, vhen our Cause seemed lost, Germans came here, in these old coal tunnels that you see all around, and built a fortress. An underground fortress of forty-five sqvuare kilometers. The Germans named it *Die Riese*, The Giant."

I was getting it. Germaniacs built this place.

"Back then they vere our friends. Ve hugged and kissed like there vould be no tomorrow."

I remembered the Mediterranean kissing thing from Juarez and tried to imagine Jack doing the same with World War Two Nazis, and failed.

"Even vhen the Third Reich vas collapsing, and its enemies closed in from all directions, the Germans continued to vork on The Giant, pouring their last resources from all across the Third Reich into their project. Against all reason. Their last concrete, their last electric power, their last scientists vere put to vork here. Then, my dear brothers, tomorrow arrived. Vhen the thanks of the Communisti came across the border—"

"That's 'tanks', Jack."

"Tanks?" said Jack.

"Tanks for thanks."

"You're velcome *again*, Bob."

Bob sighed and put his hands in the pants pockets of his military fatigues.

"Our German friends abandoned their plans, and abandoned The Giant."

"We know all about that, Brother Muck. We don' need a history lesson."

"Ah, but my dear Propaganda brothers, there is something that you don't know." Jack glanced behind him. "Before the Germans left, they built this device, vhich they called Die Glocke—the Bell. For years they vorked on this device, applying their best minds on vhat they hoped vould become their greatest 'Vundervaffe', Vonderveapon. Die Glocke vas the reason vhy the Germans vorked on The Giant until the very last moment, pouring all their last resources into its completion." Jack stood straight and stared up. "*Vhy*, gentlemen, I ask you? *Vhy?*"

"We know that also, Brother Muck." The Italian brass were beginning to lose patience. Moschin said, "But the Bell was a failure. They believed they could neutralize gravity and make a new generation of flying anti-gravity vehicles, and nothing can do that."

"Oh, but you do not have the complete picture, my brothers!" Jack folded his arms. "You see, there vas *another* line of investigation *besides* gravity. And vhen the first project failed, they continued vith the second..."

Jack waited for the suspense to build.

"Please to make your point, Brother Muck," General Moschin said. "Are you trying to say that this *thing* can fly?" A half-dozen skeptical looks were directed at Jack and his bell.

"Patience, my brothers. Just a little more patience. This Glocke that you see here today, my dear friends, is the original Glocke that vas built by the Germans. Some time ago, dear Bob and I came here in this empty desolate cavern, and after years of labor and many disappointments—ve found it! Before they left in 1945, the Germans had buried the Glocke, but vith instructions on how to resurrect it, how to...so to say...bring it back to life. And, after cleaning it up, that is vhat ve did."

"So you plugged in an old Nazi lamp and it still works. So what, Brother Jack?"

Jack grinned. "Dear brethren. Have you ever vondered vhy the Bell has its shape?"

Blank looks.

Jack continued. "Because the shape lends itself to the transmission of *vaves*."

The looks became puzzled.

"Waves, brothers," explained Bob.

"Yes—*vaves*. Brothers, information is contained in vaves. But these vaves are only probability. If an observer can index all probable outcomes and entangle his consciousness vith those outcomes through measurement and observation, then von can select the outcome that von vishes..."

The looks became dull.

Bob squinched one side of his face. "You're losing them, Jack."

"The bell shape, my dear brothers, is due to the reqvuirements of the *vave* transference properties as focused by certain crystals..."

"They're gone, Jack. Maybe back to the history lesson."

Jack sighed. "Okay, dear Bob." He took another breath. "Gentlemen, before the End came in 1945, the Germans completed two more projects. First, the Germans perfected vhat is today called suspended animation. That is, they learned how to suspend animation in living things by using, not temperature, but cyclotronic resonance from counter-rotating cyclotrons vith Serum 525. This Red Mercury, as it is called, vhen the cyclotrons are powered up freezes living things, but vithout lowering their temperature."

"As you just saw, brothers," added Bob. "Think of it as inverse radiation."

The military exchanged apprehensive glances. "Radiation?" one asked.

I was doubly glad to be shielded in the tunnel where I could observe in silence. Getting a Sicilian tan from radiation wasn't on my job description.

"Vhen the cyclotrons are povered up, the Serum glows purple. In rooms vith normal temperatures, this is reqvuired on a regular basis to keep the subject who is in the state of suspended animation alive." Jack shrugged. "Or *dead*. There really is no difference in relation to the suspended subject. Finally they froze the subject just to be sure."

I peered hard at the tiny frosted window in the upper half of the Bell. Suddenly I realized the identity of the 'subject'—Rickoletti, Tonya's father. No wonder she had been upset with her mother, Marm. Heck of a punishment for a failed business venture, to be permanently paralyzed by 'inverse radiation', then frozen as insurance.

"Their second project, vhich vas also entirely successful, vas the construction of a third-generation 'Vengeance Veapon', or guided missile."

The General arched one brow. "Third, Brother Muck? There were only two V rockets."

"Nope, Brother-ooney," interjected Bob. "There were three. Count 'em and weep."

"Yah, this is correct, dear Bob. The Germans completed in total secrecy a third-generation of V rockets. The V3 rocket vas the first truly intercontinental guided ballistic missile and vas constructed vith three stages so that it could be put into orbit around the earth."

Eyebrows rose among all the Italian brass. This was news.

"Vith suspended animation perfected and a three-stage rocket vhich they successfully put into orbit on more than one occasion in 1945, they vere on the brink of something truly great..."

"Both barrels, Jack," said Bob.

"And finally, dear brothers, ve come to the *core* of the matter." Jack grinned and took a deep breath. Things were going swimmingly. "Just before the thanks of the Communisti came rolling across the horizon, the Germans built a *second* Bell."

"That's two, gentlemen. One, two." Bob grinned.

"And they had learned how to entangle electrons betveen them, and not just electrons, but entire subjects in their suspended animation, using the new science of quantum mechanics."

My eyes lowered to the plastic tip on the end of my left pinky. So this was quantum mechanics in action.

"Can you say *entanglement*, players?" said Bob.

The brass shuffled their feet, blinked.

"Entanglement of the subject, dear brothers, is another vay of saying transfer from Point A to Point B, vithout any regard for distance. The only restriction is that you must have the same device at both ends and keep both devices under observation so that the initial entanglement is preserved."

Some of the brass were starting to get it.

"You mean..."

"No need to be mean, my brothers. Please forgive Bob vhen he is also mean..."

"That is..."

"Yah, dear brothers! The Germans planned to put their Fuhrer into Bell Number Von, suspend him using Serum 525, then shoot Bell Number Two to the Moon using their V3 rocket vith a suspended animation capsule inside, then transfer the Fuhrer to the V3 on the Moon, vere he vill be completely safe—neither alive nor dead but *dreaming*—until such time as vhen the threat of the Communist thanks vill have disappeared and they could svitch the power to Bell Number Von back on! They planned then to reverse the process, and have their Fuhrer back again...here, in this cavern."

"Quantum mechanics with entanglement. Can you spell that, brothers?"

Moschin narrowed his eyelids, astonished, shocked, and did I detect greedy? all at the same time. "But," Moschin began...

"But the Fuhrer changed his mind and vent back to Berlin." Jack shrugged. "And somevon *else* decided to go in his place."

"He missed his dog, Blondie," explained Bob.

"You mean?" said Moschin.

"There you go vith *mean* again. See vhat you have started, dear Bob."

"Forget it, Jack. You have them now."

The brass suddenly stood straight. "We have waited, we have hoped, we have heard rumors...but we never imagined that this tall tale could actually be true."

"Dream, brothers. It's all true," Bob said.

"Please to disregard the propaganda movies that you saw of our leader's death in 1945, brethren. That vas his doppelganger...his long-time stunt-double...a proxy."

"Then," ventured Moschin, all eagerness, "our Lodge will

again become complete. Our plans for Greater Italia can move forward once more, like in the old days."

"Ah, but there vas still a problem, gentlemen."

The brass listened closely. They were hooked. Like me. I wondered: Since 'Pinky' was used, will M&M start calling their new guests Thumb, Index, Forefinger, Ringfinger, and The Bird?

"Vhen the Germans buried this Bell to hide it from the enemy, they made an error...they broke the crystals that coordinate the v-v-vaves," Jack stumbled again over his w's, "the crystals that are vithin the Bell and vhich are reqvuired to complete the teleportation."

"Without a doubt," added Bob.

"And ve have had qvuite a time of it harvesting *new* crystals from around the vorld in order to pover up the Bell vonce more, and reestablish the entanglement."

"Gulliver and Crusoe."

"And ve have had to make some little sacrifices."

"And we're not done yet."

"Unfortunately no." Jack glanced up at the tiny frosted window.

"But only in *this* universe, brothers," continued Bob. "Only in this one. Not in any other."

"That is vell put, dear Bob. Very vell put."

"But the crystals on the Moon remain as good as ever."

"Yes, Bob. The V3 rocket had a hard landing, of course, but it vas designed to be vell-protected from such."

"Factory warranteed."

"And no vear-and-tear in the many years since."

"Unlike this Happy Dwarf salt mine."

"Many problems in here, yes, dear Bob. But our telescope keeps the Moon under observation."

Bob nodded. "And the V3 on the Moon is temperature frozen and still draws power from its micro-waved crystals."

"Yah! As vas proven by the dream thoughts that ve have received."

"Every bell gets echoes, brothers. So long as somebody holds the clapper."

"And these echoes," continued Jack, "are being the best if there is no clapper at all."

I noticed a pair of suitcases lying open under the computer monitors where Frankie sat glued to his screens, Diego now making sandwiches and drinks just like in Rick's bar. Viewing the monitors side-wise I thought I glimpsed a rocky landscape on one, black sky behind, with stars that shone bright and steady. That was no Earth landscape. As for the suitcases, they had apparently been emptied, their cargo of crystals harvested from the Blarney Stone and the Aztec Malverde statue installed inside the Glocke so Muck and Montez could finally execute their Grand Plan for Greater Italia, beginning with the P-2 Lodge and its secret branch in the Vatican Bank. I was starting to understand why Il Papa had to die.

But how exactly was their Plan to happen? And what did 'veni, vici, duce' have to do with it?

CHAPTER 34

F or some time a quiet sound had been building amidst the buzzing of the dynamo and the humming of the Glocke. In response, Jack threw a glance at Frankie and nodded. Frankie turned a large knob on a monitor—the one showing the lunar landscape. The sound grew immensely in volume. I could not help but think of Andrew and his favorite phrase: 'That's the crank!' Had I just witnessed the origin of the phrase? The sound grew deafening, yet remained soft, an almost feminine whine echoing through the chamber.

The military brass listened, and froze.

"Veni," said Jack.

"Vici," added Bob.

"Duce!" pronounced Moschin accompanied by awestruck expressions and happy nods among the generals and politicians, their right arms automatically resuming the Fascist pose.

The sound gurgled as if it were clearing its throat, though from Jack's explanation I was pretty sure that whoever the heck owned the voice was transmitting via a partial entanglement of brain waves, contacting every bell in the world like a satellite contacts cell phones, therefore had no throat, or, more exactly, its throat had been suspended in a frozen-like state by M&M's mystery radiation and then put in the moon's deep freeze, leaving only brain waves free to operate. I pressed my fingers to my forehead. All these avenues and U-turns were putting my own mind into a deep freeze.

"Is that you? My followers, is that you?"

Bob had the loudest voice. "You ain't just whistlin' Caruso."

A high machine-like whine shook the chamber as the computers added a mechanical tone to the sound, then settled into something audible as Frankie spun dials.

"How long, my brothers? How long am I to be exiled in this strange place? I am cold, my friends, cold."

Colonel Moschin turned to his companions in open-eyed wonder. One of them blurted, "It cannot be... Our leader has been dead for eighty years!"

"It must be a fraud," another snapped, lowering his arm.

"A hoax," added one of the blue-suited politicians. "Brother Muck, explain why you have done this hoax. And how?"

Jack shook his head and smiled at the loudspeakers.

"What are you saying, my brothers!" The voice rattled in a mix of Italian and bad English. *"You would accuse us of a shallow trick? You cowards, who are not worthy to shine the boots of even my worst Arditi, would accuse my beloved brothers, Signore Muck e Signore Montez, of a mere trick? They who have talked with me, they who have kept up my flagging spirits for these many years? I will excommunicate any follower from our glorious Propaganda Due Lodge, I will expel any member of our great national Fasci di Combattimento who dares to go against his leader in such matters!"* The voice grew to a shout, reverberating through the chamber into my rock-cut corridor. *"Do not be clay, my people. Rise, my blackshirts, to the call of history. Italiani! It is time to release all our frozen dead from their capsules throughout the world. The moment has come. Together we shall embrace the Steel Pact of Victory!"*

It sounded like a declaration of war, but against who and for what I could not imagine. The explosive voice resounded through the cave finally to peter out at the feet of Jack Muck and Bob Montez, who watched triumphantly with arms folded from the round platform where the Glocke rested, their black tassels on their black hats swaying.

The phalanx of right arms switched from automatic to full-volunteer and jerked erect, all fingers extended. I had not seen such enthusiasm since Gypsy Rose Lee made her comeback appearance at Radio City.

"You got em, Jack. Phase Two."

"Yah, dear Bob," Muck muttered. He turned back to the P-2 delegation and pointed at the upper part of the Bell. "Now, dear brothers, please if you vill to look at the face in the Glocke."

I knew that face. Without ever being introduced, it was clear who it was—the ever-missing Rickoletti, whose fortune Miz Marm had swiped in order to maintain her hi-flyin' status among the mobsters of New Orleans.

"The time has arrived for us to finally complete our experiment, dear brothers," said Jack.

"Just a demo, bro. Cause we know it'll work."

"This is being right, dear Bob. Ve do know that it vill vork."

Puzzled looks answered them.

"Please to step on the platform, everyvon. Yes, like that. Step up here next to the Glocke. I am sorry for the...how you say...nasty veather, but ve can no longer delay. Ve must end our dear leader's exile at vonce, you see."

The Italian brass and the two politicians obeyed, their ears still tuned for more communications from their Duce, marooned in the ultimate place of marooning, the ultimate Robinson Crusoe, and, in a peculiar way, also the ultimate Caruso, an exiled singer in a lunar Sing-Sing. In the tunnel, I rubbed my temples again. All this speculation was still making my head hurt.

"Bring Il Duce back," pleaded Colonel Moschin. "Think of the possibilities if we can once more unleash his energy in today's Roma."

"Yes, that is being the idea," Jack said.

A sudden jerk shook the platform. I had to shake my head to clear my eyes of the double-vision that Quinn and Pietro kept throwing over my sight. Frankie continued to twirl dials. How much of Duce's speech was real? I didn't put it past M&M to conjure up a speech from nothing for some ulterior motive.

The round platform popped loose from its moorings and began to rise—in the roof of the cavern, a circular band appeared and it dawned on me (and everyone else in my basement) that the sky had become visible and that the platform was elevating the Bell into the midst of the storm that was thrashing the Owl Mountains, torn remnants of cloud soon chasing each other about the opening to the cave. I pictured Bob saying, "Can you spell Frankenstein, brothers?" Maybe he did—the rapid rise of the noisy gears and the wind whipping inside the cavern drowned all voices.

The band of night, lit by flashes of lightning, grew, then narrowed, then vanished. The platform had joined with the cave's ceiling.

I realized that I was practically alone. Frankie remained huddled over the computers, watching whatever events were unfolding above unfold in virtual time, Diego nervously kept Frank's mint julep filled. Only Muck's poodles stood between me and the elevator which could take me up, take me to the action where I could witness the Grand Event.

One of the dogs barked.

I had taken not a single step. Looking closer, I noticed that the dogs remained quiet, heads on paws, and that the bark had not come from them. Another bark—still none of the poodles had moved.

More fakery. Whatever Jack had done with his real dogs, these weren't them.

Ignoring the mutts, I walked swiftly and with my head lowered, presenting my back to the computer area, hoping not to be noticed by the humans. Humans? Hell, for all I knew they too were fake, just like M&M themselves back in Querque. In fact, who knew how much of all I had seen inside the cavern was real, and how much just another grand deception, another Miracle in the Desert, the kind of deception that M&M loved to play on naive dupes.

On the other hand, what if all this were real? Then Muck and Montez would have no more tricks left up their mariachi sleeves. Then I would *have* them...

I rolled the dice.

I made it to the elevator. One dog looked briefly up, then put its computer programmed snout back on its paws. I entered the elevator and the door quietly closed. The car jerked up. For a moment it also occurred to me that this might be my last way out, that the elevator might be my final chance to zap my way clear of M&M's webs.

I threw it away. I sensed something real in all they had done this night—web or no web, I would have it out with them, once and finally, get an answer as to what they had done with Tonya, what they had planned for her father, Rick.

The elevator door opened inside the Milkow Museum. Through the window loomed the Henge, the huge concrete structure, now lit up by activity. *Deed* I had walked all the way back again from where the taxicab had dropped me at the Milkow entrance, and it was certain that the taxi driver had deliberately misled me.

The circus rose inside the Henge. As I looked, wind and rain pelted the actors and the stage scenery finished emerging from the depths of Dante's underworld. The ground inside the Henge, which I had glimpsed earlier that evening and which had seemed entirely natural, turned out to be no more than a giant manhole cover, which pulled aside to make room for the rising platform.

The rain was not heavy but the wind rose and through occasional flashes of lightning I watched the drama unfold as it had down below, the mad scientist Jack Muck and his sidekick Bob hovering about the Bell while their guests, the cream of Italy's elite, covered their eyes with flattened hands to shield them from the rain. Jack and Bob got busy—taking each of the chains that drooped down the side of the Bell, they attached each chain to a pillar of the Henge. There being twelve chains to match the twelve pillars, they soon had matched them all.

Bob flipped a lever and the chains grew tight.

The Bell yanked into the air. Suspended like a balloon, in response to another flick of a switch by Bob, the two rotating plates in the bottom of the Bell resumed their counter-clockwise spinning and the Bell again went through its cycle of imperial colors: red, then purple, then back to red, though longer this time, and I found myself peering up to pierce the clouds as if unconsciously searching for a glimpse of that distant object that was the terminus of this crazy train—the Moon. Finally the plates stopped spinning and Bob hammered the two switches back into place, and he and Jack one by one unhooked the twelve chains.

The platform began to sink.

The rain had not been heavy and the actors studio standing on the platform were not entirely soaked, though the water made their faces glisten as the light from the cavern burst from below and reflected on them. For a moment I wondered how much graft Jimmy the Geek back in Brooklyn would have to buy in order to get such a device permitted. I knew lots of guys who might like a long vacation in a lunar crater while their statutes of limitations ran out.

Outside the Museum, I heard a squeal as of brakes suddenly applied. I looked. The taxicab had returned. Ahmed jumped out and opened a back door, attempting unsuccessfully to hold a miniature umbrella over three figures as they spilled out of his taxi. The umbrella accomplishing nothing, once his passengers had exited, Ahmed jumped back in and sped into the night. Just like old times.

The three figures took one look at the circus inside the Henge, which had already descended several feet in its course back down to the cavern, then turned and bolted for the Museum—that is, straight at me.

I had no time to think.

Dashing into the cloud-gush night, drops of water biting into my face, I clutched my hat and rushed out a back exit, around the Museum's side, and into the Henge, dropping over the edge to alight on the sinking platform just behind the Bell. The noise from the storm and the gears and the dynamo was so great that I figured I had a good chance of not being immediately detected.

The platform clumped back into its bower on the floor of the cavern, Frankie turning his face to confirm the results of the mechanical operation. The Italian delegates stepped off, shaking off water.

From behind the Bell, I saw Muck and Montez turn their own faces upward to stare at the little opening near the Bell's top where the silent inmate slept, and the delegation from Propaganda Due, over their damp uniforms, covered their hearts with their palms as if the fate of nations hung in the balance, tilting on what may happen next in that little frozen capsule.

At that moment, the elevator opened and expelled three people into the cavern—the same three characters who had almost run into Yours Truly in the real world above, where the birds sang sweetest and the rain fell wettest. Marm shook the drops off her ample purple dress and silver rings and pearl necklace, Licia right beside her did the same, still sporting 'her' red and black-fringed feather-rimmed black jacket, still coughing into her fist. Behind them lightly stepped a third figure—Tonya—whom I recognized instantly despite the strange thick and plain white gown that hid the magical cliffs of Dover.

Marm, or Angelica Massolini, whipped out a white embroidered square cloth and tied it around her ample waist with the attached rope belt. She hurried to join the Italian delegation, which stepped off the platform to meet her.

"Who told you to start without me?" Marm cast her usual ugly frown at the lot. "You have spoiled everything, as I knew you would! Now stand aside and let someone with an actual brain in her head run things." She elbowed her way to the front and smoothed her Masonic apron. Leave it to Marm to push her way even into male-only clubs, I thought.

"My dear Mrs. Massolini, it is being so good for you grace us vith your presence—"

"Drop the charade, Mr. Muck. As the grand-daughter of our leader, Benito Mussolini, I have more right than anyone to know if he still lives and if he is going to rejoin our movement." Licia and Tonya stood obediently behind her, looking meekly down, hands by their sides.

"As you say, Mrs. Mass...uh, Mrs. Mussolini." Jack's brows climbed up his forehead.

Colonel Moschin interrupted: "Look!" He pointed at the face in the Bell. Hidden behind the Bell, I could not see the face, but my ears worked as well as ever. And I could see the faces of the Italian brass as they gazed upward. I gathered something wonderful was happening.

"Success! Yah!" yelled Jack—only the second time I had ever heard him shout.

"We done it!" Bob added. "Rick has been transferred!"

Jack grinned at his open-eyed audience. "Gentlemen. I hereby present: *Il Duce!*"

The Voice returned. Amplified by Frankie's computerized side-show, Mussolini's voice rumbled through the cavern like an earthquake, somewhere between clearing his throat and whining like a brat. The computer threw onto a large monitor an image of the small faceplate. Better than watching the real thing. I was certain that I recognized the square jaw, the large eyes, the hairless head. This face surely was different—not at all the thin gaunt face that I had seen in the faceplate up till now.

The eyes flickered.

Like a TV screen coming to life, the face quivered. Slowly the eyes opened. For a moment they stared up—then sideways—then down. Recognition flowed there as well. A grin gradually transformed the image until it became the same forceful arrogant face that I knew from ancient newsreels. Could these two Brain-ensteins have actually pulled it off? Who back in the Bronx would believe it?

Bob pressed a button on the side of the Bell and the lower door pulled aside to reveal several hand-rungs. The face lowered from the little window. A moment elapsed and a stolid figure filled the Bell's interior behind Montez & Muck.

A dozen arms rose in salute.

The figure stepped out of the Bell.

Moving backwards, it stepped onto the platform, and stretched its arms, its calves. He bent over and gradually touched his toes. Pretty good for a 135-year-old man, I thought. And if Benito Mussolini can handle that, I suppose he can also handle a re-launch of Fascism using the Vatican Bank and his private Masonic lodge, Propaganda Due, now that the Pope was out of the way.

A new future awaited.

The man turned...

Everyone sucked a breath.

"How. . ?" blurted Marm. "*Rick!*"

Jack frowned. "Vas there a fly in the transporter?"

"No, Jack," said Bob, "It's Rick, all right. A hundred percent."

"Rickoletti Costa!" yelled Marm. "What are *you* doing here?"

"Los moros en la costa," warned Bob, squinting half his face at Jack.

"And, unfortunately, dear Rick not being a true Mussolini..." added Jack.

"Only by marriage, Jack," rejoined Bob. "Only by marriage."

"Don't misunderstand me, my dear Rick. I am happy to see you again, of course," said Marm as a tear coursed down one cheek to soil her pancake base, "but..."

Rick let his gaze stutter across the chamber. "My god, Angelica, where have I been? I was in a happy land dreaming...none of the strife and anger and chaos that has engulfed us in our long struggle with..." Rick's eyes stopped—fixed on a single person.

Tonya took a mincing step forward. Her green eyes flashed, her brows lowered, her body went rigid.

"Tonya," Marm hissed, and extended an arm.

Before Marm could stop her, Tonya rushed onto the platform. Snatching a small knife from the floor where Bob and Jack had laid their tools, she leapt up—raised the knife overhead—another second and the knife would plunge into Rick's chest.

Rick lurched back. Fear wrenched his features into a grimace.

"Halt!" Jack yelled.

"Someone stop the li'l gal," joined Bob, "She's at it again!"

Marm clasped her hands to her mouth. "My dear Rick! Look out—oh my dear Rick!"

The knife plunged—grazed Rick's chest, ripping his shirt. Blood spurted.

Colonel Moschin jumped up and, accompanied by Licia, succeeded in grabbing Tonya by both her arms and pulling her back. Together they forced the knife out of her hands and it clattered to the wooden planks of the platform.

I chose this moment to crash the party—it was time to take out the trash. Stepping casually from behind the Bell, I put my hands on my hips and rocked on my heels. For effect, I whistled Elvis's 'Return To Sender' and played air-guitar, adding a twist of my hips and letting my Elvis wave flap.

Jack and Bob stared at me with open mouths, wide open enough for a coal cart to drive into. There was no illusion in those shocked expressions.

Success!

Licia and Moschin dragged Tonya off the platform and returned her to Marm's side, where Marm extracted long rope-strings from the back of Tonya's white outfit and tied them tightly behind her daughter's back, restraining her arms. Tonya growled and jerked and threw stabbing glares at Rick. I realized that her white outfit was the kind that institutions issue for 'special' inmates.

Tonya struggled and fought, but the ropes were tied sufficiently to prevent her escape. Marm glanced at me. All her anger had gone, replaced only by sadness. "Schizophrenia, they call it. Usually she is fine and can mix in normal society. Her mania is fixed on only one person...her father, Rick. As long as he is not around she can lead a normal life, more or less, and she needs no supervision. But when she lays eyes on him... Only to Rick is she a danger. She led you to him just for this. I tried to stop you. But you would not be stopped."

The terror on Rick's face was undeniable. How long had he lived with this? How long had he been the victim of his daughter's mania, narrowly escaping her attempts to murder him? How far had he attempted to flee in order to escape his private nightmare? Yep, this family's trash was more than my little office could handle, all right, perhaps the biggest any PI had ever seen.

Marm slipped another wafer to Licia, who greedily gobbled it. Tonya too opened her mouth and Marm slid one in. Tonya relaxed and peace came over her. Marm then downed one herself, her own private escape.

Who am I to judge?

Rick had dived back into the Bell. For him, any place at all was preferable.

While my attention had been on the Mussolini family, Jack and Bob had quietly watched. Now I noticed that, acting on a wink from Bob, Frankie reached for a switch—the platform-raising switch.

The platform jumped.

In confusion, the Italian brass retreated, not knowing what to expect now that the second coming of their messiah had miscarried. I was wary—I had no doubt that M&M had more tricks up their mariachi sleeves, overlaid with blackshirts or no. I sensed another effort to exchange Rick for Il Duce on the way.

Calmly, I pulled out Saint Bernard. Or more precisely my newest Colt .45 and aimed it at the pair. No swiveling stools here and a glance at the computer monitors confirmed that no audio or 3D video projection files were playing.

I felt it in my bones—I *had* 'em.

Jack and Bob stopped moving. To my surprise, Jack actually quivered. He cast a sweaty look at Bob, then back at me. "You...you plan to *kill* us, Pinky? But vhy?"

I sniffed. "After what you've done to me? Done to so many

people? You ask that now?"

"But Pinky, to shoot us...that vould be *murder.*"

Bob seemed a little less nervous, though I could see one knee shake. Not even ten pounds of Italian Arditi uniform could entirely hide his discomfort. Imagine that. Smart-aleck Bugsy Bob, with a combo personality of Chicago and St. Louis, was actually afraid now that he himself looked down the barrel of a gun.

There was no wall behind the pair. This time there would be no 'volunteering' me by walking backward into an alternate universe. They knew it, and they knew I knew it.

I cocked the hammer. "It's murder only in this 'verse, Jack. Only in *this* 'verse."

"How about a deal, Marlowe?" Suddenly Bob was polite. No more 'little man' spilling off his smarmy tongue.

"Yah," echoed Jack. "You had so much to say in our shop in Juarez. Vhy not discuss matters? You are important to us, Pinky. And it vould be qvuite easy to fix this little blooper."

"Sorry, guys. The scene is done and the last act over. All your fancy talk is done—except for Bernie here. From now on, my piece does my talkin'."

Before anyone could move, I aimed my Colt...

CHAPTER 35

...at Frankie.

Aplatform jerked to a halt, having barely moved.
ripe tomato, his seeds spraying the monitor before him. The
nd from a good twenty feet distance, I plugged him like a

Montez & Muck—the authors of so much misery and chaos in my already miserable chaotic life, exchanged glances. I knew that look too. Something else was up. Before their latest miracle could materialize to screw me over, and the world—I squeezed the trigger.

A little too hasty. That is, the first bullet ripped through Jack's neck instead of his head. He twirled and one shoulder nudged Bob sending my second bullet into Bob's shoulder instead of his heart.

Jack fell. He attempted to crawl toward the Italian Masons who stared in shock from the sidelines as his blood spilled. I then sent Jack to the next 'verse with a third report from my gun, before putting a fourth into Bob.

Bull's-eye.

Had I done it? Could it be so? Were the twin Frankensteinians who manipulated universes like Apollo and Zeus finally, truly dead?

Behind their sprawled bodies, the door on the lower segment of the Bell slowly grated to one side and exposed the interior. I expected to see Rick, having recovered his bravery and patched his side, venture out again. Or maybe Mussolini himself, finally brought back to earth by M&M's mysterious workings.

Two bodies jumped out.

Leaping over the corpses of Jack Muck and Bob Montez, appeared—*Jack Muck and Bob Montez*—identical to their executed twins in every respect. Same combat fatigues—same black Arditi shirts—same semi-fezzes with the black tassels—same polished black boots—same salad-plate medals pinned to their chests. But they each held something different in their hands. Whatever 'verse had expelled these doppelgangers had seen fit to equip them with small silvery devices which they brandished at me menacingly. From somewhere came a new whine to accompany their penetration of Nature's secrets.

I want a hippopotamus for Christmas
Only a hippopotamus will do
Don't want a doll, no dinky Tinker Toy
I want a hippopotamus to play with and enjoy

I wasted no time singing along, but swung my Colt into action. Why must my life always be a day late and a dollar short? Red rays erupted from M&M's silver devices and simultaneously burned needle holes through my neck and chest. Was it revenge? The same wounds I had just inflicted on them were now inflicted on *mio*, I noted as my body clumped onto the wooden planks of the platform.

Again I had lost!

Bob and Jack stood over me, smiling down in their hot-shit hi-packin' way, like gunslingers in Bootlick, Arizona, their silver lasers still smoking.

A blur appeared in the corner of my eye—something emerged from the tunnel. All I saw was an ivory jacket, a fedora hat, Canali shoes, and another Colt. And behind him, another blur.

The newcomer's Colt leveled and blasted.

The bullets flung Muck and Montez backward over their own corpses.

The Bell rattled—two more figures leaped out. Jack and Bob no longer smiled, cold determination was settled on their faces, all talk of bloopers ancient history. They aimed their silvery ray weapon and sent red lasers spinning about the cavern in attempts to intercept their new adversary.

The Italian generals dove for cover. Marm and Licia yanked crazy tied-up Tonya down beside them for safety.

Again the Colt spoke...again Jack and Bob lost the gamble and fell to the platform. The growing pile of bodies made me think of ancient battles when soldiers of Christ resisted hordes of infidels on fields of ravens.

On they came—Montez & Muck rushing out of the Bell to the tune of happy hippos, two by two as from an Ark—the new gunslinger with the Elvis wave knocking them down, pair after pair, until I thought, while I watched prone on the floor with my own blood spilling faster from the holes which the first M&M had burned through me moments earlier, thinking surely this newcomer must be almost out of ammo.

Still on they came—more Mucks—more Montezes—till I wondered how many universes there could be, how many could afford to expend such energy on the transmigration of so much border-jumping flesh.

Down they went as the ivory-clad newcomer drilled each pair the moment they leaped out of the Bell.

How long could the new gunslinger keep it up? How many bullets could he still possess? The slightest pause must surely expose him to the latest pair of M&Ms who would promptly riddle him with their lethal red laser-light...

The gunslinger flipped open his Colt and glanced in the chamber—one bullet remained.

He turned to the monitors.

Inside the Bell, the latest Montez & Muck saw. And understood. Their faces lit in anger, their teeth gnashed in disappointment. Together they tried to squeeze through the Bell's small door to stop him, managing only to place one leg each through the gap.

The gunslinger fired—fragments of computer shot into the air to bounce off the ceiling of the cavern terminating all observation from this universe to any other, closing the membrane that joined the universes, breaking the entanglement...

The Bell stood empty. No more mad scientists leaped from its interior.

I lay on the floor, strangely happy that no fragments had bounced onto me. Strangely, since my time was up.

Almost.

The newcomer stood above me and stared into my eyes.

***

Another moment and I stood staring down at a dead Pete Marlowe, thinking with a sense of wonder how many times I had now experienced death. How many times I had cheated it. With a flash, all the memories of all the previous Pete Marlowes rushed into mine. Suddenly I recalled the first time that I had walked through a wall in Marm's Albuquerque mansion, when Licia had impulsively shoved me, how I had not simply walked through the wall but had stumbled through, and how after I had arrived on the far side, I had tripped over mops and buckets, having found myself in a glorified broom closet, and how after a minute or two I had again stumbled, and without realizing it had stepped backward before the hole in the wall had closed, before finally regaining my balance and stepping forward again.

That small step backward had duplicated me.

And since there had been a big delay between when Licia shoved me and when I briefly stumbled backward, my second self had appeared *much earlier in time* than when Licia had pushed me through.

Standing in Marm's guest chamber, I had found myself alone. A search of the house had revealed no one, Jack and Bob and Marm and her brood having driven off in Jack's limo to take Tonya to my office for her very first visit, as part of M&M's plan to recruit me.

When the gang finally returned, I had hidden in the stairwell and had overheard their secret conversations—the most private plans of Jack and Bob were then revealed to me, they having no idea that I was listening, that I even *existed*. But I had listened and listened well. And gradually I realized that something truly extraordinary had occurred, as extraordinary as the discovery of the Deep Sea Scrolls, and I spent endless hours staring at my pinky with its Indexer and imagining what I could do with this new device that they had implanted—that I knew they *would* implant in the *other* me the following week.

I did not wait for them to bring my first self from the Dog-Gone Show to Marm's castle, however, as I knew they planned on doing. I had heard enough to know that I needed to escape the mansion, that I needed to find a way to help my first self, knowing as I did that Montez & Muck did not intend my first self to survive their scavenger hunts for crystals to power their Bell in Milkow.

So I left Marm's mansion and evaded the garden quicksand and the gate-guards, and I thumbed a ride into town and I went to Miz Tam's and paid my rent to get her off the back of my first self, then I thumbed another ride to Rick's Americana Cafe where I knew—from overhearing M&M's plans back in Marm's castle—that they intended to kill Ugly Joe and frame my first self for Joe's murder.

But I arrived too late. I timed it wrong and, as I crept up, I heard gunshots. When I peered out of the darkness I saw Andrew and Frankie put the drugged body of my first self into the car next to Joe's body while Muck and Montez looked on.

They intended to leave my first self inside Joe's taxi parked in Rick's parking lot, but, after the gang drove back to Marm's, I managed to squeeze myself into the driver's seat of the taxicab and drive it back to the alley behind my Albuquerque office with my unconscious first self and dead Joe still inside.

I was too late to help my first self in other ways. I could not follow him to Suite Chicas to prevent his second abduction since my first self had already taken the Olds and left me stranded at Miz Tam's. I could not follow him to Rome—after all, I was still him and neither he nor I had any extra dough for plane tickets. I could not follow my first self to Juarez since he took my beat-up Olds there, too. But, since I was still him, I had access to my office safe, and, after several brief bus trips, I managed to sell one of the Modiglianis after he brought them back from Rome, with which I finally managed to pay my way to Juarez—only to discover that my first self had already been kidnapped and taken to Chapo's pyramid. So I returned to Albuquerque in the Olds depressed and helpless, hoping that my first self would survive Chapo's abduction and somehow make it back from the pyramid.

He indeed had *not* survived the pyramid—but luckily had been replaced by my second self.

After I returned by helicopter, I managed to locate and follow my second self—happy that 'I' had still survived M&M's double-dealings in Mexico, and wiser after seeing how easy it was to create still more 'selves'.

After M&M had yet again kidnapped me, my third self was

imprisoned in M&M's foul box to be preserved between life and death forever, and only managed to survive when I killed myself in another 'verse, and my third self thus transferred my consciousness to my fourth self when my third self sank into the quicksand.

Then my fourth self flew to Europe in pursuit of M&M and Milkow.

I—my fifth self, that is—had more important things to do. I flew to Rome to do some investigating of my own into the Masons in the Vatican. And, since I had all the memories of all of my other selves, I knew where to go in Rome and how to watch and listen and learn.

And follow...

Now, inside the Wenceslas cavern, as I stood over the corpse of my fourth self, my Colt still smoking, the heaped bodies of Muck and Montez bleeding on the inert Bell's platform, behind me a new figure entered, shaking off dust from the tunnels.

I knew that figure.

I threw a look of reproach, and said. "So you thought you could spy on me without knowing that I was spying on you."

Uncle Flynn stood straight, tired of stooping in shallow side tunnels. Wearing his old priest's cassock, he put his hands on his hips and cracked his spine. "Now that be a fair assessment, Nephew. That be a fair assessment. But give an old Irishman from Galwey a moment to figure out this blarney. Ye're not bein' entirely fair to me to think that I can keep up."

"Why didn't you use those river-dance-sticks you call legs to come the heck out of your hidey-hole and give me a god-damn hand with this Mongol horde of Franken-mucks?" I asked. "Didn't you see that I was fighting for my life here?" I leaned in and gave my uncle a harsher glare. "It was all I could do just to keep from warning my fourth self that you were skulking around in those tunnels following him."

Flynn threw my accusation back at me. "But apparently it warn't too difficult for ye to keep from warnin' your dear old uncle that *you* were skulkin' about followin' *him*."

"Truer than a policy flush in Harlem," I admitted.

Marm had recovered an appearance of life and the blood finally returned to her pancake face after the frantic gun play. "You," she snapped, looking at Flynn.

"In the flash and in the flesh," he answered. "Didja believe ye'd never see yer old family priest again, Angelica?" Flynn lay an engaging smile on Marm, then grew serious. "Especially seein' as how ye let yer highfalutin pals Jack and Bob recruit me to steal the Blarney Stone from the Pope seven years past? And after the Pope tossed me in his brig, the lot of ye then decided that it wasn't worth an owl's hoot to try to get me out? Ye might at least have let me in on whatever it is Nephew here has tucked up his sleeve."

"Mr. Muck said *need-to-know* only, Father Flynn. Besides," she pronounced, "rescue missions cost money." As if that was the be-all, end-all.

I marveled at this exchange between Marm and Flynn. Their pigeon coos floored me.

Marm added, "Besides, Flynn, it was *you* who lost the Stone to the Pope in the first place...just because you thought you were the best in the world at dominos. Imagine a priest playing dominos! So what if he paid you some money? It was only fitting that you should steal it back to help me and Mr. Muck." Marm primmed her mouth. Her eyes squinted at two severed legs that hung half out of the Bell, all that was left of M&M. She snorted. There would be no more rent checks from them.

"You were exceedingly easy to follow," said Flynn, raising his nose, "but you were ever the rationalizer of sin, Angelica, which is why it is now my privilege to announce to you, and to your delegation of Masons," Flynn acknowledged the clutch of Italian lodge members who were finally venturing out of their own hiding places, "that..."

Marm put her hands to her open mouth again, sensed what was coming.

Flynn withdrew from his jacket (identical to mine, I noted, signaling that Flynn continued to exercise the best sartorial taste) a letter printed on extra-formal forty-pound paper akin to papyrus. He read it aloud:

"'My dear dear Monseigneur Flynn Marlowe...'" I noted that Flynn had not only recovered his priestly status, but had risen from dungeon prisoner all the way to double-dear in the eyes of what could only be a *new* pope. "'In recognition of your efforts informing me of the existence of a branch of the notorious and prohibited Masonic Lodge, *Propaganda Due*, I hereby outlaw and ban this lodge (again) from the Vatican and I hereby also ban and excommunicate any Catholic who henceforth risks his soul by participating in such activities and organizations, within or without Saint Peter's Holy Church.' Signed—Pope Flynn the First."

I looked up in surprise. Then remembered: when I had stumbled back into the Vatican cell, clutching Flynn, not only I had been duplicated, but Flynn as well. The other Flynn must have used the secrets he learned to take the Pointy Hat for himself.

Flynn flung his thumb at the Italians like an umpire. "You are *out!*"

Blind at a Yankees game or not, I didn't care. Vatican politics still weren't my thing, though I did wonder how the Curia would handle *two* Flynns.

The delegation frowned and shuffled their feet. The new pope in the Vatican had closed the window for bringing Fascism back to power.

"Well, I guess that's about it for us."

I smiled a big one. So did Flynn.

"Take an Uber, gentlemen," I said. "You're done."

Removing their Masonic aprons, they headed for the elevator, hurrying to make themselves scarce in view of the carnage that, doubtless, would soon raise eyebrows among the local Milkow police, given that a bloat-ware upgrade and expanded version of St. Valentine's Day Massacre had just been installed in their jurisdiction.

Marm, Tonya... For the first time I felt a human-type feeling for Marm. What had she put up with over the years? What disappointment had she experienced when she had realized that her daughter's murderous impulses for her father had destroyed her family and made her marriage unsustainable? I glanced at Tonya and wondered why I had let my imagination run so wild that I fancied that all I was doing in pursuit of Muck and Montez had been for her sake? How I had even believed that Marm possessed a dungeon where she tortured her own daughter instead of a simple unadorned and quiet room where Marm would calm and attempt to counsel her insane progeny, knowing that she would always fail.

Tonya looked at me. Her face calm from the effect of Marm's drug, she smiled sweetly from her tightened jacket that restrained her arms, and I saw sadness too in her eyes. Her green, green eyes.

Pietro burst into tears and climbed down his ladder to his cellar. Quinn shrugged his shoulders and joined him while Elvis stopped singing and hung up his guitar. I opened the bag of trash and mentally tossed the entire Mussolini family into its depths.

After everyone but I and Diego had gone up the elevator, Diego reluctantly put down his cups and bottles. His hands shaking from all the drama, he flipped the power off to the computers and the Bell, leaving only flashlights with which to illuminate our way out. I gazed once more at the empty powerless Glocke and wondered what the Milkow police would do with it. Probably bury it once more, I supposed, again deliberately.

Rick was gone—who knew to what dimension or universe— though he must certainly be happier wherever he now was. Mussolini was still exiled and dreaming, never to disturb 'worshippers' on earth again now that the Glocke's entanglement had been finally, completely cut.

As Diego departed, I thrust my head inside the Bell for one last look.

From somewhere a high static whine gathered strength. Before I could step back, it formed into a barely detectable voice.

"*My Germans...my Germans...do not forget me. I demand zat you release me from zis cold in Argentina. Listen well, my volk. I am starting a new lodge called P-3...*"

I made a mental note: make sure every bell in the world has a clapper. By the light of my torch, I made my way to the elevator and rode it to a bright clear day.

***

As the sun drifted to its bower over the dry heat of Albuquerque, I pulled my old-Olds into my preferred parking spot before Suite Chicas. The familiar neon glittered in my brain, sending signals telling my cells to prepare for relaxation and entertainment in

the form of beverages and eye-candy. No one was manning the door.
I sauntered in.

Sidling to the bar I deposited my usual stack of verified two-bits.

"Gimme the usual, Diego."

"Coming up, Pete." The barkeep from San Miguel turned and got busy with breakables and booze and soon slid a cold white-frothed glass to me. He stepped closer and leaned in. "By the way, Pete. I heard your Ex got your gift. She's really happy."

My brows rose about a quarter inch. "That's good, Diego. That's real good. I hope she likes riding in style."

I sipped my White Zombie and swiveled my chair to watch the show. The place was filling with smoke from cigars and e-vapes and the corners of the guest room grew darker, making it hard to see who was who, and what who was up to, my Wild Strawberry e-cig adding to the mix.

A giant loomed in front. At first his simian brain that loved open stretch shirts and gold medallions didn't register recognition. A sneer came over him—King Kong put out a foot and with an idiot grin deliberately stepped on my toe.

I put down my Zombie and e-cig.

Slowly I stood. Slowly I turned on one leg until my shoulder was under his big-shot chin.

My free leg snapped behind in a karate kick I had learned in Bangkok—his knee cracked. In another moment I was climbing the mountain, karate thrusts pounding his stick-and-twigs, bread-basket, and Zeke's Zuchini, followed by an open hand to his grinning, big-shot nose.

Blood sprayed—King Kong staggered.

I pulled a silvery device from my pocket. Aiming at roof struts, I pressed a button and a red ray zapped the girders, carving through supports—a section of ceiling collapsed, laying Kong out like Sonny Liston's worst day.

Whistling Richard Diamond's Blues, I picked up a small guest table and placed it over Kong, and pulled up a chair. As I sat to watch the show, I thought of Wendy and Green Eyes, and as the Mylar back curtain appeared, I thought about what might have been and remembered all the 'verses out there in that great big MultiVerse—tomorrow's birds always sing another song.

I pulled down my hat, propped up my feet, and thumbed for another Zombie.

#OldTimesIsOldTimes. #I'mJustThatKindaGuy.

About the Author

Glenn Lazar Roberts is an international attorney and writer of sci-fi, horror, satire, and adventure fantasy novels. Glenn has taught college, professionally translated Arabic and Russian, and credits an eclectic group of famous writers for inspiring him to write, including Jack Vance, Robert E. Howard, Edgar Rice Burroughs, Mervyn Peake, H.P. Lovecraft, Ray Bradbury, Arthur C. Clarke, Isaac Asimov, and H.G. Wells, among many other Masters of the Art. "I love language. I am perpetually afloat on a sea of script." Roberts has edited the work of other aspiring writers and hosts a writing critique circle. When he's not writing he enjoys swimming. He lives in Houston with his wife and kids.

Enjoy More Science Fiction and Thrillers from TWB Press

The 13th Power Quest, Book 1 (TWB Press, 2011)
A sci-fi thriller novel by Terry Wright
http://www.twbpress.com/the13thpowerquest.html

The 13th Power Journey, Book 2 (TWB Press, 2011)
A sci-fi thriller novel by Terry Wright
http://www.twbpress.com/the13thpowerjourney.html

The 13th Power War, Book 3 (TWB Press, 2012)
A sci-fi thriller novel by Terry Wright
http://www.twbpress.com/the13thpowerwar.html

Alien Apocalypse – The Storm (TWB Press, 2011)
A sci-fi short story by Dean Giles
http://www.twbpress.com/alienapocalypsethestorm.html

Alien Apocalypse – Genesis (TWB Press, 2012)
A sci-fi short story by Dean Giles
http://www.twbpress.com/alienapocalypsiegenesis.html

Alien Apocalypse – Payback (TWB Press, 2014)
A sci-fi short story by Dean Giles
http://www.twbpress.com/alienapocalypsepayback.html

The Tournaent (TWB Press, 2012)
A sci-fi futuristic short story by Dean Giles
http://www.twbpress.com/thetournament.html

The Grief Syndrome (TWB Press, 2011)
A sci-fi futuristic novel by Terry Wright
http://www.twbpress.com/thegriefsyndrome.html

The Duplication Factor (TWB Press, 2011)
A sci-fi human cloning novel by Terry Wright
http://www.twbpress.com/duplicationfactor.html

The Galactic Circle Veterinary Service (TWB Press, 2014)
A sci-fi novel by Stephen A. Benjamin
http://www.twbpress.com/galacticcircle.html

Extinction: The Galactic Circle Veterinary Service Book 2 (TWB
Press, 2016)
A sci-fi novel by Stephen A. Benjamin
http://www.twbpress.com/extinction.html

The Pearl of Death (TWB Press, 2011)
A historical thriller novel by Terry Wright
http://www.twbpress.com/thepearlofdeath.html

Black Jack (TWB Press, 2014)
A detective thriller novel by Terry Wright
http://www.twbpress.com/blackjack.html

Lunacidal (TWB Press, 2015)
A sci-fi short story by Pete Martin
http://www.twbpress.com/lunacidal.html

www.twbpress.com